Badger Games

Also by Jon A. Jackson:

The Diehard

The Blind Pig

Grootka

Hit on the House

Deadman

Dead Folks

Man with an Axe

La Donna Detroit

Badger Games

Jon A. Jackson

ATLANTIC MONTHLY PRESS
NEW YORK

Published simultaneously in Canada
Printed in the United States of America

FIRST EDITION

Library of Congress Cataloging-in-Publication Data
Jackson, Jon A.
  Badger games / Jon A. Jackson.
    p. cm.
  ISBN 0-87113-851-4
  1. Conspiracies—Fiction.   2. Drug traffic—Fiction.   3. Montana—Fiction.   I. Title.
PS3560.A216 B33 2002
813'.54—dc21   2001056494

Design by Laura Hammond Hough

Atlantic Monthly Press
841 Broadway
New York, NY 10003

02 03 04 05   10 9 8 7 6 5 4 3 2 1

For Leonard Wallace Robinson . . . forgive me Nardo,
I know not what I do.

A Babe in the Woods

The first time Franko saw her she was walking around Tsamet, clicking snapshots of the minaret like any American or German tourist. She was tall and attractive in a curious mixture of exotic and wholesome. She had her hair pulled back, and the baseball cap she wore had a little opening that allowed her hair to billow out in a brownish-red ball. It reminded him of the hole in the pants of a cartoon character, through which Brer Fox's tail waved.

She wore faux expedition gear, lots of khaki with many snaps and epaulets and pockets. She left the top buttons undone on the shirt, revealing a formidable cleavage. The pants were relaxed fit, but the seat was well filled out.

When he got back to his crofter's cottage, up on Daliljaj's farm, he made a couple of quick pencil sketches of her. They weren't quite right—he hadn't gotten the nose or the eyes—but the wide mouth and full lips were okay. Later he had a chance to correct these sketches and ink them in.

He saw her a couple more times in town, or near it, in the next week or so. In the meantime, he went fishing, as usual. It was handy for making his connections with the smugglers. The farmers hereabouts were used to seeing him walking in the fields, or the woods, along the streams, usually after parking his battered old Subaru Outback near a little stone bridge. He would have his knapsack with his sketchbook and lunch in it, binoculars for bird-watching, his creel, and his fishing vest and would carry his rod. And soon he would be casting into the stream, wandering across the fields, climbing fences, stalking trout, birdwatching, sketching. "The Naturalist," they called him.

Under the bridge he would find the goods that had been left for him. They would go into the creel, or the backpack. Later, usually far upstream, where the stream ran through the wooded glades, he would encounter the young fellows to whom he passed the goods, with their instructions for delivery. Then he would go on.

He caught many trout. Very few people fished for trout in these parts. He was fascinated by these fish. They were small and easy to catch. He tied his own flies streamside, based on the insects he observed, using a handy portable device. And he would sketch the little trout. Some of them were an undescribed species, or at least a subspecies, that he couldn't find in the taxonomic records. They had greenish flanks with unusual vermiform markings on their backs. Most of them he released, but he always kept a few to give to his landlord, Daliljaj. He drew meticulous pictures of their guts, their organs, the insects they were dining on. He measured them carefully, and weighed them with a little hand-held instrument.

He sketched everything on his almost daily fishing hikes: the views of the mountains, the houses, the farmers, the farmers' kids, the bridges, the haystacks, the stiles that got one over the rough stone fences—each farmer built different kinds of bridges, stacked his hay differently, had his own idea of a proper stile. But mostly he sketched wildlife: birds, marmots, foxes, the rare badger snuffling through a field, and especially the fish.

One day he was sketching a small trout and he'd brought along some watercolors, to try to capture the vividness of the green flanks, the red and blue flecks, before the color faded, as it did too quickly. He was in a little sunny clearing in the woods, barely a foot from the pebble-bottomed stream where he'd caught this fish—sitting on a crude bridge over it, in fact.

This was a bridge he'd sketched before: just some roughly hewn logs thrown across the stream and planks nailed to it. But the farmer who used it to get from one meadow to another had made a rough railing with extra logs, perhaps to make sure that his reckless sons didn't drive the tractor into the creek, and had planed off a place to sit.

The stream skirted the edge of the woods. It was only knee-deep in most places, but there were chest-deep pools, one close by, where he had caught the trout. Small, colorful stones lined the stream.

He was concentrating and didn't see the woman until she stepped onto the bridge. It was the American woman, whom by now he had learned was a representative of the American foreign-aid agency.

"Hi," she said, and sat on the opposite railing to watch while he quickly finished the sketch and made some daubs of color in the proper spots, as a guide for later.

Franko set the book aside with the pages open to dry and said, "Hello."

"Can I see?" she asked, coming across to reach for the book.

He let her have it. "That paint is still a little wet," he said. He was gratified to see that she handled the book carefully, holding the freshly painted page open and merely glancing back at other pages. Up close, he saw that she was at least partly African-American, but her skin was very pale, like old ivory, and she had freckles. Her eyes were brown, with gold flecks.

"Is this me?" she said, finding an earlier sketch. "Do I really look like that? What a big butt you think I have!" She turned her rear toward him, mockingly. She was wearing khakis, as usual.

"It's just a quick sketch," he said. "Here, let me fix it."

"Oh no, you're right," she said, smiling. "I do have a big butt."

"Not at all," he said.

"Some men are crazy for big butts," she said. "Ah, here's that Romeo kid. He's very handsome. What eyes! Oh ho, and here's a buxom lass. What's that line of Walton's, about the trout in the milk?"

"It's Thoreau," he said. "'Some circumstantial evidence is very strong, as when you find a trout in the milk.'"

"Is that from *Walden*? Maybe that's how I got it wrong."

"I think it's from the *Journal*," he said.

"Well, this picture is a trout in the milk," she said. She showed him the picture, which he knew well. It was of a farm girl named Fedima—Daliljaj's daughter, in fact—and she was nude from the waist up. She was washing her upper body by a stream. "You don't want this to fall into the hands of the farmer."

He looked rueful. "It was quite an innocent occasion, I swear. I just happened to see her. I couldn't resist the sketch—when I got home."

"I'll bet," the woman said. She handed the book back. "So, what are you doing up here, spying on farm girls?"

"I'm not usually that lucky," he said, setting the book down beside him on the railing seat. He bent down to wrap the fish in ferns and started to place it in his creel. Instead, he said, "Would you like a fish?"

"My best offer of the day," the woman said. "But no thank you. It's way too circumstantial. Well, what are you doing?"

"I'm fishing," he said.

"Is that why you meet the young men in the woods?" she said. "You're not gay, are you?"

4

"Certainly not."

"I didn't think so, with your eye for farm girls. I was just trying to get under your skin."

She was quite close, propped on one knee on the seat to look over his shoulder at the picture of the trout again. He was uncomfortable, but he didn't want to move away.

"Would you like to sketch me?" she said.

"I'd love to." He picked up the sketchbook. "This picture is dry," he said, leafing over to a fresh page.

She sat down across the way. "Maybe you can get the nose right," she said.

He began a preliminary line with a pencil. In a moment of daring, he said, "Or the butt."

The woman laughed. "You're asking to see my butt?"

"Just joking," he said.

"I don't mind," she said. She stood up and began to unbuckle her belt, then looked about, cautiously. "Perhaps not here. There's always someone around that you don't notice until too late, isn't there?"

But there was no sign of anyone. They were alone on the little bridge. A copse of willow trees blocked the meadow to the west, and the little dirt road, after crossing the bridge, disappeared into a thicket to the east.

The woman stepped down from the bridge and wandered along it. He hastily assembled his gear and followed. She came to an old stone wall, now generally fallen down. Here she stopped, glanced around, and swiftly removed her boots, her pants, and her shirt. She wore no underwear. It was all he could do not to gasp. She had a fine, full-figured body.

"How's this?" she said, sitting in the sun on some moss. She leaned back gingerly against the rough wall, stretched her arms along the stones, and languorously extended her legs. She spread them well apart, one knee drawn up, assuming a frankly wanton posture.

The sexiness of the pose was enhanced and mocked by the fact that she hadn't removed her baseball cap. He sketched very rapidly, eager to capture her careless sensuality. He was also fighting to suppress an uncomfortable erection. His problem was not unobserved by his model.

"Should we do something about that?" she said, with a sly smile.

He sketched the smile. It was perfect. "Do you think that would be a good idea?"

"Too late," she said, rising to her feet abruptly. She nodded toward the bridge, not so very distant. A tractor could be heard approaching. "What did I tell you?" She sighed and stooped to gather her clothes. Before she stepped into the shelter of the trees to dress, she looked over her shoulder and said, "How's the butt? Too big?"

He stood and stared after her, unable to think of a suitable reply. Should he go into the woods with her? Was this an invitation? But no, she was dressing rapidly.

"Ciao," she said, and disappeared just as the tractor issued out of the copse of willows and started onto the bridge.

Franko glared at the tractor with real loathing. The man on it did not see him. He was turned on the seat, his back to Franko, to make sure that the old and decrepit wagon that dragged behind, loaded with fire logs, tracked properly. He was quickly over the bridge and out of sight.

Franko looked back into the woods, hopefully. The woman was gone, of course.

It had become a habit of Franko's to take his morning coffee in the yard, literally the barnyard of his landlord, Vornuto Daliljaj. This was not as unappetizing as it might seem. It had been a long time since the barnyard had been used by animals, although a faint and not unpleasant aroma was still detectable. It was a large, open ground nominally enclosed with a dilapidated wooden fence as well as the battered walls of some sheds, the old barn, and the cottage. It was a staging area for farm implements, but it had an aspect of privacy. One might almost describe it as a kind of bucolic plaza, populated by a few strolling, garrulous chickens and the silent, prowling cat.

The east wall of the old stone cottage Franko occupied also served as part of the enclosure. In fact, if one looked closely one could see where an overlarge doorway or opening in this wall had been reduced with later stonework, not quite in the style of the original, less crude and using a finer mortar. A conventional door was mounted in the newer opening.

Franko figured that animals used to be housed in the stone cottage. He wondered if it had been the bullpen, in fact, where a cow was introduced to the sire of her calves. Probably the entry had been reduced at the same time the wooden floor was installed, to create housing for farmhands, or another family. There was a definite air of the byre about the cottage. It also had a front door, which gave onto the area outside the barnyard.

Franko had found a weathered wooden bench that he set next to the barnyard door. The crude, unfaced stone wall behind the bench had been plastered with stucco in some long ago past, so that now it had a pleasant tawniness that took the morning sun very well, warm but not glaring. It was nice to sit on this bench and lean one's back against the warm stucco, particularly now, in this good fall weather when there was a hint of frost in the morning air.

From this bench Franko could look past the barn, the tackle shed now used to store tractor parts, a dilapidated jakes, and down the sectioned fields to the east, down the mountainside to where a minaret poked up above the treetops. Then one's eye rose to distant ridges, other farms half-hidden among the trees. There was often a wisp of mist rising out of the trees, mingling with smoke from chimneys, and generally, as one's eye approached the horizon, the air thickened and blurred into a grayish blue.

"Look away, look away . . . Dixieland" were the words that came to his mind when he saw this. But it was hardly a southern landscape—almost exactly the same northern latitude as his native Montana, six or seven thousand miles to the west.

Franko sometimes brought out his notebook and sketched the view. He thought moments like these were made for smoking a pipe. But he had never taken up smoking. So he just gazed and thought, allowing himself to come fully awake.

Montana was also mountain country, but it was not much like this. These mountains were not as large as the mountains around Butte, not as clearly a part of a huge, distinct range. But maybe it only seemed so, he thought, because these valleys were smaller, not so grand and sweeping. The mountains here were rugged and precipitous, but somehow not such massive structures. And then, he thought, it could be that it was just lower here, with the Adriatic not more than eighty miles away, as the raven flew, beyond another mountain range at his back.

These thoughts were pleasantly dislodged by the appearance of the daughter of Daliljaj, very pretty and dark-eyed Fedima, who was only eighteen and looked remarkably elegant to Franko's mind in her head scarf, blue jeans, heavy sweater, and rubber Wellington boots. She was the crown of his morning pleasure.

She tramped across the old, rough, but well-flattened and sunbaked yard carrying his coffee in a little brass pot. She had ground the beans herself, he knew, in a tubular brass device with a handle on the top, and had poured the hot water over it to steep. It was very strong, but Franko had learned to like it. It was also too sweet, but he tolerated that as well.

It always happened, he noticed, that within a few moments of Fedima's appearance around the stone side of the old granary, another person could usually be seen—remote but not too far off, not so close as to require even a casual wave, ostensibly uninterested in the conjunction of Fedima and Franko. Often this person was old Daliljaj himself, though frequently it was his wife, or even one of Fedima's brothers. But there would be someone, just a black image on the perimeter of Franko's vision, a crow or raven, as it might be, attending to some useful but not evidently pressing business.

Today, it was old Daliljaj, repairing part of the fence that formed the other part of the entry. He was winding a length of baling twine from an old fence post to the gatepost. And at that moment, the world changed forever.

A large, brutal-looking man in a paramilitary uniform walked up to Daliljaj and kicked the gate free of his hands.

"That your fucking tractor out on the road, *balija?*" the fellow demanded loudly.

The old man gaped. Nobody, not even a Serbian cop, talked to the old man like that. The term *balija* was derisive and contemptuous, and hadn't been heard in these parts until quite recently. Certainly not up in this mountain village, where the Daliljajs had been farming for generations.

The cop didn't even have a real uniform, just some foolish camo outfit. Was he even an officer? What was his rank? Something about the oaf's grinning face made the farmer hesitate.

"What is the problem?" he said, careful not to address the policeman with disrespect but also not to honor him with a title like sergeant or lieutenant, which might not properly apply.

"The problem is that it's parked in the road," the cop said. He looked about the compound in a way that suggested he was taking inventory. He raised an eyebrow at the figure of Daliljaj's daughter, Fedima. Like a good Muslim woman, she immediately vanished into Franko's house, leaving behind the coffeepot sitting on the bench next to Franko. A moment later she exited from the other door and presumably went to the farmhouse, via a route shielded from the eyes of the men in the yard.

"Who are you?" the cop said to Franko, who stood up and approached the gate.

Franko was cautious. He'd heard about this fellow from Captain Dedorica, the police chief in Tsamet. He was called Bazok, and he was the informal leader of a handful of such men, sent down from Belgrade to "assist" the local police chief. Captain Dedorica's information had been sketchy. Franko had meant to press Dedorica about it, but he'd forgotten.

"I live here," he said.

Bazok nodded. "Oh yeah," he said. "You the one they call Franko? I want to talk to you." He turned to Daliljaj. "Move the tractor. You can't leave it on the road."

"Nobody ever complained before," Daliljaj said. "There is no traffic—it's not in the way."

"Move the fucking tractor, *balija*," Bazok snarled, the smile icy now. When Daliljaj went off, he turned to Franko and said, "Where's your place?"

Franko shrugged and led him back through the gate and across the barnyard. He stopped and pointed to the old stone cottage with a new metal roof. Suddenly seeing it through a stranger's eyes, Franko thought it didn't look like much—a miserable hovel. The stone had been laid in a style that he had known at home as "pudding stone"; that is, a crude frame of wood was erected, and stones were simply dropped into a thick pudding of cheap, sandy mortar. These old walls had a tendency to fall down after fifty or sixty years, but someone had kept this one repaired. Of course, if it had been a bull pen that would account for the extra-thick walls.

Bazok gestured for Franko to go ahead and took a step toward the house himself, but stopped when Franko did not move.

"We can talk here," Franko said. He wasn't sure how receptive he should be to this fellow. Was he actually a cop, or some kind of unwarranted deputy? In Montana a man didn't just walk onto another man's land in the way that Bazok had, unless he was armed and visibly authorized with a badge and a uniform, to say nothing of an official, legal paper. This guy looked to be about twenty-two or twenty-three, big and beefy but with a few complexion problems still and not too handy with a razor. Even so, one was not in Montana. It wouldn't hurt to play along, tentatively.

Bazok looked at him, sizing him up. Franko was not a big man, not within six inches of his own height or fifty pounds of his weight, but a sturdily built man in his late thirties. Like most of the men in these villages, he had black hair, dark eyes, a thick black mustache. Bazok was not impressed.

"Come," Bazok said. "I have to discuss private things."

Franko realized then that Bazok was not a Serb. He spoke the language all right, but there was something unnatural about his usage, as if he was not quite comfortable with it. It occurred to him that the man was an American. In English, he said, "What's the big deal?"

Bazok broke into a genuine grin. "All right," he said, in good American. He grabbed Franko's right hand with his own and clapped him on the shoulder. "They didn't tell me you were from the States. Where you from, dude?"

Franko managed a faint smile but wrenched his hand free and stepped back from Bazok's near embrace. Without glancing around he gauged whether there were any Kosovars anywhere near. He didn't think so; none of Daliljaj's sons or cousins would be in the compound at this time, and he was pretty sure that Fedima had gone to the house. Still, it wouldn't do to appear too chummy with this clown.

"I'm from out West," Franko said. "Butte."

"No shit," Bazok said. "I been there. I rode a freight through Butte once. Burlington Northern, eh? Friendly people in Butte, they don't hassle you. So what're ya doin' here, hangin' out with these hankyheads? You don't look like no Taliban—you ain't a fuckin' terrorist, are you?" He laughed and prodded Franko's stomach playfully.

Franko frowned. "You must have heard about me, from Captain Dedorica," he said.

"Oh, sure," Bazok nodded. "You're the friendly neighborhood dope peddler. That's why I stopped by."

Franko suppressed a sigh of depression. So that was it. This oaf wanted to be cut in on Dedorica's "business tax." He considered it. He supposed he had no choice. If Dedorica had seen fit to inform this guy, then it probably meant amending the agreement. The question was how much, and whether this meant that Dedorica now got correspondingly less for not keeping his mouth shut. But. . . . He had a second thought: who was this guy, really? Why an American? Something was amiss.

He nodded at the door, a slight motion. "If you insist," he said in Serb. As he'd hoped, the cop caught on. He pushed Franko forward, his huge hand on his back. Even if no one seemed to be around, there were always eyes. Franko was more comfortable with an appearance of being coerced. He could not afford any suspicion from the Kosovars.

Like any such house of its type and vintage, Franko's croft was not well lit. There were few windows, and the electrical wiring was a single exposed conduit. It ran an old battered refrigerator, and there was an outlet from which extension cords served a radio, a reading light by the so-called easy chair, and another reading lamp clamped to the bed frame. A single light bulb dangled from the center of the ceiling.

The interior was essentially one room, perhaps four paces wide and twice as many long. The kitchen area took up one end, with a sink and a counter for preparing food. A narrow window looked out onto the path that led around the granary toward the main house. There was no running water, no drain system, and certainly no toilet. A bucket stood on the rough wooden floor near the sink. Another bucket under the sink caught the waste. Around an old, scarred wooden table covered with an oilcloth stood some mismatched wooden chairs.

At the other end of the room stood the metal frame bed with a single mattress, some rumpled blankets. In between was a ratty old overstuffed chair with a table next to it, on which were stacked a few books—a Serbian dictionary, a mystery novel with a black cover and a French title. A reading lamp stood nearby. It had a battered paper shade. Clothes were scattered on the floor, more hung from a rod affixed in a corner.

"Pretty cozy," Bazok said, with no apparent sarcasm, peering about with interest. Suddenly, he thrust out his hand. "Hey, the name is Boz." He pronounced it "Bozh." "Back in the States, they call me 'Badger.' But over here, it's Bozi Bazok."

"Badger?" Franko said. "Is that what that animal is?" He gestured toward the ferocious, snarling beast on the patch that decorated Bazok's baseball cap.

"Yah," Bazok said, proudly. "But I got the name from this." He lifted his cap to reveal thick black hair that was cut in a stiff brush. In the center of the brush was a tuft of white hair. "I had that since I was a kid," he said, "so in Georgia, they called me Badger. Mark of the beast, my old lady used to say. It fits." He grinned, displaying a lot of white teeth.

He pointed at the loft, to which a ladder led. "What's up there?"

"Storage," Franko said. He leaned against the counter. "Go ahead, look."

Bazok climbed the ladder until his head was above the level of the loft floor. There were boxes, a suitcase, an old television set. "What's in the boxes?" he called over his shoulder.

"Junk—it was here before."

Bazok climbed down. "How long you been holed up here?"

"Six months, maybe more."

"You don't watch the tube?"

"They don't carry the ballgames," Franko said, sourly. "I'm not interested in propaganda." Lately, the Serbian television stations had been spewing anti-Muslim "news" broadcasts and special programs extolling the regime.

"Nice radio," Bazok said, nodding at the fancy Telefunken broadband radio sitting on the kitchen table. Franko didn't respond. "So, where do you keep the shit?"

"What shit would that be?"

"The dope."

"I don't have any dope," Franko said. He was sure that Dedorica would not have suggested to the young cop that narcotics were readily available here. But maybe the cop was just asking a cop question. "When were you in Butte?"

"A couple years ago." Bazok aped a southern accent: "Just kickin' around the country. Ah'm from Atlanta, originally."

"Really? You speak pretty good Serb," Franko observed.

"Actually, I was born in Yugoslavia," Bazok said. "I think. I got adopted by an American lady. Grew up in Atlanta. But I got tired of it and hit the road when I got old enough. You grow up in Montana? That's nice country. I liked it. It's a little like this, the mountains and all."

"I wouldn't exactly say that," Franko said. "This is more like West Virginia, Appalachia, don't you think?"

Bazok nodded. "Yeah, I can see it. Well, listen, we gotta talk."

"What about? I'm happy to meet a fellow Yank, even one from Atlanta, but I've got to be cool. These folks don't exactly dig Serb cops, you know."

"Hey, I'm cool, dude. I'm not gonna blow your cover, Frankie. The deal is, I know the bros, in Belgrade. Ziv and them. They said to look you up."

"Zivkovic?" Franko was suprised. "How do you know these people?" He thought it was interesting that they hadn't told Bazok that he was an American. It suggested that they hadn't been totally open with Bazok, for whatever reason, but he didn't bring that up.

"I met 'em in the States," Bazok said. "That's how I got to this fuckin' shithole country. I'm part of their posse. Then I got into this vigilante gig." He gestured at his outfit. "It was Ziv's idea. It's a good scam." He laughed. "I'm kind of diggin' it. But it's a long story."

"I'd like to hear all about it," Franko said. He was sincere. "But not here, not right now. Maybe I could meet you in town, in Tsamet. At a beer garden, maybe. Or, I know, I could come by the station. We could talk."

"Yeah, that's okay," Bazok said. "But the news is there's some heavy shit going down. You wanta get your show ready for the road. In a couple of days you don't wanta be here."

Franko was stunned. "What kind of operation? When?"

"I'm not sure, but it'll be heavy, is the word," Bazok said. "The army will be along pretty quick, in a day or two, maybe sooner. I got the feeling, though, that they'll have me and some other outfits like mine do the dirty, at first anyway. Ziv found out about it, he called me." He tapped his breast pocket, evidently where he kept his cell phone. "You got one of these? What's your number?" Franko gave it to him. "All right, I'll give you a buzz."

"I've got to know how soon," Franko said. He looked out the kitchen window toward the barn, the lane, the orchard. No one seemed to be about, but he felt uneasy in the house with the thug. The big question was how much Zivkovic had told this guy. "I've got shipments, things scheduled. I can't just pick up and run."

"It's gonna get jungly," Bazok said. He sounded excited. He came over to where Franko was and stood too close; his breath was foul. "They'll be putting up roadblocks pretty soon. Your shipments won't be coming in or going out. You gotta think like you might have to just walk, leave everything. I'll try to get up here first, make sure there's nothin' too suspicious layin' around. Prob'ly have to torch the house. See what I mean?"

This was serious. Franko thought of Fedima. He'd have to get her out. That wouldn't be easy. He had to think. Maybe he could get Daliljaj to go too. That would probably be best. Get up into the hills, to the KLA (Kosovo Liberation Army), maybe. Daliljaj would have contacts; they could get over into Montenegro, maybe, or down to the coast. Maybe get out through Albania.

"I can't just walk away," Franko said. "There are people due in here, valuable goods to consider."

"I gotcha," Bazok said. "But like I say, I doubt that your people will be gettin' through. When the shit starts, it'll come down like a storm outta the hills. You don't want to be thinkin' about your business. C'mon, let's get outta here."

Outside, the cop took a deep breath of the mountain air. He looked around. "That your car?" He nodded at the beat-up Subaru Outback. "I thought you'd have something with some jump to it— you're makin' a ton here. A Cherokee, maybe even a fuckin' Humvee."

"It runs," Franko said. "That's what passes for a good vehicle in these parts."

"Ah," Bazok said, nodding, enlightened. "You don't want to make too big a scene out here in the sticks. But you got to be thinkin' about haulin' your shit down to the barracks, tonight."

"Tonight!" Franko didn't like the sound of that. Deliver close to a couple hundred thousand dollars' worth of raw opiates to this doofus in his barracks? Not likely.

"It's happenin'," Bazok said. His face was big and grinning, like a jack-o'-lantern. He was not an ugly guy, if he could think to keep that menacing grin off his face—the teeth mirrored the badger image on his patch.

"What about my people?" Franko said.

"What people? I told you. . . . oh, you mean these *balijas*? What the fuck do you care? Whoa, I get it. You're shaggin' the ginch. I seen her, not a bad little piece of ass. What's her name, Fatima or something?"

Furious, Franko stepped toward the grinning oaf, fists clinched. Suddenly the cop's boot shot out and slammed Franko's right leg on the side of his knee, causing it to buckle. The cop caught him by the hair, burying his powerful fingers in it, while his other hand wrenched Franko's right arm around behind his back.

"You fuckin' dog," Bazok growled loudly in Serb. "I ought to kick your fuckin' ass and haul you down to the station." He bore Franko to the ground, facedown, with his knee on his back. He knelt to rasp in his ear, "How can you fuck something like that? I'll bet she's as hairy as a coon." He stood up but held Franko down, pinned with a heavy boot. "You get your ass down to the station this p.m., shithead. Don't make me come back up here lookin' for your sorry ass. And you," he snarled at Daliljaj, who had come around the side of the barn, "did you move that fuckin' tractor? All right."

He kicked Franko playfully in the butt, then strode off, taking a lazy swipe at Daliljaj, who ducked. He laughed and walked out to the road and got into his police jeep and drove off.

Daliljaj rushed to help Franko up. "Are you all right?" he asked anxiously.

"I'm okay," Franko said, standing up and brushing himself off. "Filthy bastard. He didn't hurt me."

"What did he want?"

"Just throwing his weight around, I guess," Franko said. "Listen, my friend, I must go down to Tsamet. It'll be all right. Dedorica won't allow anything serious. But I'm concerned about you, and your family. This man's behavior concerns me—something unpleasant must be happening."

"You don't worry about us," Daliljaj said. "You mustn't say anything to Dedorica." He looked fierce. "We can take care of ourselves. We have friends." He looked toward the forested mountains about them. "These pigs, they will pay."

The old man was not really very old, just into late middle age. He was short but stocky, a powerful man. He knew that Franko was dealing contraband, but he wasn't sure what it was. It didn't pay to inquire too closely. He also suspected that Fedima was attracted to the man, but he didn't believe that it had gone very far. He could not allow that, although he liked the American. Franko was not a Believer. It would not do. Still, the patriarch understood women: they had no control over their passions. A man had to govern them. The American was a good man, as foreigners go, but had no morals, of course; that was certain. It was up to Daliljaj to see that nothing foolish went on. A little flirtation, that was nothing.

Sometimes, though, he had thought that maybe Fedima should marry this American, go to his country. Things were getting bad here. He and his people would survive; they would rise up, take Kosovo. He was a Believer, but he was a practical man, after all. If the American wanted the girl and took her with him when he went—and he was sure that Franko would go, he had always known that—then perhaps that would be all right, even though the man was not a Believer. At least he wasn't a Serb—he might have the name of a Serb, but he was not a Serb. She would be safer with the American when things got really bad. A woman in Kosovo, a Muslim woman, was always in danger from the Chetniks. But the American could not have her here. That would not be right. It would make Daliljaj look bad, although the American was well liked.

"I have a bad feeling," Franko said. "This Serb, he is too bold. If he can behave like this, it means that something evil is coming."

"Oh yes, the evil is coming," Daliljaj said. "But you need not fear for us, my friend. We will be all right. Besides, the *bashi-bazouk* is not a Serb. Couldn't you tell? He's a German, I think." He was being polite, distinguishing the policeman from his tenant.

"*Bashi-bazouk*? You mean like a Turk? A terrorist?"

"No, no," the old man laughed. "That's what they call him and his men, but it is a bad joke, I think. The Chetniks will use him and his friends like dogs, to hunt the Kosovars. But they will be the first to die."

Franko was depressed by this bravura rhetoric. The farmers were fierce men, bold men, but they were farmers. He had seen what kind of weapons they had—old rifles from World War II, a crazy confidence in knives. Against AK-47s, rocket launchers, heavy machine guns, they had no chance.

He spent the afternoon relocating his goods, especially the cash. There were some secure places to stash things back beyond the home pasture, in the woods, among the caves in the rocks. He got together a practical kit of passport, money, and a handgun. It was a plausible kit, one that the foolish cop would approve. Then he drove into town.

Bashi-bazouk

Captain Dedorica knew from the start that the new guy was trouble. He was big and rough, but that wasn't the problem. He grinned in a disarming way, but he had a way of standing a little too close at times. Dedorica didn't like some big lout sticking his face into his, especially when he was supposed to be a subordinate.

That was the heart of the problem: he wasn't really a subordinate. He had been sent down from Belgrade to Dedorica's little town, Tsamet, along with five other fellows. It was supposed to be a kind of government-aid program—auxiliary police—but it was something else, Dedorica understood.

His name was given as Bozi Bazok, but that couldn't be his real name. It was a rude joke, like their insignia patch, which depicted a cartoon beast said to be a badger. The glaring, teeth-baring badger with the white blaze on its forehead clutched two lightning bolts crossed before it in a way that unnervingly suggested the old Nazi swastika—another layer of confounding imagery, evoking the hated Ustaše, the Croatian collaborators of the last war. A fake Latin inscription—CAVE TAXI—under the cartoon completed the joke: Beware the Badger.

Dedorica had a bad feeling about all this bizarre playacting. He had no illusions; he knew what was going on. But what was the point of confusing the situation by borrowing all this flummery and playacting from your enemies and then making it into a new bogeyman? It was the same old business wasn't it? Maybe it had to be made new, somehow. Still, it had nothing to do with police work.

Not that Bazok and his pals made much pretense of being working cops. They never pulled regular shifts. Mostly, they hung out in the taverns and caused trouble. They got drunk, made loud statements about "filthy *balijas*." Very soon they were an all-too-visible presence in Tsamet and the neighboring villages. And the funny thing about Bazok: he looked like an Albanian himself. He was darker, more Mediterranean, perhaps, than a Slav. And it couldn't be ignored that he didn't speak Serb all that well. It was rumored, in fact, that he was an American.

Bazok didn't seem much like an American to Dedorica. In his view, Americans were rich, didn't speak Serb at all, or any languages but their own, for that matter. The Americans he'd met seemed so easygoing, cheerful, and confident, but not in the menacing way of Boz. There was Franko, for instance, who despite his Serbian name was clearly of that easygoing, practical, and enterprising Yankee style. Or the US AID representative who had hung around town for several days this summer, asking all sorts of impertinent questions, so bold—in a friendly way, of course. And so tall, such long and slim legs, and what an ass! She was frank and open, in the famous way of American women—a whore, doubtless, but vivacious, amusing, and sure of herself.

Still, Dedorica could hardly complain about Bazok. As police chief, he was always asking Belgrade for help. This, however, was no help. This only exacerbated the problem. The half dozen Kosovar policemen on the force had quit, probably to join the resistance, or maybe even the KLA. So he was no further ahead, was he? Actually, it was worse yet, since tensions in the community had risen, thanks to the new guys. *Tako je*—that's the way it is—was the only thing you could say.

Franko was amazed at the traffic, the nervous mood in town. There were soldiers everywhere, lounging about, automatic rifles slung carelessly. How long had they been around? There had been new roadblocks on his way in, but they'd not stopped him, just waved him through when he slowed. He hadn't been paying attention lately, he realized. Had he been dreaming? He'd been too isolated, too distracted by Fedima . . . and the American US AID worker, who had gone now, it seemed.

The police station was filled with people, Serbs and Kosovars, everybody complaining, talking loudly. A Serbian army officer—Franko heard him called a major—seemed to be running things. He was ordering people about. Since Franko was not accompanied by an officer, not under arrest, not complaining, he was ignored. But he caught a glimpse of Dedorica, who stepped out of his office, looked about him in poorly disguised dismay, and retreated back into the room, quietly closing the door behind him. Franko followed, knocking and then slipping in quickly.

Dedorica tried to put a good face on, but he was shifty. "*Tako je*," he said, with a shrug. "What can I do? I didn't send the Bazok up there. I didn't even know he'd been. Of course, he asked about you."

Franko started to say, Why didn't you mention it? What am I paying you for? But he settled for "I thought, as we had an agreement, that you would keep me informed. What was he asking?"

"Well, that's just it," Dedorica said. "He asked nothing of any consequence. He said he'd heard there was a foreigner living around here, who was he, what did he do? That sort of thing. Any policeman would ask that. Not that Bozi Bazok is any kind of policeman." This last was muttered under his breath, but Franko overheard it.

"Well, who is he?" Franko asked.

"He's just a thug from Belgrade," Dedorica insisted. "It has to do with the army. So perhaps they are like the *bashi-bazouks*. They preceded the Ottoman army, created terror, and by the time the army arrived, the people welcomed them for bringing order and protecting them from the horrors of the *bashi-bazouks*. So it's not as crazy as it looks."

"Did you tell him about our arrangement?"

"Never! Why would I do that? I told him that as far as I knew you were a scholar."

"A scholar! What sort of scholar?"

"A *biolog*, a naturalist." The captain shrugged. He was a pleasant enough man, well into middle age, with a wife, children, and a mistress or two. He had impressed Franko before as a typical, fairly competent police officer, corrupt in the way of police but not venal. He was a Serb, but had lived in the region so long that he thought more like a Kosovar. It was clear that he was in despair, realizing that his life here was never going to be the same again, and perhaps only now understanding that it had been a better life than he'd thought.

"He has no notion of a scholar, anyway," Dedorica said. "He said you were probably a spy. That's what Major Kaporica thinks, too."

"He's the one running things?" Franko said, nodding toward the hall. "What should I do?"

"You're asking me, my friend? I'm sorry, there is very little I can do for you. The major is busy. He has left you to the Bazooks. But don't worry, you're in no danger. Just cooperate with the lad and I'll do what I can to see that you're not . . ." He hesitated.

"Not what?" Franko said.

"Not molested. You'll tell him a good story. He likes money, I think. Perhaps . . ." He made the universal gesture of rubbing his fingers with his thumb. "He's not very bright, you know, just a kid. What does he know about politics, about spies? Offer him some money. You'll be all right. But don't make him angry. No, no." He shook his head. "That wouldn't be wise."

Then he took Franko down into the basement, to a room that was very much like a cell, where Bazok was waiting with a couple of his men. They looked like Bazok, young and burly and full of themselves, in the same outfit with the goofy cartoon arm patch, except they weren't so dark. They were big and blond. There was shouting down the hall, voices raised in fear and protest, the sound of curses, blows. Franko didn't like it. He assumed there were other cells down here, where things weren't quite as calm as in this room. A piercing scream was suddenly muffled.

"I'll talk to him," Bazok said to the captain. "Go on back to your office. If I need you I'll buzz." When the captain had left, he stepped close to Franko, literally nose to nose, and winked. Then, still in Serbian, he said, "What's your real name, spy?" and he struck him in the face with his fist.

Franko was stunned. The blow had come from nowhere. He lay on the damp concrete floor. He wondered if his cheekbone was fractured. He drew up his legs to protect himself from a kick, but none was offered. One of the other Bazooks hoisted him to his feet roughly. They were laughing at his shock.

"That should get his attention," Bazok said, smiling. He pinched Franko's neck with his iron fingers. The pain was intense, but Bazok quickly relented. "Sit down, take it easy," he said, suddenly too kindly, in the ominous way of cops. To the others he made a head toss toward the door. "Leave us. He'll talk more freely to me, alone. If I need you, I'll call."

When they left, he spoke in English, a more amiable tone. "No offense, Frankie. I had to make it look good. Okay, what you got for me?" He picked up the valise that Franko had brought with him to the station and opened it on the metal desk. He looked at the passport, tossed it aside, handled the Browning 9mm automatic pistol admiringly, then laid it aside. He sat down and counted out the money, bundled into packets of one thousand dollars. There were ten of them.

"That's it?" he said, looking up.

Franko shrugged. He slumped in his metal chair, hands in his lap, docile and defeated. "It's all I have," he said.

"Don't shit me," Bazok said. He tossed everything back into the valise, latched it, and set it on the floor next to his chair. "Where's the junk? Ziv said you had tons of it."

"Tons? Never. A kilo, now and then. But I've nothing right now," Franko said. "I sent a shipment a couple of days ago, with a trucker from Banja Luka. I don't leave it around, you know. The idea is to keep it in transit." He was betting that Vjelko Zivkovic would not have told this punk much.

Bazok made a sour face. "We'll see," he said. He sat in thought for several minutes, occasionally clasping his hands and cracking his knuckles. He brooded over his fist, kneading it, licking at it. No doubt it had hurt to strike Franko like that.

Finally, he said, "I think it'd be best if you split. There's no point in hanging around here. I'll take care of things up at the farm." He smiled menacingly. "I'll take care of the pussy personally, don't worry. I'll see she isn't raped too much."

Franko stared at him. "I don't think that's funny," he said. "Vjelko and I go back a long ways. We're partners."

"Is that so? That's not what I heard."

Franko shrugged. "You wouldn't know," he said. "Vjelko wouldn't tell *you*. The point is, there's bigger guys behind Vjelko, guys you wouldn't know about. They won't like this."

"They're there, I'm here," Bazok said, smiling. "The shit's about to fly. Just a matter of hours. Things'll start to get confused.

You could end up in a pile. It'd be outta my hands." He spread his hands, palms up. "I tried to protect you, you wouldn't listen. You got caught in the sweep. You see?"

Franko saw it. With a calmness that surprised himself, he said, "Don't make trouble for yourself, Badger. Don't put yourself in a position where you have to explain things to guys who don't like hearing excuses. Vjelko sent you in here to look out for his interests. His and others'," he added, warningly. "If you're on the ball, you'll make out. You've got a phone there, call Vjelko." He rattled off the cell-phone number.

Bazok wasn't smiling now. He was pensive, his face stupidly slack, mouth hanging open idly, gazing at Franko with narrowed eyes. "No," he said, after a long minute. "I don't want to call Ziv. He's not expecting me to call. He don't like calls." After another long minute, he got up and went out, taking the valise with him. He locked the door behind him.

Franko slumped on his chair. What a mistake coming down here! What had he been thinking? But he hadn't been thinking, just reacting. It was time to think. He felt he'd made some kind of impression on the dolt, but he wasn't sure. Bazok was probably calling Vjelko in private, but maybe not. He went back over his own words. He had simply told the lout what he hadn't been able to figure out for himself. He was concerned, however, by the fact that Dedorica had essentially washed his hands of him, had even implied that he, too, thought that Franko might be a spy.

So now what? He got up and walked about the little room, examining it. The door was locked; there were no windows. There was a drain in the floor. He supposed he could piss in that, if he had to. There was no cot, just the desk and a couple of chairs, a light bulb hanging from the ceiling. He sat down to wait. He listened to the muffled shouts, the screams. Doors slammed, clanged. People were taken in and out, protesting, though sometimes it sounded as if they were being dragged. He heard some distant shots. He'd heard shots earlier, but he had not thought of what they meant, preferring to believe they were fired by soldiers, just high spirits. Who knew what was going on out there?

After an hour, Bazok returned, with the valise. He tossed it at Franko. It was much lighter. "You better get your ass on the road," he said. "You got your keys?"

"Go where?"

"Wherever you want," Bazok said. "Italy. Albania. I don't give a fuck, long as it ain't back up to the farm. You got a passport, you can probably get by the checkpoints. I can't give you a pass of any kind. I'd be careful about the back roads. Itchy fingers on the triggers out there," he said. "I left you some cash. That'll help." He smiled.

Franko considered the man and his words. It wasn't a good offer, it was just a bait. The suggestion of itchy trigger fingers might be authentic, an attempt to get him to make himself into a running target. He said, "I don't think so."

"No? Last chance to bail," Bazok said. "You don't want to end up in a pile with a bunch of *balijas*. It don't smell so good. Smells like shit. They fill their baggy pants when you line 'em up. Blood all over everything. It's a mess. Sure you don't want to skate?"

"I need to go to the farm," Franko said.

"No way. Too late."

"It's not too late," Franko said. "I left some stuff up there."

"Aha! Okay, now we're talking. Tell me where it is, I'll run up there and get it. It'll be safe with me. In the meantime, maybe I can talk the major into giving you a pass. You could drive to Bosnia . . . be there by morning, I bet."

Franko shook his head. "I don't think so. I have to go up there."

Bazok looked at him shrewdly. "You still thinking about that pussy? That's it, ain't it?" He shook his head, wonderingly. "The power of pussy! It's stronger than money, they say, but I never thought so. Well, all right—what all you got up there that would make it worth my time and the hassle to ride you up there? 'Cause that's the only way we're gonna get through the troops, bro. We could take the jeep."

"There's some uncut H," Franko said. "Some cash. What the hell, you might as well have it, instead of the troops or the KLA. Somebody will find it, eventually. And while you're taking care of your newfound wealth, I'll just take a walk up into the hills."

"Now you're thinkin'," Bazok said. "See? That wasn't so hard to figure out. If you'd been smart we could of took care a business when it was still easy."

The situation had worsened while he'd been in the basement, Franko saw. Now there were troop trucks in the town, covered with tarps but with soldiers looking out. He saw an armored vehicle with an antitank gun mounted on it. Civilians were scarce.

"That stuff you told me about being adopted," Franko said, as they cleared a roadblock and drove up the mountain road, "was that true?" They passed houses that had Serbian markings on them, buildings with sandbags in the doorways. There were little outposts with machine guns and more sandbags.

"Sure it's true," Bazok said. "You think I'd lie about that? Thelma, she was like a mother to me. The only mother I ever knew. She picked me up on the street in a town near Jajce, somewhere like that."

"You don't know?"

"Hey, it was a hundred years ago! All right? She worked for US AID, one of those agencies. Say, that reminds me—d'jou see that babe that was here this summer? She was a US AID worker, she said, but that was bullshit. You fuck her, too? I had her a couple a times. She was fuckin' wild! Couldn't get enough of the old two-ball injection." He grabbed at his crotch and laughed.

Franko tried not to show his utter disbelief of this adolescent boast. "How old were you," he asked, divertingly. "I mean when Thelma found you?"

"Shit, I don't know. Ten? Twelve? I don't remember much before Atlanta. Just a lot a noise and cold and not much to eat. She was a good woman. A nutcase, but okay." He drove too fast but tensely alert, looking about constantly.

"These hills," he explained, when he noticed Franko watching him, "they're full a snipers. They smell the blood. Nah," he went on, reverting to his story, "I just as soon forget all that shit. Forget Atlanta, too, after the old lady died. Things went to shit there, too. But this"—he gestured at the dark countryside—"this is cool. This is more like it! Somethin's happ'nin', man! Don't you dig it?"

Franko didn't dig it. But he could see that Bazok was excited. He'd seen plenty of young fellows like this, Serbs and Kosovars alike. Rootless, ready for action. He figured the disturbance that so bothered him turned them on—the smell of war, the hint of violence in the air. Maybe it was the promise of an end to the humdrum everyday life that pumped them up.

He was worried about Fedima. He wanted nothing more than to extricate her from the incredible brutality that was sweeping this country. She was too young, too innocent and fragile for this. She didn't deserve to have her young life shattered by this wretched madness.

The smell of war must reek of sexual license for the young guys, too, Franko thought. Maybe that was why there was so much rape. They were turned on by the violence, aroused. It was inexplicable to him. He could not imagine being sexually aroused by the brutal humiliation of a helpless, terror-stricken woman. How were they even able to perform sexually, especially before others?

"Where did you get this goofy Turk name?" Franko asked.

Boz laughed. "You don't like it? The Serbs think it's a hoot. I made it up."

He was driving too fast for these roads, Franko thought. It had begun to rain and there were many huge potholes. If one didn't avoid them there was a risk not only of crashing but of shearing off a wheel, or at least breaking the steering gear. But Franko understood the impulse to speed: in these woods and hills, on a black night like this, there could be not only KLA snipers but independent random shooters—the hills were full of angry people ready to fire a casual shot at a passing vehicle.

"I was riding the rails," Boz continued, his voice loud over the roar of the engine. "It might even've been in Montana—I'm not sure where I was, just out West somewhere. And I met this crazy old fucker in a boxcar, he was reading one a them men's magazines, you know? *Saga*, or something like that? And he was laughing, and I axt him what was so funny, and he reads me some shit, an article about the German air force, the Luftwaffe, you know? This writer is talking about the Stuka dive-bomber, which he says was invented by a Professor Stuka. The old guy thought that was a fuckin' riot. He says, 'Maybe the bazooka was invented by Basil Bazook.' And he laughed his ass off. I don't know what was so funny, but I liked that Basil Bazook."

"There was no 'Professor Stuka,'" Franko said.

"No? Then what's the point?"

"That's the joke," Franko said, pedantically. "'Stuka' is short for *Sturzflugkraft*, or something even longer. But 'bazooka,' that's a made-up word. The weapon was named after a kind of joke kazoo that George Burns pretended to play on the radio."

"George Burns? The guy who played God?" Boz hunched, peering out through the rain. A stiff wind had come up and the rain had intensified. It was appallingly dark, visibility down to just yards, and he had slowed to avoid rocks that had rolled from the hillsides, either washed down by the rain or with human assistance. Some of them were big enough to smash a transmission.

"I like that," Boz went on, "God invented the bazooka! Anyways, I liked the sound of it. When I met Vjelko, in Chicago, I told him that was my name—Badger Bazooka. I put it on my social security card, only he had me spell it B-o-z-i B-a-z-o-k. Vjelko said that was a better spelling—the social security clerk would just think it was foreign, not made up."

Jesus, Franko thought. "How long ago was this?" he asked.

"Three, maybe four years back. So, you see, I known Vjelko a long time."

"Three years is not a long time," Franko said. He braced himself as the jeep whirled around a bend and narrowly missed a tree limb that had blown down.

"Long enough. Now what the fuck is this?" Boz slammed on the brakes and they skidded to a halt near the stone wall that surrounded Daliljaj's compound. The old man, or someone, had parked the tractor squarely across the entrance. "I told that shithead to get his tractor off the road, but I didn't mean he should barricade the drive."

Franko was instantly wary. "I wouldn't stop here," he said sharply. "Move on. Turn out your lights."

As if in reply an automatic rifle flashed and at least three bullets hit the jeep. Boz, swearing furiously, stamped on the gas, and they shot by the entry. He doused the lights, but unable to see in the pitch blackness, he also hit the brakes. The shooter keyed on the brake lights, and more shots hit the vehicle.

"Goddamn!" Boz roared. He let off the brake and they coasted away, apparently beyond the view of the shooter. There were no further flashes, and Boz let the vehicle roll to a stop near some wind-tossed trees. He seemed uncertain what to do. "Should we get out?"

Franko was already out. He hurled himself at the shelter of the stone wall and crouched at its base. Boz quickly joined him. "What now?" Boz asked. They were drenched instantly. The gale was blowing the rain sideways, huge drops of rain that impacted like soft bullets.

"Let's get the hell away from the jeep," Franko said and scuttled along the stone wall in a duck walk that under less compelling circumstances he would have found impossible. This wall was not very well made, a mere repiling of stones laboriously removed from the fields and tossed along the perimeter. He'd sometimes thought that Daliljaj, or his ancestors, were poor wall makers, but he had come to see this as their practical way to clear the fields; the repiling of the stones was something they could be doing in some hypothetical leisure moment that never seemed to come. He had gotten used to this style of farming. Here and there, where the stones were not sufficient to provide a real barrier for grazing animals, they had erected posts and strung strands of mended, recycled wire and baling twine. He found one of these places and slipped through into the field, with Boz close behind.

When they reached a large boulder, well out in the field, Franko crouched in its lee. Boz hunkered down next to him, a massive Glock in his hand. "Was that Daliljaj, you think?" Boz asked.

"Shooting, you mean?" Franko shook his head. "He doesn't have that kind of firepower," he said. "Must be KLA, or somebody. They're coming down out of the hills, I guess. They want to take advantage of the storm. I'd guess they're looking to ambush a patrol or something."

"Well, shit. Time to get the cavalry in here." Boz had fished out his cell phone.

"No, no." Franko stopped him. "You want to get the goods, don't you? It could get complicated if you call the troops in. There's probably just a handful of KLA, or whoever they are. They'll be watching the road. We can slip around the back."

Boz seemed to grasp the wisdom of this, but then he said, "What about my jeep?"

Almost in answer, there was a boom and a flash back beyond the stone wall. "Looks like they got it," Franko said.

"Now what!"

"We can always find a vehicle," Franko said. "Come on." He stood up and headed off into the storm, toward the compound.

"Where the hell you goin'?" Boz demanded. He grabbed Franko by the shoulder.

"Whoever they are, they'll be checking out the vehicle, to see if we're still in it. But first they'll have to wait for it to cool down. With any luck they won't hang around to make sure, or come looking for us. I'm going to check out the house."

"Fuck the house," Boz said. "You still thinkin' about that ginch? Jesus! Let's get the shit and get out of here. We go near that house and we'll get our asses shot off."

There was something to what Bazok said, Franko realized. "Okay, but we better check out my place, anyway. We'll need a flashlight."

"Can't we get by without it?" Boz said. Clearly, he didn't relish the idea of going anywhere near the compound.

"No," Franko said. He hurried on. They stumbled across the field, the rain lashing them. As he'd expected, his little house was dark. They drew nearer and waited, listening. There was some activity out near the road, shouts, a few lights. Franko took a deep breath and ducked into the door. Immediately somebody jumped on him.

He gasped with relief when he realized it was Fedima. The girl was clutching him desperately, and he almost fell. When she saw his companion, however, she leaped back. In the pale light from the doorway, just about the only light available in this gloomy interior, her eyes seemed huge and panic-stricken. Her mouth fell open, but she did not say anything, just backed into the darkness.

"He's with me," Franko hastily assured her. "He'll help us get out. But what are you doing out here?" He seized her by her arms, then hugged her. She was tiny and felt frail, but she instantly responded, her embrace tight and fervent.

"My father sent me to find you, to warn you not to come back. The"—she glanced at Boz—"the Chetniks are coming!"

"Where are your father and your brothers?" Franko asked her. "Who is in the house?"

"They are with the fighters," she said. "My mother and the others have gone."

The "others" would be the extended family, Franko supposed—her grandmother, some cousins. "Gone where?" he asked. But before she could reply, he asked how many armed men there were.

Fedima wasn't sure. Perhaps there were twenty-five or thirty "freedom fighters" who had come down from the hills. They were expecting the Chetniks to come, she said. They were waiting for them.

To Franko that meant that they were going to ambush a Serbian force, probably by going farther down the mountain road. They must think that they had a chance of defeating them. He glanced at Boz, but he seemed indifferent.

A more important question for Franko was, What had her father meant by sending Fedima to him?

"He told me to wait for you, to flee to the cave if the Chetniks came before you returned," she said.

"Yeah," Boz interjected, "to the cave! Let's go there." He looked about him anxiously. He didn't like the idea of being trapped in this little house with a couple of presumed KLA collaborators when the army arrived. He still brandished his Glock.

Beyond that, of course, he had other concerns, Franko knew. "Yes," he decided, aloud, "we must go to the cave." He had felt a little shock at Fedima's offhanded revelation that the old man was aware that the cave would be someplace known to him. How much did the old man know about his activities? Did it include the trysts in the cave? He pushed these troubling thoughts from his mind while he searched for and found a large flashlight. "Come," he told them.

They slipped out into the howling wind and rain. Franko led them at a half run along the path that led through the rear barnyard gate and into the fields and then the woods. The way was wet and slippery, climbing over rocks, up the hill. It took them the better part of a half hour to reach a spot where Franko thought it safe to pause.

They were fairly high up now, perhaps a couple of hundred feet or more above the farm. The visibility was poor, but they could occasionally catch a glimpse through breaks in the storm of the flames flickering around the jeep. They could not see any people around it, nor any sign of vehicles approaching the farm on the old road.

"Where's this damn cave?" Boz gasped, panting. "I'm fuckin' freezin', wet to my balls."

"This way." Franko led them around more rocks, over fallen trees, until finally they were able to push through some protective brush and into the low opening of a cave. Inside, it was pitch-black but dry, with the inevitable cave odor of dust and dirt, not quite the mustiness of the cellar . . . but there was something else, as well. Franko stopped. Fedima held him by the waist, crouching.

Boz bumped them. "What is it?" he whispered.

Franko snapped on the flashlight. One after another the pale faces of Fedima's family gleamed in the light. Franko almost cursed. Instead, he took a deep breath and let it out. Boz cursed for him.

"What the fuck are they doin' here?"

"What do you think?" Franko said. They spoke in English. Now, in the Kosovar dialect, Franko said to the people, "Come, come, you mustn't stay here." He shooed them toward the back of the cave. Fearfully, they rose up—an old woman in multiple skirts and babushka, the grandmother; younger women with children, the sisters and cousins. There was only one man among them, an old toothless grampa; Franko wasn't sure he was even related to the family, but he must have had some ties. Altogether, there were fifteen people. They followed Franko and Fedima and the flashlight deeper into the cave.

It was just a few moments of head-bent walking until they entered a larger chamber, the size of a small barn, perhaps, in which they could stand erect. There were a number of boxes, bundles, and artifacts of human presence stacked along the walls. One of the first things Franko did was to find a Browning automatic pistol in one of the boxes and thrust it into his belt, pointedly. Boz started to comment, but shut up.

"What are we gonna do with all these people?" Boz said. Franko had gestured to their guests to take places along the opposite wall. He pushed over some of the boxes for them to sit on, and got out some blankets for others.

"They'll be all right," Franko said. "They won't bother us. They had to go somewhere. The only thing is, how many people know about this damned cave?" In particular, he wondered how long the old man had known that he and Fedima had used the cave. There was their pallet, an air mattress that he'd bought in town, along with some blankets, lying revealingly against the wall.

"Light some candles," he said to Fedima.

"Where's the stash?" Boz asked, impatient with all this concern for the refugees.

Franko pointed at four small hard-sided suitcases. They looked like the kind of older Samsonite cases that once were popular with travelers.

Boz picked one up and carried it to the far corner of the chamber, away from the people. "Shine your light," Boz said. He squatted and opened the unlocked case. It was filled with plastic bags stuffed with white powder. "All right," he said, exhaling with relief. He glanced up at Franko. "All pure stuff?"

"What is it?" Fedima asked, peering around Franko, her hands locked about his arm.

"Our ticket out of here," Franko said. "Right, Boz?"

Boz closed the case and made sure the latches were secure. He stood up. "Right," he said. "But the question is, How do I get it out of here? I can't carry all this myself."

"That's your problem," Franko said. "If it was me, I'd say leave it here and come back for it. In the meantime, the girl and I will hike out over the mountain."

"Are you kiddin'?" Boz objected. "What about all these people? I'm sure I'm gonna leave this stash in here with them. Forget it. Besides, somebody's got to go down there and see what's happenin', and I'm not leavin' this stuff here where you and the broad and her cousins can haul it off. There's gotta be a couple hundred grand's worth in each one!"

"Not that much," Franko said. But he could see Boz's point, all right. Boz was still holding his Glock in his hand, though not pointed at anyone. The man's concern was understandable. He looked at Fedima. She was soaked and bedraggled, obviously in a state of great emotional stress, although he sensed that she had considerable physical reserves left.

Himself, he felt exhausted—physically, mentally, and emotionally. This morning seemed years ago. How could so much happen in a day? He felt that he had been asleep, enchanted, for the past year or so, then suddenly and rudely awakened by shouts—"Do something! Save yourself, save these people!"

He wanted to lie down and close his eyes and make it all stop. Instead, he asked Boz, "What do you suggest?"

Boz was getting angry. "I think you better come up with something before I just waste this whole batch of *balijas* and make you and the broad pack my goods out like a couple a fuckin' donkeys. Get it?" He hefted the Glock.

"You're forgetting that there's twenty or thirty KLA down there, including this girl's father and her brothers," Franko said calmly. Bazok's anger had the odd effect of making him feel calm, in fact. "They're between you and whatever Serb outfit is driving up the road. That outfit's going to be up to its ass in bullets and blood before they get here. If they get here."

"They'll get here," Boz said. "They got tanks, cannon on half-tracks, rockets, all kinds of shit. They'll have their hands full for half an hour, maybe, but they'll blow these peckerwoods away."

"But then what?" Franko said. "Will they find you sitting here with a bunch of refugees and twenty kilos of pure heroin?"

"Twenty kilos?" Boz's eyes bugged out. He began to calculate mentally, but soon stopped. "What do you think?" he asked.

"There's other caves," Franko said, "but . . ." He sighed and nodded toward Fedima, who was ministering to some of the children. "Obviously, there are no secret ones."

Franko saw there was no way to get Boz to leave, not by himself, anyway. If there had been only one or two suitcases of heroin . . . what a stupid mistake. Was there any chance that the KLA could take the Serbs, or even hold them for a while? He had no idea what kind of armament the KLA fighters had, probably some shoulder-mounted rockets, some AK-47s. What he needed to do, he knew, was take Fedima and hike out over the hills, probably before the KLA started to retreat, those that were left. He had studied the maps and had a pretty good idea of the task that would be. He'd prepared a couple of backpacks for them, containing water, food, money; he'd stashed them near the entrance to the cave.

"I'll go down and check on the situation at the farm," he suggested to Boz. "You can wait here. Who knows? Maybe the army will chase the KLA in some other direction. There'll be a vehicle you can probably use to get back to town, with your goods."

"Now you're talkin'," Boz said. "In the meantime, I'll hang on to the chick, so I know you're comin' back."

"I'll be back," Franko said. "Don't do anything stupid." He said good-bye to Fedima and told her to be patient. They would get away.

"Will I go with you?" she asked. They had walked into the passageway. They embraced and kissed. Her tears were wet on his cheeks.

"Oh yes," he assured her. "We'll go to Montana."

"Montana," she said. He had told her about Montana.

Then he left. The wind had dropped considerably, but it was still gusting, with periodic bursts of buffeting gales. And the rain had moderated, but still fell steadily. He hiked back to the farm quite rapidly, taking not more than fifteen minutes. There was no one about, to his surprise. No lights, no voices. Nonetheless, he skirted the compound and crossed the road above where Boz's jeep still smoked, a charred ruin at the side of the stone wall. He was used to walking on steep hillsides. It was not a great problem for him, despite the weather. He scrambled around the hill to a place where he could get a view of the road as it wound below. He saw nothing, so he continued to make his way down the mountainside, and eventually he got to a position where he could see something. Thanks to his position on the hillside, the presence of good cover, and the rain, he was able to get within a couple of hundred feet. A very steep hillside, practically a cliff, fell at least a hundred feet below him to the road.

The battle, if there had been a battle, was over. There were groups of uniformed troups dispersed here and there, in watchful, wary positions, but the main business concerned a cluster of men in civilian clothes. They were standing in the road, hands on their heads. There may have been more, shielded from his view by the cliff's precipitousness. These, Franko felt sure, were the KLA, or what remained of them. They had been captured. There were eighteen men that he could see. What had happened to the others was in no way apparent. There were no bodies lying about.

He saw that one of the men in the cluster was the old farmer, Daliljaj. He stood still, neither defiant nor defeated in his demeanor. Franko couldn't be sure, but he thought that two of Daliljaj's sons were also there.

A Serbian officer spoke to what looked like a couple of sergeants off to one side. The NCOs signaled down the road and shouted for trucks. Then they all turned, along with a squad of soldiers, and forced the civilians to the side of the road, under the brow of the hill and hidden from Franko's view. The soldiers suddenly opened fire, blazing away at the hill. There were screams, but Franko did not try to get closer, to witness the slaughter. The minute the guns began to sputter he turned and raced back the way he had come.

He ran as hard but as warily as he could, for fear that he might encounter some escaped KLA men, who would, naturally, be eager for revenge. But he encountered no one. He was panting and scarcely able to speak when he found the hidden entrance of the cave, but as soon as he was inside and had crept nearly to the chamber he stopped.

Something was wrong. With great effort he managed to suppress his panting, to lie quietly until he could breathe with some control. There should have been a light, some little sound. But it was utterly dark. He went forward on his hands and knees. There was a very bad smell. It was not just the odor of feces and urine, but perhaps of blood, of burnt hair, it might be. And then, of course, the acrid scent of gunfire.

He put his hand in something wet. Something very wet, but sticky, as well.

Comrades

"**W**e ran north every night," the colonel said. He was reminiscing. Joe didn't know where all this was heading, but he listened and didn't say anything. He'd heard the colonel's war stories before.

They were sitting on the deck of a restaurant that looked out on Lake St. Clair, sipping drinks after dinner. The colonel was drinking straight whiskey in a glass; Joe was nursing a bottle of Stroh's beer. The other members of the party had withdrawn after dinner. It was warm, still summer. There were a lot of boats in this marina, their masts like so many leafless trees. Joe supposed that the moon on the lake had evoked this nostalgic mood, but he was sure that there was some deeper point to it. The colonel liked to talk about his days in Vietnam, Joe knew, but there was always a point.

There were still a few pleasure boats on the lake, their running lights twinkling, people partying. Occasionally a powerboat would come roaring up from the lake, then throttle down and motor slowly into the dock at the restaurant, and young people would hop out, laughing. Joe had a boat, a Sea Ray that was moored in its slip a few hundred yards away, among the masts.

"I loved the moon on the tops of the clouds," the colonel said, nodding toward the lake. "There were almost always clouds. But once in a while you could see the forest, the jungle. No lights down there, though. Except for the cockpit lights, the moon and the stars were the only lights you'd see. Nothing but night below you, blacker than Hades, except for a river, maybe, gleaming in the moonlight.

"I had a little tape player. I'd slip the earplug device inside my helmet. I had to do it. My backseater liked rock. The first time we went up he played some Rolling Stones crap, something like that. Drove me nuts—I had to make him turn it off. The next day I got my own tape machine and earplugs for both of us, so I could listen to Bach and he could hear his rock on his machine."

"Bach?" Joe said.

"My favorite tape," the colonel said, "was one I'd made off a French LP—*The Cello Suites*, played by Fournier. Or for a change sometimes, I'd play another tape, one by Glenn Gould, of the *Well-Tempered Clavier*." He was silent for a long moment, staring out at the lake. People at the other tables around them laughed and called to one another. The colonel did not hear them. He was listening to something else.

"There's nothing like it," he said. "Riding that Thud up Route Pack Six, listening to the cello with the moon on the tops of the clouds. I love those suites, especially the preludes . . . this statement of theme, then the elaboration, the argument. A solo cello can sound like many voices, at times . . . babbling, conversing with itself . . . then the solitary voice, winding and sonorous. The piano pieces are different, of course—fugues. But I prefer the suites. Have you ever listened to them?"

Joe said that he regretted that he hadn't.

"After the prelude," the colonel said, "come these stately or lively dance figures. It's very civilized music, formal but it has an implacable drive. It was amazing to listen to them while you were flying up to Hanoi, to bomb. Nobody's talking in the strike force, just this rushing background sound of the engines, the breathing noise of the oxygen, the occasional remark from the backseater, noting a turning point, pointing out a site we'd bombed a couple of days earlier.

"The tape would stop just about the time things got interesting. Just about the time the backseater said, 'I've got five rings, probably a SAM.' That meant you were being tracked by enemy radar. Then you'd have to run down Thud Ridge into Hanoi. Everything blazing away at you. Two minutes of pure hell, the Cong screaming on the radio, dodging SAMs, Fire Cans, Fan Songs—those were kinds of anti-aircraft guns. Guys in the strike force yelling out on the radio. Then the MiGs as you came out, down the river, running for your life. Plenty of light then, lots of explosions, aircraft on fire—guys yelling again: 'I'm hit! I'm on fire!' Then the dark again, as you climbed out. And I'd start the tape. I'd be almost calm by the time I got back to Korat."

"What about your backseater?" Joe asked. "Was he calm?"

"Him? No. He was wired. He was jumping around, eager to go again. But," he said, "one day he didn't come back."

"What happened?"

The colonel drank off his whiskey. "Come on," he said. He picked up the bill, and Joe followed him out. The colonel paid in cash, tossing in a huge tip. They walked along the concrete abutment toward the wooden catwalks that would take them through the maze of boats to where Joe's Sea Ray was moored. The colonel took out a cigar, but he didn't light it. There were too many signs forbidding smoking about. But once they reached the boat and went aboard, he clipped the cigar and lit it. They sat in the tall cockpit seats beneath the canopy. It was dark here. The bluish lights on tall poles, and those that reflected from nearby boats where others were relaxing aboard, didn't really illuminate the cockpit where Joe and the colonel sat.

"That kid," the colonel said, "my first backseater, he went down with the plane."

"No shit," Joe said. "You were shot down?" Joe recalled another version of this story, from when he'd first met the colonel. In that version, the colonel had spent some time in a Vietnamese prison.

"Yeah. It wasn't like you see in the movies, the newsreels. We weren't in B-52s, six miles above the war. We were in the Thuds, F-105s. We rolled in on target, diving down to a thousand feet or so, then pickling the bombs and hauling ass down river. Going downtown, we called it. Did it every day. Anyway, what the newsreels don't show is that Hanoi was the most heavily defended target in aerial war history. In the news shots you see these big 52s, way up there in a silent, empty sky, releasing thousands of bombs like dropping handfuls of pretzel sticks, then turning away and flying safely home to Guam. It wasn't like that, at all."

"It wasn't?" Joe said, more or less on cue.

"That was down south," the colonel said. "They were up around thirty thousand. They could release bombs from the DMZ. No MiGs, no SAMs south of the DMZ, see? The real war was 'going downtown' every day. Besides all the missiles, the guns, they had every kid in Vietnam who could carry a rifle lying on the tops of buildings, or in the parks, firing up at us."

"With rifles?" Joe laughed.

"You don't think a .30-caliber rifle bullet can bring down an F-105?" the colonel said. "Well, they can't, or not often. They don't hit anything. But once in a while you'd get a hit. It's a sharp rap, like a stone hitting the windshield of your car on a dirt road. Only those bullets penetrated the skin of that plane. It might do no harm; usually it didn't. But it could tear up the wiring, puncture a fuel line, a hydraulic line. Everything's there for a purpose, Joe. You need it all. Usually, nothing happened. You'd get back to Korat and look at the plane, find the bullet hole. Usually in the wing. You might have leaked some fluid, maybe some fuel. The guys would have to go in there and check it out.

"This time we didn't get back. We started smoking on the climbout. We probably got eighty miles south before we had to eject. Only what's-his-name didn't eject. At least none of the other planes saw his chute. I never saw it. He must have ridden her down."

Joe didn't say anything about "what's-his-name." Either the colonel had forgotten the kid's name or he didn't want to think about it. "So, you were captured?" he asked.

The colonel didn't answer the question. He took a big drag off the cigar. "I landed in a rice paddy," he said. "I was lucky. You don't want to come down in those trees. I ran for high ground as quick as I could get rid of the chute. We had a radio transmitter on us, so the ResCap people could keep track of us. The militia was out, looking for me, of course. It took me the better part of an hour to get up on this hilltop, up in the woods. I found a clearing. The ResCap guys—F-4s—kept cycling back, off the tankers, strafing the militia. They could see their flashlights. I could hear the militia troops calling to each other, coming up the hill. I figured I was about due for a long stay in the Hanoi Hilton. They got pretty close. Then I heard the chopper. He came in just above the trees, turned on some big lights, and down came the ladder. I jumped on that thing and held on for dear life! Away we went! The bastards didn't haul me up into the chopper until we were away from there.

"Jesus!" The colonel shivered. "You ever ride through the treetops at a hundred miles an hour, clinging to a ladder? My God, I thought they'd kill me."

"But they never found wh— your backseater?"

"No. They ran missions out there for days, but no sign, no signal. He must have augered in. They could see where the plane went in, but finally the Vietnamese carted it off."

"Did you go on the missions?"

"The ResCap? Oh, no. No, I was back up on the run the next night, new plane, new backseater."

"They didn't send you home?"

"Eventually. But I wasn't hurt, just a little bruised. No, we couldn't spare the pilots. We had something like a thirty percent loss rate in that squadron. No, I went downtown on my regular rotation."

They sat silently for a few moments, Joe mulling this story over. The previous telling had been different, with no mention of the backseater, and there had been at least a strong suggestion that the colonel had endured some heavy time in the infamous Hanoi Hilton. He had no idea how much of it was true, if any of it, although he believed that the colonel had flown in combat. But why was he being told it in the first place? The last time, out in Salt Lake City, the story had been part of the colonel's cover. But that situation had long been superseded.

Finally, the colonel said, "Yeah, the rescue guys, they were pretty thorough. They looked every day for . . . I don't know . . . weeks, I guess. The air force must have spent thousands . . . well, hell, maybe a million, on that operation. The kid never showed up at Hanoi. We didn't forget him. But eventually, you know, it was clear: he hadn't gotten out. There was a formal hearing. I testified."

Joe had found some beers in the boat's refrigerator. The colonel hoisted his, saying, "Here's to fallen comrades."

Joe drank. This was it, he thought. He was right.

The colonel was very direct, after this long prelude. "So, what happened to Pollak?" he said.

"I told you about Pollak," Joe said.

"Tell me again," the colonel said.

Joe told the story. He and Pollak had gone up Lake Huron, in this boat, to an island off the Bruce Peninsula, in Ontario, a few weeks earlier. They were after an escaped mobster who had faked his death. When they found the man, Humphrey DiEbola, he was dying—ironically, he'd caught a stray bullet in his escape. Joe had argued with Pollak that they should leave the guy to die. Their mission was simply to make sure he was dead. Evidently, Pollak had believed that "making sure" meant shooting the mobster. But DiEbola, according to Joe, had enough life in him to shoot Pollak first.

"The old devil had a gun under the covers," Joe said. DiEbola had popped Pollak, who was leaning over the bed. Joe had fled. A Detroit police detective, Sergeant Mulheisen, was on the island and was expected to show up any moment. Joe hadn't had time to remove Pollak.

It was a simple story and Joe stuck to it. The colonel obviously didn't buy it.

"The inescapable fact is," the colonel pointed out, "that Mulheisen didn't find Pollak there. If he had, we'd have heard about it. But nothing. He found DiEbola, dead, as you say. But Pollak hasn't reappeared, dead or alive. So where is he? It's been weeks. Your story isn't acceptable, Joe."

Joe shrugged. "I have no idea." This was not true. Pollak was, at least for the time being, at the bottom of Lake Huron. Joe had shot him and carried off the body, with the help of DiEbola's bodyguard, Roman Yakovich. It hadn't been a very good plan, disposing of the dead man at sea, so to speak, but Joe couldn't very well afford to have the body autopsied. So far, it hadn't washed up, or been found if it had.

Joe's plan was to avoid seeing the colonel ever again. That hadn't worked out. He'd dropped Roman Yakovich off at Port Huron. He should have walked then, himself. But he'd taken a chance that the colonel wouldn't be expecting him back so soon. With any luck, he'd thought he could slip into the St. Clair Shores Marina, park the boat, and get away in his car. Unfortunately, the colonel and his friends were waiting for him at the mooring. Joe had made his report and then he'd hung around, waiting for the other shoe to drop. The meeting tonight looked like it might be the occasion, but instead they'd had dinner and then the others had gone.

"Joe, we just can't overlook this," the colonel said. He tossed his cigar into the dark water. "You know the nature of our group. Pollak wasn't on an official assignment with us. Hell, we don't even exist. He was in town, officially, with Immigration. That's what I'm doing here, officially. We weren't on any assignment that can justify or explain Pollak's disappearance. So far, nobody knows he's missing. But that can't be sustained any longer, Joe. Eventually, somebody will come asking. They'll come to me. That will threaten the Lucani."

The Lucani was the amusing name that the colonel and his people had dubbed their organization. It was based on the origins, in Italy, of DiEbola's family. The rationale behind the group's existence was their dedication to ridding the world of people like DiEbola. The members were made up of agents in various federal crime-fighting agencies who had become disillusioned by official policies. They had decided to take matters into their own hands.

That was the story Joe had been told, anyway. It could be true or it could be crap. He had thought about this on the long trip back across Lake Huron. Maybe they were acting officially, after all. Maybe the Lucani gag was just that, a cover story they had concocted to convince him to help them get DiEbola, who had been his one-time employer. He had no idea how many agents were involved—assuming the Lucani pitch was more or less true—but they seemed to have plenty of resources. His initial impression was that it was just five or six disillusioned agents. But others kept popping up.

"Joe, the guys have put themselves at risk, for a purpose," the colonel said. "It's a purpose we believe in. It's what we got into the service for, but found we couldn't—weren't allowed to—do. They got you out of that hospital in Denver. You were looking at years in a federal pen—if the mob didn't have you hit first. They put themselves out for you. If it was you missing, we'd be looking. We wouldn't leave you hanging—pardon the allusion."

Joe shrugged. "Maybe Mulheisen's got him. Maybe the Mounties, or the FBI. Maybe they've got some reason not to talk about it."

"All the more reason," the colonel said. "We can't ignore this. We've got to know. Maybe you dumped him."

"And if I did?"

"We'll have to deal with that, Joe. I don't know what the group would decide, but at least we'd know. Maybe they wouldn't do anything. It depends on the circumstances. Pollak can be a difficult man. If you felt for some reason that you had to take him out, the group might decide that you were justified. But we have to know."

Joe wondered: Was "we" the Lucani? Or was it just the colonel? If there was such a group as the Lucani, every member's ass would be equally at risk. Yet it was always the colonel who did the talking. And there were other disquieting factors. Joe was confident, for instance, from some things that Pollak had let drop, that one of his missions was to get rid of Joe. Whose idea was that? Fortunately, it hadn't worked out that way. Joe didn't have any bad feelings about having popped Pollak. The way he saw it, it was him or Pollak.

Joe was content to believe in the Lucani: they had helped him escape. But now he was a fugitive. With their resources they could keep him more or less safe from the law. He had done an earlier job for them, getting rid of a Colombian drug dealer. It was like making your bones with the mob, he thought. In return, they had promised to remove him from the national police computer system. And there were other ways available to them to keep him on the loose. But if they chose to expose him, he'd be in a tight corner, he knew. At best, he'd find himself forced deep underground. That prospect didn't delight.

"So, where are we?" Joe asked.

The colonel stared at him. He was a pleasant-looking man, but he didn't look pleasant at the moment. He had a hint of a military manner, but it was the easygoing, practical manner that one associated with pilots. Otherwise, he had the appearance of a worldly, intelligent, and competent middle-management type. He could be an executive of a large corporation, a director of a research group, perhaps a scientist. He seemed to be something between fifty and sixty years old, a trim, fit, weathered fellow.

"Where we are, Joe, is at one of those crossroads," the colonel said. "Whether we go on from here is up to you. We can't continue . . . you can't continue with the Lucani until we resolve this issue."

"And if I can't resolve it for you," Joe said, leaning forward, his voice dropping, "what do you do?"

"Why, we'd have no choice," the colonel said. He didn't seem tense, despite Joe's manner. "We'd have to pull the plug."

"Pull the plug? On me, you mean?"

The colonel didn't answer, just gazed at Joe.

"Blow the whistle?" Joe said. "Sic the dogs?"

The colonel sat back in the tall seat and sipped at his beer. "Joe, you understand the nature of this group. We really can't afford to turn you over to the police." He gazed calmly at him. "No, I think we'd have to consider other, more permanent measures."

"If I thought you meant that," Joe said, "you'd never get off this boat, Colonel."

"Nor would you, Joe." The colonel didn't move, but he seemed somehow to be larger to Joe, as if he had acquired a host of hidden backers, squads of shooters waiting in the night.

It didn't faze Joe. "I don't care," he said. He slipped his hand into the pocket of his jacket. It was an all-weather jacket with large pockets. There had been some talk at the table, folks saying it was warm, why didn't he take off his jacket. But Joe hadn't taken it off.

The colonel shrunk, at least in Joe's eyes. He looked a little bleak. They stared at each other for long seconds, then the colonel nodded.

"Okay, you don't know anything about Pollak."

"That's right," Joe said.

"We'll just have to accept that, I guess. Until further information comes to light."

"So . . . now what?" Joe said.

"I'll have to think about that, talk to the others." He stood and handed his empty beer bottle to Joe. Joe ignored it. After a moment, the colonel looked about for a place to set the bottle. He set it in a holder next to the instrument panel, one of those devices designed for holding the driver's drink. "Ah," he said.

As he prepared to leave, he remarked, "I suppose that one question in my colleagues' minds would be, What to do about Miss Sedlacek?"

"Really?" Joe said. "Why is that?"

"Well, she inherits the mantle of DiEbola," the colonel observed. "And it won't be clear to us what your relationship with her would be. That is, are you with us, or are you with her? Something for you to think about, eh, Joe?"

"I haven't had a chance to discuss it with her," Joe said. "But my impression is that she's getting out of the rackets. I don't think she's cut out for that kind of activity."

"Well, I hope so, for her sake. But I'm not so sure I believe it. It's not so easy to get out, as Mr. DiEbola found. And Joe," the colonel said, "it might take a while to see whether it's true. But you could find out."

"Yeah, I could."

"And if she wasn't out . . ." The colonel let that hang for a moment, then spoke what was on his mind. "Her father was in it. She's pretty well positioned. She could even take over. If she did, or if it looked like she might . . . she might be a good way for you to prove . . ."

Joe laughed. "You guys never give up, do you?"

The colonel managed a smile. "No. No we don't, Joe."

"Are you speaking as a federal agent, Colonel? Or as a Lucani?" Joe was interested.

"In my experience," the colonel said mildly, "the feds do let people go. That was the problem, as we saw it. No, it's the Lucani who can't afford to let things drop. Too much at risk, you see." He turned to go.

"One minute," Joe said.

The colonel stopped in the act of climbing onto the dock. He looked back. "What is it?"

"Aren't you forgetting something?"

The colonel looked blank. "What?"

"The money. The 'fee.' I think we said one hundred thousand dollars."

"Ah yes, I forgot that about you, Joe. You like to be paid. I think I mentioned that you were free to help yourself to Mr. DiEbola's ill-gotten gains."

"And I rejected that," Joe said. He was smiling, but he still had his hand in his coat pocket. "Anyway, we didn't have time to look around, and then Pollak kind of made it necessary to leave in a hurry. So I'll settle for the fee."

"Well, I don't have it on me," the colonel said. He held his hands out, open, as if asking Joe to search him.

"Put your hands down," Joe said, sharply. He moved more deeply into the shadows. "Come, sit down, like you were."

The colonel complied. He perched on the high seat, his hands in his lap.

"That's one of the things I hate about this work," Joe said. "You always have to ask for your money. Well," he admitted, "not with Fats—DiEbola. He always brought the money to the table. But his old boss, Carmine, didn't. That's what started all this . . . this stupid shit. He always made you ask. I don't want to get in the same situation with you. Where's the money?"

"I can get it," the colonel said. "It's back at the hotel. You needn't get excited, Joe. I thought, in the way of these things, that I'd debrief you and then, if everything seemed okay—which it doesn't, quite, but we'll let that go—then we'd meet later at the hotel and you would be paid. Okay?"

"You've left it for quite a while already," Joe said. "So let's go get it."

"Now?"

"Why not? Have you got a date?"

"Well, it's a little late," the colonel said. "And we're both tired. . . . But if you want to. . . . Why, sure, why not?"

They walked down the wooden catwalk, Joe staying close but slightly to the rear. When they reached the parking lot, Joe let the colonel lead the way, but still stayed close. He walked in the direction of Joe's car, an ordinary Ford rental. Joe let him walk. When the colonel stopped a few cars away from the rental, as if to wait for Joe to get into the car, Joe said, "Where's your car?"

"Mine? I thought you'd prefer to drive."

"No, you drive," Joe said. He'd had experience with these guys. His car was probably wired.

"But then," the colonel protested, "I'd have to drive you all the way back. The hotel is all the way over on the northwest side of town, out in Southfield. Handy to the airport," he explained.

"That's okay," Joe said. "I'll be rich. I can afford a cab. Hell, maybe I'll buy a new car. In this town, there's probably a place that's open all night for car shoppers."

The colonel's car was rented too. But it was a Lincoln. Joe liked that. Among other things, he reasoned that if the colonel was on official business, he'd have an official car. So maybe this was Lucani business. Besides, the car was comfortable.

On the way, once they'd reached the expressway, the colonel said, "Actually, now that I think of it, Miss Sedlacek could be a useful ally. That's assuming that she is, as you say, not interested in the rackets."

"How's that?" Joe said, surprised. "You mean, join the group?"

"Not exactly, but maybe as a sort of adjunct member. She's a Serb, isn't she?"

"I'm not sure," Joe said. "I think her mother is, anyway. So what?"

"I'm sorry if I seem obsessed about this business of recovering missing agents," the colonel said. "But we've got another, similar problem. Unrelated to this present business. We had a man in Kosovo. That's in Serbia."

"I've heard of it," Joe said. "They've had a lot of trouble. A war."

"Yes. Well, this fellow—let's say his name is Franko—was working on a drug case. There was a pretty brisk trade in hard drugs moving up through Bulgaria, into Kosovo, then out along the coast, and so on. The drugs were not destined for Serbia or Kosovo—they were processed and moved on. I dare say some got siphoned off en route for local sales, but we weren't concerned with that. It was an official DEA operation, infiltrating, tracking. It wasn't a Lucani operation, per se, though there were some connections. But then along came the war, and the DEA bailed out. Only Franko was still there. Now it appears he's not."

"What happened to him?"

"We're not sure," the colonel said. "He was a bit of an odd duck. He may have been arrested in one of the early sweeps by the

Serbs, when they were 'ethnically cleansing' Kosovo. He may have been posing as an ethnic Albanian; we're not sure. He could have been executed. They did a lot of that, you know, the Serbs. Especially young able-bodied men. Though, come to that, they weren't too picky. They shot everybody sometimes."

Joe was interested in this story, but he said, "I don't know anything about Serbia, Colonel. I wouldn't be much use to you over there."

"No, I know you wouldn't. But Miss Sedlacek—"

"She doesn't know anything about the old country, either," Joe said. "I remember her saying something about that."

"The point is, Joe—let me finish—it looks like Franko could have gotten out. We don't know that for sure, but we've had some information. It's not very reliable. But—"

"If he got out, you'd know, wouldn't you? He'd contact you."

"Not if he'd been turned," the colonel said. "Or if there were some other circumstances that we don't know about. If he's still on the case . . . it might not be prudent for him to contact us."

"So where would he be? Italy? France? I don't know anything about those places either."

"You had a place in Montana, didn't you?" the colonel asked. "In Butte, or near there? It burned down, I understand."

"Yeah. So what?"

"There are a lot of Serbs in Butte."

Deathgrip

Joe Service was into simplification. The rest of the world, it seemed, was not. His ultimate simplification was this: I am. After that, things got complicated. Lately, even the first premise was modified. The modifier was Helen.

Sometimes he thought it had started with being shot in the head. He'd been a little confused afterward; it was no simple thing to say "I am." He felt he'd succeeded. But then he began to think that the complications had begun even earlier, when he'd met Helen. He'd been a fairly simple person up until then. Now he wrestled.

They wrestled. It always ended with grappling. It might start with a workout in the gymnasium in the basement of her late father's mansion—the weights, the fancy machines, or just intense aerobic exercises—or it might be a grueling game of racquetball. They were well matched: what Helen gave up in power she gained in mobility. Joe had incredible stamina, however, now that he had regained his physical fitness. He could wear her down. But whatever they played at was only a prelude to wrestling.

Neither of them were particularly skilled at wrestling. They both had some experience with tae kwon do, but that isn't wrestling. What they liked was the physical contact. They tried different holds, writhing their slick, naked bodies against each other like snakes—it was difficult to tell where one left off and the other began.

They were superficially similar physically, although Joe was an inch or two taller and more heavily muscled. But to others they seemed like brother and sister, fraternal twins, perhaps. Helen was very fit, with almost no bosom and slim, boyish hips. She had a heart-shaped face with a great volume of black hair. Joe's facial features were heavier, but like hers strong and handsome, with a well-defined nose, a firm mouth, and sensual lips. They were both of an age, about thirty.

The wrestling started casually, as if they were panther cubs, tussling. It would get more intense, sometimes becoming quite serious, as with their utmost energies and strengths employed, each gained a position of superiority at least briefly. But it always ended the same way—with sexual penetration.

Without ever discussing it they had arrived at a commonly held conceit: that they shared a phallus. This notion stemmed from Helen's gradually acquired ability to seemingly relax her large muscles, to submit to Joe's driving force, only to contract her vaginal muscles so as to grasp his member so firmly that when she drove her buttocks back into his groin he actually experienced a kind of penetration of himself. It was a sensation that initially surprised, even shocked them, but which they had both come to enjoy.

On this occasion, however, he had wrestled her into a face-down position and had pinned her arms behind her. They were on a thin mat beside the pool in the dim light. She groaned quietly, struggling, expecting him to enter her now, but when she thrust her buttocks upward he did not allow her to gain her knees, but lay along her back, forcing her into the mat. His right arm encircled her neck. He tightened his grip, choking her.

She waited, sensing something a bit different. It was always different, of course. No sexual act could be precisely reenacted. But this was different yet. He pressed her brutally against the thin mat. She couldn't breathe well. She struggled now, but he only tightened the crook of his arm across her throat and forced her face more firmly into the mat. She tried, in a panic, to free her arms, but his grip was fierce and the pressure of his body further restrained her arms.

"Mmmf!" She grunted, but it was muffled. She felt an awakening fear. This was going much farther than she liked. Then suddenly he seemed lighter. He didn't release her but he braced himself with his elbows and knees, relieving the weight and easing the pressure on her head and her neck. She turned her head to the left and gasped.

"What are you doing!"

"Killing you," he whispered hoarsely into her ear, panting from the exertion.

"Why?

"They want me to."

"Who?"

"The Lucani," Joe said.

Unable to see Joe's face Helen couldn't tell how serious he was. He sounded serious, and her situation felt very serious. She was afraid that she might lose consciousness.

"If you kill me . . . that means you're one of them?"

"Something like that," he rasped, allowing his weight to rest fully on her now. She was finding it extremely difficult to breathe.

"All right," she grunted. "But let me die happy."

"What a good idea."

It was not a frenetic coupling but a long, drawn-out thrust and counterthrust, until finally they seemed to merge into each other and both felt the thrilling pulse of fluids pumping through the conduit that joined them.

They collapsed onto their sides, embracing. When they had regained their breaths they rolled to their feet and dove into the adjacent pool together, side by side like dolphins. They swam back and forth, pushing and playing with another. Joe was in a swirling underwater swoop, looking up at the underside of the surface, intending to break through it and breathe, when he felt her arms encircle his legs and she drew him down.

He was more buoyant than she, with his greater lung capacity. Still, she drew him down. It occurred to him that she might have taken a breath before her attack, whereas he was now desperately short of breath. She was clearly kicking down, carrying them both toward the tiled bottom. He could not free his legs, and he clawed with his arms. This was a payback, he knew. He forced himself to relax, to yield to her superior force. And graciously, she responded, releasing him so that they both shot to the surface.

They came up gasping. He pushed at her. "You almost drowned me!"

Helen splashed water at him, retorting with nearly as little breath, "You almost choked me!" They chased each other around the pool like otters, racing from one end to the other. At last they clambered out and padded into the sauna.

As they relaxed in the dry heat, sitting on the aromatic cedar slats, Helen lifted her head and spoke. "They really asked you to kill me?"

"It was more a suggestion," Joe said.

"And you gave it a try?"

"I wondered how far you'd let me go," he joked. "You knew I couldn't resist one last fling. And once I did that . . ."

"You were lost," she said. "But, were you tempted?"

"In that death grip of yours? I'd never have been able to get out of you."

"That's right," she said, her dark eyes gleaming. "Never. I'll never let you go."

He lifted his head, not so much wearily but from utter relax-
ation in the heat. He smiled slightly.

"Are they crazy?" she asked.

"Oh yeah," Joe said. "Crazy as wasps in honey."

"What is it?"

"They've had a taste of some kind of weird power trip, juiced
up by danger and fear. They're wrestling, too—like a couple of
octopi. Too many tangled arms to unravel. They can't break off . . .
they can only go on. That's my guess, anyhow."

"They are a danger," Helen said, her hand unconsciously rising to her throat. It was still a little sore. "Not just to each other,
but to others—us."

"That's it," Joe said. "And now they've had some success, but
not enough. They want more. Still, they could be useful to us. They
have a scheme. It's not very clear, not focussed. But then . . . they
weren't very clear what they wanted or how to go about getting what
they thought they wanted in the Humphrey deal. Now they want
us to go back to Butte."

He told her what he'd heard from the colonel. Helen was
interested. She knew that Joe still felt bad about losing his place
out west, near Butte. Conceivably, this new scheme would make it
possible for him to rebuild, to establish a safe haven—never safe
enough, of course, as long as the Lucani had leverage on him. Still
. . . the potential was there. If they were clever, and had luck, they
might be able to recover some lost ground.

Colonel Tucker
was thinking, Joe Service was a mistake. Maybe an irreparable mistake. Fatal.

He had first met Joe in Salt Lake City, where the colonel was
conducting a stakeout of the residence of Helen Sedlacek. She had

been observed converting large amounts of cash into bank certificates—nothing illegal, restricting her purchases to amounts just under the limit that required Internal Revenue notification. But an alert bank official had notified the IRS of her suspicions, who had, in turn, notified the colonel.

At the time, the policy was to allow the suspect to continue the process; indeed, there were no grounds for intervention, despite a strong indication of illegal intent.

The point of the stakeout was to observe the suspect's activities over a period of time, identify her associates, and if suspicions were confirmed, swoop in, confiscate the remaining money, and interrogate Sedlacek and her confederates. It was a joint operation of the DEA, the INS, the FBI, the IRS, and the Treasury Department. The idea was to fund the war against the drug barons with their own loot: they would never attempt to recover the confiscated money, because establishing its provenance would be self-incriminating.

The amounts seized were small change compared to the staggering profits of the drug trade, and the "smurfs" were rarely seriously prosecuted—except for incidental, unrelated violations—but the project had a win-win nature that was much admired in law enforcement circles. As a matter of fact, Colonel Tucker was one of the architects of this program, and it had been very successful in the short time it had been running.

In the meantime, his crew would run their checks on Sedlacek and try to get a fix on what her activities had been, what was the source of this money she was "smurfing." Early returns were promising: she was associated with known mob figures in Detroit; her father had been involved in various criminal activities for years before being assassinated, evidently in a dispute about drug collections. It was believed that Helen had played a role in the revenge assassination of the Detroit mob boss, Carmine Busoni, who was thought to have ordered the hit on Sedlacek's father, but the Detroit police had come up with no convincing evidence of this.

Prior to the Busoni assassination she had not attracted the interest of any agency. She had been in a legitimate business, a partnership with another woman, consulting in interpersonal communication for large corporations and government or educational institutions. She had studied to do this in college, achieving a master's degree.

But the chief reason to be skeptical of her as a putative assassin was the fact that she was not only still alive but active. It even appeared that she had reestablished friendly contact with Humphrey DiEbola, Busoni's successor. That didn't look like she was in trouble with the mob. A Detroit police precinct detective, a Detective Sergeant Mulheisen, had some different theories, but Tucker didn't buy them. A colonel was not inclined to accord much credibility to a municipal police sergeant's theories.

One day when Helen was away from her Salt Lake City residence, the stakeout team was excited to observe a stranger attempting to break in. The colonel intervened, as a "concerned neighbor." After a few questions and a surreptitious check of the man's credentials, the colonel had apologized to Joe for bothering him and had let him run free, but with an electronic tag on his vehicle. In due course, this exercise backfired. The colonel found himself trapped by Service and Sedlacek. It was a humiliating episode, and one might have thought that the colonel would have been furious, would have pursued Service and Sedlacek vindictively, seeking his own revenge. But Tucker was a pragmatist. He had respect for his opponents, something he had learned in Vietnam.

Another lesson learned in Vietnam was a distrust of his masters. Like any loyal, patriotic soldier with a genuine dedication to duty, Tucker had a deep need to believe in his mission. He had been brought up to respect and honor his government. As he saw it, the

American government was unlike other national governments. It was a flexible, ever-changing organization. Policy could rarely be exclusively attributed to one faction or another; it was subject to constant curbs and influences from opposing factions. To be "in power" was merely to be nominally in control. Despite this, somehow the country managed to muddle through, more successfully than other countries, in fact. Whether this was due to the seemingly flawed system, to luck, or to the will of the Almighty (or some other suitably nebulous superior principle) sometimes occupied Colonel Tucker's mind. After Vietnam, he didn't often waste a lot of time on the "why" of such things, however. His motto was, If it won't fly, fix it; if you can't fix it, find someone who can.

Vernon Tucker had been born and raised on a modest ranch in northern Montana. His family owned a few thousand acres and leased many more thousands, on which they ran cattle and grew wheat and occasionally some other grain products. When he was twelve he contracted scarlet fever and was forced to spend many months in bed. This was a critical moment in his personal development. He became a reader, for one thing. His mother was a schoolteacher, or had been. She made sure he kept up with his studies, and also, for a while, was able to reassert the primary control of his upbringing, after a typical early boyhood that was mostly spent outdoors, hunting, fishing, and working with his father and older brothers. Now she was able to guide his reading, play classical records for him, and answer his questions, big questions, about Life, the Universe, and Meaning.

She was pleased that at least one of her four sons took to literature so eagerly. He'd been, like her, better at math and science. But mostly, he'd been good at riding, shooting, and fishing—in fact, just about anything he tried. He was also crazy about airplanes. He'd started flying early, with his father, who was accustomed to traveling the country in a Cessna. The other boys were happier on horseback.

It was inevitable that the boy would enter the air force. The big fear was his heart, but evidently he had not been seriously affected by the bout of fever. He was not a large man, which from the point of view of cockpit space in a jet airplane was a blessing.

Vern Tucker loved Montana, but he had no interest in ranching. He tried, a couple of times, particularly when he came back from Vietnam, and again when he quit active flight duty. But it just didn't appeal. He still loved to fly-fish, but ranch life was not for him. As much as he'd loved riding as a boy, as a man horses annoyed him. They looked smart but they weren't, and they could never really do what you thought you could make them do. Now an airplane . . . you could figure out an F-105 and it would do what it was supposed to do.

He also got interested in the administrative duties of the squadron, especially in the legal aspects. He had an interest in education, as well. When he was looking around for something to do after his active flight duty ended, an old squadron buddy popped up, a fellow trout fisher. This buddy was now in Air Force Intelligence. He got Vern in. Vernon proved good at it. At one point he worked with the DEA on a narcotics case. From there he moved into the field. Increasingly, the complex, international character of the drug trade made interdepartmental cooperation a necessity. Tucker liked that. It gave him a degree of freedom to work with various agencies, at first on an at-loan basis, but ultimately as a kind of roving superagent, almost an agency of his own.

What he hated about military service in Vietnam continued to affect him in his work in the intelligence services, however. Very often, he found, he would pursue some drug criminals to a point where legal action should ensue, only to be thwarted by international policy complications, domestic political concerns, or corruption. Cases were sidetracked or abandoned; or he'd be transferred to another investigation. It was frustrating.

Before long, he met other agents with similar complaints. In the course of off-duty socializing they would express his own frustrated attitude, and often, very often, the suggestion would be voiced that they "ought to do something."

In due time, when he found enough like-minded agents that he could trust, he proposed forming an informal direct-action extra-official task force. This group, "the Lucani," carried out a handful of cautious actions to achieve at least a measure of what they saw as justice.

This was where Joe Service entered the picture. Service was a shadowy operator in the organized-crime world. As best as the Lucani had been able to determine, Service had a long and ambiguous career in organized crime. He didn't seem allied with any of the major families, but he had good relations with all of them. He seemed to be primarily an investigator, like the Lucani themselves, but one often called upon to carry out sanctions. The crime world, it appeared, like all large, loosely affiliated organizations, had internal problems, interdisciplinary problems, so to speak. A nominally independent agent was required, someone all sides more or less trusted and respected.

Independent operatives are of value in any field—it was one of the justifications the Lucani claimed for themselves. The advantages are clear, the results widely applauded, and if the operator has the sanction of the organization (as the Lucani, obviously, did not) the organization congratulates itself on having had the wisdom to create such a useful internal organ.

But soon enough, the infatuation fades—independence is all well and good, as long as it doesn't annoy the ruling faction. Organized crime, perhaps even more so than legitimate enterprise, is riddled with factions and, inevitably, with corruption. The censor, as one might term the internal investigator, comes to be resented, suspected of acting not out of disinterested evenhandedness but of being corrupted by invidious factions, and so on. The role can't last, as Joe Service had discovered.

Service had made a good living out of this for some time, and might have continued for at least a little longer, but he fell in love with Helen Sedlacek. Tucker didn't have much experience with these attachments, distrusted them as human motivations, but he had concluded that it must be a genuine factor in this case. There was no other explanation for the behavior of the two young people. The two had essentially destroyed their heretofore promising careers in favor of a joint activity that was, apparently, neither lucrative nor productive. They both seemed to be interested in money—always a reliable motivation in Tucker's eyes—but then they would do things that ran counter to their financial interests. Or so it seemed. Their activities had also been highly dangerous, which might be seen as an attraction to young and daring operatives, but these two were practical-minded souls.

Tucker believed that it was Joe Service who had killed Busoni, perhaps with Helen's help, or at her urging. What would drive a man to do that, if not love? It hadn't helped Joe's career, obviously.

But it was a good thing for the Lucani, he'd thought at the time. When they encountered Service they were looking for just such a man. The Lucani had a familiar problem for intelligence agencies engaged in proactive operations: insulation and deniability. Someone had to carry out these actions, someone who, if caught, could not be associated with official (or in their case, unofficial) policy.

Joe Service was a criminal. He was, at the time, in a Denver hospital recovering from complications of being shot some months earlier. He was due to be tried for several crimes. It was unclear how strong a case there was against him, but there was the likelihood of a long prison term. The Lucani debated his recruitment and decided it was worth a chance. The colonel had been mightily impressed by Joe's cunning, his quick-wittedness, his tendency to act expeditiously but judiciously, and his success ratio. Best of all, he appeared eminently susceptible to their control: if he screwed up, they could easily betray him to the usual law agencies, or they could terminate him in other ways; and his association with them was easily deniable.

They decided to help him escape. And it paid dividends: the foreign drug dealer was neutralized, in a way that made it seem that it must be an action by rival criminals. The mission had the inestimable value of being completely deniable by legitimately constituted authority—indeed, the issue never even arose.

Subsequently, Joe was employed in an action against the powerful Detroit mobster DiEbola. Here again he had succeeded, at least to the extent that DiEbola was indeed neutralized. But now it wasn't clear to Tucker just how that had been carried out. Worse, the unaccountable loss of one of their own had raised dangerous warning flags. And Joe's behavior about the money was also objectionable. He had an appearance of being a rebel, an uncontrollable servant. Worst of all, he might be a rebel clever enough to mask his rebellion.

Naturally, at this juncture, the colonel was forced to consider a judicious removal. Some of his fellow Lucani were frankly scared of Joe Service. Others, however, notably Dinah Schwind, the agent who had recruited Joe in Denver, were opposed to purging Joe. Colonel Tucker considered whether Schwind might not be, herself, romantically or at least physically attracted to Service. But knowing Schwind to be a sensible, level-headed agent, he was inclined to think that was nonsense. She knew Joe best, had spent the most time with him—he was her protégé. Naturally, she was protective.

This was always the difficult part of administration, the colonel knew. As in the past, he tended to fall back on his experience in the squadron. You had to think of the mission first. Then you had to consider your resources. He had known good pilots, brave and intelligent men who were not good strike leaders, or even good wingmen. He'd known, on the other hand, pilots in Vietnam who had lost confidence in their mission, who no longer believed that it was right to bomb Hanoi. One or two of them had continued to fly, however. They would go on the missions, carry out their responsibilities as wingmen, but never drop their bombs until they were out of the target area. Astounding behavior. They put themselves at risk, apparently solely for their comrades, unwilling to let them down. Nothing was said, although everyone knew about it. Such a pilot, of course, could not be asked to lead the strike force.

Now what about that? Tucker had been impressed by these men, honored them for their faithfulness to the unit. But it had been troubling. Others, he knew, had despised them. Tucker could never do that; he knew these men. In MiG Alley, he wanted these guys on his wing. He had this same feeling about Joe.

He contrasted Joe with Pollak, the man who had not returned from the DiEbola mission. Tucker had a feeling that whatever had happened up there, it hadn't been Joe who had precipitated the mischance, such as it was. Pollak, now, he was one of those hard-nosed types, a guy who saw himself as the leader in any situation, the guy who would make the tough decisions. Unfortunately, he didn't always have good judgment, and he was likely to have made decisions that were not his to make. Joe was a guy, the colonel felt, who could react coolly to unforeseen developements. Joe's first priority would be to survive, but he'd also do everything possible to save the mission—and, of course, the mission had been accomplished. You wanted to be close to that guy, in any kind of scrap.

The colonel had been nervous about Pollak before this. He had considered him dangerous. If Pollak ever lost faith in the Lucani's mission, he'd be the one to blow the whistle on all of them, and there would be no warning. He was competent, but he might not be a good comrade if the basic premise was seriously challenged. Until this episode, from which he hadn't returned, Pollak had never given the colonel reason to object. When the operation was proposed and planned, Tucker had agreed with Pollak's volunteering to go, mainly because he had figured that whatever problems there might be with Pollak, Joe's presence would probably override those problems. In other words, without actually saying as much to anyone, including himself, he'd seen Joe as the de facto leader of the operation.

He'd made a mistake, though. He realized it now. Before they'd left, he'd said to Pollak, "If anything goes wrong, make sure it's you who comes back." What he'd meant by that, he thought, was simply that Joe was the expendable one, the guy who would have to take the fall for a failed mission, the cutout, the insulation. That was Joe's role from the beginning, wasn't it? But, he considered, Pollak might have taken that another way. Maybe that was what was eating Joe. Maybe he thought that Tucker had meant for him to be neutralized, that it was an integral part of the plan, rather than a prudent option.

Tucker sighed. The simple fact was, something had gone wrong and it wasn't Pollak who had come back. Maybe it wasn't a disaster, but now he would have to do the cleanup, disinfect the situation. Was Joe a mistake? He hoped not.

In the meantime, he had other concerns. One of them was Franko. Another disappearance. Unlike Pollak, Franko's disappearance was eminently explicable. The intelligence community had pretty much accepted the notion that Franko had been caught up in a Serbian militia operation and been killed. There were a lot of people missing over there. The problem was if Franko hadn't been captured or killed. Where was he? What was he doing?

Lieutenant Colonel Vern Tucker was a man of action, of course. He had already put some actions in train to find out the whereabouts of Franko Bradovic, his man in Kosovo. The trouble was, nothing had come of it. The actions had turned up nothing. The only fallback was some suspect information about Butte.

So, he was back to Joe. He didn't want to think about Joe anymore tonight. Joe had gone off with a pocketful of dough. He had a feeling Joe was like the cowboys he'd known in his youth, the hands that came and went on the ranch. When you paid them on a Saturday, you knew some of them wouldn't be back—at least, not until they got rid of their pay, which didn't always take longer than Saturday night in Great Falls. He had a feeling Joe was right now in bed with Helen.

Damn Helen, he thought. Joe without Helen was just about the ideal tool. With Helen . . . who knew what they'd get up to? To hell with it. If he were home now, he'd pour himself some of that ancient single malt he'd acquired, get out some reports to read or maybe study up on the history of Serbia, and listen to some Bach. He wasn't at home. He was stuck in a hotel in Detroit, albeit about the best the city could offer, but still sterile and not very accommodating to a man of sophisticated tastes. Still, he had picked up one of those clever little clamshell CD players with some decent earphones. He had been surprised to find Tureck's splendid version of the Bach partitas in a large music store in the nearby shopping center. There was some commercial Scotch in the minibar. He could tough it out with that. He settled down with Michael Sells's interesting text on the religious aspect of the Bosnian strife.

The wind must have changed, he thought a half hour later. The airliners were making their approach to Detroit-Wayne just west of the hotel. An old pilot notices these things, almost unconsciously.

Every Bend

"'**R**ound every bend / A crooked man will lie" goes the old blues tune. But Joe Service figured that every straight road has a crook in it, eventually. You didn't want to get lulled into going too fast when the kink suddenly popped up. And Lieutenant Colonel Tucker's projected routes were never as straight as they were sketched, Joe knew. But this one was no more than a cursory gesture, a vague line into a far, hazy horizon. There were no markers at all.

Of course, it wouldn't be the colonel who missed the turn. "Go on over to Butte and find this Franko," he'd said, more or less.

Find who? Joe said to himself. He was used to clients not knowing *where* he could find someone—that was *his* job, after all. Typically, some usually trustworthy fellow had decided to take $X and run—or, more likely, $XXX,XXX. Without guys like that, Joe would be looking for a career change.

But his old clients rarely said, "Find so-and-so." Well, in the nature of things, they sometimes didn't know exactly who had taken $X, and they would ask Joe to find out who it was—but there was always a shortlist of suspects. The colonel seemed to know who he wanted found, a missing agent who "maybe" was in Butte. His name was Franko. The Butte location was just a guess—somebody had said the guy was originally from Butte. To be sure, the colonel had checked out this Franko in all the official files. There wasn't any Franko from Butte.

Joe and Helen were sitting in the colonel's hotel room, where they had gone to discuss this project. "You must have a file on the guy," Joe prodded the colonel. "An application for employment, maybe? With family history, educational background, blood type, fingerprints . . . a picture . . . a description, shoe size for crying out loud?"

They had a file, the colonel explained, but it wasn't much use. No one in the DEA, the CIA, or any of the other agencies from which the Lucani drew their members had ever actually met "Franko." At least, not as far as they knew. So, yes, they had a file, but it was a file derived largely from information provided, at a distance, sight unseen, by the subject of the file: Franko. So, no, they didn't have a real file.

The problem was that Franko had not been recruited in the usual way. Indeed, he hadn't been recruited at all. He had contacted them. This wasn't unusual, Tucker explained. U.S. agencies were often contacted by foreign citizens, volunteering their services. Some of these were more or less clumsy attempts by foreign agencies to infiltrate American agencies or particular spying campaigns. In the old days, of course, these attempts were invariably attributed to the Soviet Union. What was different about this voluntary spy was that he claimed to be an American living abroad, and that he offered invaluable information about narcotics smuggling while insisting that he was not himself engaged in narcotics trafficking in any way. Furthermore, and most important, he had contacted the Lucani.

Joe didn't understand that. "How could he contact the Lucani?" he asked the colonel. "What are there, billboards in Bosnia—'The

Lucani seek a few good men . . . Uncle Sam wants you!' Do you have a number in the phone book?"

The colonel looked patiently suffering and said it wasn't quite like that. But it was an important question, and the colonel understood it as such. Had Franko contacted them as a group known to him as the Lucani? Or had he simply approached someone who he thought might be an American agent, who just happened to have a somewhat tenuous connection to the Lucani? The link from that agent to the Lucani wasn't the problem, he felt. But Franko's motivation and the extent of his knowledge about espionage wasn't clear, not to them, and they wanted to be clear about it.

They had first heard about Franko from a contract agent named Theo Ostropaki—himself not an American—who had subsequently disappeared and was now presumed dead. He had been last heard from in Mostar, in Herzegovina, more than a year ago. He was supposed to be meeting some people who, like Franko, were involved in the international drug trade. But they had heard nothing since.

Ostropaki had reported his initial contact with Franko to the DEA. He'd suggested that Franko might be a prospect as an agent or at least a source of information. He seemed like a reliable guy, an American from Butte, presently living in Bosnia or in the bordering hill country, at a location that might have been actually in Kosovo—jurisdictions were a little fuzzy up in those hills sometimes. Franko, he said, was intelligent, fairly young, able to move around. His occupation and his reason for being there weren't clear. Ostropaki was asked to clarify that. Either he didn't know what the guy was doing up there and didn't take his explanations seriously, or there was something else, something Ostropaki wasn't communicating. He hadn't been able to do much research, for reasons that were later explained, though he was satisfied that Franko was fairly well known in the local area, but . . . how to put it?

Sometimes a stranger can come into a small, remote, clannish community, with no discernible connection there, no good reason to be there, and be accepted. His reasons, at least his initial reasons, for being there were not germane. The local people liked him and accepted him.

That hadn't been good enough for the DEA. They'd passed on the offer. Ostropaki had turned to the colonel, who, at the time, was working with the DEA. He'd been impressed with Ostropaki's intuition regarding Franko, and intrigued.

The colonel had seen a scenario such as Ostropaki had suggested occur in Montana. It wasn't usual, that was for sure. The world over, villagers are almost painfully aware of strangers, perhaps more so when the stranger doesn't seem to have any reason to be there. But he remembered a fellow who had come to the High Line when he was a kid, on the ranch.

Everybody talked about this Rick, wondered about him. He'd stayed for a couple of years, perhaps longer. Rick wasn't a cowboy, he didn't farm, he wasn't a construction worker, although he fixed up an old house a mile or two out of Sun River and did a good job, folks said, meaning it was workmanlike and not too fancy, no sun roofs or geodesic-dome additions.

When Ostropaki had shrugged off the DEA's concerns about Franko's ostensible purposes, the colonel had immediately been reminded of Rick. He'd been surprised that he'd so completely forgotten this fellow who had occupied his boyish imagination more than a little bit.

Rick was a tall, good-looking man, if not exactly handsome, not movie star handsome. He had gotten the presumably dry well working at the old Ford place, which he'd rented. He kept a good bird dog. Was friendly but not nosy. Had a good pickup, but nothing too new. He hunted a little bit with some of the boys, for upland birds and deer, and seemed to know what he was doing. Fished a little in the Sun, a fly fisherman. He was good enough at those pursuits to need no guide, no advice, but took it cheerfully.

Some people called him "Perfesser," because he talked a little formally and seemed to have an education, but that handle didn't really take. The waitress at the Stockman's Grill said he could park his boots under her bunk any night, but nobody thought that he did.

Occasionally, a few of Rick's friends would show up, people from back East. They'd stay a few days and he'd take them hunting or fishing, drive them around; they'd have drinks and a steak in the Stockman's. They were people who didn't announce themselves as rich or famous—they seemed like ordinary fellows, possibly farmers or reasonably well paid working folks from back wherever they came from. One was rumored to be a writer, but nobody had ever heard of him or of his putative books. So it was assumed that Rick was of that larger world, somehow, but no one had ever heard him talk about writing or wealth or anything but what folks usually talked about—hunting, fishing, the weather, crops.

The colonel couldn't remember now if Rick had left before he did, but he thought he had. He'd made no lasting impression on the folks in that part of the country, but he was well regarded. Colonel Tucker wondered if it hadn't been the same for this Franko—who, incidentally, was also said to be a fisherman.

The colonel wondered now if he hadn't accepted Theo Ostropaki's inability to provide any substantial information about Franko because he had known Rick. He pushed the thought aside. After all, the peaceful world of the High Line was not much like a remote Balkan village, but then, it was his impression that the hill people in Kosovo hadn't yet seen much of the turmoil that later caught them up. Country people, he tended to think, were much the same the world over.

"As far as Theo could find out," the colonel told Joe and Helen, "Franko was accepted in the community. Just one of those guys, it seems, who gets along and pretty soon people forget that he's a stranger. He's a little helpful, but not so as to make people dependent on him, or beholden to him. He doesn't ask questions . . . he just *gets along*." He paused for a long moment, thinking. "Of course, that could all be bullshit," he said. "Maybe he was just a hell of a good agent. That's something I hope you'll find out, when you catch up to him."

"Well, what did your guy find out?" Joe asked. He didn't express any particular concern about this paucity of information, but he wanted to know what there was to know.

According to Ostropaki, the colonel said, Franko had stumbled on the existence of a smuggling operation that was involved in the drug trade. That seemed plausible enough—smuggling was a traditional occupation in those hills, with the borders so close and ill-defined. Franko had become friendly with some of the younger men who were involved. From them, he had heard about Ostropaki, who they suspected was a government agent of some kind, though not for the Serbs. Interpol, maybe. At the time, the colonel informed them, Ostropaki was in fact working for the DEA. That's how the colonel had gotten on to this—he was the controller on this operation.

Ostropaki had gone to the village, in his role as a contact for suppliers in Belgrade, but the people he was supposed to meet hadn't shown up. As he was leaving he'd been flagged down on the road back to Montenegro by this fellow, Franko. His car had apparently broken down. He was leaning into the opened hood. When Ostropaki came to look into the engine compartment, Franko confessed that there was nothing wrong with his car. He said he wanted to warn Ostropaki that there were some men a little ways farther on, at a lonely spot, who he suspected were waiting for the agent. He had seen them as he came down and recognized who they were. Maybe it was nothing, he said, maybe they weren't looking for him, but he thought he should warn him. Ostropaki went home another way.

"Theo was—is, as far as I know—a good agent, a real professional," the colonel said.

He was standing, looking out the hotel window. The flat landscape of the city sprawled to the south. He said something about visibility having dropped to about six miles. "Haze," he observed. "Might be some fog come nightfall. I think we could have a drink. It's that time."

He poured some good Scotch for them in the glasses provided by the hotel, added ice and water.

"I met Theo a couple of times, in Athens. Smart fellow, looked like he wasn't all that bright, which is always good. You'd take him for a middle-level manager type, a sales-force supervisor—in fact, that was his cover: he sold construction supplies for a Macedonian firm. I told him we were interested in his Franko, but that the agency couldn't see his value. But I trusted his judgment and if he thought the fellow was . . . you know, genuine—and useful—that maybe we could work something out. But for now, it had to be just between the two of us. He should report to me through a separate link. I told him I could supply him with some funds and that if Franko worked out, why then. . . . I left it at that, and Theo never brought it up again.

"Theo never went back into those hills, after his initial contact with Franko," the colonel went on, when he was settled again. "He made inquiries, found out who the fellow was who had stopped him and sent him some brochures, or something, I imagine. That would be his style, but he never told me. He heard from the fellow a few weeks later, by phone. Franko had come to Belgrade, where Theo had infiltrated the drug trade. They met in a café. That's when he learned about Franko's distaste for the drug trade—said he thought it was bad for the people, the young fellows who were involved. Smuggling the usual goods was one thing—it was a tradition, almost a rite of passage for the young men, one way and another. But when you mixed drugs into that, things changed. Drugs were too volatile;

too much money was involved, too much violence, and people in-evitably started using what they were hauling over the mountains. And the local smuggler became a link in an international trade— foreigners got seriously interested in your activities. It was no good.

"Specifically, he said he had some information about a trans-fer of goods. He didn't want his people, his friends, caught, but maybe if the trade was damaged, maybe the big dealers would quit using this route. That was the premise, anyway. They set up a com-munication system. The information was accurate. We intercepted the goods, well down the line—in Italy, I believe.

"Over a period of time, thanks to more good intelligence, some of the smugglers were picked up, or otherwise eliminated. Not the mountain boys—the coastal ones, intercepted on the sea." The colonel glanced away, unwilling to expand on that last piece of information.

"A new plan was worked out, a departure from the original scheme. Franko was supplied with information about the trade; he got personally involved with the smugglers. He advised them, and his advice was good. He became more important to them, even-tually becoming the chief contact in the area for the suppliers, a gang out of Belgrade headed up by a Vjelko Zivkovic. It was a nice piece of work. Franko's information was delivered to Ostropaki, who forwarded it to an answering service in Paris, informing us of ship-ments of narcotics. The information was always dead accurate. The DEA was able to interdict these shipments, always at some point far from the Balkans."

The communication technique was familiar to Joe. He used similar systems, actually a chain of such services, each of them an-other barrier to identifying the person who originated the message. It could be cumbersome at times.

"I thought you guys were into codes and drop boxes, that kind of stuff," Joe said.

The colonel caught the underlying current of Joe's remark. "As far as the DEA knew, the information was not ostensibly from Franko," he said, with no particular emphasis. "The agency had declined him, forgotten about him. He no longer existed. This info was coming from Ostropaki, who had presumably gotten it from nameless Serbian or Kosovar contacts. Theo, naturally, thought I had overcome the agency's reluctance, but he understood that the provenance of his information was still not to be mentioned to anyone but me."

"Still," Helen spoke up, "you must have been hot to know who Franko was."

"Oh, indeed I was! I pressed Ostropaki on every available occasion to find out more about him. The best he ever came up with was a last name, which came to nothing in our research."

Helen remarked, "I thought Franko was the surname."

"So did we, and it may turn out that it is. But I suspect that, like the surname Ostropaki came up with, it is also fictitious. Oh yes, we turned those names over every which way, looking for some clue to his real identity. Frank, Frankenheim, Frankenstein, Frankovic, Francis, Franjo—there's a world of related names to check out in existing files, compare to customs records, border listings of passages, airline reservations, passport applications . . ."

"What was the other name?" Helen asked.

"Bradovic," the colonel said. "Or some variation thereof. It was simply a name that Ostropaki had heard attached to his pet agent. Franko himself always went by, simply, Franko."

"Bradovich," Helen said, "or Bradovitz, maybe."

"Fratovic, Pratovic," the colonel offered, "and Voradovic. We didn't get anywhere with it."

"And then Ostropaki went dead on you," Joe said. "I bet that was a—what would you call it?—a sticky moment when you heard about that." Joe had a clear notion of that kind of moment: when someone, say a cop or a superior, lays that kind of heavy dope on you. You look at him and wonder how you're supposed to react. Surprised? Even interested? Puzzled? Thinking to yourself, first, Can it be true? Is this a trap? How much does this guy know?

The colonel knew what Joe meant. "We were spared that, for better or for worse," he said. "We'd received another of the messages, ostensibly from Ostropaki. We acted on it, with the usual good results. A day or two later we heard that Theo had not been heard from since a time that *probably* would have precluded him sending the information. Then, I suppose, there was one of those airless moments . . . waiting for the other shoe to drop. But it didn't. We just kept getting the good product."

"How long did you wait before you sent someone to find him?" Joe asked.

The colonel shrugged. "Where would we send an agent? And to whom?"

"Um," Joe said, and held up a finger. "If I followed you, Ostropaki was not in the Lucani?"

"He was a prospect, but," the colonel said with a shrug, "I don't think any of us really seriously considered bringing him in. He wasn't . . . not to put too fine a point on it, one of us. I mean a federal agent. We all of us are in this for essentially the same reason, and somehow that didn't include Theo. But I interviewed him in Athens, later on, when things got going so well, to get an idea of his attitude. I liked what I heard and saw—he seemed to share our feelings about the failings of the system—but there wasn't any compelling reason, really, to open up to him, to expose ourselves. You see? And then he was gone."

He sat back and gestured with his hand, opening it with a little wave, as if releasing a bird.

Helen did not see. "You mean, because he wasn't an American? But it was okay to use him . . . sort of like . . . ?" She gestured at Joe and, by implication, herself.

The colonel thought for a long moment, then said, "We don't know if authority—the agencies we work for—is aware of us. I expect that someone may be curious why certain things happen that seem to have no firm explanation—disappearance of various figures, of goods. We try to provide adequate, plausible scenarios, usually premised on the notion that it's internal, that crooks are ripping off each other, hijacking, protecting their respective turf. That's about as far as we can go. An action has to be explained, you see, and it seems there is always some rival organization at hand who can be blamed. But at some point, someday, someone is bound to notice that quite a few events are not substantiated by interrogation of those who were thought to have been responsible. As far as I know it hasn't happened yet, but we may not be aware of official suspicions if they exist.

"So far," he hastened to assure the two, "we haven't detected even a rumor of the existence of the Lucani. Which is at least one reason why we've been successful, thus far," he murmured.

After a moment, he observed further, in a donnish manner: "The history of the Balkans is rife with secret organizations, of course—the Black Hand, the Brotherhood, and so on. They were generally associated with secret movements of national liberation, revolutionary groups. But it's something that people are familiar with in that part of the world. In a way," he mused, "it may have unconsciously inspired our own group. Unconsciously, let me emphasize. We have no political ambitions." He dismissed any such vagrant thoughts that may have been conjured in the heads of Joe and Helen with a wave of his hand. He seemed a little surprised at the thought, himself.

"But the point here," he said, "is that security is Principle One in this kind of activity. Theo Ostropaki was an agent involved in dangerous business. We did not endanger him further, as far as we can tell. Indeed, by keeping him on the outside, as it were, we protected him from . . . *contamination*."

"Sounds like he got contaminated," Helen said.

"Well, we don't know that, do we?" the colonel said. "That's a corner where Franko could cast some light. If you find him. But—point two—your situation is not analagous to Theo's. I, we, initiated a relationship with you, Joe. We saw that your services would be helpful to us and we could be helpful to you. Ms. Sedlacek, your involvement is a consequence of your relationship with Mr. Service."

He gazed at her pleasantly enough, but Helen felt that the colonel had barely stopped himself from saying something that might have been less amiable.

"Wait a minute," Joe said. "Back up here. First you said that Franko may have known about the Lucani. Then you said that Ostropaki didn't even know about it. So what's the prob? Franko is just a nameless source, now missing."

"Yes, it's confusing and mysterious," the colonel conceded, "but it's not really a contradiction. It's possible, from some intimations Ostropaki had made when I interviewed him, that he'd had some notion of the existence of a group like the Lucani. But I concluded that he knew nothing and I didn't enlighten him. Still . . . you see, this is where it gets sticky . . . there was always the possibility that Franko was actually a probe from another agency, one that had heard rumors of the Lucani, and his approach to Ostropaki was part of an internal investigation. Wheels within wheels. I essentially gave up on that notion, especially when Franko began to provide such good information."

"And it's just on the basis of Ostropaki," Joe said, "that you want us to go to Butte?"

"Well, you know, there have been some refugees who have shown up in Butte," the colonel said. "And I know that you two have some connections there, some reason to be there. I thought it serendipitous, and it might be convenient . . ." He let the idea drift in the air. "There is no very pressing urgency about it, you know. Take your time. At present, things have turned somewhat more positive, politically, in Serbia. As far as we can tell, the NATO war disrupted the drug traffic, as did the revolution that brought down Milosevic."

"What is this guy supposed to look like," Joe asked, "according to Ostropaki?"

"Theo said Franko was about thirty-one or -two, but he could be much older, maybe as much as forty. He's about one point seven five meters, weighs about seventy-five kilos or so . . . say, five-eight or -nine, about one sixty-five pounds. Dark hair, worn medium length, the usual mustache but no beard, no glasses. Dark complexion, brown eyes. Looked like a Kosovar, you might say. Dressed neatly, in the style of those hills. Good sturdy shoes, slacks, a sweater, an old tweed wool jacket. No hat. I mention all this not because he'd still be wearing those clothes, but because it gave him a local look, though you wouldn't mistake him for a farmer. Theo said he looked like he could be a schoolteacher, maybe, and talked like it. Spoke Serb and the local Albanian dialect well, if not quite like a native, but also English like an American."

Joe Service sighed, but said nothing.

The colonel said, "Thin-lipped, lean face, no prominent cheekbones, dark eyebrows but not particularly heavy, ears small and close to the head, which is round, not elongated, hair close but not dense or wavy or crimped, prominent brow and large, smooth forehead but no widow's peak. Walks like a city dweller, confident stride, knows where his feet are landing, but doesn't choose to stride rapidly. That sort of thing?" He raised an eyebrow at Joe.

"Not very helpful," Joe said, "and I try not to get too firm an image. By now, he could be limping, or had an ear shot off. Probably no mustache, but maybe a full beard. Who knows? It sounds like, if he's alive—in Butte—that he was blown but managed to escape."

"Not an unreasonable assumption," the colonel agreed.

"You said something about Ostro's notion of what Franko was doing up there," Helen said.

"Yes, the agency didn't buy it," the colonel said, "and it didn't amount to much. He thought he was a scholar."

"A scholar?" Helen said. "What kind of a scholar? You mean an ethnologist, or something? Some kind of social scientist?"

The colonel made a slight grimace, almost a frown. "No," he said, "maybe something more in the way of an amateur, a fellow who is just looking at things, a man of curiosity. I can't say I bought it, either. I just don't know. Maybe he was—or is—a bird-watcher."

The colonel was amused to observe Helen rolling her eyes.

Joe was thinking about Butte. It was a city of about twenty-five thousand, he thought, and maybe another five or so in the surrounding valleys who might show up from time to time. He was supposed to hang around and hope to see someone he couldn't really identify if he did see him.

"What the heck," he said, "it can't be that hard."

Frenchy's Forque

Joe Service owned property down in the Ruby Valley, thirty-five or forty miles south of the city of Butte, as the eagle flies, fifty by highway. The nearest town was a village called Tinstar. Joe's property was situated on Garland Butte. The Garland family had ranched a sizable spread there for at least three generations, but the Garlands weren't there anymore. Old Mrs. Garland, a widow, had died in a tragic run-in with a crazy woman she'd befriended.

A couple of years before her death, Mrs. Garland had sold a section of her property to a young man named Joe Humann. This was one of Joe Service's aliases. The turbulence surrounding Joe Service had caught her up, though only a few realized that Mrs. Garland's death was linked to Joe's problems.

Joe Service certainly knew it. He was not big on remorse, but he'd liked Mrs. Garland. She was the best kind of neighbor, helpful but not nosy, rarely to be seen or heard. His chief regret, however, was for his hideaway in the mountains of Montana. It was the ideal retreat, a place he could flee to after his typically hectic forays into the affairs of the mob, in Detroit or Los Angeles or points in between. The colonel had exploited Joe's unabashed affection for the place when he'd offered the Butte mission. But now, the closer they got to Butte, the less attractive it seemed.

There had been some excellent moments on the road from Detroit—not a straight road by any means. The weather was good. They had a new vehicle, an SUV that Helen had insisted on buying. Joe had preferred a Toyota 4-Runner, or a Range Rover . . . but Helen had put her foot down. There was no way she was buying anything but Detroit iron—the very thought! She opted for a powerful Dodge Durango, a take-no-prisoners four-wheel-drive outfit— hardly a useful feature on the interstate. But at least he'd talked her out of the red one. Cops stop red cars at least 50 percent more often than black ones, was his theory. They got one in bottle green, although it was called something else. And, after all, they had driven some "blue highways," through Wisconsin and Minnesota, and even gotten onto some fairly rough tracks in back country in the Dakotas and eastern Montana . . . just lollygagging, sightseeing.

Helen thought that as long as the colonel wasn't in any hurry, neither should they be. Joe's initial eagerness to get back to what he called his "Hole-in-the-Wall" had begun to modulate into a classical approach/retreat syndrome by the time they got to the Yellowstone River.

He discussed the matter with Helen. "The colonel says we're secure," he observed, "but what does that mean? Do you trust him? I'm not even sure what we're supposed to do with this Franko when we catch up to him. As for the Hole-in-the-Wall, the last time I was up there was after that deal in Salt Lake. I was kind of riding a high, you know what I mean? And I was just there for a few hours. It was fine—the place was a mess, the house burned down and all— but the hot pool was nice."

Helen had been thinking, too, and especially about the hot pool. It was an idyllic spot, a beautiful little thermal spring just over the ridge from where Joe's house had been. But her memories of the pool weren't entirely pleasant. She had been attacked and almost murdered in that pool. In the event, she had overcome her attacker. But it would never be the same. She didn't know if she could bring herself to plunge into that pool again, certainly not with the same blithe confidence as before.

She realized that she'd been avoiding thinking about it. It was good that Joe had brought it up. "What are you thinking?" she said. "Just forget about the place?"

They were in a hotel in a small town in central Montana, an hour or so west of Billings, no more than a three-hour drive to Butte. They were sprawled naked on the queen-sized bed in a room on the second floor. It was the oddest hotel Helen had ever stayed in, or even heard of. It was an old cowboy hotel, they decided. There was a sink and a toilet in their room, but the real bathroom was across the hall. This wasn't much of a privacy problem: nobody else seemed to be in the hotel. It was clean and decorated in an amusing mélange of cowboy chic and 1920s moderne—cane furniture, Charlie Russell prints on the walls, but art deco slipshade chandeliers.

The great draw here was clearly the restaurant downstairs. It was reputed to be great, and it certainly had been occupied for one seating at least. Good rack of lamb, excellent wines. They were told that movie stars stayed here when they were filming nearby, which was fairly often. Hunters and fishermen also kept the place booked, but they were just between seasons, it seemed—"Come November you couldn't get a room here for five hundred dollars," the desk clerk had claimed. Besides elk hunters, a movie was scheduled in a few months, when Redford was due in town.

But for Helen's money, the thing that would bring her back was the massive bathroom with its enormous shower and the sauna. This was as modern as it could be, showers with jets at all angles, heat lamps, great fluffy towels on heated racks, lots of mirrors, and good lighting. She was grateful to the movie stars, if they were re-

sponsible for the decoration. The sauna was brilliant, with its aromatic cedar paneling and benches.

"There's no place to stay there," Joe said, idly stroking her
back. "I have bad feelings about it. The folks around there may
not be so friendly. Maybe we should just avoid it. Find somewhere
new. It'd be all right to take a run up there, clean out some stuff
I've got stashed." He was thinking about an abandoned mine,
above the house site, where he'd stored a few useful things, like
money, some guns, and—he had a vivid flash—the desiccated
corpse of an unknown man.

"Hate to give up the hot springs," he said. "When I was there
I took a long soak and didn't give a thought to the problem of returning, or rebuilding. I was too out of it. There's some cops around,
too . . ."

"You mean Mulheisen," Helen said. "He's in Detroit."

"He knows about the place," Joe said. "The colonel might be
able to head off the other cops, but I don't think he can do anything about Mulheisen. And there are some local cops, sheriff's
deputies. I'd bet Mulheisen made some good contacts there. They'd
sure give him a buzz if they find out we're back . . . and they'll hear,
probably within hours. Hell, I don't even know if we ought to stay
in Butte, though it's not so likely that we'll be noticed there."

There was also a woman in Butte, but he didn't mention her
to Helen. He was pretty sure that Helen had no knowledge of the
nurse, Cateyo. She'd been a useful ally when Joe was extricating
himself from his problems. He wasn't eager to encounter her again.
He'd made a few promises . . .

Helen saw his point about the place, all right. Mulheisen was
a real cop, a detective on the Detroit police force. Seemingly a
simple, not too bright fellow, just a precinct sergeant, but somehow
always in one's way. "We can find someplace," she said. An idea
occurred to her: "Maybe we could stay here."

"You mean rent this room?" Joe thought about it. "It's too far from Butte, almost two hundred miles. Quite a commute."

"How much time do we actually have to spend in Butte?" she asked. She suddenly didn't have much appetite for this. It had seemed like fun, in the beginning, but now she felt an uncertain dread. Maybe she was picking up Joe's vibes.

Joe considered. A few days poking around, maybe another few days following up leads. If they weren't going to fix up the old spread down in the Ruby Valley, maybe they wouldn't be spending so much time in Montana, after all. But if not, why had they come? He had plenty of money. Helen was loaded as well. They could go to . . . South America. He'd never been to South America. Brazil seemed suddenly attractive, maybe Argentina. Buenos Aires? Chile?

"What about the colonel?" Helen said.

"Gotta say good-bye to him someday," Joe said. "Funny, but the farther I get from that guy, the less I look forward to seeing him again. Let's just bag it . . . fly to Hawaii."

Helen was game. But for some reason, they didn't go. Neither could be accused of conventional attitudes toward duty, but . . . perhaps it was nothing more than curiosity. Instead, they wrestled.

In the morning, they lingered over the remains of their elegant breakfast of omelettes and toast and fruit, gratefully restored from the exertions of the night. At last Joe said, "Well, if we're going to find our wandering scholar, let's do it." Some three hours later, the fancy Durango swept around a curve coming down off the Homestake Pass, and the entire Silver Bow Valley opened up before them, a thousand feet below.

Butte was unlike most cities: from any of its approaches you could see the city laid out across an enormous canvas before you. It sprawled from the mountains in the north down into the valley. A Detroit or a Los Angeles was just endless habitation and industry, stretching into a haze, even when you approached from twenty thousand feet. They were vastly larger cities, of course, and that's the problem: one can see no end of city. It can seem to be an inescapable trap to its citizens.

Joe Service considered that one attractive aspect of Butte was that you could see it all in its physical setting, the city in the frame around the canvas. The mountains and highlands on either side, especially the great, craggy ridge of the Continental Divide to the east, which they were now descending. But there was no ignoring the enormous abandoned pit mine, smack in the heart of the town. And now there were extended terraces of a new, active pit.

The golden dome on Holy Trinity Eastern Orthodox Church gleamed in the sun. The rest of the city sprawled up the great hill, surrounding the monstrous open-pit copper mines. A few old gallows frames—old hoists left over from more than a century of underground mining—also caught one's eye from the highway, and then the chalk-white towers of Immaculate Conception Catholic church, and beyond that the extensive brick campus of the state technological university—the "School of Mines," as it was inevitably known.

Butte was not the typical modern western town, aglow with the familiar icons of American popular commercial culture, the fast-food emporia, the big box malls. It had those, of course, and contemporary neighborhoods of modest ranch houses and working-class bungalows, but there were also the older brick apartment buildings, the hotels and department stores, now run-down. It was a place that evoked an earlier industrial culture, dominated by a single enterprise—the mining company—now long gone, but its imprint still visible. An odd mixture of the old and the new, a sense of a history. It resembled eastern rust-belt cities, though it was rapidly giving way to the new consumer culture. Still, it was quintessentially a working-class town.

Joe and Helen were depressed, despite the brilliant sunshine, the clear air, and the magnificent sweep of the massive Continental Divide. They had occupied themselves for several days with a kind of goofy American tourist travel, visiting natural monuments, enjoying the remarkable scenery from the Great Lakes, across the forests, the Mississippi and Missouri Rivers, the plains. Indeed, just moments before they had still been in the great American back country, driving through a spectacular panorama of jumbled rocks and canyons, the forest looming above them, the mountains rearing on all sides. They'd been carefree, on vacation. Now all of a sudden, here was the workaday world. They had to go to work, and they weren't eager for it.

They checked into the old Finlen Hotel, uptown. It stood in the very midst of the old city. It wasn't very popular, they found. Most people stayed in the big motels down near the interstate. But the Finlen had been refurbished fairly recently, it appeared. They had a large, pleasant room, with good views of the city and the mountains, the pits.

Ordinarily, when working for the mob, Joe would have been provided with more local contacts than he wanted. Usually, he'd avoid them, preferring to dig out things on his own. There were people here, he knew, who had mob connections—no doubt they could provide him with useful information. But he had no intention of contacting them. It would just be a further complication; he still had some unresolved issues with the mob.

No, as usual, he'd do his own research, find out about these Serbian refugees the colonel had mentioned, visit the church, talk to the Serbian priest, look through the phone book and figure out where the Serbs lived, who they were. It was just that, for once, he felt a little uncertain, a little too isolated. But he had Helen, he reminded himself. She could certainly help him with the Serbian community.

Helen could see Joe was still a little down. "Why don't I go over to the church?" she suggested. She could talk to the priest; she was familiar with these churches from childhood. She could even speak Serbian. She'd visited the church when she'd been here before, although she had not told Joe that. She remembered the priest as being from Detroit, in fact.

Joe readily fell in with that plan. "I'll go see some realtors," he said. "Maybe I can get a line on some property. Maybe even a house out in the hills. I don't know how long I can take this old hotel."

Helen agreed with that. They would meet later, for dinner. There was a restaurant on Main Street, near the power company. It looked like the kind of place that had a modern eclectic cuisine, vaguely French by way of California.

Joe wandered around uptown on foot. He began to feel better, just getting out, getting active. It was odd, he realized, but even if one has spent a significant amount of time in a place, once you've been away for a while you fall back on a kind of mental image or general impression of it. And when you return it seems neither as nice nor as awful as you remembered. The harsh necessities of everyday life are oppressive, at first, with their disregard for esthetics. Butte had plenty of that. But overall, he thought, the image lacked the interest of the real. The small dramas and successes assert themselves. The ways in which the city accommodates its aspirations to its needs begin to seem interesting.

He liked the old town's mixture of Cowboy West, Mining West, and New West. People casually used the word "pardner" when you asked directions and cheerfully pointed out the way. It was a battered town, but remarkably upbeat. Just walking a few blocks uphill from the main business district, he came upon a remarkable stone chalet that had, according to a plaque, been erected by one of the copper barons. It had been purchased in Europe, dismantled, and rebuilt here.

He had turned away from contemplating it with amusement and was standing on the corner, undecided about which way to go next, when an SUV pulled over to the curb and its driver, an attractive blond woman, called out.

"Looking for something? Can I help?" She may even have said, "pardner"; he wasn't sure.

Carmen Tomarich was a big woman, at least a head taller than Joe, and she looked like she'd dress out nicely in a brass brassiere and a horned helmet. Instead, she was decked out in full western rig, complete with tooled cowboy boots, flared slacks, and a fringed buckskin vest over her prominent bosom. She looked to be in her late thirties. She had a throaty contralto voice and a big smile. Joe mentally dubbed her Queen of the Rodeo.

As it turned out, Carmen was the proprietress of her own real estate agency. "Just the gal I was looking for," Joe said, pleased.

Carmen was more than happy to drive him around to look at some homes. They were just a few blocks from some real bargains, she said, if you liked old mansions with fifteen rooms, beautiful hardwood floors, cut-glass chandeliers, and curving staircases with splendidly crafted banisters. They also had, she pointed out, ancient furnaces, poor insulation, suspect plumbing and wiring, crumbling foundations, steep roofs that needed reshingling, rusty rain gutters, and brick chimneys that could use repointing.

Alternatively, she would love to show him some spectacular newer construction "out in the flat," meaning the area spreading around the bottom of the hill, out into the valley. It was the modern part of town. She had some bargains in the "hundred-fifty to two-hundred-K range."

Joe said "the flat" sounded more his speed. He didn't have any problems with the "two-hundred-K range." He hopped into Carmen's fancy new vehicle. He liked Helen's Durango better, but he said Carmen's "outfit" was nice.

They drove out past the airport and up into the grassy, tree-less foothills to look at a large, rambling house with far too many bedrooms but a lavishly modern kitchen and a vast open basement that was decorated as an entertainment room, with an enormous fireplace. The house sat on five acres of not very private lawn; no fences out here.

"You'll need a riding mower," Carmen said. "There's one in the barn." She pointed at a small utility shed artfully tucked away near the back. "It doesn't come with, but the owner will sell it for peanuts. He's moved to Helena. Got elected our new attorney general."

She led him across the lawn along a path shielded by evergreens to a small, rustic-looking structure. "Ta-da!" she said. "Your own sauna. It's a beauty, too." It was. Helen would love the sauna, he knew. Joe hated the place. He didn't like the deck, the high upkeep, the general hugeness of it. It wasn't him. And the thought that it belonged to the new attorney general wasn't appealing. But he didn't say so. He said he'd have to bring his wife out to look at it.

On the way back into town, he asked, offhandedly, if there were a lot of Serbs around here. He said he thought he'd noticed an Orthodox church on the way into town.

"Oh, gosh, yes," Carmen said. "People are always asking me if *I'm* Serb, but we're Crotes. Well, my mom's Mexican, which is why I'm Carmen."

"Croats?" Joe said.

"Yeah," she said, "you can't always tell by the name. Some Tomariches are Serbs, though. The Crotes are Catholic, the Serbs are Orthodox. Everybody gets them confused. There's plenty of Serbs in Butte." They were passing a large car dealership on the road back into town. "That's one, there."

Joe looked at the sign. "O'billovich," he read out loud. He smiled. "Irish?"

"I'm pretty sure he added the apostrophe," Carmen said. "Lots of Irish around here. Fabulous Saint Pat's Day celebration. You may have heard about it, even down in Salt Lake."

"I didn't live long in Salt Lake," Joe said. "I'm from back East, really. But is that a real Serbian name?"

"Or Crote," she said. "I went to school with some of them. Tomjanoviches, Kapariches, that kind of thing. There's a lot of them around. There's more than one Obillovich family. I'm not even sure if they're all related."

A thought suddenly occurred to Joe. "Do you know a Frank Obradovich?"

"I think I've heard the name," Carmen said. "How old is he? I might have gone to school with some of his relatives."

"You think so? I'd love to find Frank," Joe said. "I knew him back East. He's about thirty-five, medium height, kind of dark. That'd be something, to run into Frank out here! I'd forgotten all about him. He said he was from Montana, but I never made the connection."

"I could ask around," she said. "Realtors always know every-body, especially in a town like Butte."

In fact, it took about ten minutes in her office, on the phone. There was a Frank Oberavich, who had returned to the Butte area a few years ago, she was told. Her informant wasn't clear. He'd been living out of state, maybe in California or Washington. But he'd come back. "They always come back to Butte," Carmen said. "That's the old saying."

"Not Obradovich?" Joe said. "But Oberavich?"

"You don't pronounce the *e*," Carmen said. "Ob'ravich."

"Well, it could be," Joe said. "Where does he live?"

That wasn't so clear. Carmen said it seemed like he hadn't stayed in town long. He'd found a place up in the mountains, up

toward Helena. "Kind of a reclusive fellow, I guess," she said. "I don't
know if I've ever met him. Most of the Oberaviches I know are real
friendly, social kind of folks. My friend Trudy—she's a realtor, too—
knows him. Is your friend, um . . . I don't mean to pry, and no disrespect, you know . . . as far as I'm concerned, everybody's got a right
to his own, ah, choice—"

"Gay?" Joe said, with a disarming smile. "You know, I never
thought of it, but"—he shrugged—"it could be, I guess. Is your
friend's Frank gay? Maybe it's not the same guy."

"Maybe not," Carmen said, "but it's not too common a name,
is it? Anyway, he lives out in the brush, not too far from a little town
called French Forque." She spelled the second part of the name. "It's
over the pass, north. Trudy doesn't know just where the house is,
but you could ask in the town. Ask a realtor. Let's see . . . that'd be
Denny, Les Denny."

Joe practically ran to the restaurant to tell Helen his discovery. She had some great news, too, she said, "But you first." They
were sitting at dinner, eating a very good veal parmigiana.

When Joe told her about Oberavich Helen's face fell. "That's
what I was going to tell you," she said. The priest had told her about
"Franko Bradovich," correcting her pronunciation of the name and
confirming her hunch.

But they were pleased with their joint discovery. Helen said
they were just like Nick and Nora Charles, in *The Thin Man*. Joe
wasn't familiar with the movie, but Helen filled him in, mentioning that Myrna Loy had played Nora, to William Powell's Nick. Joe
said that was auspicious, because he'd just been told by Carmen that
Helena was the birthplace of Myrna Loy, and that was the direction their investigation was headed.

The next morning they drove north, over the pass, and took
the turnoff to the little village of French Forque. Most people just

called it Forkee, they'd been told in the bar of the restaurant last night. In fact, there were ruder versions of the name, based on a "fork-you" pronunciation. It was an old mining town, now in considerable decay, located in a well-wooded gulch, through which flowed Frenchy's Fork of the Boulder River. This was a beautiful little twisting stream, easily wadable except during the spring run-off. It was lined with alder and, according to locals, "very trouty." Many miles farther down, where this gulch opened into a much broader valley, the stream flowed into the Boulder River, which in turn flowed into the Missouri. But Joe and Helen were not interested in fishing.

Carmen had called ahead to Les Denny, the local realtor, who was also the owner and bartender of Frenchy's, the one remaining tavern of a dozen or more that had catered to the deep thirst of hundreds of gold and silver miners in the area. The mines were all closed now, although Denny said that there were still some prospectors working claims. An unlooked-for business had developed, he said: "radium treatment" mines. These were old mines with a fairly high radiation level. People paid good money to go sit in these mines, some of which were outfitted comfortably, to "take the cure."

"Personally, I think they're nuts," Denny said. He was a pleasant man, burly and with a bushy beard that covered the open neck of his plaid shirt. "Hell, you're more likely to get some kind of radiation sickness, I'd say. Wouldn't you? But these are desperate people, mostly. They already got cancer, or had it, I guess, and they've had radiation therapy, so maybe they're not so dumb. But it can't be the same thing, you reckon?"

Joe agreed. Denny was happy to pour them whiskey and draw beers and talk about the fishing and the mines, but when it came to discussion of Franko, as Denny called him, he became more guarded. There was no one else in the tavern at this hour of the morning, but Denny dropped his voice.

"You know, I'm not a close pard to ol' Franko," Denny said, "but I known him a while and he's a guy who likes his privacy. Y'gotta respect that up here. Are you a friend of his?"

Joe fed him the Franko Bradovich story that he'd told Carmen. Joe said he and his wife, Helen, were from out of state, just passing through, but they were impressed with the country. It might be nice to buy some property, maybe even move out here. They were in a kind of on-line consulting business that didn't require them to live in a city, the way things were these days. And then he'd stumbled on this Oberavich thing. It looked too good to pass up. Joe just wanted to meet this Frank and see if he wasn't the same guy. And who knows? They might even see some property that would interest them.

"Well, it's damn nice back there," Denny conceded, "and I do know about some property, right on the crick. But you gotta know that there ain't no electricity back there and not likely to be anytime soon. Great place for a hunting or fishing cabin, maybe, but if you're doing anything in the computer business, you're gonna want power."

Joe said that consideration could come later. Mainly, for now, he thought it'd be interesting just to take a look and meet Frank.

"The thing is," Denny said, his voice dropping again, "Carmen referred you, but she admits she don't know you from Adam. You see what I mean? You got Michigan plates on your rig, you look like good folks, but . . ." He shrugged. "You got any identification?"

Joe fished out his wallet and showed a Utah driver's license in the name of Joseph Humann. He also had one in the same name from Montana, as well as a couple in different names from California and Colorado, but he thought the Utah one more consistent with the story he'd told Carmen. They'd bought the vehicle in Detroit, he explained, and licensed it there for convenience, until they decided where they were going to settle.

Denny nodded at all this while staring at the Utah license. Finally, he said, "Well, it's you all right," tapping the picture on the license. "But I don't know . . . ol' Franko's pretty much a hermit. . . . I feel kinda like I should give him a call, first."

"Oh? So there's phone service back there?" Helen said.

"Well, he's got a cell phone, of course," Denny said. "You guys doing okay with those beers? I'll be right back." And he went into the back room.

"Hm," Helen said, "he's damn cautious. What do you think?"

"I think we're on to something, Nora, my dear," Joe said. "If this doesn't work, we'll just take it in good humor and ask about property and then go on our way. We can always locate the guy one way or another. In fact, it might be bet—" He broke off as Denny reappeared. "You get hold of him?" he called out.

"Yeah," Denny said, lifting his eyebrows quizzically. "He says come on back. Funny thing is, he don't know no Joe Humann. But that's how it goes with these hermits. . . . I guess he's feeling like company today."

"That's great," Joe said. "I guess he forgot me. It was a while back. He'll recognize me, though, if it's him. Listen, I appreciate your being careful and all that, and I'm sure Franko does, but isn't this a little, uh, mysterious? What's the big deal?"

Denny made a defensive, apologetic grimace. "Oh, well, he said it was all right," he said, "but. . . . Look, I'll be straight with you. You aren't cops, are you?"

Joe's surprise must have been convincing. Denny smiled and said, "He grows a little pot, maybe, nothing big. He doesn't sell it or nothing, but you know how it is . . ."

Joe and Helen both laughed, relieved. "Oh, for cryin' out loud," Joe said. "That sounds like Franko, all right."

Denny drew them a crude map on a bar napkin, showing the road that ran up Frenchy's Fork. They had to take another road, this one not so good, and it soon got much worse, becoming a mere two-track that angled up over rocky humps, ran along bluffs above the stream, and wound through scrubby pine thickets. But they had four-wheel drive and were pleased with an opportunity to use it. Just when the road dropped down to the stream—which may not have been Frenchy's Forque anymore, for all they knew—and seemed to promise to angle into a valley, it would climb up into the hills again and into a different drainage. They forded streams twice and carefully crawled over some pretty rough knobs and ridges before the road let down into a beautiful valley that opened out before them, backed by craggy mountains beyond. Altogether, it was a good ten miles back into the brush before they came out onto an open meadow.

They arrived at a well-constructed barbed-wire fence line, at last, and a gated cattle guard. There was no sign of a house, just a rising meadow filled with brown bunchgrass waving in the steady breeze and an occasional pine tree. Joe got out to try the gate and look around. It appeared that there was a bluff off to the south, presumably fronting the stream. The rising land crested a quarter of a mile before him, and a couple of modern-looking windmills poked their tops over the ridge, their huge propellers spinning briskly. Joe supposed that beyond that might be the house they were looking for. But there were no signs. And when he tried the gate, which wasn't chained or padlocked, it didn't yield.

"Now what?" he said to Helen, who had gotten out to join him at the gate.

"Maybe we have to climb over and walk," she said.

At that moment a voice spoke from a concealed speaker somewhere nearby: "Yes?" it said. "Mr. Humann?"

Joe looked around. The best he could make out was that the voice emanated from a pile of field rocks about five feet high beyond the gate. He peered at it. There could be a television camera there as well, he thought.

"That's us," Joe said, loudly.

"Come on in," the voice said. There was a buzz, and the gate swung open on oiled hinges. "The house is just down the road. You'll see it."

They found the house all right. They drove up the road, accompanied by four large Rottweilers, and stopped in a yard in which were parked three four-wheel-drive pickup trucks of vintages ranging from old to current. The dogs waited patiently, tongues lolling, not barking, but watching.

The house was impressive, essentially a rustic greenhouse. It was more or less oval, sheathed in rough cedar, with a roof that was covered with solar-collector panels and a lot of skylights. It even had a tower. The southern exposure and parts of the east and west sides were glassed in and all but bursting with cultivated greenery. It looked like Frank Oberavich grew more than just a little pot.

The man who came out to greet them, shushing the Rottweilers, was not anyone Joe or Helen had expected to see. This man was short and slight, heavily bearded, with long blondish hair gathered into a ponytail that trailed out from beneath his battered old cowboy hat. He squinted at them in the bright sunlight through glasses mounted in clear plastic frames. His thin, wiry arms were deeply tanned, and he wore baggy frayed khaki shorts and mocassins with no socks. It was sunny, but cool in the fall air, and his stained T-shirt was inadequate. He crossed his arms on his narrow chest and rubbed his elbows. He was none too clean, and when he smiled they saw that his teeth were stained brown.

"Hi," he said, in a soft voice. He addressed Helen, who was in the driver's seat. "I guess you must be Mrs. Humann?" He turned to the nosing dogs and told them to get back. They retreated but looked on with interest. Joe and Helen got out, warily eyeing the dogs.

"Don't worry about them," Oberavich said. "They recognize dog people. They're very reliable that way."

"I never thought of myself as a dog person," Helen said. "I had a puppy once, but he got run over by a car, and I was so heartbroken I never got another one."

"I don't think it's necessary to actually have dogs," Oberavich said, "just be . . . I don't know . . . *okay* people." He smiled uncertainly, as if embarrassed.

"Well, I'm Helen," she said, thrusting out her hand. "Sedlacek, actually. It's more convenient to say Mrs. Humann. You know?"

"Sid-logic?" he repeated. "You're Serb?"

Helen shrugged. "Could be. I'm not sure." They both laughed lightly.

This was not Franko, Joe was sure. Not Colonel Tucker's Franko, anyway.

But he was amiable. He invited them in, and while they sipped some wine, which they'd brought along on Denny's recommendation (and at his extravagant price, for California jug wine), he enthusiastically showed them around his amazing greenhouse. It was plenty warm inside, and moist. There were plants everywhere, huge and small. One walked through and among them on a slatted walkway. Besides magnificent marijuana plants he had flowers, many kinds of cacti, and some ornamental shrubs. He had devised an elaborate watering system, run off the solar-power-generating system. A radio played classical music from a distant station.

They got along very well, right away. He had a truly interesting house, albeit considerably disheveled and disorderly, except for his plants. There were books everywhere, dishes in the sink, clothes tossed about at random. Although there were a couple of bedrooms and a bath, it seemed that he lived in one large room, basically, except for a delightful tower room, which one reached by climbing a ladder. Here there were more books, a stereo system, and many recordings, mostly CDs of Mozart and Haydn. The tower room had a bench running about it at desk height. The room was barely large enough for the three of them to stand in; there was only one chair, a pretty good upholstered leather desk chair. He had a typewriter buried under some books and papers, and a very up-to-date laptop computer with the lid open, running a screen saver that displayed constantly changing geometric shapes.

There were windows all around, and one could look out on a splendid panorama of mountains. The stream, Frenchy's Fork, was beyond the line of scrubby pines, he pointed out. The bluff dropped down about a hundred feet, but there was a good path. If they liked, they could walk down there. The fishing was very good, he said. Fly fishermen came up there from time to time, but not many knew about it or were willing to drive back in this far.

Joe was intrigued. How did he keep all these things going, the pumps, the stereo, and so on, without commercial power? Oberavich eagerly showed them his power system. It was multifaceted, employing not only solar converters but the windmills and even a couple of small stream-driven turbines, and was backed up with a bank of batteries. All of this, in turn, was connected to a very deep well that provided heat and water and served as an energy reservoir. It was fairly complicated, a little capital intensive, but totally reliable and over time almost free to run.

"I never have power failures," Oberavich said proudly. "The power company is always breaking down. Not me."

From there the conversation went on to topics like flowers, music, books, and so on, mostly conducted with Helen, while Joe drifted about, nodding and remarking approvingly. Oberavich built furniture, he raised vegetables, he had been studying the stars. Soon he was urging them to stay for dinner. Joe and Helen readily accepted. While he was preparing dinner they went for a stroll over to the bluff and looked down at the stream below. They could see up a narrow canyon, from which the stream issued, towering cliffs on either side.

When they came back and sat down to a decent spaghetti with a marinara sauce, they asked about the canyon. You could walk up it about a mile, Oberavich told them, and it was spectacular, but eventually it got to be pretty tough going. There was nothing beyond it but more mountains, as far as Deer Lodge, he said. He owned several hundred acres of this, he added, shyly. How many hundreds? Actually, a couple thousand or so.

Developers had been after him to sell for years. They'd bring in power, sell large acreages to wealthy Californians. He wasn't having any of it. He was well protected, with a state forest and BLM land adjoining his. He didn't think there would be any development in his lifetime, although across the river was some property owned by an old lady in Great Falls, which might eventually be sold. But the bluff isolated him from that. "I don't need their power," he said, smugly.

Joe was enraptured. This was a Hole-in-the-Wall indeed! He was already trying to figure out how to get into this paradise. But he didn't mention it to Oberavich. That would take some doing, he realized. A long, careful campaign would be required. He didn't mind; he could be patient.

After dinner, Oberavich was comfortable enough with them to roll some huge spliffs of his best stock. It was dynamite grass, potent but mild to the palate. They went out and sat on the grass in the yard, smoking and drinking the last of the wine. It had turned quite cool, and as night had fallen the sky had filled with an almost oppressive number of brilliant stars. Oberavich was mellow, relaxed in long pants now and a heavy sweater. He pointed out the constellations to Helen.

Joe and Helen were having trouble focusing. They were absolutely swelling with good feeling from smoking so much powerful marijuana. Although they had discussed Joe's quest for his old friend earlier and had dismissed it as a lost cause, Joe cautiously brought it up again. He vaguely described having met Franko Bradovich "back East." They'd worked together, he said, on a "re-search project." He said it was a "nature thing," trying to organize some research materials for computers. It was too complicated to go into. But he hadn't really known Franko very well. In fact, he hadn't given much thought to the guy since, but after coming to Butte . . .

Oberavich didn't press for details, fortunately. He was obvi-ously feeling pretty mellow himself. But he did ask what this Franko looked like. When Joe provided the description given them by the colonel, however, Oberavich said, after a very long moment in which they all just sat back in the now cold grass and stared at the billions of stars, "Sounds like my cousin."

"Really?" was all Joe could think to say.

After another long moment, Oberavich said, "Yeah. Paulie's into that stuff, that research. Eco stuff. He's the smart one in the family. Always traveling around. India. Got up into Kashmir. Loved Kashmir. Went to the poppy fields."

"Poppy fields?" Helen said. "You mean, like opium?"

"Oh yeah," Oberavich said. "He said it was bitching stuff. Too good, he said. Scared him, I think. He left, went to . . . I don't know, somewhere in Yugoslavia. He spent quite a while there, I think. Another great place. But then they had the war, you know. Whew! Are you guys as fucked up as I am?"

They all laughed at the incredible wit of the comment, almost uncontrollably. Eventually they staggered to their feet and went inside. It was warm indoors. They were amazingly hungry again. But when they'd devoured the remains of the spaghetti, they were sopo-rific. No way they could drive out. Oberavich invited the visitors to sleep over—an extra bedroom that he used for storage had a mattress on the floor, and he had blankets. Joe and Helen fell asleep in seconds.

Goods

The next morning there were the usual awkwardnesses, inevitable in such situations. The parties realize that they've experienced an unanticipated intimacy with someone they don't really know. It was surely more awkward for Oberavich. Two strangers had waltzed into his life and he had fallen into perhaps a too familiar easiness with them, unusual behavior for him. He couldn't be sure how much he had said. But he didn't think he had said anything too revealing. If it had just been the grass, he thought, but there had been all that wine. He had more than a slight hangover.

As it worked out, the three people were quite agreeable to one another, and the awkwardness soon dissipated. Oberavich, with Helen's assistance, cooked up an enormous breakfast of bacon and eggs, with plenty of coffee and toast. They fell on it like famished dogs, and it was only in the eating of it that they recalled that they had polished off all the leftover spaghetti before bed. But that didn't stop them from mopping their plates clean.

After that, however, it became apparent that Oberavich was eager to get on with his normal routine. Joe and Helen politely refused his invitations to linger, and they left after pitching in to help him clean up. Helen and Joe drove away promising to come back soon and declining a generous offer of a grocery sack of the excellent grass. Nobody had as much as mentioned Paulie.

Nothing may have been said to Oberavich, but it was the major topic between Joe and Helen as they sped back to Butte. Joe was sure there was something worth pursuing here. He recalled very well the things that Oberavich had said. He had drunk very little wine, leaving the greater quantity to Oberavich and Helen.

"There were several things about Paulie that were too good to ignore," Joe said.

"Evocative, you mean?" Helen said. She was driving, as usual.

"Exactly. That stuff about poppies, opium, and then Yugoslavia, and the fact that the description fit. Paulie could be our guy. Maybe, for who knows what reason, Paulie used a version of his cousin's name while he was in Kosovo. He probably entered the country on his own passport, as Paul Oberavich. That's why they didn't catch it."

"Not that they tumbled to Frank Oberavich, for that matter," Helen pointed out. "We should get the colonel to check both names out."

"The next, obvious question," Joe said, "is, Where do we go from here? Where is Paulie, assuming he's the guy we're after? We've got to be gentle with Frank. He's a little skittery."

"A little! I kept cringing every time you brought up the subject of buying land."

"I didn't think I even mentioned it," Joe said. "Did I? Was it obvious?"

Helen said it was obvious to her that he coveted Oberavich's property, but Frank might not have noticed. "He was bombed," she said. "Anyway, you didn't push it, thank heaven."

"It's true, though," Joe said. "I'd love to get a foothold back in there on the Forkee."

Helen thought it would take some doing. Joe agreed. It was obviously a delicate issue. But he thought it could be done.

"How?" Helen asked.

"You," Joe said. "He's got the hots for you."

"Oh, bull," Helen said. "The guy's probably gay," and she cited Carmen's hint. "He didn't display it, but he's probably one of those deeply closeted guys, afraid of his attraction to men. If anything, he's probably got the hots for you. He was hanging on your every word."

"I thought you said he didn't notice my hints about buying land? No, no, there were no vibes. Hey, I've been around gay guys," he said. "I know when I'm being hit on. Frank is just one of those guys who are so leery of attachments of any kind that they find it much more congenial to be a hermit. There are plenty of guys like that. But that doesn't mean that he wasn't attracted to you. I saw the way his eyes followed you around the room. He pitched almost all of his talk at you."

"I wonder why it is that men so hastily reject the idea that another man could be gay and might be interested in them?" Helen observed. "Is it some fear of homosexuality in themselves?"

Joe scoffed and reiterated his belief that Frank was interested in her. She didn't like where this was heading.

"What are you suggesting?" she demanded. "I should seduce him? So you can have a place in the bush?"

"Hey, I'm not pimping you," Joe said. "You don't have to go to bed with the guy. . . . But if the attraction is there, why ignore it? Every guy is in a more agreeable mood when a woman he likes is being nice. It's an angle, that's all."

Helen's glance was severe enough to convince him that it was a topic that had better be dropped.

In Butte, while Helen took a shower Joe went down the street to an outdoor phone booth with a pocketful of quarters, to check in with Tucker. But for some reason, once they were connected, Joe didn't report their success to the colonel. He merely suggested that the Lucani use their contacts to check out Oberavich as a variant name for Franko. He said nothing about their meeting with Frank, or about Paulie. A check on the name would do for their purpose. Other than that, he told the colonel, they had just gotten started in Butte. The colonel seemed satisfied, even pleased.

In the afternoon, Joe checked in with Carmen Tomarich. He was curious about the property across the creek from Oberavich, he said. He told her he'd met Frank, who wasn't his old buddy, but they'd gotten along quite well. Frank had mentioned something about plans to develop property up that way. She said she hadn't heard anything about that, but she'd check it out.

"Are you thinking of building?" she asked. "I've got loads of good building sites, private and picturesque, but much more convenient than clear out on the Forkee—accessible roads year-round, with power, wells already drilled, sites laid out."

Sure, he was interested, he told her. He meant it. But he told her that the inaccessibility was part of the attraction. If there was one such place like Frank's, perhaps there were more. You just had to look. Montana was a huge place. As for commercial power, Frank got along without it. In fact, Joe pointed out, Frank's system was probably less likely to fail than the power company's.

Carmen was skeptical. "To me, power is something you get when you plug into the wall. He probably didn't tell you about all the days in the winter when the sun doesn't shine."

Joe assured her that he had. But, he conceded, he wasn't as obsessed with self-reliance as Frank was. "I like good groceries," he said.

"Well, I'm glad you guys got along," Carmen said. "I'm just sorry Frank didn't turn out to be your long lost pard. But it's funny, last night I bumped into my friend Trudy at Gamer's restaurant?

And she says when she called around for me, to find out where Frank was? Well, somebody else is looking for him, too."

"No kidding?" Joe said. "Coincidence, I guess. But then, Frank is pretty reclusive. Probably a bill collector."

"It didn't sound like it. Some guy like you, an old acquaintance. Trudy said her friend, the guy who knows Frank, said when she asked that Frank must be getting popular in his old age, somebody else was asking about him."

"Maybe it's his high school reunion organizer," Joe said. He didn't want to seem too interested. After all, his ostensible reason for finding Frank had gone bust. Unless, it occurred to him, there was another Frank Oberavich in town. "Or maybe there is more than one Frank Oberavich," he said.

"There's plenty of Oberaviches," Carmen said, "but no other Frank, that I know of. There's Gary, Vic, Jim, and, let's see . . . Bill."

"How about Paul?" Joe asked.

Carmen didn't think so. "Who's Paul?"

"I was just thinking," Joe said, "my pal used to talk about a cousin, or maybe it was an uncle, named Paul. But now that you mention it, there are a lot of possibilities, aren't there? Frank never said he was from Butte, just from Montana. I imagine the Oberaviches have spread out to other cities. Oh well, this is getting to be too much trouble. Heck with it."

"Sorry it didn't work out," Carmen said. "But you might want to call Gary. His wife, Selma, is one of those whatchacallems, always tracking down ancestors and relatives. If there is another Frank on the planet, or a cousin Paul, Selma would know where. I've got her number." She looked it up and gave it to Joe. "When do you want to look at some of these other properties?" she asked.

"I'm beat today," Joe said. "We're going to do some sightseeing, go to the mining museum, that sort of thing. I'll give you a call in the next few days."

There was no Paul Oberavich listed in the phone book. After a few moments of thought, he dialed the number Carmen had given him for Gary and Selma. A woman's recorded voice on an answering machine said that Gary and Selma were unable to come to the phone, but if this was Publishers Clearing House calling to tell them they'd won a million dollars, leave a message. Or anyone else, the voice added.

Ah well, it was good to be patient, Joe thought, hanging up. He'd give it a try later. But now he felt the old urge to dig. He considered making contact with someone from the mob. If Frank was dealing marijuana, no doubt the local mob could at least give him an angle on him. They might even know Paulie. It might be worthwhile to make some tentative inquiries.

An answering machine in Chicago told him to leave a message. He gave the number of the phone booth and said he'd return in fifteen minutes. That would allow his contact on the other end to make some contacts of his own, and it would also relieve him of the necessity of waiting around the phone booth, which was located on a street corner near a bank.

He took a little stroll around town, just to get some fresh air. To his horror he almost encountered the one person in Butte he didn't want to see: Cathleen Yoder, better known as Cateyo. She was a nurse at St. James Hospital. She was walking down the street toward him, some two hundred feet away. He looked for a handy store entry, but nothing was available. He had just about decided to brave it out and was preparing an eager grin, when she turned into the entrance of the power company, a look of concentration on her pretty face. He exhaled in relief. She hadn't noticed him. He turned about and walked back to the phone booth, where he huddled with his back to the door, pretending to look up a number in the book until the phone rang.

"Joe," his contact said. "Whattaya doin' in Montana? Last I heard, you was in jail, or the hospital. You all right?"

"I'm fine, Deke," Joe said. "Just hangin' out, coolin' it. I'd appreciate it, though, if you didn't spread the news."

"Hey, you know me, Joe. What can I do you for?"

Joe asked for the names of some contacts in the area. Deke told him that the only guy he knew about who was connected out that way was a Smokey Stover, who ran a bar. Deke could find the number if he wanted it. Joe said that was all right—he wasn't planning to be in town more than an hour or two, so maybe it wasn't worth calling the guy.

Deke was a good friend. Joe knew he wouldn't broadcast the news about his whereabouts, unless somebody important asked him. That was about the best Joe could hope for. He also learned that there wasn't any particular interest in him, as far as Deke knew. That was good. Deke didn't mention DiEbola, or Mitch, or any of the other people with whom Joe normally did business. Good.

Joe hung up and took off, keeping an eye peeled for a blond who might be out and about, relieved that the mob had little concern with him, despite his problems with them. Presumably, DiEbola had squared him with the mob, reinstated him, so to speak. He felt considerably easier, even more confident and somehow more . . . what? Connected. He realized that for some time, without thinking about it, his world had become more constricted, less connected.

He strolled down to a bar on Park Street and had a beer, asking the barkeep if he knew this Smokey Stover. "Ask Smokey who told Father Nick he stole the wine," the guy said. He gave directions. Joe left and walked another four blocks down the hill to a place called Smokey's Corner. It was an old-fashioned neighborhood joint—smoky, reeking of beer, not very well lit, with pool tables, a pressed-tin ceiling, a long oak bar with a brass footrail, and a high, ornate, beveled-mirror back bar. An older man with a bit of a paunch and smoking a corncob pipe stood at the end of the bar, talking to the bartender, a young, muscular fellow. The older one looked at Joe with baby blue eyes under a polished bald dome. He smiled at Joe and made a rueful grimace that was evidently an attempt at an ingratiating smile.

"I'll be goddamn," he said. "You don't know me, but I'm Bernie Stover." He held out a big, calloused hand. "And you're Joe Service. I knew your boss. Sorry to hear about his passing. I guess you guys made up, eh? Let me buy you a drink."

He signaled the bartender and had a couple of shots of Jack Daniel's poured, with beer chasers. He tossed his back, saying, "Here's to Humphrey—may he be safe in heaven while the devil's busy in Butte."

Joe said, "Here," and took a sip of the whiskey. He wasn't fond of whiskey.

"What can I do for you?" Stover asked.

"Just stopping by, Bernie," Joe said. "So you knew the Fat Man? He was . . . well, he was all right. Things went a little sour for him, finally. That's all. But you're looking all right. I met a guy, said ask you who told Father Nick you stole the wine."

"Jim Tracy, that rotten bastard." Stover laughed.

They chatted like this for several minutes, establishing carefully who they were and making it clear that there was no animosity, no issues between them. But at long last, Joe asked about Frank Oberavich.

"Weirdo" was Stover's opinion, and it was plain that he didn't have much use for him. "He grows a little weed, I hear. I don't mess with that shit, you know? It's a pain in the ass. The cops are too freaky when it comes to even a little of that."

"Weed?" Joe didn't know much about the trade. "What's all the beef about weed?"

"It's the entry drug, the cops say, where the kids start. Anything with kids is poison. Anymore, the cops get so much of their funding from the drug program that it's all they think about. What

do you want to know about him? Christ, don't tell me you're thinking of getting into that shit." He puffed his pipe, emitting little
clouds of not very aromatic smoke.

No, no, Joe assured him. He'd never had those kinds of interests. He was just looking for some property to build on.

Stover hastened to assure him that he'd had nothing to do
with Joe's place getting trashed, down in the Ruby. This was surely
a lie, but Joe had never gotten the full story from DiEbola. It had to
have been Stover or his men who'd done the job. Some of them, of
course, had perished in the process. It was a topic worth avoiding.
But Joe was glad to plant the notion that he was looking for property.

Stover knew the Oberaviches, all of them. A couple of different families, he said they were. Frank was wacko, but the others
were okay. Gary, for instance, he was a straight hand. Worked for
the railroad. He didn't know what his relationship with Frank might
be, but he thought they were uncle and nephew. Paulie? Never heard
of any Paul Oberavich. The only Paulie he could think of was Paulie
Martinelli. Nice guy, a professor or something. He might be a friend
of Frank's, although Paulie was a bit older. Stover didn't know him
well. If he had to guess, he'd say Paulie was at Montana State, over
in Bozeman.

Joe listened to all this with an air of casual interest. Finally,
he said, "You know, Bernie, I'm glad I came in here. I want you to
know, as far as I'm concerned, all that stuff with Humphrey and
those other guys—I don't even know who they were!—to me, it's
all history. You know what I'm saying? That was Humphrey. He's
gone. I got no beef with you. Okay?"

Bernie shrugged and drew on his pipe. "Okay with me, Joe,"
he said. They shook hands again.

"I'm retired, Bernie," Joe said. "I'm not doing any business
around here. All I'm interested in is my own peace and quiet." He
looked Bernie in the eye.

The old man didn't try to evade his gaze. He held Joe's gaze for a significant moment, then nodded as he scoured out his pipe. He stuck it in the pocket of his baggy old suit coat and fished out a fresh one, also a corncob. "Peace and quiet is all we got around here," he said, as he reloaded and lit up. "If a guy keeps his own peace. It wasn't so quiet when you were around before. I'm not saying that was your fault, I'm just saying it."

Joe started to retort, but swallowed his irritation. "That was Humphrey," he said. "He's dead, God rest him. I'm just asking if there's any reason I shouldn't relax. Nobody been around, asking about me?"

Bernie shook his head.

"Good. Now what about this Oberavich? He in any kind of trouble? What I mean is, if I did any business with him—I mean legit business, buying property, maybe—it's not going to attract someone's attention? I just ask, 'cause if he's some kind of high-profile outlaw or something, the feds will be keeping an eye on him. Right? And they'll notice me. And Bernie"—he laid his hand quietly on the older man's arm—"I'm not just making noise here. I don't want *any* notice."

Bernie nodded. "I hear you, son. The only thing I can tell you is the guy is known to the local cops. That means he's also known to the feds. But as far as I know he's a pretty clean operator. I said something earlier about not wanting to have anything to do with him. That's true, as far as it goes. But the fact is, he never approached me. I don't know how he operates, where he sells his stuff. Maybe he's smart and sells it out of state. But if it was me, I wouldn't go near him. If you don't want to be noticed."

That was a fair enough warning, Joe thought. "Nobody else interested in him? Other than cops?"

Bernie puffed his pipe. This one smelled a little better; perhaps it was newer, cleaner. "There was a guy, maybe a week ago. I wouldn've give it a thought, but you put me in mind of it. I didn't talk to him. But I was here. Nobody I knew. He didn't push it, just asked the bartender if he knew him. The answer was no. He left."

"You think he was connected?"

Bernie puffed. "He was connected to somebody, I'd say. He didn't drop any names and my man didn't ask any questions. Like I say, I don't want no part of that business. If I gave it any thought at all, I think I took it as some outside operation, maybe just checking the competition out."

Joe asked what the guy looked like. Bernie described him as big, young, a wise guy.

That was good enough for Joe. He thanked Bernie for the drink and left. He knew that word would now be relayed to the rest of the mob that Joe Service was back in town. Joe didn't like the idea, but he didn't think there were any consequences to be feared, especially since he didn't plan to hang around town. But it wasn't ideal, he knew. He thought he'd probably made a mistake in initiating contact. Still, he'd made his point with Bernie; they understood each other.

On his way back to the hotel, thinking about whether he ought to call the colonel and ask if he had another man on this beat, he almost walked directly in front of a car sitting at a light and being driven by Cateyo. Horrified, he saw her first and turned away, down another block. She hadn't seen him, he was sure, but this was twice in a matter of an hour. This town was too small, he realized. He hurried back to the hotel.

He didn't mention Cateyo to Helen, but he told her about the guy who was looking for Frank. "We ought to blow," he said. "Helena would be safer. It's only thirty or forty minutes from French Forque." Helen agreed.

Joe hauled their bags to the parking lot while she handled the bill. He was confronted with two large chunks of carved wood, all but filling the back of the Durango. Helen came out to find him tying the statues, or totems, onto the top of the vehicle.

"Oh no," she said. "Those are my chain-saw sculptures. They go inside." Joe insisted there wasn't room for bags and sculptures, but Helen won. There was room for both.

"What are they supposed to be?" Joe said.

"What do you mean? It's an owl and a bear. I think they're really neat. Don't you like them?"

Joe leaned over the seat for another long look. He sat back with a sigh. To him a statue was carved out of marble or cast in bronze. It wasn't hacked out of a bull pine with a Stihl chain saw. "If that's art," he started to say, then shut his mouth. Instead he asked Helen what her thoughts were on the unknown snooper.

Helen suggested that it could well be a federal investigator, from an agency unknown to the colonel. "If your friend Smokey says Frank is growing grass," she pointed out, "he's bound to attract federal attention. The colonel can't know about all the investigations going on, can he? Maybe we should ask him."

Joe wasn't so sure. "Bernie's description didn't sound like a professional snoop," he said. "It could be just an old friend of Frank's. Bernie seemed to think the guy was connected, but he didn't recognize him."

Helen didn't understand. Joe explained that the man's manner must have led Bernie to think that he was not a cop but another bent guy. It could be a subtle thing, he said, but people in the life usually recognize their fellows.

"The life?" Helen said.

"The Street, the Biz, bent," Joe said, impatiently.

"Do I seem to be 'in the life'?" Helen asked.

"No, of course not," Joe said. "That's one of the things I like about you. I try to avoid that, too. It's a dead giveaway. It's like I walk into Smokey's and even if I didn't already know, I can see right away that Smokey's into it. The squares, the straights, they don't know. What do they know? They're out buying chain-saw statues. Of course," he hastened on, "it's not always obvious. You can make mistakes. And it's hard to know about yourself, how you come across to others, I mean. Do I seem different to you?"

"Oh yeah," she said with a smile. "I like the outlaw in you, Joe."

He wasn't sure if she meant it. But as they were approaching the exit to French Forque, he said, "Maybe we ought to drop in on Frank."

"Do you think?"

"Yeah, I do."

A half hour later they pulled up at the gate. Joe got out and looked around. It was a fine fall afternoon. Warm enough in the sun, but there was a briskness in the air. The windmills were spinning busily over the ridge. A posse of long-tailed magpies swooped across the field, lighting in a scraggly cluster of crab apples. Joe looked at the pile of rocks. No sign of the dogs. Helen got out and stood next to him. After some thirty seconds, a voice called out, "Joe! Helen! Come on back."

Frank was clearly delighted to see them. They apologized for dropping in on him, saying they were headed for Helena and couldn't resist another quick visit. They'd only stop for a few minutes. But Frank would have none of that.

"Oh, heck, no," he insisted, "stay over. I was hoping you'd be back. I got to thinking about it—we should have gone down to the hot springs last night."

Helen was certainly agreeable. It took them an hour to prepare a picnic, pack it into a couple of backpacks, and set off for the Forkee. It was not an arduous trek but it was much farther than the half mile Frank had promised, though Joe reckoned later that if they'd walked directly there it would have saved at least a quarter of an hour. Instead, they wandered across the meadow and down into a small hidden hollow, with the dogs racing ahead, chasing magpies. Frank pointed out an old site where a miner or an early settler had built a log cabin, now long gone except for a jumble of rotted logs, some of which were still marked by the white clay chinking.

Eventually they came to a small creek, easily jumpable, and walked down a path through a twisted gulch, descending to the Forkee. At last they were there, by the sand and gravel banks of the stream, perhaps twenty yards wide here. In places, the river under-cut towering cliffs on the other side, which soared straight up at least three hundred feet.

"There's usually lots of swallows," Frank said, "but they've gone for the season."

"Where's the springs?" Helen asked, looking around, disappointed. There were wisps of steam here and there, obviously some thermal springs, but no sign of a pool, such as they'd enjoyed up on Garland Butte.

"They're all around you," Frank declared. He was watching her expectantly. "See? These little tubs?" He pointed out where the creek they'd been following flowed in a shallow sheet across the wet sand to the river. Here and there were small depressions in the sand that looked natural, at first, but when examined proved to have been scooped out by human hands and lined with smooth rocks.

He shucked off his clothes unabashedly and stepped into one. Joe and Helen looked on while he scooped his "tub" out with his hands and settled down into the clear water. "See?" he cried. "Try it! You can let in more cold water, if you want"—he pried out a rock to let in some of the cold stream water—"or you can let it fill up with the hot." He replaced the rock. The tub soon filled.

In a moment, Helen had slipped out of her clothing and was digging out her own tub. Joe noticed that Frank's eyes were fixed on her lithe form. He got undressed himself and found his own tub nearby.

"Oh, fabulous!" Helen cried. She set about fashioning her tub to suit her, deepening it, setting the rocks just so. Soon enough she was submerged but for her head.

Frank had gotten out and distributed cold beer from the backpacks and rolled spliffs of his marijuana. They all lay back, inhaling deeply and staring into the pure blue sky above the awesome cliffs.

There were a lot of these little hot springs about, Frank told them, but these were the most convenient to the river; plus it was such a great place to just lie and soak and stare at the sky, especially when the stars came out. In fact, although the sun was below the cliffs it was still pretty light out, but already they could see a few of the brighter stars.

After a while, as it grew darker, Frank got up and slipped on a sweater and his shorts and moccasins, to gather firewood. He made a good-sized fire and passed around the sandwiches and cookies. From time to time, Joe or Helen would emerge and wrap themselves in towels or their clothing, to sit by the fire. But they would soon be back in the tubs, trying each other's and experimenting with new ones. Eventually, however, when it was quite dark and the sky was ablaze with stars, it was too cold even by the fire, and they lay basking in their tubs and drawing languidly on the endless spliffs.

They talked about the stars, Greek gods, Indian myths, and other soon-forgotten things. Then they fell silent. The fire died to coals. And soon, to the amazement of Joe and Helen, they were visited by ghostly deer, at least three does and a couple of yearlings that wandered among them, actually stepping over them, to lick at the rocks. The deer seemed all but oblivious to their presence. Frank whispered that they were after the mineral deposits on the rocks.

They lost track of time. At last, Frank dragged himself out and built up the fire. He had dressed and picked up their litter. Joe and Helen took the hint and got up themselves. They felt wiped out. They had no idea how much time had passed—several hours, a couple?

Suddenly another man stepped out of the dark. He was dressed in khaki pants and a sweater, with a jacket over it.

"Paulie!" Frank said. He introduced Joe and Helen. This was his cousin, he said. Paul had a camp about a mile upstream, they learned. He'd heard their voices and smelled the smoke. Not the grass, but the fire, he said. They all laughed, except for Paulie. He seemed relaxed, but somber.

"I also saw the dogs," Paulie told Frank. "I told them to go home."

They sat around the fire, chatting. Joe let Helen recount their cover story. It concluded with their abandoning the casual search for Franko Bradovich and heading for Helena.

When the fire had been put out and the backpacks hoisted onto Frank's and Joe's backs, the revelers felt more up to the hike home. Paulie said he would come back to the house with them, "for a cup of coffee." Frank had provided flashlights. He and Helen went ahead and Joe and Paulie trailed after.

"What kind of research were you doing with your friend?" Paulie asked as they climbed up the gully to the meadow.

Joe said something evasive about "nature stuff," but Paulie persisted. What kind of nature stuff? He was interested, he said. He'd done quite a bit of research of one sort or another himself.

Joe said that he hadn't done any research; he was just helping put it in order, doing the "computer stuff."

"Compiling a data bank?" Paulie said. "What kind of material was it? Geological? Field studies on animals? Birds?"

"Mostly data on birds," Joe said. He hoped he didn't sound too stupid.

"Habitat?" Paulie persisted. "Migration?"

"Oh, it was technical stuff," Joe improvised. "Measurements, numbers of one sort or another."

"Ah, I've done some of that," Paulie said. "Who was this for? Who had compiled the data?"

"Gee, I can't really recall," Joe said. "There were several groups that provided the information. I didn't pay too much attention. It was all over my head."

They had gained the meadow and were strolling more comfortably now. Frank's and Helen's lights were swinging along far ahead of them. They could even see the lights of the house.

"So, did you organize it by families, species, subspecies?" Paulie asked. "You know, Fringillidae, Gruiformes, that sort of thing?"

"That's it," Joe said. Mercifully, Paulie dropped the topic.

When they reached the yard, Paulie stopped to look at Helen's Durango. "Are those Detroit plates?" he asked. Joe said they were and told the story about picking up the vehicle in Detroit. He said they'd relicense the car when they found a place to settle.

Inside, when the coffee was made and some Miles Davis was playing on the stereo system, Helen and Frank went to arrange the bedding. Paulie suggested to Joe that they go up into the tower. Joe settled on the one chair and looked out, while Paulie squatted nearby. They had not turned on a light, so they were able to see the stars.

"I'm not normally a nosy person," Paulie said, after a moment, "but I'm a little anxious for my cousin. He's not used to company, as I'm sure you've noticed. He can get a little overfriendly, maybe, almost like a . . ." He hesitated.

"A puppy?" Joe said, an edge of impatience creeping into his voice.

Paulie didn't reply, just looked out into the darkness. Joe could barely make out his face. Paulie looked down at his cup between his knees. After a moment, he said, "So you and your friend, Bradovich . . . I guess you set up this data bank on a mainframe, what—"

"How was Kosovo, Franko?" Joe cut in quietly.

Paulie sighed. "I was afraid you were here about that," he said. His voice was soft and gloomy.

"Well, at least I'm not here about Frank's dope," Joe said. "I'm working for a Colonel Tucker. Know him?"

"I may have heard of him," Paulie said. "What does he want with me?"

"He just wants to know what happened."

"Is that all?" Paulie said, the bitterness evident in his voice. "I don't know what I could tell him. I haven't really come to grips with it. I'm not sure I want to."

"How long have you been here?" Joe asked.

"Since last spring," Paulie said. "I guess I convinced myself that nobody would be coming, that nobody knew who I was, what I'd seen."

"The colonel's not the type to just forget," Joe said. "I don't know what he wants to know, to tell you the truth. I'm just a finder. I tell him I found you, he takes it from there. I guess he'll want to see you."

Paulie didn't reply. He gazed out at the darkness. Finally, he said, "What if you don't tell him? That you found me. I mean, until an hour or so ago, you hadn't."

"Ah," Joe said. "That could happen, I suppose. But if 'Franko' isn't found by me, I'd guess that he'd send someone else. In fact, there is someone else."

Paulie looked at him. "Who?"

"I don't know," Joe said. He told him what he'd heard.

Paulie was alarmed. "A big guy? Kind of loud?" Then he said, "I have no idea who that could be, do you? I mean, why would the colonel send another man without your knowledge, when you've barely gotten here?"

Joe had to agree it didn't make much sense. He admitted that he didn't think the other guy was sent by the colonel.

Paulie said, "Listen, I can't offer you any money . . . I don't have any. But if the DEA comes in here . . . I mean, look, you know what would happen, with Frank. I know you like Frank."

"Frank can take care of himself," Joe said. "I'm sure he's got some kind of plan, for when the narcs come around. He's pretty sophisticated, with his fences and cameras."

"Yeah," Paulie conceded, "Frank'll be all right. But . . . look, what's all this to you? Isn't there something . . . ?"

Joe took thought. "Who owns all this land?" He gestured out the window.

"Who owns . . . you mean this property? I do. Well, me and Frank. We inherited it, from our gramp—grandfather."

Joe smiled and spread his hands. "Well, there you are."

Paulie knitted his brow. "Ah," he said then. "You're inter-ested in land. Yes, you said as much, earlier." He nodded, several times. "Yes, I see. Well, anything's possible, of course. But what about this other guy?"

Joe said, "That's another thing. Maybe it's nothing, just some old pal of Frank's."

"I don't think so. Look, can you come back to my camp? We need to talk this over."

"Sure," Joe said. "Let's talk. What about Helen?"

"She can entertain Frank," Paulie said. "I've never seen Frank so interested in a girl before."

Joe thought he'd detected a hint of an emphasis on "girl." "Why not?" he said.

They clambered down out of the tower. Helen and Frank were looking at some flowers and Frank was enthusing about them. Joe took Helen aside.

"Bingo," he said. "He wants me to go back to his camp. I think he's got plenty to tell. He doesn't want us to expose him to the colonel."

"What am I supposed to do," Helen said, "hang out here with lover boy?"

"You'll be all right," Joe said. "Just don't get too intimate."

Helen grimaced. "Well, at least after hours of soaking, he's clean. You be careful. Paulie may not be too stable. Are you armed?"

"I was in a hot tub, remember?" Joe said. "Of course I'm not armed. But don't worry, it'll be all right."

Home Guard

Clark was a lady-killer. Tall, well built, handsome, with the tight auburn curls that the babes loved. At twenty-five he had the world by the tail. He was also the night bartender at Smokey's Corner and was thinking positively. The old man had stayed a little late, for him, until after six, drinking too much, shooting the shit with old buddies who stopped in. Which meant that he wouldn't be back. He'd go home and settle in before the TV and fall asleep. About ten, he'd wake up and call the bar to say he was going to bed and was everything all right? And if the crowd was as nonexistent as Clark figured, he'd be out of here himself by midnight, easy. Maybe even eleven.

The after-work crowd was long gone. The only sports on the tube tonight was wrestling. There wasn't that much interest in wrestling in Butte. Please, please, Clark prayed, don't let a bunch of goddamn bikers or late-quitting construction workers come in and settle down for a night of boozing. It was a weeknight, not many people out and about. It looked very much like he'd be out of here in time to drop by Nancy's pad—she'd let him in because it wouldn't be too late for her to get her "beauty sleep." And they'd be porking on the couch by midnight. He was almost positive that he'd timed her period right: she should be just about due, but not for a day or two. A good Catholic girl, she hated condoms and wouldn't use the pill, so it was the rhythm method or take a hike. And if she didn't let him in, he had some other numbers he could call.

In fact, things went even better than he'd hoped. Nobody even asked to see what was on the tube. Nobody came in but a few regulars for a quick shot and a beer, and still nobody came in, and Smokey called before ten. He sounded like hell, just woke up. He was going to bed. No way he could come over to check the receipts, no reason. He had full trust in Clark, who, like all of Smokey's boys, was not so dumb as to think it might be all right to skim off a canny old crook like Smokey.

"Kinda slow tonight?" Smokey inquired.

"A fuckin' morgue," Clark said. "Hasn't been anybody in for damn near an hour. Okay if I shut her down early?"

"Give her 'til 'leven," Smokey said. "It's prob'ly the same all over town. If Pat & Mike's shuts down early, and the Racetrack, and the Helsinki, there'll be guys running all over town looking for a drink."

"The M&M's always open," Clark pointed out. He was amazed that the old man gave a shit about the convenience of Butte's drunks. Lord knows, at least a half dozen other bars up and down the hill would be open until two A.M.

"Well, give her 'til 'leven," Smokey said. "If you ain't got no business, lock her down. I'll see ya tamorra. And be sure the cases are all stocked before you leave."

"They're already stocked, boss. I finished half'nour ago. I was just gonna put the chairs up and sweep." In fact, Clark had already put the chairs up on the tables and even the stools onto the bar. He'd done damn near everything, in fact, except turn out the damned sign. After the boss finally hung up he started to count the till.

And then the door banged open. Wouldn't you know it? Clark saw that it was the big guy who had been in the night before. "We're about closed," he called out.

"Aw, it's early," the guy said. He yanked a stool off the bar and sat on it heavily, as if he meant to stay. "Gimme a shot a that . . . lessee," he said, scanning the back bar. "You don't have no sliv'vitz. No? All right, make it the Stoli. Make it a fuckin' double, Jack. Er, pard. That's what you say around here, ain't it?"

He hauled out a fistful of bills and dropped some fifties on the bar and on the floor. He bent down to pick up the fallen bills, one hand covering those on the bar. When he straightened up Clark was holding the Stolichnaya and a double shot glass and making a face. "What's the prob, Bob?" the guy said.

"Aw, hell," Clark said. "I just counted the till. I ain't got change for that. Here, I'll pour you one on the house."

"Well, shit, pard, I'm gonna need more than one," the guy said. He fumbled in his pocket again and found a ten.

"There's other bars up the hill," Clark said. He poured the shot glass full. "There, drink that up."

The guy picked up the shot glass and emptied it in one quick jolt. "Ah, yes," he said and drew in his breath gratefully. "Another." He shoved the glass forward.

Clark shook his head. "Sorry, pal."

"Hey," the guy said, leaning forward. His eyes were watery and he wasn't focusing well. He probably shouldn't be served, Clark thought. But the guy concentrated now and said, in a low, ominous tone, "I'm try'na be nice, pard. Just a customer. I can pay." He shoved the ten forward.

Clark glanced up at the clock. He had plenty of time. This guy wouldn't need much. The only thing was, he feared, the longer he stayed open, the more likely that someone else would come in. But—he sighed—it was probably less time-consuming to give this bird his shot, or two, and get rid of him that way—avoid a hassle. So he smiled and shrugged and poured another. "On the house," he said.

"I like that," the guy said, with a grin. "Price is right." He tossed the shot down. "Another," he said.

Clark sighed again. "Tell you what," he said, "there's . . . what?" He held up the bottle and shook it. "A good half a bottle here. I'll sell you the rest for ten bucks." He pushed the bottle over.

The guy grabbed the bottle and poured himself another shot, slopping it over the top. He eased the glass aside and leaned his big head down to suck up the spilled vodka from the bar with a slurp. Clark was tempted to crack the oaf over the head with the bottle. Instead, he patiently said, "Go ahead, take the bottle." He waved toward the door.

The guy picked up the shot glass and tossed down the vodka. "Wow," he said and gave a little shudder. "I just wanta ask a question," he went on when he'd regained his composure. "Pour me another one, my hands are a little shaky."

Clark poured another. This time the guy let it sit.

"I was in here last night and I ask you about a guy named Franko Bradovic. Only, I find out he goes by Frank Ob'ravich. 'Member?" When Clark nodded, the guy went on, "You said you din't know him. But I seen the way you said it, you did know him. Then I seen you look down the bar"—the guy cast a glance down the empty bar in demonstration—"and there was this old fart standin' down there and he gave a little sign, with his head. But I seen it."

The guy paused and drank down the shot of vodka and gestured for another. Clark complied. Again, the man let it sit.

"So, you do know Franko. I was gonna come back, but I thought . . . well, what the fuck does it matter what I thought? Anyways, I'm back. So tell me about Franko." He folded his arms on the bar and looked at Clark.

Clark considered briefly, then said, "You're a friend of Frank's?" The guy didn't look like any friend, but Clark didn't know Frank all that well. This guy was younger than Frank though probably not by too much, and kind of rough but wearing what looked like a cashmere turtleneck and a fine dark leather coat. Obviously he wasn't a bum. Maybe someone Frank had met in California. What the heck, Oberavich could look after himself, Clark thought. Still, there was a rule: if anything funny happened with Frank and Smokey found out he'd told the guy. . . . But how could Smokey find that out? The important thing, he decided, was to get this yahoo out of here before someone else came in.

"Me'n Franko go way back," the guy said.

"Are we talking about the same guy?" Clark said. "What does this Franko look like?"

"Jesus," the guy said with a sigh. He propped his head between his hands, his elbows on the bar. He groaned and held his head tightly. When he looked up he seemed less drunk, obviously concentrating mightily. "I'm just askin' 'bout a ol' buddy," he said. "You wanta know, he's about thirty-five, medium height"—he held his hand out at his side at about a foot less than his own six feet and a few inches—"dark hair, a mustache. Not a bad-looking fella, if he'd lighten up, once."

"Nah," Clark said, shaking his head. "Frank Oberavich I know is, oh, not quite thirty, blond—dishwater blond, you know? He's skinny, 'bout five-six or -seven. Wears glasses, or used to. Different guy entirely. Here, here's your bottle, pard." He pushed the Stolichnaya forward.

The guy sat back with a puzzled look. He reached out absently and picked up the full shot glass and drank it off. This time he didn't shudder, just looked thoughtful. "No shit," he said, finally. He looked at Clark closely. "No shit?"

"No shit," Clark said.

The guy thought for a second, then said, "Well, where's this fucker live?"

"Out in the boonies," Clark said. "North of here. He's got a place way back in the hills. I couldn't begin to tell you how to get there. It's way up French Forque, somewhere."

The guy looked confused now. "You got his number?"

"No, I sure don't," Clark said.

"Who would have it?" the guy asked.

Clark shrugged. "His family, maybe. His uncle Gary works for the railroad. You might be able to get hold of him."

"You got *his* number?"

Clark eyed the man calculatingly, registering a description, in case it became necessary: big guy, about twenty-five, drunk, open face, dark hair with a white patch in front, alternately amiable and hostile. . . . He searched for an apposite term, but the best he could come up with was *bombastic*, which didn't quite say it. "Who's asking, pard?" he said, temporizing.

"Just a ol' pal of Franko's," the guy offered, breaking into a disarming grin. "All's I want is to give him a call."

Clark nodded, resting his hands on the bar. "So, what's the deal, your name a state secret? Next time I see Frank in town I'll say, 'Hey, did what's-his-name ever get in touch with you?' Give me a break."

The guy leaned forward with a belligerent look on his face, but Clark stepped away and dropped his hand down out of sight. The guy hesitated. He had learned that bartenders were not good people to mess with, especially big, athletic ones like pretty boy here. He had a feeling that there was something useful to a bartender at hand back there—a bat, possibly a gun, a shotgun even. He started to slip his hand into his coat pocket but realized that pretty boy was watching him very carefully. Instead he reached out for the vodka bottle and took a jolt from it directly.

"It's a long story," he said, when he had swallowed the good smooth, warming liquid. He sat down on the stool again and Clark relaxed, folding his arms and leaning back on the back bar. "Franko had a chick," the guy went on. "She run off with me. Franko was pissed, natcherly. I felt bad about it, but what can a guy do? A babe makes up her mind, she does what she wants. But then we broke up. I just happened to be going through town and I thought I'd look up Franko, tell him what happened, maybe bygones will be bygones. See?" He spread his hands openly. "No big deal."

Clark shook his head and looked disgusted. Was this asshole ever going to leave? "So, do you have a name or not?" he asked.

The guy rolled his eyes and looked about him as if appealing to an invisible audience, his hands spread in innocence and long-suffering patience. "Jeez! I all's heard Butte was a friendly town. Okay, tell him Badger was asking after him. All right?"

"Badger? That a last name or a first name?"

"Just Badge. Or Boz. Yeah, tell him Boz." He pronounced it Boze. "Franko'll know. So what's his uncle's number?"

Clark opened a drawer in the back bar and brought out the telephone book, opening it on the bar. He paged through it, then read out the number. Boz reached over and tore the page out from under his hand.

"Thanks," Boz said. "Lemme use your phone."

Clark had lost patience. "Get the fuck out of here, pal," he said. He reached under the bar again, and this time he came up with a Little League baseball bat. A very handy and dangerous-looking weapon.

Boz started back, his hand going to his coat pocket. But then he grabbed the bottle and stalked out, shouting over his shoulder, "Thanks for nothing, dickhead!"

Clark blew out his breath in relief. He quickly locked and bolted the door behind him and switched off the sign. He glanced at the clock. Plenty of time. His agile mind turned instantly to more lustful thoughts.

Boz drove his rented car uptown—very carefully, after a Silver Bow sheriff's car cruised across an intersection before him. He realized he didn't know where he was going. He parked the car uptown and went into another bar, the M&M. This place was live-lier than Smokey's. It had a keno game going and a lunch counter. He'd been in here before. They hadn't known Frank Oberavich, either. Friendly Butte, he thought, bitterly. This time he stepped up next to a fellow at the bar who looked a little tattered and worn, gazing forlornly at a half-empty glass of beer.

Boz called out, "I'll have a double shot of Stoli and a beer. And give one to my pard here."

The bartender said, "No Stoli. Smirnoff's. That do?"

"Sure," Boz said. He smiled at the little guy next to him. "Whattaya say, pard? Smirnoff?"

The little guy smiled back; he lacked a few teeth. "Kessler's, if you don't mind. And a beer."

Boz nodded, and the bartender brought the beers and the drinks. Boz lifted his shot and nodded to the little guy. "*Nasdravie*," he said, tossing down the shot.

The little guy sipped his Kessler's and replied, "Smooth as silk."

Boz said, as soon as they were comfortable, "You live around here, pard?"

"All my life," the fellow said.

"Where's this Quartz?"

"The street? Just a couple blocks over," the little guy gestured. "What number?"

Boz gave a number, not the right one. He figured if he could find the street he'd find the address. A few minutes later he left, having bought his friend another drink, as well as one for himself. He found Quartz easily enough. It wasn't too difficult to locate the house, an older two-story behind a little picket fence, with neighbors an arm's reach on either side. Boz took another swig out of the vodka bottle and went up to the house.

There were lights, including the telltale flicker of the television in the front room. A little dog yapped. A man's voice shushed the dog, and a man came to answer the doorbell. He was in his fifties, dressed in sweatpants and a sweatshirt with NAVY stenciled on it. He was a good-sized man, hefty, bald, wearing steel-rimmed glasses. "Yanh?" he said as he opened the door, holding the little dog back with his slippered foot.

"Hi," Boz said, leaning on the jamb. "Say, I'm sorry to bother you, but I'm looking for a fella—they tell me he's your nephew."

The man looked Boz over and frowned. "Which one?" he said. "It's kinda late, you know."

"Frank," Boz said.

"Whattaya want with Frank?" the man asked. Then he said, "Maybe you better look him up yourself, tomorrow." He started to close the storm door.

Boz caught the door. He smiled broadly. "Oh, say, pard, I drove clear out here to see Frank. All I want's his phone number, tell him I'm here, where I'm staying."

The man pursed his lips with annoyance. "What's your name?" he said. "Where you staying? I'll tell him in the morning."

"All I need's his number," Boz said. "Don't mean to bother you. I'll call him tomorrow, after I rest up a bit."

"He don't have no phone," the man said. "You better go sleep it off." He tried to close the door, but Boz had stuck his big shoe into the opening. "Hey, asshole! Beat it!" the man said. He reached through the opening and shoved Boz backward.

Boz lurched but didn't remove his shoe. His hand came up with a large brushed-metal Glock 9mm automatic. He held it pointed at the man's head. "I tried to be nice, fucker," he said. He yanked the door open and entered the house as the man backed into the living room, his hands held up.

"Whoa," the man said. "Be careful with that thing!"

The little dog, a tiny ball of white wool, dashed forward. Boz kicked it across the room. It squealed and ran behind the couch, whining and mewling. A comedian on the television was grinning and talking; people were laughing. A woman came out of the back of the house, wearing a robe. She was gray-haired and stout. She saw the gun and started to retreat.

"Come back here!" Boz ordered. She crept back into the room. "Sit down, both a you." He gestured with the gun while he extended his arm behind him to close the heavy front door. He stepped into the living room again and glanced at the front windows. They were large, double-hung casement windows, covered with lace curtains. Boz didn't think he could be easily observed from the street, but he thrust the gun into his coat pocket with his hand on it.

The couple sat on the edge of the couch. The woman was frightened, but the man was angry. He put his arm around his wife. "What the hell you want?" he said belligerently.

Boz was excited. He started to yank the gun out of his pocket, but instead he just swore. "Goddamn it," he said, "I didn't want to. . . . All right." He paused to get hold of himself. "All I want, I mean. . . . I been trying to find this fu—" He stopped. "This guy. He's a buddy. Franko. Your nephew. He's a friend of mine. I swear. No harm. See?" He released the gun in his pocket and held both hands out to his side, palms open.

The woman looked horrified, but the man glared. "You better beat it, guy. I mean it. Just get on out of here and no harm done. You scared my wife." He glanced at her.

"Gotta have that number," Boz said stubbornly. He stuck his hand in the coat pocket.

"I told you," the man said, "he ain't got no phone."

"Then, where does he live?"

"He lives way the hell out in the brush," the man said. "You'd never find it, drunk as you are. You better go sleep it off." With the last phrase his voice had lost some of its sharpness. He was a man familiar with Boz's condition. He knew how to handle drunks. "Come see me tomorrow. I'll take you out there, personally. You okay to drive? You don't look too good."

"I can drive," Boz said. "Draw me a map."

"I don't think so," the man said. He stood up. "I'm gonna call the cops if you don't leave. Go on back to your motel, or whatever, sleep it off."

"Jesus," Boz said. He drew out the gun. "What the fuck is it with you people? Draw me the fucking map!" His voice had risen to a near shout. The little dog, which had peeked around the edge of the couch, withdrew.

"All right, all right," the man said. "I have to get a pencil." He made as if to leave the room.

"There's a pencil right there," Boz said, pointing to a half-finished crossword puzzle in the daily newspaper, folded and lying on the coffee table in front of the couch. "And turn off that goddamn TV."

The woman reached out and picked up the remote. She switched off the television and sat back, watching while her husband began to sketch a map on an envelope that lay on the table.

The man said, as he drew, "You go on north on the freeway, toward Helena. Get off at the French Forque exit." He described the turns, the roads not to take, and ended by making a cross on the paper. "You won't be able to get in that gate, and it's a mile back to the house. You'll just be sittin' out there in the dark."

Boz had replaced the gun in his pocket and now leaned forward to look at the map. The man took his glasses off and set them on the table, then suddenly grabbed at Boz. The woman screamed. The two men grappled, Boz clawing at his pocket. The two men fell to the floor, knocking the coffee table sideways. The older man had gotten a powerful arm around Boz's neck and his other hand on Boz's right wrist. The little dog had dashed out and was tugging at Boz's pantleg.

"Jesus!" Boz yelled. He kicked at the dog but missed it. He groaned as he tried to writhe out from under the heavier man. Suddenly, he wrenched his arm free and fired the gun.

The older man cried out and rolled off him, then lay still, on his back, his mouth open. The woman screamed. Boz got to his feet, panting. "Shut up!" he bellowed, but the woman screamed on. Boz shot her. The bullet struck her in the chest and she was knocked sideways on the couch, then rolled onto the floor. She was crumpled in a heap at the base of the couch, her varicosed legs exposed, the remote still clutched in her hand.

Boz turned to the dog, but it ran behind the couch again. Boz yanked at the couch back, but the woman's body prevented it from moving, and the dog retreated around the end, whining.

"Fuck you," Boz snarled at the dog. He turned to the couple. He shot the man again, and then the woman, their bodies jumping at the impact, then subsiding into final rest. Boz snatched up the envelope from where it lay on the floor and lurched out.

The air was cold and refreshing. He stood on the little porch and looked around. There was no sound, no commotion from the neighbors. He let the storm door bang behind him and stumbled down the walk to his car. A few minutes later he found himself driving down the hill on an unfamiliar street, with no idea of how to get to the freeway. He reached across, found the bottle of vodka and drained it, then tossed it out the open window. Shit, he thought,

I gotta get some more booze. He had no idea how long it would take him to find Frank's. He had no notion of driving around all night with nothing to drink.

Through sheer luck he glanced down a cross street and it seemed familiar—Smokey's! He pulled up in front of the bar, got out, and tried the door. Locked. Then he realized the tavern light was off and the lights in the bar had been reduced to just the back bar, which glittered with lots of bottles of booze. He kicked at the door and cursed.

When he stepped back and looked around, disgusted and angry, he saw a light go on upstairs. Maybe it was that fucking pretty-boy bartender, he thought. But he saw a woman peering out. The building was brick, and the three upper stories were evidently apartments. Someone was bound to call the cops if he kept raising hell.

He drove off, and either through sheer luck or gravity, he kept heading down the hill, and shortly he saw the freeway. Even better, he saw a lighted tavern sign just beyond it. The bar had a pool table, at which some young guys were playing. Others sat in booths or at the bar. There were three or four women, as well. A jolly evening at the pub in Butte. Boz bought a fifth of vodka and left. Miraculously, he got on the freeway in the right direction and soon he was zooming north, toward Helena, climbing up toward Elk Park. Before long the lights of Butte had disappeared and he was in total night, under a sky sparkling with stars.

He drove with confidence now. It was odd, he thought, how he could feel drunk and confused at those people's house, but now, having taken a few fortifying swigs of vodka, he felt calmer, quite clearheaded. Those fucking people! he thought. What were they thinking? Assholes! People like that got what they deserved. Always fucking around, stalling. Ask a simple question and all you get are more stupid questions. Then they start getting pissy. Well, they weren't getting pissy now! He laughed. He felt damn good. He regretted not popping that fucking little dog.

The Home Guard, that's what the 'boes called the squares. The old 'bo he'd met on the train, years ago, when he was last out in this part of the country, the one who told him about the Stuka and the bazooka—Boz couldn't think of his handle, if he'd ever known it—had told him about the Home Guard. The ones who stayed home, who pulled the daily job, pissed their whole lives away in some shithole, afraid to get out and see what the world was really like. And yet, they thought their shit didn't stink. They worked for wages, day after day, got a mortgage, married some fat whore, had a bunch of kids, maybe got drunk at the bar once a week. Jesus, what a fucking life! And they thought that was what it was all about! Fuckin' suckers.

He rolled down the window and stuck his head out into the cold rushing wind and shouted at the top of his lungs, "Fuckin' suckers!"

The right front wheel went off the road, the car pulled violently to the right. He managed to swerve back on, but then the car fishtailed and he nearly lost it.

Whoa, he thought, and slowed down. That was fuckin' close! He took another hearty hit of the vodka and felt better, more like his own self. Then he began to think, How far did I come? Did I miss the road to this French Forque? He slowed to a crawl, alternately peering at the crude map and out at the road. He hadn't passed or met a single car since he'd come over the pass from Butte, and thought, Where the fuck am I?

Then, like magic, there was the reflecting sign that indicated the exit to French Forque, one mile. He got off and cruised slowly through the village. Hardly a light was on. Frenchy's bar was closed. Too bad. He hoisted his bottle again and drove to a stop sign. This was the road he wanted.

The road turned to gravel. He drove on. It became dirt. He found the turnoff. Still not a single light, not a car. The Home Guard went to bed early out here. It occurred to him that the little dog was the real Home Guard. He laughed. That was a real dog, he decided. He ought to go back and get that dog. He'd never had much luck with dogs, but he could tame it, he was sure. That dog would become his dog. His best friend. Faithful, feisty. He'd name it Home Guard. He'd call it Homes, for short.

"Here, Homes!" he bellowed out the window. He laughed. The road turned rough, then rougher. All of sudden he came on a turn too fast and bounced right off the road and into some heavy brush. The car stalled. He sat there for a minute, dazed. He drank some vodka. The car started right up. At first he couldn't back out, and the brush was too heavy to go forward, but the ground was not boggy, and soon he was able to back far enough that he was clear of the brush and he was able to turn and go forward and get back on the road.

This road was a nightmare, he realized. There was a damn good chance that this rental sedan would never make it to Franko's place. The road angled up, switching back to get over a rocky knob, and at the high point he saw a light. He stopped and got out.

The light was distant, maybe a yard light. As dark as it was and not knowing the terrain, he couldn't be sure just how far that light might be. A mile? Five miles? Closer to five, he thought, but at least it was a light, and this road had to be going there. He'd just drive as far as he could and walk the rest.

He got almost two miles before, in his drunken state, he let the right front wheel drift off the narrow rutted road. The car slid sideways and down into the ditch, coming to a rest on its side. There was no moving it now. He was lucky, he knew, that he hadn't been going fast. The car was at such a steep angle that he had to push the door upward until it stayed open. He found the vodka bottle at the bottom of the car, up against the righthand door, and he clambered out.

Okay, he thought. Now it's walk. It was chilly, but his coat was adequate. What a night! He stood in the middle of the road and stared up at the billions of stars. He took a long drink of vodka. He still had at least half a bottle left. That was comforting. But man, what a night, what a sky! This was a very big place, he realized.

He checked his pockets. He had the gun and a couple of spare clips. If only he had his dog, faithful Homes. He set off. There was enough starlight to see the road, although he stumbled a good deal. At the bottom of the hill he had to ford a stream, which was almost enough to make him despair. A good pair of shoes ruined, he thought. He'd spent two hundred dollars on these goddamn shoes! Well, Franko would pay for this. He trudged on.

He began to think about what lay ahead. He was still baffled about this Frank Oberavich crap. There was always the chance that he'd made a big mistake, but he didn't think so. The minute he'd heard the name from that dumb bartender he'd known this had to be the guy. That jerk had thrown him for a minute, with his description, but then he'd realized that it was just part of the crap the Home Guard always puts in your way. He should have shot the bastard, he thought. Maybe he still would, when he got back to town. That cheered him up.

No, he was sure he had the right guy. And when he found him he could take care of business. Item number one: get the rest of the goods that the sneaky fucker had stashed. Boz could sure use the money. Item two: make sure the fucker didn't testify to no goddamn war-crimes tribunal. Vjelko had made that clear.

He came to the gate. It was locked. No sweat. He had one leg over the top rail of the gate when the lights came on, high up on poles. He was surprised, but more glad than frightened. He clambered over and set off up the road. He hadn't gotten more than a hundred feet when the dogs arrived, barking madly. Boz got the gun out in time. They attacked and he clubbed the first one and shot the second one. The other two ranged off.

Boz stood there, raging. His good coat was ruined. The one dog had taken a sleeve and nearly destroyed it, but the coat had saved him, Boz realized. The other two dogs stayed well away, racing about beyond the edge of the bright light, but occasionally showing themselves. It would be futile to shoot at them. He replaced the clip with a fresh one. Who knew what lay ahead?

Incoming

The dogs had accompanied them about halfway across the meadow before Paulie ordered them back. Away to the north were some dark, wooded hills; an owl was hooting over that way. "*Strix*," Paulie said. He was walking with a steady sureness along a path, but paused to listen.

"Who?" Joe said, and gave a low laugh.

"*Strix varia*," Paulie said. He gestured with the large, dry-cell light toward the distant woods. "Barred owl. You don't know the birds at all, then?"

"I know robins and crows," Joe said, "and pigeons."

Paulie snorted, almost a laugh. He moved on. "What's your deal with Tucker, Joe?" He spoke over his shoulder, slowing and looking back.

Joe explained that it was a contract. He didn't work for the DEA. "It's a little complex."

"Ah. Yeah, I had the feeling that it was not, uh . . . well, you don't seem like a federal agent. So, what kind of land are you looking for?"

"Something just like this," Joe said. "Not all this much. A few acres. What I was thinking, maybe we could strike some kind of deal. I'm a little concerned about Frank's operation. It's going to attract the law, if it hasn't already. I don't like that."

"Down this way," Paulie said. He led Joe down the gulch again, but before they reached the stream, he set off up along the bench. "Why are you concerned about Frank?"

"Who wants the threat of a raid?" Joe said. "Personally, I'm not bothered by him growing grass, but . . . it's a bother. Maybe, if Frank isn't too tied to this dope business, I could make it worth his while to drop it. I'd need his help, anyway, to set up my place."

"Just between us," Paulie said, "I don't think he makes much, if anything, off the grass. He isn't really a dealer, if that's what bothers you. Once in a while, he sells some to people he knows in Butte, or wherever, but he probably gives away more than he sells. The cops wouldn't see it that way, I'm sure, but that's the truth of it."

"What does he live on, then?" Joe asked.

"He inherited some money from Gramp, like me, plus he's got another little trust fund, from his maternal grandmother, so he doesn't really need much, but he spent a lot on his infrastructure. Sometimes I think that's what he's really interested in, besides the plants, of course—fiddling with his 'systems.' A little capital might interest him, but so would the prospect of setting up another system. He's got ideas about tapping into the hydrothermal potential around here for heating and power generation. He'd love the chance to dig some holes and lay pipe."

Shortly, they came to his camp. It was a large, wall-sided canvas hunter's camp tent set up in a copse of aspens, well back from the stream on high ground but still within hearing of the tumbling water. Paulie led Joe in and lit a kerosene lantern. It didn't give a lot of light, but Joe could see a camp table and a cot, a large footlocker that served many purposes, and a couple of folding camp chairs.

"I've got a generator and lights," Paulie said, gesturing with the flashlight, "but most of my domestic arrangements are outside.

Frank would love to make it all interlocking and self-sufficient, but I've resisted. A certain crudeness and discomfort attracts me, I guess. The deer come around, and raccoons, so I've got to keep all the food in those coolers, inside. There's bears, too, but I haven't seen them. They'll be going into hibernation soon, anyway. But so will I, up at Frank's. I thought about trying to stick it out through the winter, but winters are just too brutal up here, even for my discomfort index. I should have used my time better, built myself a little cabin."

Joe looked about. "All the comforts of home," he said wryly, "almost . . . *cozy*." He made a shivering gesture with his shoulders. It had been warm enough hiking, and they were both adequately dressed, but the tent offered no real comfort other than a windbreak.

"Exactly," Paulie agreed. "It was fine when the days were long. Reading with mittens on isn't so much fun. But I got well here, or at least I got better. Peace and quiet." He began to pump up the fuel tank on a Coleman camp stove to heat water for coffee. "Frank tried to talk me into excavating into the hillside, with hot-water heating piped in from a thermal spring. But it seemed too . . . cavelike."

"You got well? Were you sick when you came back from Europe?"

Paulie looked up. "I guess you want to know all about that."

Joe was only casually interested in Paulie's adventures. As far as he was concerned, his job was done. He'd found the man. But, as always, there was more to the job than anticipated. Paulie was his ticket to reestablishing himself and Helen in this country. The more he thought about the possibilities, the more enthusiastic he got. Frank's way of thinking was very congenial to him. If Paulie wanted to talk about what had gone wrong in Kosovo, Joe was content to listen.

"Yeah, well, it seems a little odd," Joe said. "You were doing okay, then everything goes silent. You come back here and spend months hiding out in the bush."

Paulie filled the kettle and set it on the burner. Then he sat down on the footlocker to grind the coffee beans with a tubular hand-crank brass device.

"I haven't talked about it," he said, "not even with Frank. He never asked. I just showed up and he could see I wasn't too . . . jolly. He helped me set up this camp. After a while things got better." He cranked away as he talked.

"What did you do?" Joe asked.

"Went for long walks, fished, read. Had some long nights . . . woke up in sweats, that kind of thing. A lot of bird-watching. Thinking."

"What about in Kosovo?" Joe asked. "What were you doing there?"

"Nothing."

"Nothing?"

"Just looking around, fishing," Paulie said. "I don't know, maybe I was looking for a place to light. I guess you could say I was observing."

"Hell of a place for loafing," Joe observed.

"It was all right, at first. I had a good situation there," Paulie said. "It couldn't last, of course. The war was getting closer. We were up in the mountains, like this, kind of, only it's a smaller place. Those folks, they don't know remote like we know remote. But it was back in the hills. The war would get there eventually, but I tried to ignore it. Then I got involved with these smugglers, kids really. I should never have done that. I should have just left them to their . . ." He hesitated. "Games," he went on. "I guess you could call them games. It was their life, really."

Joe sat patiently in the camp chair, listening with half his mind. A breeze had come up, fluttering the canvas. He supposed one was more aware of it in a tent. He wondered what it would be like to live in a tent. It might get pretty old. But the Indians did it, full-time.

They must have figured out how to make it comfortable but still portable, since they moved pretty regularly. How did they keep warm? You couldn't have much of a fire inside a tepee, and most of it would go out the top . . . which would be why they were so tall, maybe . . .

". . . Bazooka, he called himself. He was trouble," Paulie was saying. "I could see that right away. Coffee? It's pretty strong, if you're not used to it."

Joe tried it. Paulie served it in a tiny cup. It was strong all right. You could float an axe in this. It was also very sweet. He sipped and nodded. Handy way to make it though. You'd have to develop these kind of systems, he thought. Grind your coffee by hand, get used to fetching water. It was primitive, in a way, but Paulie wasn't a slave to it, he could see. He'd gone to the trouble of finding good equipment, like that lightweight but sturdy cot, a really good sleeping bag, maybe take your clothes to be washed at Frank's.

Joe had caught a glimpse of a bike of some sort, probably a top-of-the-line mountain bike. Laptop computer. Run on batteries, but not for long—generator. Have to have some kind of converter, don't you? For direct current. Maybe not. Frank would know about that.

". . . do you? I mean, privately?" Paulie asked.

"Privately?" Joe said. "Well, yeah, basically. I always worked for large outfits. This deal with the colonel is private. That is, I'm not a government employee. Just a contractor. Contract for Service, that's me." He smiled. "But I'm not like a private detective, with an office, taking clients who walk in off the street. What'd you have in mind?"

"Bazooka," Paulie said.

"I thought you didn't want anything to do with all that, just peace and quiet," Joe said, recalling the story he'd half-listened to.

"I've had the peace and quiet. Now I'm able to think about it again. Just talking to you has cleared up my thoughts on it," Paulie said. "But I can see I'd been coming to this. I made a mistake getting involved over there, but once you intervene it seems like you have a responsibility, to see it through. I was thinking we could work out a deal—for the land, I mean."

"I thought the deal was I wouldn't say anything to the colonel, about finding you."

"That's for openers," Paulie said. "We haven't discussed how much land you want, or where. An acre by the gate? Ten acres up in the woods? On the creek? There's lots to talk about."

"So, we're talking," Joe said. "No hurry, the colonel can wait. I was just thinking . . . what if you didn't really want a fixed living site—just to move seasonally? Low-impact kind of thing. How much land would that entail?"

Paulie didn't know. He said it would depend on how comfortably one wanted to live. A person could drag a trailer from one site to another, put in some minimal facilities like solar-power support, maybe septic tanks. But he wasn't interested, Joe could tell.

"What about this other guy?" Paulie asked.

Ah, thought Joe, that's what's bugging him. "You thinking it might be this Bazerk character?"

"It sounds kind of like him," Paulie said.

"Why would he be looking for you? Isn't it the other way around? You want to find him?"

"Yeah," Paulie admitted, "now. You're right, it wouldn't make sense for him to come looking for me. You'd think I'm the last guy he'd like to see."

"I'll say," Joe cut in. "The guy screws up your act, waltzes off with your goods . . ." Joe hesitated. Paulie's story hadn't quite gotten to that point. It seemed headed that way, though. You don't ever want to leave a guy alone with your goods. "Did he?" he asked.

"Oh yeah, he took the goods," Paulie said. He got up and went to the tent flap. He stepped out, partially, listening. "You hear something? I thought I heard the dogs. I hope they're not running deer."

Joe hadn't heard anything. "Maybe it was Strix, the owl," he said.

"Maybe," Paulie said, but he didn't come back in. "He killed them all," he said. He spoke it to the wind, to the night.

Joe wasn't sure he'd gotten this right. "The people in the cave, you're talking about?"

Paulie came back inside. His face had a new look. It was haunted, but determined. "It took a long time to get that out," he said. "Another mistake. I tried to hide it, even from myself. It's a shameful thing, to be a part of that."

"You weren't a part of that," Joe said. It irritated him when people took responsibility where it didn't belong to them.

"I left him in the cave," Paulie said. His eyes were glowing. "Those people were there because of me. Because Fedima thought they'd be safe, with me. He butchered them."

"All of them?" Joe was surprised to find that his breath felt short.

"All but Fedima. He took her with him," Paulie said. "I don't know what happened to her. He probably killed her somewhere on the mountain, or he may have traded her to brigands, to help him get out. There are a number of possible scenarios. I've had a while to think them all out."

I bet you have, Joe thought. "Are you sure *he* got out?"

At that moment they heard the shots.

"Uh-oh," Joe said. He followed Paulie out of the tent. They looked off into the night. There were no further shots, but there was barking, very urgent barking with a keening sound.

Paulie grabbed the bike, but Joe stopped him. "Forget it," he said. "You can't go rushing back there. It's better if we go together. Have you got a gun?"

Paulie had a shotgun. He fetched it hastily. "Maybe you should take the bike," he said. He was leaping with impatience.

"No, you lead the way," Joe said. "I wouldn't get twenty feet on that thing in the dark. But watch that light. We don't want to be seen."

They set off as fast as Paulie could go, with Joe loping along behind. Clouds had moved in, at least partially obscuring the stars and diminishing the available light. That slowed their progress, considerably. Both fell more than once, but they quickly ran on. It took them at least twenty minutes, Joe estimated, to reach the crest of the meadow, from where they could see the house. They'd had to douse the light earlier, so as not to alert anyone to their coming.

From the crest they could see lights on at the house, including the orangish-pink yard light that Frank had turned on when they left. Nothing seemed amiss, except that one of Frank's vehicles was gone. Joe thought it was the older pickup that had been parked next to where Helen had pulled up the Durango. Paulie noticed it too.

"Somebody must have shown up at the gate," Paulie said. "Frank must have gone to check."

But the shots? That gripped both their minds. They raced to the house, but as they approached, Joe held Paulie back. "Wait," he said. "I'll check it out. You cover me from here." He pointed to another of Frank's vehicles.

Joe didn't like entering the ring of light provided by the yard light, but he felt he had to arm himself. He raced to the Durango and rolled under it. He peered at the house and surroundings. There was no sign of any activity. He crawled to the back of the vehicle and opened that door as quietly as he could. He dared not open one of the side doors, as that would turn on the interior light. The back of the SUV was jammed with gear and Helen's damned chain-saw sculptures. But he found his canvas gun satchel and dragged it out.

He scurried back into the shadows, away from the car, and extracted a couple of favorite pieces. One, a nice flat Smith & Wesson .380 automatic, he jammed into his waistband at the small of his back, after making sure it was loaded. The other, a big, hulking Dan Wesson .357 magnum, he carried in his hand.

Joe crept around the house, keeping to the shadows, moving cautiously. He was almost to the greenhouse part when he thought he saw something inside the house. He sat and watched, praying that Paulie would not become impatient and do something stupid. At last what he took to be a human figure moved enough that he was sure it was Helen. She was standing against one of the huge posts that supported the beams. She was in shadow, but he could see a gleam of metal in her hand, held down along her leg. Very smart, he thought. It was also encouraging. It indicated that she was alone in the house, that she was not under the control of another, hidden, person. The problem was to prevent her from firing at him, if he appeared.

He picked up a pebble and tossed it at a window, well away from himself. Helen instantly turned her head. He tossed another pebble. She understood. She said something, or at least her mouth moved, forming an "O". He thought it was his name. But she hadn't said it aloud, or the heavy, double-glazed windows had muffled her exclamation. Joe felt it was safe to show himself. He stepped into the light, just for a second, long enough for her to see him, and then stepped back.

A moment later she was out of the house and around the back. Joe called to her softly. They embraced briefly. She quickly filled him in.

The alarm had sounded, she explained. Frank had come to where she had already turned in. He had still been up, puttering with his plants. The dogs were out. Normally, he'd have put them in the pen to keep them from running deer at night, but they had gone with Joe and Paulie, so he'd assumed they were still with them. On the monitors he'd seen a man inside the gate. The lights at the gate had gone on automatically. Just a guy, apparently alone, and no car. Maybe a lost drunk.

"A drunk?" Joe said, skeptically.

"Well, he was staggering, Frank said. The dogs had come up and attacked him and the guy had shot one and clubbed another. Frank took the pickup to go sort it out."

"Did you watch the monitors?" Joe asked.

"Yes. I saw Frank go down there, to the gate. He got out and talked to the guy. On the speakerphone I could hear them arguing, but I couldn't make out what they were saying. They were too far from the mike. But it looked like they calmed down. I could see Frank was angry. He put the dead dogs in the back of the truck. Then the guy got in the truck and the two of them went out through the gate."

"What about the other two dogs?" Joe asked. Helen said they were still out, down by the gate.

Joe decided they should go in the house. He called to Paulie, and when they met on the porch he explained what had happened. They went into the house and checked the monitors. The two other dogs were standing at the now closed gate, looking down the road beyond.

"What do you think?" Joe asked Paulie.

"It sounds like what Frank said," Paulie replied. "Some drunk got on the wrong road, probably ditched his car, and stumbled on the gate. But . . ." He looked worried.

"You're thinking it's your pal Bazooka," Joe said. Paulie nodded. "What did this guy look like?" Joe asked Helen.

"They weren't that close to the cameras," she said, "and the light wasn't that great. He seemed big, much bigger than Frank, wearing a dark coat. He looked excited, pacing around, but not threatening or anything. I didn't see the gun. Frank didn't seem very leery of him, once he'd calmed down. I'd say the guy was drunk. He tried to pick up one of the dogs when Frank was picking up the other, but he looked clumsy, dropped it. Frank just came back and put his hand on his arm, then picked up the dog himself. Then they stood and talked for a few minutes, gesturing back toward town."

"What do you think?" Joe asked Paulie, who shrugged his shoulders. "Well, it's been a half hour, at least. We better go see," Joe said. "Do you know how to switch off those lights? Good. It'd be safer for us without them."

Helen stayed at the house, where she could watch the monitors. She could maintain contact with Joe and Paulie by cell phone, or with Frank, if he should call—although the phones didn't always work that well.

Joe and Paulie drove down to the gate in one of the other four-wheel-drive pickups, a big old Dodge Ram—Joe thought it better to leave the Durango for Helen, just in case, and the pickup had the key in it, which was customary out here. There was a broken vodka bottle lying by the side of the road. They got out to check, and the dogs came eagerly. Paulie ordered them back to the house and they withdrew, but he didn't think they went far. Paulie had brought an electronic opener for the gate. The dogs didn't attempt to follow them, and the gate closed behind them, automatically. They drove on toward town.

In a few minutes they came upon the rental car, down in the ditch. But there was no sign of the pickup, nor the two men. It appeared that they had stopped—there were two sets of footprints in the road.

Paulie and Joe discussed it as they drove on, slowly but steadily. The best scenario was that the intruder was, in fact, a lost drunk—the broken bottle on the road bolstered that notion—and Frank had decided that it wasn't a good idea to try to help him extricate his car from the ditch. At any rate, it was down so far that it really required a wrecker. In this scenario, Frank might have elected to drive the drunk to town, or even home.

"An armed drunk, out here?" Joe said.

"You have no idea how many guys go armed in these parts," Paulie said. He seemed hopeful. "It's so common no one even discusses it. He may not have been carrying it on him, just had it in the car, but when he had to get out and walk, at night . . . most of the guys I know would have taken the gun out of the glove compartment. Bears, you know, and mountain lions."

Joe thought Paulie might be trying to convince himself of the innocence of the incident. It had a plausible feel, but Joe was skeptical. He didn't say as much to Paulie, just cautioned him that they shouldn't proceed as if it were simply a road accident. Paulie accepted that.

They cruised around the village, searching for anything that might look out of the ordinary. There was a gas station, but it was closed, as was Frenchy's bar. Paulie said the nearest town where there would be a wrecker was Basin, ten miles down the interstate. There were no lights burning in the town, except for a few yard lights of the type that go on at dusk. But Paulie didn't think there was much point in calling the road service in Basin: Frank could have called them, if that was what he had in mind. No, he was leaning on the theory that Frank had driven the drunk home—which could mean as far as Butte. Possibly, Frank had recognized the guy.

"Is there a bar in Basin?" Joe said. He glanced at his watch; it was getting toward two A.M., official closing time.

There was a bar. Paulie called Helen and told her what they were planning. She said no one had called.

"I don't know," Joe said. "If Frank had to drive the guy home, wouldn't he have called? Just to reassure Helen?"

"Maybe he thought it wouldn't take long," Paulie said. "And if it was an acquaintance, his fears would have subsided."

Joe nodded. "Maybe you should stay here, in case Frank comes back. If we both drive down to Basin we could miss him." He left

Paulie pacing on the dirt road to the upper Frenchy's Fork and headed for Basin.

The road was a four-lane freeway. At times the opposing lanes diverged fairly widely, due to the difficult mountain terrain—one couldn't always see the other lanes. Joe caught a distant glimpse of a couple of vehicles headed the other way, but he couldn't make out what they were, just headlights in the distance. Joe was fuming. Here he had all but sealed a deal for what looked like his dream retreat. Only if anything happened to Frank or Paulie, the deal was blown. Anything, that is, that couldn't be easily concealed or conveniently explained away. It was too cruel to contemplate.

In Basin, the tavern was closed. The sign had been turned off. But Joe could see the bartender inside. He pounded on the door until the fellow came. "No way," the man said. He was a big guy, a regular Paul Bunyan of a man with a bushy black beard, wearing a red watch cap. Joe explained that he didn't want a drink. He was worried about a couple of pals of his who had gone off against his advice. One of them was all but falling-down drunk. The other was Frank Oberavich.

"Oh yeah," the lumberjack said. "Frank was in here, not fifteen minutes ago. I didn't see the other guy. Maybe he dropped him off. I sold Frank a bottle of vodka. Don't know that I ever seen Frank drinking vodka, now you mention it. Maybe they had a party to go to." To Joe's query he said that, no, he hadn't noticed which way Frank drove when he left, but anyway, he probably would have gone on down to the interchange, to get back on the freeway. From there, he could have gone to Helena or Butte.

Joe raced back to French Forque, annoyed that he hadn't brought the cell phone. In fact, he'd thought of it but decided that it might be more comforting for Paulie to have, alone in the dark. When he got to the exit and then to the road, however, Paulie was nowhere to be found. He cruised about, but there was nowhere to look. Evidently, one of the vehicles he'd seen coming from Basin had been Frank. He must have picked up Paulie and taken him home. It was, after all, quite cold out, probably dropping down to near freezing at this altitude, which Joe estimated must be close to six thousand feet. He wouldn't have relished standing about here, in the night. But they could have left a sign, at least. What, though? A yellow ribbon 'round the old oak tree?

He drove back to the gate, which took a good half hour. The gate was locked and the dogs were gone, but the lights were on again. Joe had to get out, of course, and stand in the cold for thirty seconds before Frank's voice called from the box in the rocks, telling him to come in. "Thanks for waiting, bastards!" Joe called out and drove on through.

The house was all lit up and the dogs barking in the pen. Joe bounced out of the truck and ran up the steps. He could see Helen in the kitchen, looking at him. He had opened the door before he realized that something was wrong. Now it was too late.

A Glock automatic appeared from the shadows behind her, aimed at her head. "Come on in, Joe," a man's voice called.

Joe let the door close behind him. "Just put the gun on the counter, with the others," the man said. He shoved Helen violently aside, and she sprawled on the floor.

"You the one they call Bazooka?" Joe said. He stood with his hands held up, just above waist level.

"Call me Boz," the man said and grinned. "Come on in and have a drink with me and my new pals." He gestured with the Glock in his right hand and a bottle of vodka in the other. On the floor beyond him Joe could see Frank and Paulie, their hands secured behind them and their feet bound with duct tape. "Those jerks don't drink much—they're no fun," Boz said, clearly delighted with his coup. "But this sweet little ginch, she might like a sip before you wrap her up."

Boz prodded her in the ribs with his shoe. "Smile, honey," he said. "Your old man's home." He set the bottle on the counter and picked up a roll of duct tape that lay next to an ominous butcher knife. He tossed the tape to Joe, who caught it deftly. "Go ahead, wrap her hands good and tight. But not the legs." He leered and picked up the bottle of vodka, jostling the butcher knife away on the counter, and took a drink.

"You okay?" Joe asked Helen. He knelt beside her.

"I'm okay," Helen said. He could sense her fear and anger as he took her hand in his. She squeezed his hand.

Boz stood off a few feet, wary but swaying, undoubtedly drunk. Joe watched him while he picked at the sticky edge of the tape, to free it from the roll. The man was large, and none too agile at the moment, but he was alert.

"On second thought," Boz said, setting the bottle down on the counter again, "I think it'd be better if she tied you up, Joe." He laughed, a thick gurgle. "I wasn't thinkin' straight. Musta had one too many." He laughed. "She did a good job on those wimps. She can do the same for you. Here, in here." He gestured with the automatic toward the living room. "Tie him to the post, darlin', hands behind him." He indicated one of the posts that supported the lofty beams.

The post was round, roughly peeled fir, some six inches in diameter. It was securely fastened with steel plates, top and bottom, Joe knew. There would be no dislodging it, not that it would help. This was looking bad, he thought. Grisly, in fact. He had a flashing image of that butcher knife. A bloody slaughter. Slashed throats, perhaps disemboweling. He couldn't help thinking of Paulie's account of the carnage in the cave. This crazed, drunken beast was capable of anything.

"Put your fuckin' arms around the post, behind you, asshole," Boz commanded, aiming the Glock at his head at arm's length but keeping well back. "Wrap him tight, bitch."

Paulie and Frank looked on, their eyes wide with fear. Frank was bruised about the face, his lips puffed up. There was a severe laceration across his brow. It had bled a good deal but had stopped. His nose appeared to be broken. Paulie didn't look so bad. Evidently, Boz had not felt compelled to beat him. But from the look in Paulie's eyes, Joe knew that what was coming would not be something that anyone wanted to witness.

"Wrap the tape around the left wrist first," Boz told Helen, "then run the tape to the right one. And do it tight!"

Helen did as instructed, but in moving around the post, away from Boz, she fumbled, and Joe's right hand slipped away from hers. He sagged clumsily, almost falling, but seemed to catch himself. Then she saw the .380 in the waistband, as Joe had intended.

"Whoa! Watch it there," Boz said, brandishing the pistol. "That's better."

Joe extended his arms backward, to facilitate her wrapping of the wrists, but also to keep himself clear of the post. Helen tried to keep the bonds loose, but the tape had an appalling tendency to grab onto itself. Still, she did the best she could, keeping the post and Joe between her and Boz.

With her right hand she snatched the .380. But what now? It was too risky to shoot. If she missed, their chance of survival was gone. She instantly placed the pistol in Joe's hand, for him to hold, while she went on with her task. From a certain sagging of his shoulders she knew that it was not what he had hoped. But it was the best she could do, for now. With any luck there would be an opportunity for her to get it, later.

Joe made a subtle gesture of tensing his forearms, as if surreptitiously trying his bonds. It was not lost on Boz, who laughed, seeing that Joe was securely bound.

"That's enough, sweet thing," Boz said. He picked up the bottle and swigged, then said, "Come over here." He set the bottle down next to the knife and grabbed her when she came near and wrapped his great arm around her neck, lifting her off the ground, her back pressed against his chest. "Ha, ha," he cried, "look at her squirm! Relax, bitch." He lowered her, but did not release her. "Quit that fuckin' kickin' or I'll let some air into your head."

His eyes gleamed as he lurched forward, holding her in front of him, the gun pressed against the side of her head. "You know why I had her tie you like that, you fuckin' piece of shit?" he snarled at Joe. A piece of his saliva hit Joe on the cheek. "I wanted you to have a ringside seat while me and this little bitch have some fun! Ol' Boz ain't had no pussy in a week. How 'bout it, sweetie?" He looked down at her. "You ready to scuffle? Hey, I tell you what, let's start with some head. Come on, get on yer knees."

He thrust Helen down until she was kneeling before him, his fingers clutching her by her heavy mane of black hair. He looked around wild-eyed, checking that all three of the men were watching him. There was no doubt that the presence of a rapt but helpless audience was a tremendous turn-on for the man. He held the huge gun at Helen's head as she looked up at him. She seemed very tiny at his feet, her face blanched with terror. Each of them, including Helen, knew with certainty that whatever acts he might compel her to perform, whatever outrages he might enact on her, it would end with killing. They would all die here, but not before he had his insane pleasure.

Boz released her hair, momentarily, to fumble at his fly. But he suddenly narrowed his eyes when he saw the look in Helen's eyes. "I know what you're thinking, you bitch!" he shouted, seizing her hair again and twisting it violently. He raised the gun threateningly, but didn't strike. Instead he pointed it at her face. "If you so much as nip me I'll blow your head apart like a fuckin' melon!" he raged. Helen didn't blink. She stared defiantly back at him. He recoiled from her, holding her at arm's length, warily.

Joe watched. He felt cold and strangely calm. He saw that the madman was having second thoughts. That gun's barrel would be very close to Boz's penis. If she bit and he shot, even a little wildly. . . . Joe laughed.

Boz was shocked. He released the crouching woman, thrusting her from him. She fell forward onto her hands, but didn't move as he backed away. He hoisted the vodka bottle and swigged deeply. He gasped and absently tried to set the bottle down next to the butcher knife. It tumbled over, and he scrabbled momentarily to set it upright.

"What the fuck are you laughing at, you bastard!" Boz literally shook the Glock at Joe, who was laughing freely now. Boz's eyes were wild.

"You know what they called her in high school?" Joe managed to gasp out between laughs. "Sonya!" He laughed more wildly. "Sonya—" He doubled his body down as far as the bonds would permit, presumably incapable of restraining his hysteria. "—Sonya Bitchacockoff! She bit a guy!"

Boz looked down at Helen, aghast. "You what?"

"She bit his goddamn cock off!" Joe shouted, laughing. He was so infused with mad hilarity that he couldn't speak, or even stand. He was leaning forward, bobbing in spasms of glee. The other two men looked on in horror. "And you . . . you damn near stuck your dick into a meat grinder! You fuckin' idiot!"

"Joe!" Helen snarled, turning on him, as if enraged at his betrayal.

Boz stared at her, his mouth open. He was drooling, but he didn't know it. He had almost . . . sure, her head would have been blown away, but his dick. . . . He could not conceive the wickedness of some people!

Joe suddenly writhed far to his right, pivoting like a bullfighter so that his left knee touched the floor, and he shot Boz from behind his back. The bullet appeared to strike him in the right side.

Boz uttered a shocked grunt, and the Glock clattered to the floor as he clutched his side. His mouth was open and his eyes wide in surprise. Helen pounced on the automatic and rolled away. Joe fired again but didn't hit anything. The noise was great. The first blast had been so stunning that none of them had really registered it. This one they heard.

Boz lurched away, crashed through the kitchen door, and tumbled down the steps. They could hear him get up and stumble off, roaring with pain and rage.

Helen started after him, but Joe shouted at her. "Helen! Get me free! The knife!"

She snatched up the knife from the counter and raced to him. She started to slash at the tape, but Joe said, "Calm down. Calm down. I don't want my wrists slashed, for God's sake!"

Boz had gotten the Dodge Ram started. By the time Joe ran outside the truck was careening down the drive and then onto the road, racing away. Joe had the fleeting, remorseful thought that he'd left the keys in the ignition. He scrambled around to the Durango, but the keys weren't in it. Helen had them, of course. He ran in to get them. She had freed the other two.

"The keys!" Joe yelled at her. She fumbled in the pocket of her jeans and tossed them to him. By the time they got to the gate they realized that it was probably hopeless. The big Dodge had left the gate in a tangled mess. Their only chance was if the drunk had an accident. They drove on.

"Damn you, Joe," Helen was saying. "Why'd you have to hit on that old story?" But then she laughed, almost hysterical now with relief. Joe laughed too.

But when they reached the town and still hadn't caught up with Boz, they were more sober. They could go on, of course, except that it wasn't clear which way he might have gone. Helena? Or Butte? Or had they, somehow, missed him? It seemed impossible, but they didn't feel they could take the chance with Frank and Paulie still back at the house. If Boz had tricked them, somehow. . . . They turned and drove back.

Helen was talking excitedly, relieved. "What a shot!" she said. "An impossible shot!" She hugged him and kissed his cheek.

"What? You think I haven't practiced that shot?" Joe said. "I used to practice with handcuffs on. Not with a pole at my back, though."

"Oh, come on," she protested.

"A man's got to be ready," Joe insisted. "It's too late to practice when the deal is going down. You remember I used to go out shooting left-handed? It's all part of being ready."

"What is it about men?" she said, folding her arms. "They're all heroes. In their minds."

Joe rolled down the window. He was bathed in sweat, he realized. The cold air felt great. He drove more carefully now. Not far away he could hear an owl hooting repeatedly.

Jammie

Agent Dinah Schwind was looking at a file, actually a printout of a computerized file, from the Immigration and Naturalization Service. The file had been obtained in the usual way, except that the INS had no record of it having been requested by Special Agent Tucker, Vernon. He was sitting across the table from Schwind while she looked through it, in a newly opened restaurant on Telegraph Road, in a northern suburb of Detroit.

Ms. Schwind was an athletic woman in a business costume of blue suit jacket and blue skirt. The colonel was intrigued that Dinah looked more attractive than formerly. She had a square face with a square jaw, not very full lips, but seemingly fuller these days. She had done something about the faint shadow of pale facial hair that she didn't used to be concerned about. Her hair was still short, but now it was more blond than brown. The short cut revealed tiny diamond studs in her neat little earlobes. The colonel wondered if she had a boyfriend. She was one of the charter members of the Lucani.

"Quite a nasty boy," Dinah said, looking up. "Not so little anymore. Harold Hartsfeld, a.k.a Barry Barsouk, later Bozi 'Boz' Bazok. Age"—she leafed back, found the page—"approximately twenty-five. Last seen in Belgrade . . . possibly the same individual who entered the United States two weeks ago, using a stolen passport registered to a Swedish businessman named Ake—"

"The name doesn't matter," the colonel interrupted. "Handsome Harry, busy Barry, boisterous Boz, nickname 'Badger.' It's the same guy. He's back. Bozi Bazok is the object of some interest to the INS, also to the FBI, but especially, the international tribunal on war criminals in the former Yugoslavia, in The Hague. He's come a long way, our Harry."

Dinah riffled the pages. She glanced at them but she had already absorbed the useful information. Harry was an orphan, adopted by an American aid worker named Thelma Hartsfeld, now deceased. Somehow, this never-married woman had managed to assert her will over obdurate bureaucracies of various foreign and American agencies to become the mother of a child thought to be eight years old that she'd found on the streets of Salonika. She had raised the child in Atlanta. He did well in school, seemed a good boy. Unfortunately, Thelma had died when he reached twelve. Evidently, whatever disease that had taken Thelma at the relatively young age of forty had struck her very suddenly and swiftly, and she had been unable to formally provide for the boy.

Distant relatives of hers, in Texas, had intervened. Harry's further upbringing had been taken over by them, but they hadn't done a very good job of it, apparently. There was a suggestion in the file of abuse, neglect, misuse of his mother's estate, and alienation. He had attended a private school in San Antonio for a while, had not done very well there, he'd had some minor scrapes with authorities, and then had run away. According to this file, his name had popped up on police blotters in California, Montana, Wyoming, Illinois, and Michigan. Vandalism, delinquincy, minor alcohol and narcotics violations . . . nothing requiring more than a few weeks of incarceration and desultory attempts at reform.

At some point, he had taken the name Barry Barsouk and had even obtained a social security number. No known record of employment, though. Vagrancy charges, then some harder raps, like possession of firearms and a minor assault or two, again with only a few weeks of incarceration and suspended sentences.

Thought to be a "runner" for known narcotics dealers in Chicago, later on. Left the country and reappeared on Interpol lists in Italy, then Bosnia, and finally Belgrade. A notation of "dangerous" was attached to some later files. Should be approached with caution, thought to be habitually armed. Known associate of narcotics dealers.

And then a member of a paramilitary group in Serbia. Thought to have murdered no less than fifty individuals. Dinah Schwind was a hardened agent in the war against crime. She had seen a lot of horrendous behavior. But this was a stunner.

"What's our interest?" she asked, in her best blasé style. By "our," she meant the Lucani, and the colonel understood it as such.

"I believe he may be in Montana," the colonel said.

"That's where Joe is," Dinah said. "Didn't he and what's-her-name go off in the sunset, to stay out of trouble until we figure out what to do about him?"

"You mean Helen," the colonel said. They fell silent as the waiter brought dessert menus. Nothing looked particularly interesting, unless one were a devotee of crème brûlée. They ordered coffee. "Actually, I asked Joe to look into a few things for us, just to keep him busy," the colonel resumed, when the coffee had been brought. He looked, possibly, a little uneasy. "Nothing serious," he assured Dinah.

He explained the Franko affair, some of which she already knew. Joe and Helen's task, he said, was merely to inquire about the background of this mysterious Franko.

"Joe *and* Helen," Dinah said, surprised. "What's *her* involvement? She doesn't know about the Lucani?"

"Under the circumstances," the colonel said, "I couldn't very well keep her totally in the dark. I told her that she and Joe would be operating on the behalf of a sub-rosa governmental agency—well, a *quasi*-governmental agency. I had to assume, as a matter of caution, that Joe had probably told her something about his new employment. I'm confident that it's not a problem."

He didn't look that confident, Dinah thought. The problem really lay with the rest of the Lucani. There was no way Helen should have been brought in without discussion with the group. Or had there been some discussion, to which she had not been privy? She asked if the others had been consulted.

"Not as a group," the colonel said blandly. "I broached the possibility to a couple of them, Bernie and Edna. The others weren't available. They didn't see any problem with Helen." He watched her carefully, sipping his coffee, to see how she took this.

Dinah was a professional. She was good at concealing her feelings. She asked, "When we talk about 'others,' how many and who are we talking about? To me, it's just us and Bernie and Edna and Dex, now that Pollak's . . . missing."

"Pollak's dead," the colonel said, bluntly. "Joe killed him. I thought you had figured that out."

Dinah had been leaning toward that hypothesis, but to her knowledge no one had actually said as much. "Did he admit it?" she asked.

"No. But it's obvious. Pollak doubtless overreacted at the scene, with DiEbola, and Joe had to do what he had to do. I blame myself. I wasn't as concise in my instructions—my advice—to Pollak as he required. He read too much into it. It was my fault. I can't blame Joe."

My God, Dinah thought. What have we become? "What are we going to do? That is, what should we do?" She realized that she had slipped into the habit of thinking of the colonel as the chief, the unquestioned leader. This was what had gotten them to this state, she thought.

"I've managed to cover up Pollak's disappearance," the colonel said. "I had to call in a few favors. It appears that he went off on some quite unrelated wild goose chase, another case entirely, with which none of us are associated—in Central America, actually. What happened to him there, well, we don't know. He was seen by a couple of agents, at a distance. Presumably, he was meeting some known gunrunners, in Belize, or nearby. Such a hothead, Pollak, a loose cannon."

Dinah digested this. It couldn't really be washed down by coffee. She'd have to sort it out later. "How many are we?" she asked again.

"Dinah," the colonel said, quietly, "don't get alarmed. 'We' are just who we've always been. But the group, by its nature, is fluid, to a degree. We all know at least a half dozen others whom we've wondered about, considered for inclusion, vetted, as it were. For all we know, there may be several other groups just like ours, informal 'posses,' as the kids might say. We are who we are. I've always considered a few others as sort of peripheral adjuncts, so to speak. It's a collegial kind of thing." He mentioned a few names that had come up in discussion in the past, particularly Jamala Sanders, a candidate that Dinah had herself proposed.

"Well, Jammie . . . sure," Dinah said.

"Jammie is invited, it's my pleasure to inform you," the colonel said. "All the others have agreed. I polled them. That's one of the things I wanted to talk to you about, today. You should meet with her and 'bring her in.' If your schedule permits, I could arrange it this afternoon. I think you could meet her in Cincinnati, tomorrow. Would that work?"

Dinah was happy about this. She saw Jamala as an ally. But now she had some misgivings about involving her in the group. It no longer sounded like quite the tightly knit band of like-minded pals that it had once seemed to be.

"It's this thing with Joe that I'm concerned about," the colonel said. "If our Harry turns up in Butte, it could complicate things. The question in my mind is, should you go out there to deal with it, brief Joe, et cetera, or mightn't this be a good opportunity for Jammie to get her feet wet? What's your feeling? I know you have a certain . . . rapprochement . . . with Joe. I'd like to advise you against any proprietary feelings, however."

"I have no 'proprietary feelings' toward Joe," she said, briskly brushing aside the implication of a special relationship. Immediately, however, she felt regret. The prospect of seeing Joe, even with Helen lurking about had momentarily lifted her spirits. But she saw that it was impossible. Had the colonel maneuvered her into this? It would have to be Jammie.

"But I'm not sure why Harry is a problem for Joe," she said.

The colonel explained that there was reason to believe that one of Harry's victims, in Kosovo, had been Franko. Possibly Theo Ostropaki, as well. The speculation was that Harry might have coerced some information out of Franko, the nature of which they could not know at present, but which had driven him to go to Montana, to Butte, in fact.

"Here's what you have to do," he said. "Bring in Jamala, sound her out on her schedule, her feelings about an assignment, and if it looks propitious, have her look in on Butte. The thing to keep uppermost in your mind is that this Harry is not just dangerous—the record shows that, heaven knows—but he's running from an international tribunal. So he's like a wounded bear. Doubly dangerous. To say nothing of the fact that he could be leading other investigators into our sphere."

* * *

"**W**e may have a problem," said Dinah. She was talking to Jammie at the airport in Cincinnati. They were old friends, had been at the CIA's training program together, years ago. Between them, they had worked for or with a veritable alphabet of federal investigative agencies and bureaus, sometimes as partners or associates. Presently, Dinah was temporarily attached to Immigration and Naturalization Service, and Jammie was with the Secret Service, assigned to counterfeit-money investigations.

They were sitting in the main concourse, chatting across a table, in one of those islands of padded chairs for the weary travelers. They appeared to be two travelers who were not known to one another, passing the time of day until the next flight. Dinah looked athletic in a stretch pants suit and a fleece jacket. She had a kind of clean, square-jawed, all-American, white-bread look.

Jammie was not so ordinary looking. One had to examine closely that pale, lightly freckled complexion, the slightly broadened but still aquiline nose, the darkish full lips, and the hair that was either curly or frizzy or kinky, to decide if she was African-American or Mediterranean, possibly Semitic. Her brownish-red hair was pulled back and secured with a colorful elastic band so that the bulk of it formed a buoyant ball at the nape of her neck. She wore ordinary, drugstore dark glasses, presently propped in her hair; neat tapered gray flannel slacks; a dark green blazer; and expensive leather walking shoes.

At first glance, one might think her a secretary, a business-woman, the director of a service agency, perhaps. They both were surrounded with purses, briefcases, laptop computer cases—the usual paraphernalia of traveling businesswomen. They both had large paper containers of the ubiquitous latte confections available especially in Seattle but now spreading across the country, particularly in airports. Jammie had flown here from Europe to meet Dinah,

who had flown in from Detroit. This was an excellent place to talk
very privately, with crowds surging past, oblivious, constantly changing. The only better place might have been in a rental car, but
neither was staying in Cincinnati; both would be catching flights
in different directions within a couple of hours.

Dinah had just concluded her pitch to Jammie about the
Lucani, a name that she hadn't used yet, however. Jammie's interesting reply had been, "I was wondering if you were ever going to
ask me in."

Their intense conversation soon revealed that while Jammie
didn't know anything at all about the Lucani, per se, she knew about
it, or about similar groups. She was eager to be accepted, that was
clear. She quite approved of their purpose. And she was happy to
hear about the colonel, whom she knew quite well.

Dinah could not shed her misgivings. She felt honor bound
to voice them to her friend. She said she was wondering lately if
the group wasn't becoming too dangerous an association.

"Any group like this is dangerous from the git," Jammie said.
"What's new?"

"It might not be the best time for getting involved," Dinah
said. "Things seem more *fluid*." This was the colonel's usage. "It
won't be so easy to distance yourself, if it is discovered."

Jammie wondered aloud if it was ever possible to detach one-
self, once one was admitted to such a group. "Where you gonna go?
Where you gonna hide? If they tumble to us, it'll be because one of
us blew the whistle. We'll all be fingered. Unless . . ."

It wasn't necessary to finish the thought. One could eliminate
the Judas, if one could determine that there was one and who it was.

"You don't think, then, that we could be discovered otherwise?" Dinah asked.

Jammie doubted it. "There might be suspicions of some kind
of extralegal or out-of-school collaboration," she opined, "but that

wouldn't necessarily lead anywhere. The brass has to assume that the grunts are always up to these kind of tricks, anyway, no matter how they try to discourage it. Every posse's got circles within circles. Well, look at the two of us . . . that's what we're doing, isn't it? I mean you and me, within your—our—group. The colonel probably has his own confidants, I guess. . . . You aren't sleeping with him, are you?"

Dinah laughed. "No. He's never even patted my butt. Are you?"

"Maybe he's gay," Jammie said. "He's never even winked at me. You might be more his type. I always thought you were his protégé."

"My God! You think?" The thought had never occurred to Dinah. "If it's anybody, it would have to be Edna. Seems like they work together a lot."

"Edna? Edna Payne? She's in? I knew she was in INS. . . . Isn't she kind of . . . cold?"

"Edna's nice," Dinah protested. "I mean, I never really *talked* to her, you know? Maybe she is a little cold."

"Maybe Tucker likes that," Jammie said. "Some men, they go for the icy type. You know, this guy is starting to be like one of those dentists, got a whole harem running around the office. That why I'm coming aboard?" She shook her head in wonder.

Dinah laughed. "It's nothing like that," she said.

"Forget Tucker," Jammie said. "Who *are* you sleeping with?"

Dinah told her about Joe Service. Jammie had been working in Europe for months and hadn't seen Dinah to gossip. No, Dinah swore, she hadn't actually made love with Joe, although it had been a near thing at her apartment, in Chicago, a few months back.

"You were actually naked? Both of you, in a bed?" Jammie said, feigning shock. "And you didn't knock the dude over? Honey, was the man alive? I mean, was he functioning? 'Cause, otherwise I can't imagine *you* not having your way."

Oh, no, Dinah assured her, Joe was functioning, all right. She declined to describe his equipment, except to say that it looked more than adequate for the purpose. A minor digression ensued, about the unfunctionality of so many men, some offhanded discourse on preferences in that area, before they returned to the chief topic.

Dinah gave her a succinct briefing of the situation with Joe, his recruitment. Jammie was concerned to hear about Joe's integration into the group and, especially, the absorption of his friend Helen. She judiciously passed over the obvious: Joe's unwillingness to sexually engage with Dinah because he already had a preferred partner. The more serious problem was what the presence of Joe and Helen meant to the group.

"I'm beginning to see what you meant about 'fluid,'" Jammie said. "But don't feel bad about asking me in. Anyway, it's too late now. I'm in."

She went on: "I can see the usefulness of someone like Joe. But it's so dangerous! We're really at his mercy. Didn't the others object? Have you discussed it with them?"

Dinah explained that there had been a formal meeting, with a quorum of members present. The objections voiced by Jammie were raised and dealt with. The feeling was that Joe was so utterly dependent on their good offices that no overriding reasons to betray them could be envisioned. The consequences to him would be disastrous, no matter what happened to the group.

The affiliation of Helen, however, was another matter, Dinah felt. The group hadn't had the opportunity to interview Helen, nor had there been an occasion to debate the issue with them, unlike the case with Jammie. As Dinah saw it, they had no adequate sanctions on Helen. What if, for instance, Helen had a falling out with Joe? Who knew what might result? Was she even stable?

Jammie listened carefully, watching Dinah. "You hate her ass, don't you?" she said.

"I don't hate her," Dinah protested. "I hardly know her. I talked it over with the colonel, but I didn't have a chance to discuss it with the others. The colonel is confident about her. He says she's smart, she's totally attached to Joe, she's very level-headed, can be very useful to Joe and to us—"

"But you don't trust her," Jammie said. "I don't blame you. I wouldn't trust the bitch if she wore a lead chastity belt under a brick apron. Well, why'd the Old Man take her on? He got the hots? Is this another recruit for the harem?"

No, that was impossible, Dinah said, brushing the thought away. But it was disturbing that the colonel had maneuvered around them this way. He had committed them to this woman *before* he'd discussed it with them. Apparently, he felt very strongly that they needed Helen's assistance, that Joe would be able to control her, that there was no danger. It was quite unsettling. She went on to describe the Pollak incident and the Kosovo affair.

Jammie was keenly interested. After Dinah had finished, Jammie went off to fetch them refills of their latte grandes while Dinah kept watch over their stuff. When Jammie returned she said, "Pollak doesn't faze me too much. I worked with that bastard in Colombia. I'm surprised that he was a member. To tell you the truth, Dinah, the fact that you guys thought he was all right makes me a little nervous. Not to sound like a ho, but that dude was a bad john. This Kosovo thing, though, that's another matter. This Franko deal sounds like found candy. So the guy drops out—so what? It was good while it lasted."

"The problem is Theo Ostropaki. Remember him? It seems the colonel might have approached *him* about the group."

Jammie said she vaguely recalled Ostropaki. She didn't know him, hadn't met him, but knew about him and had heard something about his success in the Balkans. She hadn't heard anything about

Ostropaki's disappearance, except that he'd run afoul of some gang
in Serbia.

"Whew," she said. "You're right, this outfit is a little spooky.
No wonder you're upset. Who else has the colonel decided, on his
own, to invite? Maybe we should start thinking about the colonel's
stability, about retiring *him.*"

"Exactly," Dinah said. "You know, at first we were all on the
same page, but over time we kind of delegated de facto leadership
to the colonel. He seemed better placed to coordinate things, he
was older . . ."

"I hear you," Jammie said. "So, what are you thinking? Maybe
getting the others together, without the colonel, and discussing it?
I mean, it's everybody's ass. You know that. We got a right—and a
responsibility—to get this straightened out."

Dinah didn't think that would do. Eventually that might become necessary, she thought, but not yet. It was enough for now to
take a closer look at the Joe and Helen situation, as well as the Franko
business. There was yet another complication: the colonel anticipated other pursuers of Franko, in Butte. She told Jammie all she
knew about Harry.

She reiterated the colonel's briefing and analysis. One point
had struck her, she said: if Franko could attract the attentions of
Harry, mightn't others be interested, as well? The possibilities
seemed to be: one or more of the agencies were growing suspicious
and had initiated an investigation of the Kosovo connection; or the
Ostropaki disappearance was connected to the Franko disappearance, and whoever had engineered the one could be pursuing the
other—and it might not be Harry; and finally, there might be some
wholly unrelated reason for unknown persons to pursue Franko. As
far as the colonel had been able to discover, the Kosovo connection was a dead issue, a closed case. But now that they were in the

game—had put Joe and Helen on the case—any other searcher for Franko had to be dealt with.

The colonel had come up with one additional possibility: the international war crimes tribunal had stumbled on Bazok—Harry's *nom de guerre*—who was an American citizen. They might have connected him with the disappearance of Franko—another American citizen. There were elements in the tribunal not particularly pro-American. They might have someone investigating Franko as a connection to Bazok, or at least for someone who could provide evidence against him if he resurfaced. Any involvement of Americans in the tribunal's field of inquiry could be highly political.

Jammie found that plausible, even probable. She also saw where this was leading. "You want me to go to Butte?" She thought for a moment, then said it could be done. She had just finished the report on her counterfeit case—"Honey, you wouldn't believe it—they're color-xeroxing money and passing it! Stupid, but they succeed enough to make a dent." She could cut out some time to get to Butte, possibly by tomorrow.

"And don't worry, honey," she told Dinah, "I'll be checking out the frame on that Helen bitch."

Kibosh

Joe was enumerating the tasks at hand. One, they had to find out where Boz had gone. Two, they had to remove his rental vehicle from the ditch and stash it somewhere. And three, they had to figure out some way to explain all this to Colonel Tucker without exposing Paulie. This also meant finding the stolen Dodge Ram and keeping that out of the cops' purview. The gate would have to be fixed, of course, and they'd have to keep a standing guard, a watch.

Some of these things could wait until tomorrow, had to wait, in fact. But others needed doing now, tonight. They were all tired, not to say exhausted, but they couldn't rest. Well, Frank could rest. He had suffered the most. Boz had targeted him for abuse, perhaps as an object lesson for Helen and Paulie, to ensure their cooperation. Joe was surprised, in fact, that Boz hadn't simply shot him out of hand, but perhaps he'd felt that he needed him to operate the security system, at least until Joe got back and was taken care of.

The others wanted to discuss these matters, and Joe wasn't opposed to that, in a way, but certain things needed to be done. Now. A watch, for instance. They were sitting in here in a lighted house in a vast, unlighted near wilderness, totally exposed to Boz if he was out there. And he was out there, somewhere. He might not be close, but who knew?

"It'll be more complicated if he gets picked up," Joe pointed out. "He's drunk, driving a stolen vehicle—or at least one that he can't demonstrate ownership for. He's shot. He's also an accomplished liar—hell, he convinced Frank that he was just a lost partygoer, and he'd killed two of Frank's dogs! He got Frank to help him get some booze, and even return here to 'sleep it off.' The guy's a menace, but a survivor, and he has charm. I know," he said, "he didn't seem all that charming at the end, but that's how he got us to that point."

What he didn't voice, but knew he would have to discuss with Helen, was why he and she had to stick around. They could call in the colonel right now and presumably get some help, wrap up their involvement. But the fact was, Joe had fallen in love with the idea of hiding Paulie and establishing himself in this ideal mountain lair. Helen, he knew, wasn't going to be too excited about all this, but he thought he could convince her if he had a chance.

"I think we should call in the colonel now," Helen said. So there went Joe's chance.

"Call the sheriff" was Paulie's opinion.

To Joe's relief, Frank vetoed that idea. Frank was not feeling very chipper, but he didn't relish the idea of the sheriff and, unquestionably, a posse of DEA agents being invited into his marijuana plantation.

"The colonel can deal with that," Helen said. "Hell, he's DEA himself."

Joe winced. That wasn't information he wanted to discuss with Frank and Paulie. Frank wasn't privy to the notion that Joe and Helen were involved with a federal authority. He looked shocked. He'd assumed that this whole thing with Boz had been strictly about Paulie. But now they had to take valuable time to bring him up to speed. In the meantime, as Joe pointed out, Boz was still out there.

Maybe there was too much to do. Maybe Helen was right: the situation had escalated beyond their ability to deal with it. A crazed killer was on the loose out there—a menace to society. He had to be dealt with. Maybe . . . but no.

"We can deal with this," Joe said forcefully. He looked at them, gathered in the kitchen, at the scene of a near disaster. The butcher knife, for instance, still lay on the counter. There was blood on the floor. Joe could see that Paulie was with him, and Helen would go along. Frank? Frank didn't want the cops in.

"We've got to get that gate back in place," Joe said. "Get the dogs out, to help patrol. Then we've got to figure out where Bazok went, where the truck is. Okay? Well, let's get going. We can discuss some of these problems while we work."

Joe felt they had adequate arms, for now. He had five handguns, counting Boz's Glock, for which he had 9mm ammo that would work. Frank had a .30-06 deer rifle and a 12-gauge shotgun, a Remington pump. Paulie had his .410 popgun. Later, if he had time, Joe could run down to his old place, where he had a veritable armory stashed, including AK-47s. For now he put Paulie up on the ridge to watch, with the dogs, while he and Frank tried to get the gate functioning. Helen could stay in the house and monitor the system, act as a command post. They could communicate using the cell phones.

The gate was a mess, but with some hammers and crowbars they managed to get it remounted and working within an hour. Fortunately, the electronics had not been trashed.

"Who comes up this road?" Joe asked Frank. Helen had made coffee and brought it down to them with some sandwiches. They sat in the truck and ate. "The mailman? UPS? FedEx?"

"No, I get my mail in Forkee," Frank said. "UPS and FedEx know to call me first. I run in to Butte to pick up. Nobody lives out here. Fishermen come in, but not this time of year. Maybe a hunter. The thing is, more people come around than you expect—just looking, bird-watching, or lost. We get kids who drive out here and park, to screw, or have a party."

"We better get Boz's car out of that ditch then," Joe said. "Someone will spot it and call the sheriff, for sure. I want to take a look at it, anyway."

It took the four of them the better part of an hour to drag the white Ford Taurus up out of the ditch, using a chain and the four-wheel-drive power of the Durango. When they got it up, finally, with Helen at the wheel of the Durango and the others pushing, it was a great disappointment to find that while it started all right, the right front wheel was badly damaged, the steering gear smashed. It couldn't be driven. Frank figured out that with the aid of his tractor, which had a front loader for picking up hay bales or scooping up gravel and the like, he could hoist the front end of the car onto the back of his old pickup. They drove slowly back to the house and maneuvered the vehicle into Frank's barn, out back.

Joe could find nothing in the vehicle except for the paperwork in the glove compartment, which said it had been rented to one Harry Hart, of Atlanta, Georgia. Joe took that and stacked hay bales around the car to further hide its presence. Then he went into the house.

Paulie and Frank had gone to bed. Joe was not sleepy. He was excited. Frank had described his security system in greater detail to Helen before retiring. She explained that Frank's fence was electronically sensitive for all of its extensive perimeter. Already tonight Frank had shown her the electronic signature of a deer leaping the fence. They were fairly secure, for now. A careful and measured attempt to breach it could be accomplished, especially in some of the more distant reaches, where it was little more than a single wire strung over rocky outcroppings. And there were approaches from the backcountry, where no wire could be strung. But you would have to be more thorough and careful than Boz to find those places.

"I don't think there's much to worry about tonight," Joe said, "if the nut has found someplace to crash. Pardon the expression," he said with a snort. "He'll be wanting to sleep, that's for sure. But we don't know how badly wounded he was. If he's not too bad off he'll go back to his motel, or whatever, and rest. With any luck, the bastard will die in his sleep. That'll be a problem if the truck is connected to him, and then to Frank. But we should be so lucky."

"If I knew where he was, I'd kill him myself," Helen said. She was serious. Joe knew that she was capable of doing it. "Joe, why are we fooling around with this? Let's call the colonel."

Joe explained why that wasn't such a great idea. He filled her in on what Paulie had told him about Kosovo, about the cave. "I don't know what the colonel really wants here," he said, "but my gut tells me that Paulie won't come out of it whole. I'm not just thinking about Paulie. The potential for us is great here, if we can only hold it together for a few days. I'm not ready to give up on it. But we've got to locate this bastard and get to the bottom of this."

They discussed it further, in more detail, but he could see that she was about out of it. He convinced her to go to bed. He would stand guard until daylight. He found a warm jacket and went out to patrol above the house, on the ridge.

Well before daylight, Paulie came out, bringing coffee. "I can't tell you how grateful I am," he told Joe. "If it hadn't been for you, we'd all be dead. I owe you an explanation."

Joe let him go at it. The whole story of Ostropaki and Boz came out. Paulie was glad to unburden himself, at last. In the end, he opined that Boz was driven by at least two factors: he thought

Paulie might have more "goods"—he had demanded as much, in the time before Joe had gotten back from Basin. But there was something else. Paulie had figured out that Boz knew that Paulie could finger him for the cave massacre, to the war crimes tribunal. The people he worked with in Serbia had probably made it clear to Boz that he had to get rid of this witness. Paulie endangered them all.

Joe wasn't so happy to hear this angle. It meant, if he judged Paulie right, that Paulie would be going back, cooperating with the tribunal. That could have a big effect on Joe's plans. The press would be interested in what Paulie had been doing in Butte, where he'd holed up, and so on. Beyond that, he wasn't sure what the colonel's take on it would be. Maybe, he thought again, Helen was right: it was time to bail. But no . . . it was too soon for that. First things first. Find the man.

Joe probed Paulie carefully. "I understand what you want to do," he told him.

"What I have to do," Paulie corrected him. "I should have come forward before, but . . . I wasn't ready. Now, I have to do it. For all of them, especially for Fedima."

"You don't even know what happened to Fedima," Joe pointed out. "When we get Boz we can find out that much. For all you know, she's still alive somewhere. A guy like that, he could have sold her into slavery. This might be her one chance to be liberated, you don't know. Once we learn that, we can figure out what to do next. You'll go back, don't worry. I'll see to it. But we have to work out the best way to do it."

Joe was already thinking of a plan. Maybe Paulie's Butte background could be kept quiet. He could be provided with another history, possibly. It wasn't relevant to the tribunal. Only his activities in Kosovo meant something to them. The colonel could help there, and he'd be eager to do so, Joe felt. But first things first. He got Paulie's agreement to keep this confidential, for now at least.

This government work was dicey, Joe thought. But interesting.

When dawn came, Joe and Paulie went in to find that Helen and Frank were up, looking rather awful but at least a little more rested. Joe got them fed. There was no television in the house, Joe learned, but there was a radio. He was eager to find out if the news had gotten on to Boz, for any reason. But there was nothing about him. The sensation of the day was a double murder in Butte, overnight. A man and his wife. The police were not releasing names, yet, "until they'd notified family."

Within a half hour there was a new crisis. An uncle of Frank's called. Had he heard? Gary and Selma had been murdered by a burglar. The sheriff wanted to interview anyone from the family. Funeral arrangements were being made. Frank and Paulie would have to come in and be interviewed. The officer the uncle had talked to was Jacky LeBruyn. Frank remembered Jacky, didn't he? Jacky wanted to talk to him. The uncle had told Jacky that he'd get hold of Frank—he knew Frank wouldn't want a bunch of cops knocking on his door.

"You've got to go in," Joe told Frank when the uncle rang off. "You don't want the cops out here. Paulie will go with you." The question was, What would they say? It was immediately apparent to both men that their uncle and aunt could have been the source of Boz's information about where to find "Franko."

Frank seemed dazed. "I don't know, man," he said, running his hands through his hair ceaselessly, tugging at his unruly beard. "What'm I gonna say? They'll see my face. What'll I tell them, man?"

Helen started to go to him, to comfort him, but Joe shook his head to warn her off. Joe leaned against the counter and let the man ramble in near panic for a moment or two. Then he said, calmly, "Well, you'll just have to belt up, Frank, and do what you think is right."

Frank stopped pacing and stared at Joe. So did the others. Joe hadn't spoken unkindly, but with confidence.

"But what *is* right?" Frank asked.

"You'll figure it out, Frank. You always do. I'm sorry about your aunt and your uncle, but for all you know this has nothing to do with Boz. If the cops thought it did, if they suspected anything, they'd have been out here by now, don't you think? I imagine they've been looking for an excuse to visit you for some time, anyway."

Frank thought about that and nodded. He seemed a little calmer. "Me and Paulie will have to go in, the sooner the better, I guess. I could always tell them I fell, digging a trench, or something, and banged up my head."

"That's right," Joe encouraged him, "and Paulie helped you fix it up. You could even tell them you wanted to run over to the doctor's office, or the hospital, to get it properly looked at."

"Yeah, that's good," Frank said. Paulie agreed. It would probably relieve Frank of any serious grilling, if any such thing were contemplated by the cops.

Not likely, Joe thought, but didn't say so.

"You ought to clean up, look your best," Helen suggested. "I could trim your hair and your beard." That offer was gratefully received.

While they were gone, Joe counseled Paulie. "Remember, you and Frank don't know anything about Boz. There was no mention of a suspect on the radio, or from your uncle. Just tell them what you know, which is nothing. Frank had an accident. You're his witness, and he's yours. You were both out here, all night—hell, you've both been holed up here for weeks. It's nothing. Don't panic. In the meantime, Helen and I will get after Boz."

"But what if the cops find him?" Paulie said. He seemed calm. "What if they find the truck? Frank's truck?"

"If Boz was involved in that killing," Joe said, "he had to be driving the rental car. If they're on to that, they're not on to a man driving a pickup truck. If, somehow, they're looking for Boz and they find him and connect that truck to him, well you didn't even know it was missing. You'll know if they ask about the truck. Tell them that, as far as you know, it's still parked down by the gate, where Frank was doing some work. But that's all just speculation."

Joe could see that Paul was looking a little worried now; he was imagining complications. He hastened to cut them off.

"The cops don't know anything about Boz, even if they have him in the tank. He's not the kind to cooperate with them. He won't be talking. I know his kind. He's seen the inside of jails before. He'll have a lawyer in no time. But why speculate? I'd be very surprised if they have any idea who killed those people. It's much too early. All you and Frank have to remember—and be sure to discuss this with him on your way into town—is that, in truth, you don't know anything about the murder of your aunt and uncle. You can't really help them. You're bereaved. Frank needs some medical care. This other thing, your missing truck, that's your private business. Right now, your main concern is with your family."

Helen had done a job on Frank. He didn't look so bad, after all. His hair and beard trimmed and combed, an insignificant patch on his forehead, a little makeup to disguise some bruises and the hint of a black eye, clean clothes and regular shoes—the medical story might not even be necessary. His nose was sore but not broken, after all. And he seemed in much better spirits, which Joe attributed to the tender care and attention of Helen.

When they had gone, Joe talked it over with Helen. "We've got a few hours," he said. "After that . . . who knows? It depends on the cops, and Boz. But we've got to find him. It could get complicated for Frank and Paulie," he conceded, "but they're in no danger from the police. They don't know anything about what happened with their aunt and uncle. If they keep their mouths shut about Boz, they'll probably be all right."

"What do you think happened?" Helen said. She was not so sanguine.

"Boz killed them," Joe said. "But they're dead. So are a bunch of other people. Time to find Boz."

The first thing they did, after they left Frank's, was to cruise the parking lots of both motels in Basin, just in case. The truck wasn't there. They checked other motels as they drove into Butte, with no success. Joe hadn't expected to find Boz that way, but it was worth doing.

"The smartest thing for Boz," Joe said, "would be to simply drive off on one of these back roads and take a snooze. But we don't know how bad that gunshot wound was. It may have been nothing, just a graze, but he could be in a bad way, in pain, in shock from loss of blood. He could have panicked and gone to a hospital, more likely in Helena than Butte. But I doubt it."

"If he was really smart," Helen said, "he'd be driving somewhere out in Idaho, or Washington, by now."

"Do you think?" Joe said.

"No," she said. "I'm thinking he probably didn't have much money on him, and he was unarmed. He's going to want a gun and some money. He probably left both with his gear in a motel, in Butte. He'll want to recover that, even though he probably doesn't want to go near Butte. I'm assuming, like you, that he killed those people. Even if there's no gun or money there, there's always something incriminating."

Joe agreed. Beyond that, he reckoned that Boz would feel that he had to accomplish what had brought him here in the first place. He would not go too far from Frank's, or not for long.

"If you think that," Helen said, "why are we going to town? Why don't we just lie up and wait for him to come to us?"

"We've got some time," Joe said. "He won't be back before night. The wound is the unknown factor. But we've got a chance to find him first."

"How do we do that? Check every motel in a fifty-mile radius?"

"No, I've got some contacts in town," Joe said. "And you can attend to some other business."

"Like what?"

"Find this Fedima," Joe said.

Helen was taken aback. "How do I do that? Through the colonel?"

Oh no, Joe cautioned her. They had to keep the colonel in the dark, for now at least. But it was true, they had to report in. He might have some information that would be helpful. As for Fedima, he thought it might be time for Helen to call her late father's faithful lieutenant, Roman Yakovich. He was now retired and living in Miami. He'd been helpful to Joe in the past, and he was devoted to Helen.

Helen couldn't see what use Roman would be.

"Roman's a very resourceful guy," Joe said. "Once he gets on to something, he carries through until he's satisfied. He'll know something about Balkan refugees, or know someone who knows."

Boz fought sleep. He fought waking. His mind wanted neither. But another program decided that sleep was no longer an option. So Boz woke up. He opened his eyes, tried to focus. It was dark. He could hardly make any sense of where he was. His first impression was jail. A dungeon, in fact.

He sat up, too fast. He groaned. His head hurt. He swore, a long, rambling curse that took in gods, alcoholic beverages, his mother, and, finally, fate. He held his head for a moment and then looked about him.

He *was* in a dungeon, he thought. Walls of stone, a low ceiling, rough support timbers. "Where the fuck am I?" he said aloud, but not to anyone but himself.

Nonetheless, a voice answered: "Seven Dials, pardner. Remember?"

Boz looked around. He was lying on a pallet of sorts on the ground, a kind of rough mattress stuffed with something not very soft, corn shucks maybe. Nearby was a table, on which there was an indescribable jumble of pans, plates, newspaper, books, a radio, and a table lamp made out of an old Jim Beam bottle, the liter size, with a scorched shade. There were a couple of wooden kitchen chairs arranged about the table, and on one of them sat an old man.

"Who are you?" Boz said. He was rapidly regaining his native wariness. He felt weak, anxious, a little sick to his stomach, and he had a fierce headache. Worse, he realized now, he had a terrific pain in his right side. He felt it pull and stab at him, and then he remembered. His hand went to the wound. It was bandaged—not hospital neat, but pretty well done.

"Who?" he said again. He wasn't sure if the old man had responded the first time. He might have, but Boz's head was so abuzz that he could have missed it.

"Kibosh," the old man said, pronouncing it kye-bosh. "My maw called me Lester, but I been Kibosh forever, it seems like." A large, gray-brown-black cat came prowling by, disdainfully avoiding Boz, and rubbed up against the old man's high laced-up boots. He nudged her away. "That there's Mary," he said to Boz.

"Mary," Boz said. He understood none of this.

"Gotta have a cat, ye live in a mine," the old man said. His voice was raspy, as if he didn't use it much. "Rats," he said, nodding his head authoritatively. "But no rats when Mary's about."

A little bit of last night was creeping back into Boz's conscious mind. A mine. He'd driven up here in a truck. Where did he get a truck?

"Man, I need a drink," he said.

"Yes, ye do," the old man said. "Not a whole lot, but ye need about a shot or two." With that he reached behind him without looking, felt about on the shelf of some crude cabinetry he had cobbled together, and came away with a fifth of County Fair bourbon, about half full. He splashed some in a small, dirty jelly glass that was covered with pictures of children playing at ancient games like hoops. He got up from his chair and carried the glass to Boz.

Boz accepted it with trembling hands and gulped the warming liquid down. He blinked. "More," he said, holding out the glass. He loved the way the whiskey burned down his gullet.

"I don't think so, not just yet," the old man said, shaking his head. He sat down in his creaking chair again. "Let that one take hold, first. I'll give ye another in a minute. I s'pose ye'd like some water. Eh?" He dipped water out of a nearby bucket, filling a large metal cup, and handed that over. Boz drank it down eagerly. It was the best-tasting water he'd ever drunk.

"More," he said.

"Naw, jest wait," the old man said, sitting down and crossing his legs. He picked up an old cherrywood pipe and began to stuff it with tobacco from a can that said *Union Leader*. "Ye smoke?" he asked.

"No," Boz said. "I never did. Bad for you."

"Wal, a smoke in the morning can be right nice," the old man observed. "Evenin', too. When yer hungover it's real good. But there ye go . . . yer a man without comforts. What do ye expect? Yer head hurts." He nodded as Boz groaned. "Ye got vices, but no comforts. I tell ye what, I got some asp'rin."

This time he got up to peer at his shelves and rummage. He soon found a little bottle and rattled it. "Here we go!" He pried the lid off with some difficulty, cursing safety lids, and shook out three white pills. "Naw, better make it four," he said, and shook out another. He recapped the bottle, put it away, and brought another dipper of water to fill Boz's tin cup and put the aspirin in his trembling hand. "Toss them down," he said.

Boz did as directed, finished the water, and he felt that he could get up. He did, but he was shaky enough to have to prop himself against the wall, which he now saw was composed of rather dusty and dirt-encrusted cinder blocks.

"Whew," he said. He flexed his knees. He dusted off his hands and ran them through his thick hair. He stood up. His head was too near the ceiling. He could stand erect, but he wanted to hunch. "Man! I guess I tied one on last night!"

The old man laughed, a dry, raspy cackle. "I guess ye did. Ye're lucky ye got here in one piece."

"Where's the truck?" Boz said. He started toward a door, some twenty feet away, with a pane of dirty glass next to it that let light through.

The old man came forward and opened the heavy door. It was made of steel, mounted in a heavy wooden frame. The wall was stuffed with fiberglass insulation that hung out in ragged hanks.

They stepped out into a morning that wasn't as bright as it seemed at first. There was a thin high overcast of seamless clouds. But there, spread out before them, was a grand panorama of mountains that were well forested, mostly in dark green pine mixed with golden patches of larch. Rolling fields of brown grassland swept down a mile or more to the highway, along which Boz could see a semi laboring up a grade toward the pass, beyond their view.

Boz breathed in the fresh air gratefully. Down the rough road he could see the black Dodge pickup, its grill bent and one headlight smashed, but otherwise in pretty good shape. It sat square in the middle of the narrow road. A number of other old vehicles were pushed off into the sparse woods around the front of the mine, some of them missing important parts, like a rear axle, or an engine. One of them, an old Studebaker pickup truck, appeared to be operable. It was drawn into a kind of a drive, between two pine trees that had a tin-clad roof rigged from one to the other of them to shelter it.

Boz looked all around. Behind them the mountain rose up, covered with pines that soughed gently in the wind. A jay or a squirrel called, or it might have been a crow: he didn't know. There was not a man-made structure to be seen anywhere, just the distant highway.

"Where's the ranch?" Boz said. He remembered being so sleepy, battling to keep his eyes open, and then seeing a light way off to his right. He'd gotten off the highway, somehow, and found a road that seemed to lead in that direction, but what happened after that . . . he didn't know.

"Ain't no ranch," the old man said, "just the Seven Dials." He pointed up to a large wooden sign over the entrance to the mine. It was sunbleached so pale that one could barely read the name.

"I saw a light," Boz protested.

The old man pointed to a tall post from which the bark had been roughly stripped. At its top was a light fixture, such as one saw in barnyards, with a large bulb in it. A wire ran down the post, wrapping about it and disappearing into the mine.

"I keep that burning all night," he explained, "to keep the bears and badgers out of my smoker." He pointed to an old refrigerator that stood next to the door. It had a heavy web strap about it to keep it closed. "Ye hungry? Ye must be."

He went to the refrigerator, undid the buckle, and let the strap fall to the ground. He opened the door. A waft of smoke and the odor of meat drifted out. He reached in and came out with two lengths of dark, wrinkled sausage. He handed one to Boz and set the other on the top the refrigerator while he rehitched the strap and tightened it, snapping the buckle closed. The sausage on the top of the refrigerator fell to the ground. He picked it up and brushed it off, then took a huge bite, as Boz had.

"Pretty damn good, ain't it?" the old man said.

"It sure is," Boz said. It was delicious. Spicy, hard, chewy, but succulent. The grease ran down his chin and he wiped it away with a hand, then looked around for something to wipe his hand on. The old man was wiping his hand on his pants. Boz looked down at his own pants. They were pretty foul, with blood, dirt, and cat hair, but he didn't feel like wiping the grease on them. They were the only pants he had. He saw that his leather coat was all right, though the sleeve was torn. His shirt was torn, too, a mess, stiff with dried blood.

"Jesus, I'm a mess," he said, holding his hand away from him.

The old man picked up a dirty rag from the ground and tossed it to him. It looked like it had been used to clean oil from a truck part. But after he snapped it a few times in the air, Boz was able to clean his hand with it. He gobbled down the last of the sausage and wiped his fingers again, then flapped the rag at his pants and coat. Every time he flapped the rag he felt a twinge in his side, but it didn't bother him much now.

"Thanks for bandaging me up," he said to the old man.

"No problem. Looks like ye got into a jaw-t'jaw."

Boz shook his head. "I don't remember too much about it. Couple of guys, I guess they didn't like the way I was dancing with one of 'em's old lady." He laughed. "I don't even know how I got out of there."

"Where was ye?" the old man asked.

Boz shook his head. "I don't know the place."

"Unh-hunh," the old man said. "Well, I see yer vee-hicle, it's got Silver Bow plates, I figger ye must be from Butte."

"Naw, it's just a loaner," Boz said. "My car had some problems. They lent me that till they get it fixed."

"Ah," the old man said, "then ye ain't from around here?"

"What is this, a quiz show?" Boz said sharply.

"Nope, nope. Ain't no bizniss a mine," the old man said, finishing off his sausage. "Wal, it looks like a purty day." He wiped his hands a final time on his blue jeans and stood there, gazing about with his hands on his hips. "I think I'll fetch my pipe. Ye 'bout ready for another whiskey poultice? I thought ye would be."

The old man went back into the mine and reissued a moment later, the pipe in his mouth, carrying the whiskey bottle and two small glasses. The cat slipped out between his legs and disappeared into the brush. The old man set the bottle on a chunk of wood that served as a chopping block and went back to fetch a Mason jar of water. When he came back, Boz was chugging at the bottle.

"Hey, now! That's enough a that!" the old man exclaimed. He snatched the bottle from Boz, who docilely permitted it, smiling while Kibosh poured them both a reasonable dollop in the little jelly glasses. "That's fine stuff. Ye got to sip it. Pull up a stump."

He sat down himself on a chunk of firewood and motioned Boz to one like it nearby. The two of them sat, warming in the morning sun that was just beginning to glow through the thin cloud cover. The old man lit up his pipe again. Then he sipped at his whiskey.

"Now, this is the goddamn life, ain't it?" he said, gesturing at the mountains.

Boz sipped at his whiskey, as bidden. He felt much, much better. "Yer damn right," he said, unconsciously mimicking the old man, who didn't notice.

Boz sat and rested himself. His mind was working, now. He saw that he was in a pretty secure position, up here, for the time being. Little by little, the events of the night began to resurface: the hassle with the bartender, the fight with the man, the mad dogs, the crazy hippie, then . . . by God, Franko! And then that fucking Joe Service. And the girl! Jesus, she was a handful, all by herself.

"What was in that sausage?" he asked.

"Why that's elk sausage. Ye want some more? I got aplenty." He half-rose as if to get more.

"No, no, that's all right," Boz said. He smiled affably. "It was the best damn sausage I ever ate. So, how come they call you Kibosh?"

"Oh, ye know, it's a long time gone. I don't hardly 'member."

"Oh, come on, now," Boz said. "You must remember how you got your name. They call you that from a kid?"

The old man made a wry face. He got up and poured a little more whiskey for each of them. When he was reseated, puffing his pipe, he said, "Wal, ye see, I was just a young feller, younger'n you. I killed a feller."

Boz drew back in mock surprise. "Whoa! A killer! I wouldn't of took you for an outlaw. That why you live up here, by yourself?"

The old man saw he was joking and took it well. "Naw, they caught me all right. Fact is, I turned meself in. It was a fight, prob'ly like your'n. Over a girl, a course." He sighed. "Neither one of us got her, the way it turned out. He was dead, natcherly, and I went to the pen for five years, over to Deer Lodge." He gestured over his shoulder, beyond the mountain at their back.

"Five years, that all they give you for killing a man around here?"

"Well, hell, it was a fight," the old man protested. "We was both working up in the woods, at a camp on the Little Blackfoot, and the sumbitch came back from Hel'na, drunk as a hoot owl, an' started in on me about . . . her. I give him some back, an' he come at me with a damn bowie knife an' I jes' snatched up a double-bit axe was stuck in the log like that there"—he pointed to an axe a few feet away, buried in a chunk of pine—"and laid his goddamn fool head open."

"Well, Jesus, that's a fair fight," Boz protested. "Why'd you get any time?"

"Wal, the jedge said I hadn't orter kilt him, I coulda avoided it. Ye see, someone made off with that knife. Some of the fellers in the camp, who seen it, now said they wasn't sure they'd ever seen a knife. But ever'body agreed, he started it. Anyways, they give me five years. I served my time. I felt bad about killing him. But I served my time."

Boz shook his head. "That's something," he said. "But how'd you get the name?"

"Why I guess I give it to meself. I went on down there to Hel'na an' tol' the sherf, 'Lisle, I done put the kibosh on Frog Davis.' An' folks took to callin' me Kibosh. Mostly, though, they call me Kibe, anymore."

"That's a hell of a story," Boz said. "I'm proud to meet ya, Kibe." He half-stood and stretched his hand across to shake the old man's callused one. "You're a hell of man," Boz said, reseating himself. "So how long you been up here?"

"'Bout forty, fifty year. I worked in all these mines." He swept his arm around the scene. "There's hundreds of old mines out there, though ye wouldn't know it. Ye'd never find a dozen. I know 'em all. Hell, I could walk to Butte underground, I betcha. See, these mines, you wouldn't guess it, are a lot of 'em interconnected. They run for miles underground."

Boz was impressed. "What did they mine? Copper, was it?"

"Up here? Oh, hell no. Gold. Gold and silver."

"No shit?" Boz stood up and looked around. It was all mountains and forest, as far as he could see. "You mean there's gold out there?"

"Quite a bit," Kibe said. "But it's jest damn hard work gittin' it out. I work at it a bit, I kin git out an ounce er two, oncet in a while. Ain't hardly worth the effort, price a gold nowadays. But I don't need much."

Boz nodded and sat down. "Well, better you than me, Kibe. I never had any desire to go down into the earth, you know? But I see you got electric up here, and water, so you mine a bit for groceries and pay the electric bill, eh?"

"Why that's about it, only I don't pay no 'lectric. A kid I know down the way, he showed me how to rig up some solar panels on the hillside up there, and a ram in the crick for backup, that runs 'bout ever'thin', for free. I shoot me an elk now and then, make some sausage. Rest, why, a week or so of scratchin' will grub me up pretty well." He puffed his pipe and looked pretty satisfied.

"Well, I like it," Boz said. "I got a mind to kick back for a few days, Kibe. What do you say? I could pony up a few bucks, in case we run out of booze." He stuck his hand in his pocket and came out with a handful of fifties. It was more than he expected. "Hell, I got more than I thought. I figured those bastards robbed me last night. I could spare a couple hundred." He counted off four fifties and thrust them at Kibe.

"Hey, that's too much," Kibe said. "Ye can stay if ye like. Lord knows, a little comp'ny'd be nice for a change. Long as ye didn't stay too long, a course." He laughed and took one of the fifties. "That'll do."

"You sure?" Boz said. "'Cause it looks to me like we're gonna need more of that." He pointed at the nearly empty bottle of County Fair.

"Well, I'll tell ye a secret—what's your name? I never did hear it right last night. Boz? That's a good name. Boz. Secret is, I keep a little stash a this. It'll be enough to git on with." He got up and scuttled inside.

Boz shifted his log butt against a pine tree and settled back. He felt a lot better. He cupped his hands behind his head. The air was clear, the food was good, the company amiable, and the whiskey plentiful.

When Kibe returned, waving a full bottle of whiskey, Boz said, "What kind of gun you use on them elk, Kibe?"

Lying in Wait

Joe Service strolled into Smokey's Corner. It was still midmorning, not much business. Bernie signaled him from the end of the bar with a lift of his head. When Joe approached he took him aside to a small table near the back.

"Coffee?" Bernie offered, "or something stronger? Maybe you oughta take something stronger. No?" He yelled out to his regular bartender for coffee, black, as Joe had requested.

"What's the trouble?" Joe said.

"You heard about Gary?"

"Gary? Oh, you mean Frank's uncle," Joe said. "No, what about him?"

Bernie filled him in. "I hope you took my advice," he said, "and steered clear of Frank."

"Why is that?" Joe said.

Bernie told him about his night bartender's encounter with the stranger who had been asking about "Franko." The bartender had given Gary's number to the guy.

"Nothing wrong with giving a number that's in the phone book," Joe said. "Where's your bartender now? That him?" He nodded toward the man behind the bar.

"No. I told him to take a vacation. He left town an hour ago. I don't want no part of this business. But I thought you'd want to know."

"You think this guy, this stranger, is the one who—"

Bernie interjected before he could say it, with a quieting motion of his hand on the table. "He was pretty drunk, awful drunk, the kid says. He mighta gone over there, to Gary's. The kid told me that he was pretty sure the drunk—he said his name was Boz, or Badger—had some heat on him."

"Did he *see* a gun?" Joe said. "No? Well, then he doesn't know. Where did he go?"

"Just between you and me, he went to California. Driving. I told him to drive slow. See the sights."

Joe thought that was wise. "Have you talked to the cops?" he asked.

"About what? That a feller came in here asking about a 'Franko' Oberavich, and then another feller came in asking the same thing? No, I told you, I don't want no part of this."

"I wasn't thinking of that so much as I was about whether you knew anything about what the cops know about the case. But thanks for not mentioning me. I appreciate it. I just want—"

"Yeah, I know," Bernie said, "peace and quiet." He looked sour. "But just so you know, if Jacky—the sheriff's dick—asks me anything, I'd have to consider what I did know. Now, don't get your balls in an uproar. . . . I'm just thinking, this guy has prob'ly asked other folks around town about 'Franko,' and so have you. Did you?"

Joe considered. There was the realtor, of course, Carmen. And she had mentioned her friend, and her friend's friend. And there was the realtor–bar owner in Forkee. Carmen had also mentioned Gary to Joe. But all of this was really about Frank, a possible real estate deal, perfectly explicable, although he had provided a story. People remember stories. If the cops didn't connect Gary's death to Frank . . . it might be all right. But it was getting a little shaky.

"It's no problem," Joe said. "Tell me, what do you hear? What are the cops thinking?"

"They don't know shit," Bernie said. "I haven't heard nothing about Frank. One rumor says Gary was in with some bad cops, a while back."

"Bad cops? What's that all about?"

"We had some robberies around town, they never were explained, but some cops may have been involved. Liquor store, two or three drugstores. One of the cops was an old buddy of Gary's. That was, oh, ten-fifteen years back. The buddy of Gary's they found shot to death in Billings, a while back. Lot of talk about that."

"What do you know about it?" Joe asked.

"Nothing. Oh, the cop that was shot . . . he did the robberies. I don't know if Gary was mixed up in any of it, though. I kind of doubt it. But I'd guess that Jacky would be thinking along those lines. That's why Jacky is bound to come around here asking about Gary, and strangers."

Joe nodded. "But you don't know anything."

"That's right," Bernie said.

"Well, thanks for letting me in on what you don't know," Joe said. "Uh, you said 'cops,' plural. There was more than one in on the robberies, then? Where are they?"

"A couple of them got into some sticky business, tried a Brinks robbery, over in Missoula County. The robbery didn't go down—the FBI jumped the gun, the Missoula sheriff was pissed—so there was no charges. They didn't even pick 'em up. But they were advised to vamoose, and they did. I think one of them's up in Kalispell."

"What's the situation in the cop shop now?" Joe asked.

"Oh, that's all past," Bernie said. "This bunch, they're pretty straight, far as I know. Especially Jacky Lee. You don't want to try no funny stuff with Jacky."

"If this guy, this Boz, did Gary," Joe said, "and he's still around . . . I wonder where he'd be?"

Bernie lifted his eyebrows in thought. "Well, he asked about Frank. If he was really after Gary . . . ?" He let the question hang. "I'd say he's gone, but he may still be interested in Frank. I'd keep away from Frank."

Joe thanked him and left. It was too early to meet Helen, at the Uptown Cafe. He decided to make his call to the colonel. But how to play it? By ear, he supposed.

"Joe, I'm glad you called," Tucker said. "There may be a complication." He told him about Harry Hartsfeld, a.k.a. Bozi Bazok. "A man using a stolen passport entered the country a couple of weeks ago. We think he's Harry, and we think he's headed for Butte." He didn't give any particulars on how they knew this, but he gave a description that Joe recognized as Boz.

This was the spot for telling about the stranger asking around town, and possibly about the murder of Gary Oberavich, but for some reason, Joe didn't say anything. Instead, he said, "You know, that Oberavich name . . . any results on that?"

"What? Oh, no. That's a dead end, I'm afraid. But a good thought. Now, about Harry . . . I just thought you should be on your guard, Joe. This fellow is pretty dangerous. He'll also be attracting the attention of other investigators, international ones included. You follow? So step carefully. If you don't make some progress on Franko soon, it might be as well to just drop it. Are you and Helen having a good time?"

"A good time?" Joe said. "Well, sure. I always liked this country, you know."

Jon A. Jackson

"I know. I'm sorry it's gotten so complicated," the colonel said. "Where are you staying? I may have to give you a hurry-up call . . . to fold your tent, you know."

Joe explained that they had been staying at the Finlen, but it seemed a little too exposed, in a way. They were thinking of shifting over to Helena, but he didn't know where. This news about Harry suggested that a move was a good idea.

The colonel agreed. "I'll tell you what," he said, "I'm expecting some further information about Harry. It's unfortunate that you didn't call an hour later. Give me your number at the Finlen and I'll call back as soon as I hear."

Joe told him that they had already checked out. But he was meeting Helen for lunch, in a little while—she'd gone off to do some shopping. "I think she had some, ah, personal items she needed to pick up," Joe said. "You know how that is. I could call you from the Uptown."

"That'll be fine, Joe," the colonel said, and rang off.

Now why, Joe wondered, didn't I tell him about Boz? Joe hung up the phone and walked over to Carmen Tomarich's office.

"Oh my God, did you hear the news?" Carmen said. "Did you ever get hold of Gary? It's just awful!"

Joe listened to her gush for a while and commiserated with her about the Oberaviches. No, he said truthfully, he hadn't called Gary. In fact, he and his wife were interested in some of those other, more developed properties she had mentioned. Unfortunately, he said, his wife had gotten into a conversation with some woman about what a great place Missoula was, and she insisted that they drive over there to take a look. But Carmen was not to worry; Joe wouldn't make any decision until he looked at Carmen's properties. They'd be back in a day or two.

Carmen listened, of course, always attuned to business, but her mind was really on the poor Oberaviches. "I was thinking about

202

that other guy," she said, "the one who was looking for Frank. Do you think I should tell the police about that? It could be connected."

It was her way of suggesting that she was worried about Joe's interest in Frank, as well. Joe had the impression she was asking for reassurance. "Gee, I don't know," Joe said, with an innocent air. "Were Frank and his uncle close?"

Carmen didn't think so. "They were sort of opposite sides of the coin, if you know what I mean," she said. "Gary was this really straight guy, you know. Never miss a day of work kind of thing. He was friends with the police, I know. He worked with the department on their annual children's circus thing. And Frank, I guess he was sort of a hippie . . . maybe he still is."

"I wouldn't say anything," Joe said, thoughtfully. "The guy wasn't asking about Gary. Why get Frank involved, or yourself? You aren't a friend of the family, are you? It's not as if you actually knew anything about the killer, is it?"

"Me? Oh, no," she said. "You're right. I just wondered . . . if the question came up, about strangers asking questions about the Oberaviches . . . you know?"

"If the question comes up," Joe said, "I'd certainly not conceal any relevant information you had about Gary. But a businessperson has to be kind of careful about involving others, don't you think?"

Carmen saw his point. With that, he left. It wasn't very satisfactory, but at least he had drawn her attention to the fact that this might be a can of worms, something not quite nice, not worth taking a chance. He headed over toward the Uptown, a little early, but hoping that Helen would be early as well. He had begun to be anxious about Frank and Paulie. The day was getting on. He felt that they should get back.

On the other hand, he thought, the colonel's information about Boz had reminded him of the name on the rental-car papers. Harry Hart. A little detective work could be in order. It could also be the name he'd used to rent a motel room. It was worth a try. He was passing a motel ludicrously called The Palms, complete with a large sign featuring two such trees—not what one looked for in Butte. He stopped in at the desk and said, "Is Mr. Hart back yet?"

The girl checked. "I'm sorry, we don't have a Mr. Hart. Are you sure you have the right place?"

"I thought he said The Palms," Joe said. "Oh boy." He frowned. "Now what?"

"Maybe he meant The Oasis," she said. "That's clear down on the flat. Did he say it was uptown? There's The Pines. That's over on Molybdenum." She pronounced the street name "Molybdum." It was two blocks west. Joe thanked her and walked that way. The street deadended into a great mound of overgrown dirt that evidently was part of the rim of the Berkeley Pit, the huge abandoned pit mine that was such a dominant feature of Butte.

"Mr. Hart?" the man at the desk said. "I could ring. Let's see . . . one-one-five . . . nope. Sorry, no answer. Was he expecting you? I could take a message. Actually," he said, leaning out and looking down the parking lot, "I don't see his car."

Joe glanced at his watch with a worried expression. "I guess he must have meant to meet me at the restaurant. I better run. Bye!" And he quickly left.

Joe stood in the parking lot for a brief moment, as if getting his bearings. He marked the location of 115, then walked around the corner and along the street to the back of the building. There was no alley. Amazingly, the brick building was right up against the berm of the pit. It provided an excellent vantage point for breakers and enterers, like himself. He counted off the windows until he had arrived at the bathroom window of 115. He clambered up the berm, which was crumbly, clayey dirt, and was able to lean forward and look into the bathroom. It was just a motel bath. The door to the bedroom was open, and he could see the edge of a bed, all made up.

He squatted on the steep edge of the berm and considered. It was broad daylight, although—he glanced around—there really wasn't anyone who could see him. At his back was the berm, off to his right an abandoned mining structure. The berm angled around to cut off any view of the street at the other end, and at the nearest end. There were some office buildings over the way. Possibly, someone in an office on the third floor or higher could look out and see him crouched here.

But what could he hope to find? Would Boz really leave anything of interest in a motel room, where maids came and went, making the bed? The window, he noticed, was a simple sliding affair in an aluminum frame. It appeared to have double-glazing, which he'd noticed was usual in this cold country, to keep the heating bills down. Fairly stout, then. He absently tapped his pockets. He didn't have anything more than a penknife to use for a jimmy. It might work, but more likely he'd break the blade.

And then he noticed that the little plastic curtain moved slightly. He stared. He'd been looking right at this window and hadn't realized that it was slightly open, just a sliver. He leaned forward and braced himself against the edge of the building with his left hand, then tugged with his fingertips at the glass. It slid. A moment later, he was inside.

Another advantage of small size, he told himself. Boz could never imagine someone crawling through that little window. But here he was. The bed was made. The wastebasket empty. But the luggage rack had an expensive hard-shelled suitcase on it. This a penknife could manage.

There was, as Helen had predicted but Joe had not, another brushed-metal-finish Glock 9mm semiautomatic pistol and a box of cartridges, in the case. How dumb can he be? Joe thought. There was an airline ticket in the name of Harry Hart, with a return to Atlanta. There was a Swedish passport, not in Harry's name but with his picture on it. There were clothes, including military-style under-shorts and undershirts in olive drab. Socks, of course. Some dress shirts in their plastic bags as they had been purchased.

Joe glanced about. Boz was not a great reader. No magazines, no letters. Nothing. Joe pocketed the Glock and the ammo. No point in leaving that for Boz, in the event of him eluding them. He dumped the suitcase out on the bed. As he had expected, there were three credit cards, in different names. Also a thin bundle of American cash . . . five hundred dollars. Not much to get on with. What Joe had hoped for and didn't find was a notebook, or an address book. Something with names of contacts, phone numbers. But he must have those with him.

Joe glanced at his watch. He was late. Nothing more to find here, anyway. He opened the door and walked confidently away from the motel. He reached the cafe in a minute or two. He was about to enter when he saw Helen in conversation with a young woman, about her age, at the little bar where one waited for one's table. The woman was tall, her reddish hair in some kind of frizzled, bushy style. She looked fashionable, in a lustrous green suit, skirt above her knees. Nice frame on her.

Joe knew she was not from Butte. He walked away. There was a tavern on the corner with a phone booth. Joe called the colonel.

"Where are you calling from?" the colonel wanted to know.

"A bar," Joe said. "What did you find out?"

"Boz is in Butte. He flew in as a Harry Hart. There has also been a murder in Butte."

"I know that," Joe said.

"Some guy named Oberavich. Looks like Harry had the same idea you did," the colonel said. "Do you suppose it's Franko?"

"The victim? Not unless Franko was fifty-four years old, mar-ried to a woman named Selma, and worked for the railroad for the last thirty years," Joe said. "The picture in this morning's paper doesn't resemble your description."

"No, I didn't think it was Franko," the colonel said. "But there must be a connection. Is there a Frank Oberavich?"

"There is," Joe said, "but he's too young, also doesn't fit the description, and has been in town for the last couple of years. But I'll keep poking around. It may be that Harry made a hasty connection and it went wrong. Anything else?"

"No. That's it," the colonel said.

"You haven't heard about any other agents we should keep our eyes peeled for?"

"Not yet. Why? Have you seen somebody around?"

"No, I just wondered," Joe said. "It was your suggestion."

"Are you at the cafe? Is Helen with you?"

"No, I'm on my way, though. Did you want to talk to her?"

"No," the colonel said. "Just say hi. Well, keep a low profile, Joe. Check back as soon as you find a new place to stay, okay? I'll need to keep you posted. It's imperative that we not run afoul of any other investigations."

"Roger," Joe said. "Out." And he hung up. From the bar he could look out onto the street. He ordered a beer and sipped as he watched. Eventually, Helen came out of the Uptown and stood there, looking up and down the street. He started to leave and join her when he saw the other woman come out and engage her in conversation again. They talked, glancing up and down the street; then the woman gestured and they reentered the restaurant.

Well, Joe thought. Guess I'll wait. He switched to coffee and glanced at the *Montana Standard*, the local newspaper. The murder was the headline. The cops had found the bodies late last night, it said. No suspects. That didn't mean much, Joe knew. He kept his eye on the cafe. He ordered another coffee and tried to interest himself in sports. He'd never understood the fascination with sports. It was just another of those pastimes of the straight world that was alien to him.

Eventually, he saw Helen come out of the restaurant. She set off up the street, presumably to wherever she had parked the Durango. Joe stepped out of the tavern, but stood in the entry. He wasn't surprised to see the red-haired woman come out of the cafe. She paused a moment, then set off after Helen. Joe followed.

At a nearby parking lot he saw Helen's red Durango pull out and cruise slowly to the corner. She was looking around. She waited at the light, then decided to turn left and went down the hill. Red-head's gray Pontiac trailed after her.

Helen would go to Smokey's, Joe figured. That was where she had dropped him. She'd park and go in, ask. He wondered if he could get there in time. He walked briskly. He was almost on the same block as Helen before he spotted the gray Pontiac. It was parked well back from the intersection, and the woman was in it. The Durango was right in front of the bar. Joe turned down the alley.

He entered the bar from the back. There was a parking area out there; many of the customers came in that way. Bernie wasn't visible, and neither was Helen. The bartender was way up front, over among the tables, serving some beer to a table. Joe stepped into the ladies' bathroom. It was empty. But then Joe saw her shoes under the door to the commode. He opened the door.

"You scared me," Helen said.

"You don't look too scared," Joe said. He leaned down and kissed her. "Who's the redhead?"

"The . . . oh, the woman in the cafe? Says her name is Jemmie, but I think she meant Jenny. Did she follow me?"

"She's waiting out front. Gray Pontiac," Joe said. "I tell you what . . . go back to the bar. I'll be out in a sec. You'll have to move your car. There's a parking lot out back. Park next to the dumpster."

Helen got up, straightened her clothes and washed her hands, touched her hair critically, and returned to the bar. Joe followed a moment later and stood next to Helen.

"Where's Bernie?" he asked the bartender.

"Lunch. What'll you have?" the man said, wiping the bar.

Joe shook his head. He laid a twenty on the bar. "I need a favor. See that red Durango out front? Go out there with the lady." Joe nodded at Helen. "Point to the curb, the corner, whatever, and tell her to pull around back. Okay?" He lifted his hand from the twenty. He put his hand on Helen's purse, to keep her from taking it.

The bartender picked up the twenty. He asked no questions, just walked out the front door with Helen behind him. He gestured, said what he was told to say, gestured again, a sweeping arm motion, and went back inside.

Helen got in the car, drove around back, and parked. Joe slipped into the car. He squatted on the floor in the front, the back being taken up with chain-saw sculptures and several bags of groceries.

"Go get your purse," Joe said, "then come back and we'll drive back to Frank's."

When Helen came back with her purse, Joe said, "Did you see the gray Pontiac?"

"It's moving down the street, very slowly," Helen said.

"Fine," Joe said. "No hurry, just take the regular route back to the freeway."

As they drove along, Joe told her what he'd learned from Bernie, his conversation with the colonel. "This is some kind of setup," Joe said. "I let slip 'Uptown' to the colonel, but not 'Cafe.' For some reason he's sicced this woman on us. Don't talk to me, she might be able to notice. How far back is she?"

They were on Montana Street, approaching the freeway. Helen glanced in the mirror. "About a block—there are a couple of cars and a pickup between us."

"Just turn on the freeway and drive normally," Joe said. He was calm. "What's her story? No, let me guess: she's a stranger in town. She's just passing through. Stopped to visit with a friend, but the friend's not home. Is this a good place to eat?"

"That's about it," Helen said, impressed.

"Well, what else could she say?" Joe said. "Did you talk to Roman?"

"He'll look for Fedima."

"Good. I wonder why your friend Jenny felt it was okay to make contact, but the colonel didn't say anything? Maybe she's not with the colonel. Hmmm. I don't know. Could be some kind of test. He asked me if you were with me. By now she'll have talked to him on the phone. He'll tell her to stick with you."

They were on the freeway and flying up toward the pass. Helen said the car was about a quarter mile back. There were only a couple of other cars and a laboring semi on their side of the freeway.

"She could be the colonel's insurance," Joe said. "Hit person," he added, at Helen's puzzled glance. "Hit lady. The colonel's playing some kind of deep game, but I have no idea what it is. If she were here to help us, she'd come forward. He'd have mentioned her."

"What'll we do?"

"If she doesn't make a move, she'll probably follow us up the Forkee road," Joe said. "We could ambush her there."

"Ambush?"

"Kill her," Joe said. "She's no help to us. I'm not curious about the colonel's plans. She could disappear, and what could be said?"

Helen glanced at Joe to see if he was serious. He looked serious.

"What's the traffic like now?" Joe asked.

"The truck has fallen way back," Helen said. "The other cars are about where they were, between her and us. She's moved up a bit, maybe. Five hundred yards?"

"Speed up a bit," Joe said. "Get away from those other cars. See if she comes on."

After a couple of minutes, Helen said, "She's coming."

"Now drop back to the speed of the other cars—what is it, about seventy?"

"About."

"See if she continues to come on or if she stays back."

"She's coming. Now she's slowing. She's about a hundred yards back."

"Okay," Joe said. He took Boz's extra Glock out of his coat pocket and checked the clip, racking the slide to make sure there was a round in the chamber. "Found this in Boz's room," he said.

"You found his place?" She shook her head. She looked tense, however.

"Not much else there, except this." Joe flashed the wad of bills. "I robbed him. I'm a robber. Well, he's too stupid to survive. Leaving guns and money in a motel room! Okay, remember that pullout area down here a ways? It should be coming up, unless I'm completely confus—"

"I see it," Helen said, grimly. "What are you going to do?"

"Just pull in there," Joe said, "and stop. If she pulls in, which I think she will, that'll be one indication of her intentions. If she stops back of you, but not right behind you, that'll be another indication. If she then pulls up slowly, alongside, you drop down behind the door. Get that window down, now!"

Helen lowered the window and slowed to pull off the highway. In the mirror she could see that the Pontiac was slowing, too. "Shouldn't we talk to her first?" she said, her voice tight.

Joe crouched on the seat, his head still below the top of the backrest. "Let her decide," Joe said quietly. "Are you armed? Good. You don't have to get it out yet, but be ready if you need it." He glanced down to see Helen tugging at her purse and opening it beside her. He thought, Who's smart? I left her purse on the bar with a gun in it. Anyone in that bar could have snatched it. Dumber'n Boz.

"She's stopping," Helen said, as the Durango slid to a halt. "Should I turn off—"

"Leave the ignition on," Joe said. "Put it in park. Now, what's she—"

"She's moving forward!"

"Be ready," Joe said.

The Pontiac pulled alongside and stopped just as Joe was about to jerk Helen down. The woman was leaning across her seat, her passenger window open, and calling.

"Are you all ri—"

Joe leaned across the body of Helen, the huge Glock propped on the windowsill. They were no more than ten feet apart. "Don't!" Joe said, when she started to move toward the steering wheel. "Just keep your hands on the wheel. That's nice."

The woman did as she was told, resting her hands on the top of the steering wheel. "It's not what you think, Joe," she said. "I'm Lucani."

"Fuck a bunch of Lucani," Joe said. He opened the door and directed Helen to slip out. "Be careful," he told her. "Don't get in my line of fire. Check the back seat of her car."

When Helen was out, standing toward the rear of the Pontiac, peering into the back seat, her own snub-nosed Smith & Wesson in hand, Joe got out carefully. "All clear?" he said. Helen nodded.

Joe leaned one shoulder against the door of the Pontiac, partially shielding the gun as the big semi blew by. He looked in and

smiled. The woman's purse was on the front seat. Joe reached in
and plucked it out. He handed it back to Helen. "Check it," he
said.

Helen fished out a small automatic. "Twenty-five," she said,
turning it over in her hand.

Joe didn't look. "That's not her main piece," he said.

"My main piece," the woman said, "is in my shoulder hol-
ster, Joe."

"Let me guess," Joe said. "Browning nine-millimeter?"

"Very good," she said, "but no. Llama."

"Well, here we are," Joe said. "Jenny, is it?"

"Jammie," she said. "Do you want to talk here?"

"No," Joe said. "All right, I'll ride with you. Helen will follow." Joe got in. As they drove out of the pullout, Joe glanced back
to see Helen toss the guns in the window of the Durango and climb
in to follow them. "She's a little pissed," Joe said to Jammie.

"Why is that?" Jammie smiled at him, glancing over her shoulder. She craned to make sure that it was safe to pull out; then they
drove on, rapidly picking up speed.

"She thought I was going to shoot you," Joe said.

"Were you?"

"I thought about it," Joe said. "But you did all the right things.
Close, though."

Jammie shivered. She raised the windows. "Where are we
going?"

"To my mountain lair," Joe said. "So what's the story? Say,
just for safekeeping, let's have the Llama." She let him reach
across, open her coat, and withdraw the Llama. His hand brushed
across her breasts. She raised an eyebrow and suppressed a smile.
Joe grinned back at her and tossed her gun into the back seat, along
with the Glock.

"There, now," he said. "You were saying?"

"It's a little complicated," Jammie said. "The Lucani are nervous about you. And Helen. Especially Helen. When I say 'the Lucani', I'm not talking about the colonel."

"What the hell was that?" Joe said suddenly. "I'm sorry. I was . . . pull over."

Jammie braked and pulled off the road. "What is it?" she said. She looked around. "I didn't see—"

"That sign back there," Joe said. He looked back. Helen pulled in behind them. Joe motioned through the back window for her to back up. "Go ahead, back up," he told Jammie.

The two cars backed slowly, for two hundred feet or more, until they had backed past a sign. Joe told Jammie to stop and looked out his window at the sign.

It was an old, weather-beaten wooden sign, halfway up the hill on their right, advertising RADIUM MINES! RADIANT THERAPY! FIVE MILES! The faint lettering instructed cars to take the next exit and turn left.

"Judging from the sign," Jammie said, "it's no longer in business." She was right. The sign was barely standing. Another winter, a little wind, and it wouldn't be a blot on the landscape any longer.

"Hmmm." Joe mused. "Radiant therapy. Wouldn't that be sun, rather than radium?" he said, not necessarily asking Jammie. "Let's go." As they drove on, he said, "Does the colonel know you're here?"

"Ah . . . yes," Jammie said. "But he doesn't know that the other Lucani know I'm here, that they have an interest besides his. Can I explain?"

"Lie away," Joe said. He smiled cheerfully. But he listened carefully, asking a few questions. By the time he had directed her through the turns and twists and warned her of bumps on the Forkee road, he felt that he understood the situation. He told her to pull aside before they reached Frank's gate. "Helen has the opener," he said. He got out and motioned Helen to stop.

"What's up?" Helen asked, looking down from the Durango.

"Everything's copasetic, I think," Joe said, nodding toward the Pontiac. "I'll explain at the house. But we've got to be careful. Looks safe. The dogs are out, so the boys must be back."

The two Rottweilers were standing beyond the gate, their tongues hanging out, looking down the road at them.

"I don't think we should all drive up to the house," Joe said, "just in case. We can drive to just short of the ridge. I'll put the dogs in Jammie's car and then go ahead in the Durango. You come up to the ridge and watch. Take your weapons. If it's safe I'll come back out in the yard and wave. I'll wave twice, like this. You can have a chat with Jammie. She'll fill you in."

"Jammie, is it?" Helen said. She nodded and picked up the opener, then drove on through and waited.

Joe started to put the dogs into Jammie's car, but she protested. "We've got groceries in the Durango," he explained.

"No way," Jammie said. "Those dogs look like they'd eat a Volkswagen." They were standing next to her door, their tongues hanging out, watching. Jammie clung to the steering wheel, not looking at them.

Joe sighed. Some people were not dog people, he thought, recalling Frank's remark. "Okay," he said. "I'll take them in the Durango." Joe got the dogs into the front seat, and although they looked longingly at the groceries, they didn't try anything.

The two women hiked up to the ridge, well off the road, creeping the last few feet. They squatted in the tall brown grass, then sat, feeling the heat of the sun, which had the sky to itself now, the high overcast having blown away. The wind whispered through the grass, and there was a fine, clean smell of earth and grass. A raven croaked, distantly.

"Pleasant enough for government work," Jammie said. "Did Joe tell you what I'm doing here? No?" She explained.

"How did you get into this?" Helen asked.

"Dinah Schwind," Jammie said. "You know her?"

"I've met her," Helen said.

"She's an old acquaintance," Jammie said. "Not exactly a soul sister, but we get along."

"Soul sister!" Helen laughed. "Ice queen, don't you mean?"

Jammie laughed. "Don't be fooled. Butter don't melt in her mouth, but Dinah's got some moves. She's got the colonel sniffing around her tail, but I think she's got eyes for younger dogs."

Jammie rolled onto her back, her arms under her head, and gazed up at the sky. Helen stayed on watch. "Joe's very nice," Jammie said.

"I wouldn't say 'nice,'" Helen said.

"Maybe 'nice' isn't exactly what I had in mind," Jammie said. "Say . . . charming."

"I wouldn't . . . oh, forget it."

Jammie started to say something, but didn't. They lay there, almost drowsing in the sun. "Waiting," Jammie said, finally. "It's what you mostly end up doing, isn't it? Wait for some guy."

Helen didn't respond.

Soon enough, they saw Joe come out and wave twice. They walked back to Jammie's car and drove on.

The boys, as Helen thought of them, were back. Jammie was introduced as a "colleague." Paulie and Frank accepted that without comment.

The visit to the Butte–Silver Bow sheriff's office had been anticlimactic, Paulie said. The detective in charge, Jacky Lee, was a long-standing acquaintance of both men. He'd asked them if they'd been in contact with their uncle lately, knew of any reason he might have been killed, if he'd voiced any concerns, any anxieties. They couldn't help him, they'd said, and they'd left. They'd gone to the family doctor's office and he'd glanced at Frank's gash, said it looked okay to him, suggested a tetanus shot, which Frank had declined, and they'd come on home. They hadn't noticed any signs of Boz or any-one coming around. They had let the dogs out, as Joe had suggested.

Joe was pleased that everything had gone smoothly. Obvi-ously, it had relieved much of the tension. But he warned them not to become complacent, to assume that the police had no interest in them. This Lee, he told them, was probably concerned with other, more pressing details. Later, if nothing further developed on the case, he would start thinking about Frank again. As for Paulie, Joe thought that police interest would be limited to his connection with Frank. But for now, things looked brighter.

"Unless they find the truck," Helen observed.

"I have some ideas about that," Joe said. He turned to Frank. "That realtor in Forkee said something about radium mines, up in the hills. Are there a lot of them?"

Frank said there were just a few still operating, and as far as he knew they weren't open on a regular basis, more on appointment. He saw where Joe was heading. The mines would be practically ideal lairs for a wounded beast, like Boz, to lie up.

He dashed up the ladder to his tower and came back shortly with a couple of U.S. Geological Survey topographic maps of the area. He spread them out on the kitchen table and pointed out the locations. There were three or four within ten miles. "That's half a day hiking, probably," Frank said. "But you can drive up to most of the mines in less than ten minutes from the highway. This one"— he pointed to the map—"is just over that ridge, beyond the Forkee. It's occupied."

"Occupied?" Joe said. "You mean someone lives there?"

"Yeah, an old coot named Kibosh," Frank said. "I did some work for him, putting in his solar and hydro. Pretty funny old guy.

It's not really a radium mine. It's an old gold mine, called the Seven Dials. Kibosh says he still gets a little gold out of there, from time to time."

Joe looked out the window. It was early afternoon. They had time to check out these sites. Now that they had five hands, they could form two search groups. "You up for this, Jammie?"

She was leaning against the post to which Joe had been bound the night before. She looked rather chic for this work. But she said, "As soon as I can change into something more appropriate for hiking, I'm game."

"All right," Joe said. "So who'll stay here and mind the store? I think Paulie and Frank should both go, so it's up to you or Helen who stays."

The two women looked at each other; then Helen gave a little sigh and said, "I'll stay. I know the alarm system." Joe could see she wasn't keen, but there was nothing else for it.

On the way out to the vehicles, Jammie drew Joe aside and said, "I need to talk to you before this goes too far. Maybe you and I should team up."

"That wouldn't make sense," Joe said. He was conscious that Helen was undoubtedly looking on from inside the house. "Paulie and Frank know this country. They'll know how to approach these mines. If Boz is holed up in one of them, we don't want to alarm him. One of us should go with one of them."

"Okay," Jammie conceded, "but let's be clear. The colonel will really, really want to talk to Boz. It's about Ostropaki. He needs to know what happened. If you find Boz, or if I do, we'll come straight back here."

"I wouldn't want to leave him," Joe said. "He could escape. We'll call back to Helen. That do it?"

"Okay." She nodded. "No moves until we consult."

With that they set out.

Miami Jake /
Mine Jinks/

Roman Yakovich could make little sense of what Helen was telling him on the telephone. He was prepared to do anything she asked, of course. Early in life he had decided that he lacked sufficient intellect. He had attached himself, therefore, to a man who he believed had what he lacked—Helen's father, Sid. This had worked out well for Roman. In time, he had transferred his loyalty to Sid's daughter.

The "Liddle Angel" he called her, and his adoration was no less than he would have had for an angel if he believed in such things. But it was in no way a blasphemous appellation. The little angel that he had in mind was not a religious figure at all but a cartoon ghost in a comic book that he had enjoyed, many years ago—he had never picked up the distinction between this imp and a cherub, such as one saw in great paintings. In his eyes Helen was more of a sprite, or a fairy, lovely and so light that she seemed to fly on wings invisible to any but him, and she was very dear. But he didn't know what to make of this request.

She wanted him to look for and find a missing and possibly dead Kosovar named Fedima Daliljaj. This was a young woman who might have fled from Kosovo nearly a year ago, in the company of an American who traveled under the name of Bozi Bazok. Or she might have been murdered by him. Obviously, she was a Muslim. Roman had no notion of Muslims.

Roman was, nominally, a Jew—although he practiced no religion. In America, his name had become Yakovich, but it was really Jakovic, which is to say, Jacobs or Jacobson or, anyway, something to do with the tribe of Jacob. One of his parents had hedged a bet, or had been conflicted enough about Judaism, to name him Roman. But if the Liddle Angel wanted him to find this Muslim girl, Fedima, he would look.

He had been cooling his heels, as it is said, in Florida these days. One was supposed to take the sun in that country, but that was not in Roman's nature. A burly man in his sixties, he had always tended to wear black suits with a sweater vest and an expensive necktie—annual Christmas presents from the Liddle Angel. The sweater vest he had given up in Miami, but he still wore the suit, tie, and thick-soled brogans, and he normally went armed with a small cannon of the .357 or .44-magnum variety—which one could hardly conceal in a bathing suit. The beach was not a congenial place for such a man. He knew quite a few retired mobsters in the Miami Beach area, and he visited with them, playing at boccie or cards. They sat in patios under the shade of lemon trees, drinking wine and smoking cigars. He was known as Jake, though some who had known him in Detroit still called him the Yak. Either name suited him. He went to them with his problem.

The guy to talk to, everyone agreed, was Cris Tantiello. Cri-stan, as he liked to be called, was a man of middle age who contrived to look thirty. He sported two-hundred-dollar designer shades and was always impeccably dressed in handmade silk shirts and very fine, beautifully tailored silk or linen jackets and slacks. No open collars and gold medallions for Cristan; his watch didn't even seem to be gold, until you looked closely. (The maker, Vanio of Parma, made a dozen watches a year; this one looked like a bracelet until Cristan touched it with his forefinger, whereupon a glaucous face materialized briefly.) He was a more sociable man than Roman. He claimed, with a flash of perfect white teeth beneath his pencil-thin mustache, to know more or less everybody in the world, by his or her first name. Cristan listened to Roman's problem with great interest.

Cristan knew of an agency, in Miami, that provided aid for refugees, like this Fedima, presumably. This was merely a phone call; he would do it for free. Alas, it turned out they knew nothing about her. But they suggested a group in Atlanta that did some placement work. Another phone call—again, pro bono. No Fedima, however.

Cristan was not daunted. "I know a man in Brooklyn," he said. "He's Armenian. He knows everybody I don't know. But it will cost you."

They were sitting in a little bar off the beach. Cristan was sipping ginger ale through a straw from a frosted glass. A tall blond woman wearing a bikini that concealed nothing of her twenty-year-old body but nipples and pubic hair, was waiting for him impatiently on the terrace, under an umbrella, paging through a fashion magazine.

"Two C's?" Roman asked, indifferently.

"Four," Cristan said. "Come by and see me tomorrow, about this time."

"Today," Roman asked. "Three C's."

"Five," Cristan said. "Okay, *mi amigo*. But first, I must break the sad news to Claudia." He went out and leaned down to the tall girl. Her shoulders drooped; then she stood up and shook her mass of blond hair angrily. When she shook her head every man's head within visual range swiveled, because Claudia's head shake created a sympathetic vibration in the rest of her, particularly her upper torso: it was like a submarine disturbance, hidden at first and slow to build, but as it reached the surface the inertial violence threatened to rip her flimsy costume to pieces. Cristan calmed her with his hands upheld like a traffic cop's. He promised her. She folded her arms and waited while he returned to Roman.

"Ladies," he said to Roman, "they're so . . . volatile. I have to go for a drive. You wait here." He went off with the girl, jumping into a white Cadillac convertible.

Roman sat and stared at the open door of the bar. It framed an oblong of tan sand, some colorful umbrellas, the deep blue of the sea, and the paler blue of the sky. He sat there, hardly moving, patiently waiting, for almost an hour. He tried to imagine what the Liddle Angel wanted with a girl named Fedima, but he had no clue. He quit wondering. And then Cristan returned, alone but looking simultaneously refreshed and depleted.

"My friend Ari has said he will inquire of some Arab friends. We must wait. I'm sorry, Jake. He may not call back this evening."

"Who are the Arabs?" Roman asked. "I'll go ask them myself."

"Ha, ha!" Cristan laughed gaily. "You can't do that, *mi amigo*. They are in New York!"

"There are airplanes," Roman said. He took out a packet of bills from his breast pocket and counted off five hundred-dollar bills. He stopped, looked at Cristan, who was watching him expectantly, and counted off five more. Cristan picked up the bills and disappeared out the door, walking directly to his car. He drove off and was back in ten minutes. He handed a piece of paper to Roman.

"**R**adium mines?" Boz didn't get it. If the mines were radioactive, wasn't that dangerous? Who would sit in a radioactive mine?

Kibosh assured him it was so. "It's a real low-grade radiation, they tell me," he said. "Might be somethin' to it. I was talking to Frankie about it, and that kid knows just about ever'thin' about science. He brung over a whatchamacallit, one a them little gewgaws, and checked out the Seven Dials for me."

"Geiger counter," Boz said. They had moved into the mine, but sat near the open door so Kibosh's pipe smoke could escape. The cat wandered back and forth. They were on their second bottle of County Fair, and it was getting pretty low.

"Naw, it wan't a Geiger counter," Kibosh said. "This thing counts all kinds a radiation. Frankie said what I had here was a little bit a ray-don. It ain't the same. An' I didn't have anough to bother 'bout. Ray-don daughters, he said. He 'splained it all, but I didn' git the whole gist."

"Radon daughters. I could go for some daughters," Boz said. "Jesus, lookit that bottle! Time for another, Kibe."

Kibosh picked up the bottle, poured them each the same amount, about a shot apiece, and then hurled the bottle out the open door. It bounced across the gravelly yard and rattled down the hill past the pines and out of sight. He sipped his shot and got up to fetch more. He came back shortly with a bottle that was only half full.

"Thissisit," he said. "Thought I had more, but I forgot this'n'uz only half full. Wal, jist have to take 'er easy."

"Fuck that," Boz said. "We'll drive down an' get some more. Maybe we should go while it's still plenty light." He glanced out the door.

Kibosh agreed. "We could git some bread, too. I never been any good at makin' bread. I miss it now an' then. An' maybe some-thin' to dress that scratch a yers."

"Let's go, then," Boz said. He picked up the bottle. "Take this along."

Kibosh hurried after him. It was a little touchy turning the big Dodge around on the narrow road. There was a steep dropoff on one side and the embankment on the other. But at last they went bouncing down the hill, out to the highway, and soon were whiz-zing along toward French Forque and Basin.

"Pull in t' Frenchy's, here," Kibosh directed Boz as they ap-proached French Forque. "Ye want t'git it, er me?"

Boz handed him a fifty. "Get three—no, four," he said. Then he peeled off another bill. "What the hell, get a six-pack. And you might as well get some beer, too. And maybe some of them beef-jerky things."

"Aw, I got plenty a elk sausage," Kibosh reminded him.

"Oh yeah, well go on then."

Kibosh came back with a sack full of booze and beer. "I cleaned him out on the County Fair—he on'y had three bottles—so I got some brandy. All right? The rest of the stuff we gotta git down to the 'little store.'" He pointed down the road and they drove on. Here Kibosh loaded up with loaves of Wonder Bread and Twinkies, a couple of cans of salted nuts, a dozen eggs, and some first-aid supplies.

They got back on the highway, drinking and talking, having a fine time. Just as they were approaching their exit, Kibosh looked ahead to his road and saw an old pickup coming out.

"Shoot, there's the kid," Kibosh said. "He musta been up to the place. I missed 'im."

Exiting southbound traffic was provided with an off-ramp, which led to a stop sign at Kibosh's road. Vehicles on that road, headed northbound to Basin, had to pass right under the freeway, then turn onto an entrance ramp on the other side. The pickup had gone into the underpass by the time Boz got to the off-ramp. But he didn't exit.

"He prob'ly was jist stoppin' by, t'see if I was doin' all right, needed anythin' from the store," Kibosh said, craning around to catch a glimpse of the pickup as it entered the northbound lanes. "He's a good kid. Hey, ye missed the turnoff!"

"I was just thinking," Boz said, "that I need my stuff from town. I been wearing the same clothes for two days."

"Hell, I been wearing these since . . . well, I don't rightly remember," Kibosh said. "But go ahead on. In this rig, won't take a half an hour to git to town."

He was right. They pulled up to the motel and Boz jumped down, saying he'd be right back. What he found inside made him furious, however. All his stuff dumped on the bed, his Glock and his money gone! He raced to the bathroom and jerked off the lid of the commode tank. To his relief, his Star automatic, a Spanish 9mm, had not been discovered. It sat in its sealed plastic bag with an extra clip and extra cartridges. He took it out, unsealed it, and slipped it into his coat pocket.

He looked at the shower wistfully. He would have appreciated a cleanup, but now he felt nervous about hanging around here. He stuffed his gear into the suitcase, took it out to the truck, and tossed it into the back.

"That was quick," Kibosh observed as they wheeled out of the lot. "Ain't you gonna check out?"

"Fuck 'em," Boz said. "Who needs that joint? We got everything we need, eh, Kibe?"

Kibosh grinned and cracked open a can of Budweiser and handed it to Boz. "Ye got that right, pardner," he said, and got out a can for himself.

A half hour later, with the light dwindling but still present, they bounced on up the trail toward the mine. Boz drove the Dodge right up to the yard and stopped to let Kibosh out.

"I'm gonna turn her around," Boz said.

Kibosh jumped down with the groceries and went to the door. There was a note stuck there on a nail. He picked it off and stuffed it in his pocket while he opened the door and carried his goods inside. Boz turned the truck around and parked facing down the trail.

Boz sat out on the stump, sipping at a beer and enjoying the pleasant fall evening, while Kibosh bustled around inside, frying up some supper. After a bit the old man came out with the grub—scrambled eggs, sausage, toasted bread—and they set it out on handy stumps to eat.

"Damn, this is good," Boz said. "By God, Kibe, you got the fuckin' life!"

After dinner they sat back to watch the evening settle in. Kibosh smoked his pipe, and Boz sipped beer. "Where's that rifle of yours, Kibe?" Boz asked.

Kibosh brought it out and handed it over, proudly. It was a deer rifle, a .30-06. Boz hefted it and looked through the scope.

"By God, I can see the cars on the highway," he said. "How far is that?"

"Oh, a mile or more, depending on where ye're lookin'," Kibosh said. "Them lights goin' up the grade," he said, glancing at where Boz was aiming, "that'd be two mile, easy."

"I believe I could hit it," Boz said, his finger curling around the trigger.

"Oh, Jesus! Don't!" Kibosh said. He reached for the barrel, but Boz pulled it away.

"Leave off," Boz said. "I ain't gonna shoot, you old fool! But, Jeez, looks like I could." He looked through the scope again. "Too far. You'd never hit nothing at this range, what with elevation, wind." He set the rifle down beside him, leaning it against a pine.

"Them thirty-ought-sixes'll carry, though," Kibosh said. He was a little nervous about the gun staying by Boz's side, but he didn't say anything. "Folks a been kilt, from ca'tridges fired two mile."

"What was that you was telling me about walking to Butte underground?" Boz asked. "Was that bullshit?"

"Wal, as to that," Kibosh said, feeling sobered, "I mighta 'zaggerated there. Butte's a good ways. I knowed a feller in Butte, though, that claimed he could go from one end a town to t'other, underground, and I b'lieve 'im."

"So it was bullshit," Boz sneered. "How about to Basin?"

"To Basin? Wal, no. The river cuts in, see. But French Forque, hell, yes," Kibosh said. "Wal, ye'd come out 'bout a mile from Forkee, maybe a little closer. I never did it. I got through to the river, a little further up, an' come out above Frankie's place, oncet."

"Frankie. You're always talkin' about that kid." Boz frowned, then said, "You mean the Oberavich kid? Grows dope up there, up the crick?"

"I don't know nothin' 'bout dope," Kibosh said. "Ain't none a my business what he grows, nor nobody else's."

"Don't matter to me," Boz said. "I just heard a rumor. So where'd you come out at?"

"There's a ridge, comes out 'long the river 'bove his place," Kibosh said. "I got to foolin' 'round in there one day and I'll be damned if I didn't come out acrost the crick from his place. Took me the better part of the day. But I walked right back in a couple hours. See, I marked the way with chalk, so's not to git lost."

"You got a map?" Boz said. "I'd like to see where you're talking about."

They went inside, Boz carrying the rifle. He leaned it up against the shelves next to his chair while Kibosh cleared away some of the clutter and spread out some forest service maps.

"See, here we are," Kibosh pointed out. "And there's the crick. Ye can see it ain't but a mile or two, 'cept that there's a whole damn mountain in betwixt."

Boz looked at it carefully. The mountain was part of the ridge that determined the course of the Forkee. It angled to the northeast, so that the highway angled as well, before it reached French Forque. By road, it was at least six or seven miles, then the ten miles or so of twisting road that ran up and around and through the jumbled hills, to come out onto the big meadow that formed the major part of Oberavich's place. The southern bank of the river was very steep, high cliffs in some places, whereas the north side was a gradually rising block of another mountainous structure pushing down from the north. A straight line through the ridge was amazingly short. But any system of tunnels and mine shafts would not run straight through, Boz understood.

"Is it dangerous?" he asked Kibosh.

"Oh, I dunno, d'pens." Kibosh opened a bottle of bourbon and poured them each a small glassful. "Been a couple year since I been back in there any distance. I ain't noticed no falls, but ye never can tell. Durn thing could be plumb blocked off."

"Sonofabitch," Boz said, "walkin' under a whole damn mountain." The idea was scary, but he had an urge to try it, especially since finding he'd been robbed—he was positive it had been that Joe bastard. Only the thought of crawling around under an actual mountain of rock that could fall and crush you . . . old shafts with rotting timbers . . . maybe getting lost, unable to find your way out. . . . Plus, he considered, he was a little drunk.

He decided to put it off. He'd rest his wound some more, sleep on it. Tomorrow would be plenty of time. This decision made him feel better. He relaxed and drank down the good, warming whiskey.

The old man bustled about, washing dishes, feeding the cat on scraps. "Forgot to turn on m'light," he said, heading for the door.

"Leave it," Boz said. "You don't want no one up here, any way."

"That's jist it," Kibosh said. "Folks don't see the light, they know I'm dead."

"Oh, all right then." Boz poured himself another glass of whiskey.

Kibosh came back, closing the door against the night's chill. He turned on his old radio, and music crackled out.

"How in hell do you get radio in a cave?" Boz said, surprised.

"Got a aerial, runs up the tree. Purty good reception, too." He started to tune the radio. Boz reached over and shut it off.

"No radio," he said. "I hate music."

"All right," Kibosh said. He sat down and began to stuff his pipe.

"No pipe," Boz said. "I hate that stinking thing."

"All right." Kibosh set the pipe aside. The cat leaped onto his lap and he began to caress her.

"So you spent how many years in the can?" Boz said. "Five? Five years for killing a man. At that rate, let's see . . ." He scratched his unshaven chin in calculation. "I'd of been in for five hundred! Maybe more. But you know how much I spent? None. Oh, I spent a night or two, when I was a kid, but that's all. What do you think of that?"

"Five hundred years! Wal, I'll tell ye, five was plenty."

"What'd you do for five years?" Boz was interested.

"I kept to meself," Kibosh said. It was clear he didn't want to talk about it.

"D'you get fucked?" Boz said. "That's what they do, ain't it? Young guy like you was, I bet you got fucked. Some big ol' nigger, I bet. Fucked you up the ass. D'you get to likin' it?"

Kibosh didn't like the way this was going, but he didn't say anything. Boz laughed. He was feeling frisky. Also, thinking about sex, a little horny. He thought of how he'd almost had that little bitch the other night—it seemed like several nights ago now.

"Well, did you?" he demanded.

Kibosh thought about it. He'd been a pretty tough young fellow, capable of taking care of himself. He'd made the right friends, too. There were some good fellows in the pen, at least in those days, he thought. You made the right connections and played it careful, you got by. Serve your time, get out. Don't get back in, ever. He looked at this young man across the table from him. He had seen men like this in prison. He could see, now, that it had been a foolish mistake to be friendly to Boz. This was a mean one. Like a wild creature, he could turn on you in a flash, if he sensed your fear or you said the wrong thing.

"How's yer wound?" he asked. "Mebbe I orta put some a that antiseptic on it."

"It's all right," Boz said. He stretched his arm, twisted in his chair. "Yeah, it's a little stiff, but it's all right." He drank. "I had me a piece a ass last night," he said. "That's how come those guys came at me."

"Looks like someone shot you," Kibosh said, then was instantly sorry to have brought it up. He stroked the cat.

"Naw, nothin' like that," Boz said. "Fucker tried to spear me with a pool cue. Grazed me, is all. Tore my coat, though, the bastard."

Kibosh knew a gunshot wound when he saw one, but he didn't dispute the foolish lie. Better to let the man blow his horn—maybe it'd make him feel better. "Why'd he do that?" he asked him.

"Cuz his girlfriend was givin' me the eye," Boz said. "You know what I did? I took her out to the car and she give me a blow job and then I fucked her—bent her over the fender. She squealed like a pig! What do you think of that? When's the last time you got laid?"

Kibosh forced a laugh. "Oh, I kinda give that up quite a while back. Never found no wooman'd take me."

"Jesus, I don't believe I could do without it," Boz said. "Hell, I'd fuck anything when I get horny. I'd fuck that cat."

"A cat!" Kibosh held the cat more closely.

"Hell, yes!" Boz his voice rising, suddenly excited. "Cat, dog, chicken! I know guys fucked a chicken! You know how you fuck a cat? Verrry carefully!" He laughed and poured himself another glass, drank.

"The trick with a cat," Boz said, "is you gotta break her legs. Can't scratch, then. Fuck 'em up the ass. The cunt's too tight. Here, give me that cat. I'll show you."

He reached across the table but Kibosh jumped back, over-turning his chair, clutching the cat in his arms. The cat wriggled free and ran away. Boz laughed and stumbled after it, knocking over another chair. The cat whisked behind the shelves at the back of the room and disappeared. Boz laughed and turned around. Kibosh was reaching for the deer rifle.

"Hey!" Boz yelled. He took two strides and seized the old man, slinging an arm around his neck. He was much taller and stronger than Kibosh. He jerked the man up until his feet left the ground.

"You don't wanta do that," Boz breathed in his ear. He hugged the old man. "By God, I think I'll fuck *you*. You ain't had it in years, you say. You'll like it. They say an old man is almost as good as a boy. Just another asshole. Something warm to stick it in."

"Please," the old man gasped, "let me down."

Boz laughed and set the old man back on his feet. He had knocked Kibosh's old hat off. He picked it up and flapped it against his knee, wincing a little bit from his wound. "Damn," Boz said, but he grinned. He tousled the old man's thin strands of matted hair, then clapped the hat onto his head.

"Hey, did I scare you?" he said. "You sure look scared. You look like a . . ." But he couldn't think of an apt comparison and let it drop. "C'mon, sit down. Here, here's your chair." Boz righted the chair and pushed the old man into it.

He sat down in his own chair and poured them full glasses of whiskey. "Here's to you, Kibe!" He saluted with the glass and drank. "Go ahead, drink!"

Kibosh drank. It steadied him. He breathed more calmly, staring at the young man and waiting for the next eruption. It occurred to him that the crazy galoot might get so drunk that he'd collapse. He poured him more whiskey.

"No harm done," Boz said. "Right?" He drank.

Kibosh nodded. "No harm." He drank.

"So, what do you do all these long nights?" Boz said. "Got any dirty books? Don't worry, I ain't interested in your shit-smeared old butt." He grinned. "C'mon, now. Where's the dirty books?"

The old man went to his crib, a wooden bin containing a mattress and a tangled mess of blankets. He fished out a tattered copy of *Playboy* and brought it to the table.

"All right," Boz said. "I knew you hadda have something to get you through the night. Let's see, now." He picked up the magazine and began to page through it. "Go ahead," he said, "pour us another round. The night is young."

After a minute, Boz found a page of pictures of young women cavorting by a pool, in the nude. "That's it," he said. "Goddamn! Look at the jugs on that one!" He turned the magazine to show it to Kibosh. "That your favorite?"

Kibosh craned, then nodded. "Nice-looking wooman," he said.

Boz nodded. "I'll say. 'Cept for the tits, she looks like the one I screwed last night." He began to pore over the magazine, absently sipping at the whiskey while Kibosh sat across from him, tense and watching.

This went on for some time. Boz went through the magazine once, twice, studying certain pictures for long periods of time. At last, he yawned. He threw the magazine on the table and stood up. He stretched, groaned, and felt cautiously at his side.

"Well, I hate to break up the party," he said, "but I'm a little weary. C'mon, let's take a piss." He picked up the rifle and ushered Kibosh out the door. The cat streaked by him and out into the darkness. "Goddamn, look at pussy go!" He laughed.

They went out to the edge of the dark yard, lit only by the light from the door and the high, overhead light filtering through the pine boughs. Boz rested the rifle butt on the pine needles, holding it by the barrel while he unzipped his pants. "Go ahead," he told Kibosh, "take a leak. I know you're busting."

Kibosh unbuttoned his fly. He was unsure of what was going to happen. But when he saw that Boz was, indeed, pissing, he joined him. Boz pissed for a long time, then shook himself and zipped up.

"Happiness," he said, "is being able to piss off your front stoop." The rifle was still in his hand. But now he turned and looked at Kibosh in a thoughtful way. He easily hefted the rifle by the grip in one hand and let the barrel swing up until it was pointing at the old man's belly. "Be safer to just let the air out of you," he said, as if to himself, running the tip of his tongue over his lower lip.

Kibosh stood, helplessly. He had no doubt that the young man could and would shoot him if his calculation ran one way rather than another. But after a long moment, Boz racked the bolt back, catching the released cartridge deftly in one hand. He removed the bolt and dropped it into his coat pocket.

"Safer that way," he said, grinning. Kibosh felt relieved. "C'mon, Kibe. Time to lock up."

Inside, while Boz was locking the door, busying himself with jamming a chair under the handle for added security, Kibosh took the great risk of casually turning off the yard light. There was only a single window, a small pane of filthy glass with a dusty scrap of cloth hanging over it. Kibosh had put it in to tell if it was light out. As long as the light in the room was on, Boz wouldn't notice that the yard light was off, and probably not even when the inside light was off.

Boz said, "Now, where we going to sleep? I'm damned if I can take that pallet again." He sat down and untied his shoes, shucking them off, the earthy stink filling the space around him. He wriggled his toes.

"I'll take the pallet," Kibosh said. "Ye can have the crib."

Boz smirked and stood up. He drank a dipper of water. Then he prodded Kibosh over to the crib. "Room for both of us," he said. "You take the wall. Well, for Chrissake, take off your boots at least."

While the old man peeled off his boots, Boz folded up his coat carefully and placed it next to the crib. He motioned the old man in, then he turned off the light and crawled in behind him. He arranged the blankets around him and, throwing an arm over Kibosh's shoulder, he curled up against his back and relaxed.

"You know," he said, practically in Kibosh's ear, "this is damn cozy." He pulled the old man closer to him.

Boz breathed quietly for several long minutes, and Kibosh thought he was collapsing, at long last. My God, he thought, what a way t'end up. After years of livin' free, makin' a life for yerself, givin' up certain things in order to be yer own man. . . . It was enough to break a man's heart.

Then Boz began to talk, a low drone in the utter blackness of the crib. "I'm not no one, you know. I been all over the world. I seen a lot. I been a soldier. I saw terrible things. I been a hobo, rode the boxcars. A hobo ain't a bum, you know. He's a man who chose the free life. I knew a boomer tramp, an old man like you. I learned a lot from him. He called me his punk. You know what that means? He liked me. I ain't no punk, though. I come from the old country, you know. Americans think it's different over there. It is, but it's the same, you know? It's the same ever' fuckin' where. I had a lot of money, at times. Women. Women always liked me. They like that big dick." He laughed, a low chortle.

"I was in a cave like this before, in Kosovo, or maybe it was Bosnia, I ain't sure. Just like this, only it wasn't a mine. A cave, but not fixed up like you got it. We were waitin' for this guy. I got hot, lookin' at this little bitch. The bastard didn't come back. Finally, I just had to fuck her. There was other people in there, just skunks, they were. They got . . . well, they didn't like it. I had to shut 'em up. Bunch of assholes. Always something, to git in the way."

He rambled on. Kibosh listened in terror, wrapped in the ogre's arms, feeling his breath on his neck. His eyes felt wet; he blinked it away.

"You ever cut a man's throat?" Boz whispered. "Or a woman's? It's easy. They struggle, but they can't get away. It's over quick. Messy, though."

Kibosh could hardly breathe. Please, he prayed silently, jist conk out.

Frank was worried about Kibosh. He told Joe after supper, when they walked outside while Helen and Paulie cleaned up, that he had a mind to drive back over to the Seven Dials and see if he was all right.

"He never goes far from home, anymore," he said. "He pokes around in those mines up there. One of these times something's going to cave on him, or he'll have a stroke or something. I hate to think of him just lying up there, hurt, maybe dying."

Joe didn't like the idea. "Boz could be out there, anywhere," he said. "It's just inviting trouble. But, if you feel you should . . ."

They told the others where they were going, then set off in the Durango. "Maybe we should take the dogs," Frank said. They were loping along next to the vehicle as it approached the gate.

"In here?" Joe said. "No way."

"I just thought . . . ," Frank said, apparently miffed. "If Kibosh is in trouble or something, they could help find him."

"We don't even know if he is in trouble," Joe said. "Besides, Helen spent a half hour cleaning it out when I just drove from the gate with them. She won't have the car turned into a kennel, hair all over, scratching the leather—"

Frank nodded, but Joe knew how it was. Out here people took their dogs everywhere, usually standing in the back of the pickup. "They'll be more useful here," Joe said placatingly.

As they drove out both of them kept a close watch for any sign of a vehicle, or a man, but there was nothing. It was getting pretty dark by the time they reached the highway. But it was a quick run up the highway to the turnoff to Seven Dials. As it happened, they saw the light far up the mountainside as Joe pulled up to the stop sign at the bottom of the off-ramp.

"He's back," Frank said, relieved. "Let's go on up. He may have seen something."

Joe shook his head. It was a ten-minute drive up that bumpy road to the mine and then not much room to turn around. If this Kibosh had been fooling around in some old diggings all day—presumably where he'd been when they came by earlier—he'd not have seen Boz. Besides, it occurred to him now, if he drove straight back onto the freeway, he could run down to Garland Butte in less than an hour. He'd been thinking about the firepower he had stashed down there.

He wished now that Frank was not along. All these people constantly around, needing to be directed, advised, placated . . . Joe wasn't used to it. He didn't care for it. When he told Frank what he had in mind, Frank immediately hauled out the cell phone to let the others know their plan. But he couldn't get through—atmospherics, he said, or just the mountain, blocking them.

"Never mind," Joe said. "We'll be back before they miss us." He accelerated onto the highway. "Besides," he said after a mile or so, "we didn't have anything planned for tonight."

Frank was surprised. "Aren't you expecting Boz to show up?"

"Who knows?" Joe said. He sounded more casual about it than he felt. He was conscious of an unfamiliar feeling of guilt, as if he were running away from a problem rather than seeking the means to deal with it. It was easily suppressed: "I have a feeling he won't be out and about until late," he said. "That's the time to go prowling, in the hours before dawn, when people are either asleep or guards are drowsy. But we don't have any time to waste." He put the pedal down, speeding up toward the pass.

They had a fast run, but it was farther than he'd estimated. By the time he got to Garland Butte, trekked up to the old site, and brought down the stuff he wanted, they had already been gone nearly two hours. Part of the problem was that he was reluctant to expose the site to Frank. For one thing, there was a stiff in the cache where the guns were. How do you explain that? Especially when you have no idea who this stiff is, or was, yourself? He felt it was better to pretend that he was just a secretive fellow—Frank could understand that hypersensitivy to security, all right. But it meant hauling the stuff down himself in four separate trips. He brought down a couple of AK-47s, a Stoner rifle, a nifty little Heckler & Koch MP5A3, an Uzi, a couple of extra handguns, even a couple of shotguns. Plus ammo, of course. And a nondescript box of "papers," which contained approximately a quarter of a million dollars in small bills.

Frank was impressed with the armament. "You've got a regular armory here," he said.

Joe brushed it off as just a gun collection. "I've always been interested in unusual weapons," he said.

Frank was also impressed with the property. They discussed it on the way back. Joe explained why it was no longer so useful to him. The explanation had to do with the ruin of the dream house, lost in a fire, and the resulting depression. There were problems with water rights, too, he claimed. That always struck a resonant chord with Montanans. Water rights were things one could debate endlessly, even fight small wars over.

They were making good time, and Joe felt more relaxed. Perhaps it was just getting away from the women. He could talk more freely. But he was anxious to get back and make sure that they were prepared in case of an attack. They wouldn't be out-gunned, anyway.

And then Frank said, as they were descending from the pass, "I don't see the light."

"Kibosh's light?" Joe said. He was driving rather fast. He didn't know exactly where to look anyway. "Are you sure? Maybe some low clouds have moved in."

"It's clear as a bell," Frank said. "Starry night. Something's wrong."

Joe cursed silently. "Try the phone," he said. "We're still up high enough. Tell them we're going back up."

Helen and Jammie said they felt like getting some fresh air. Paulie said he would keep watch. "Take the dogs," he advised. "You're armed?" They were.

It was chilly out. The two women walked over toward the river. Helen thought she'd show Jammie the hot springs.

Boz was droning on about his career in the militia. "I had my own outfit," he said with pride. "I was the same rank as maybe a captain, in the army. The guys all looked up to me. We had our own uniform, special patches." He described the patches. "Everything was going great, the guys—good guys, we had our own barracks—everybody looking up to you. The civilians were scared shitless of us, they'd jump out of the way when we walked down the street. Even the cops! The cops didn't say shit to us. It was great. They were making a real good thing, there. It wasn't a bullshit kind of deal like I seen everywhere else. They were doing it! And then," he said with genuine regret and dismay, "that fuckin' Franko fucked it all up. He should have come back. I had all those crazy skunks on my hands, that little whore was fuckin' with my head—"

He suddenly stopped and stiffened. "What was that? You hear that?"

Kibosh listened in the dark, hope welling in his breast. He hadn't heard a car, but he thought he heard a crunch of gravel underfoot, very faintly. Then utter silence.

"What is it?" Boz whispered softly. "A bear?"

"I . . . I guess," Kibosh whispered. He strained to hear. Nothing.

Boz released him, whispering, "Keep still." He got quietly out of the crib and felt around in the pitch-black room. Then he padded away, stumbling against a chair so that it scraped on the dirty wooden floor. He moved on, to the door. Kibosh swung his legs out of the crib, tense. Oh, let it be Frankie, he prayed.

The little window was so dirt-encrusted that it scarcely seemed possible that it could let in starlight. Yet in the blackness of the tunnel it almost glimmered. Kibosh could even make out the hulk of Boz by the window. He was peering out, but of course, he'd be unlikely to see anything.

"Fuckin' light's out," he whispered over his shoulder.

"Musta burnt out," Kibosh whispered back. "That bulb 'uz gittin' purty old."

"You turned it out, you old bastard," Boz accused.

"No, I never. Ye want me to go out and change the bulb?" Kibosh said, hopefully. "I got a new one back here somewhere."

"Fuck no! Someone's out there."

Boz returned to the crib, suddenly all business. "Come on," he said. "We're goin' into the mine."

"Now?" Kibosh said. "It's the middle a the night."

"What does that matter?" Boz said. He was putting on his shoes. "You got a flashlight? Get it. You got some kind of bag, a backpack or something? Come on, get going. But be quiet, or I'll brain you."

Boz would permit no lights. Kibosh gathered some gear together and put it in the old canvas forest service knapsack that he
used when he was exploring. He threw in some Twinkies, a few
things off the shelf, the whiskey, a couple jars of water.

"How do we get into the mine?" Boz said. He was anxious.
He carried the rifle and a box of ammo that Kibosh had located for
him. He stuffed the shells into his coat pocket along with the remaining brandy and put that on. Somehow, he had a pistol in his
hand.

"We're in the mine," Kibosh said. "The entrance to the drift
is behind that cupboard." He indicated the large cupboard that Boz
had simply taken to be the back wall. It had to be unloaded of canned
goods and other items before it could be shifted. Boz prodded him
with the rifle to get after it.

Finally, it was bare. Boz slid it aside. It made a scraping noise
that clearly bothered him. Behind it was a plywood-covered frame
wall. One section of the plywood could be easily removed. Beyond
it lay a dark hole.

Boz peered into the darkness. Cool air whispered past him,
with a dry but musty odor. He didn't look eager to go in, but he was
determined.

"Okay, let's go," he said. "Be careful with that light. Don't
shine it this way." He followed Kibosh into the mountain.

Noir

The women could not resist the hot springs. Perhaps it was the liberating absence of men. They felt free to act like girls. Helen and Jammie were not friends, hardly sympathetic, but there was comfort in being alone together. Despite the general atmosphere of threat and tension, or perhaps because of it, they felt larkish in the veiling night. Let the men stand guard, play at heroes. They would soak.

Helen was already half naked. Nudity was damned chilly in the night breeze, under the icy stars. Jammie laughed and followed suit. But she carefully set her clothing and her automatic on some rocks, close at hand.

Helen was impressed by Jammie's physique. She'd looked like a slim model dressed, but dancing around naked on her long legs, bending so that her breasts swung free, she looked like a noir Barbie, gun in hand. Her silhouette reminded Helen of the logo on the old Nancy Drew books.

Helen showed her how to scoop out a tub, arrange the rocks. The incessant, gentle action of the seeping springs had already silted in the tubs they had made the other night. But it was quick work to make them deeper. The water felt hotter than before.

They squirmed down into the hot, velvety solution of caressing sand and water, the steam billowing up about them, partly obscuring the stars then scattered by a breeze.

"Oh my God," Jammie said huskily, shifting her buttocks and thighs, feeling the water flow over her belly, "this is bliss. It's cold on your face and hot, hot, hot on your bod. Mmm, mmm."

"There were deer the other night," Helen told her. "It was incredible. They just stepped over us, daintily. We should have brought some of Frank's grass."

"Champagne, you mean," Jammie said. "I can't believe those stars. I could reach up and break one off, like an icicle." The barred owl hooted, very close by, in an old gnarled cedar. "An owl? I can't believe it. It must be a male, a peeping Tom." They both laughed, Jammie chuckling deeply.

Something splashed out in the river, quite loudly. "What the hell was that?" Jammie said, sitting up and reaching for her Llama.

"Trout," Helen said. "A bull trout." They both laughed again.

"A big bull trout," Jammie said, settling back. "Long and stiff and slick." Their laughter was more like hoots. The owl laughed with them. But soon they fell silent, basking in the soporific heat.

Neither spoke for a long while, merely sighing and gently moving their limbs, feeling the feathery heat caress them. Then Jammie said, "Women are water creatures . . . of the water. We're nymphs, naiads."

Helen knew it wasn't necessary to respond. "I could be a trout," she said later, dreamily. "It wouldn't be cold if you just lived in the water, lying behind a rock, under a mossy log . . . flashing across the current . . ."

"A houri," Jammie said, "a nymph of paradise, lolling in the steamy pools . . ."

A light flickered past them, then came back. "Telephone!" Paulie called. "I'll wait up here. It's Joe."

Both women swore. "I'll go," Jammie said. "If it's important, I'll yell."

Helen started to protest, but then sank gratefully back into the warmth. "Tell him not to hurry," she said.

Jammie dragged herself out and slicked the water off her skin with the palms of her hands, shaking her hair like a dog. She glanced down at Helen, saw that she was all but submerged, so she merely picked up her clothes and gun and carried them up the path to where Paulie politely waited at the edge of the meadow. He had doused the light and stood staring up at the pierced black sky.

Jammie paused for a moment, one hand on a hip, but Paulie did not turn to look. Then she shivered. "It's too cold to play games," she said, almost to herself.

"It's Joe," he said, over his shoulder.

She shrugged and pulled on her pants, then the shirt. "Don't tell me," she said. "They found the bastard. Why couldn't he have stayed lost for another night?"

"I'm not sure if that's it," Paulie said. "The connection is breaking up. We get that all the time out here, in the mountains. The best I could make out, they found the truck at Kibosh's place. I was thinking . . . reception might be better up on the ridge, or out by the highway. I didn't want to go off and leave the house unattended."

"And here I thought you had come up with a clever ruse," Jammie said. "Oh well, I better go." She sat down on the grass to pull on her boots. "If it isn't better, how do I get to Kibosh's?"

Paulie explained. He seemed uneasy.

"What is it?" Jammie asked.

"I was just wondering," he said. "Did you ever know Boz?"

"I don't believe I ever had the pleasure. Why?"

"Just curious," Paulie said.

"How well did you know him?" she asked.

"Too well. But . . . you mean, like, well acquainted? No. Actually, I just met him the same day he . . . well, not very well. Until the other night . . . that was only the second time I saw him."

"How about Colonel Tucker?" she asked.

"I never met him. I heard about him, from Ostropaki."

"And Zivkovic? Did you meet him, too? In Belgrade?"

"No. Ostropaki was the contact," Paulie said. "Why?"

"Just trying to put everything into focus. Well, I better get going. Maybe you better go down and get Helen. Don't get wet. If I'm not back right away and I can't get through to you, I'll have gone on to see what's up with Joe. What's the problem with these phones out here?"

"Mountains," Paulie said. "You know how it is. And atmospherics. You can call halfway around the world, but not from one side of the mountain to the other, sometimes. What did you mean, 'Don't get wet?'"

"Women in their baths," Jammie said. "Naiads can be dangerous." She set off for the house before he could respond.

Boz didn't know what he'd expected, but this wasn't it. The drift wasn't anything like the living quarters that Kibosh had made for himself in the mouth of the mine. This didn't have a wooden floor, dirty as Kibosh's was. This was a jumble of rocks that you had to negotiate. The floor, if you could call it that, was muddy and sticky in places. His shoes were already a mess, wet and inadequate in support. Generally, he could walk upright, but at times that wasn't possible. In places where there had been a partial cave-in, he had to go on hands and knees.

But the worst thing was the feeling that it was all closing in on him. The ceiling dripped water, little rills of sand came cascading down, there were creaks of aging, rotted timbers. He had begun to hear distant rumbles, even feel the earth shift, then settle and compact. At first he was sure it was his imagination, but finally he had to stop. He listened, open-mouthed.

He had never experienced claustrophobia. Not the real, breath-crushing claustrophobia. Most of the time he was able to keep a grip, hold it at bay. But he could not suppress a hideous feeling of imminent entrapment. This place was falling down. This mountain was settling, constricting like an anaconda. Like a living, contracting nightmare.

Why would it fall down now, just as he had entered? It didn't make sense. These timbers had been here for generations, some of them, the tunnels and shafts had survived. But now they were collapsing! Could it be the movement of himself and Kibosh?

"What the fuck is going on?" he demanded of the little man who led him, hopping like a spry elf through the tumbled rocks and over broken posts and lintels.

Kibosh didn't know how to respond. He was pleased by Boz's fear, but he dared not show it. At an early point, when they had traversed scarcely two hundred feet, Boz had asked him how far they had come!

"Why, we ain't hardly started," he'd told him. But the dark look on the man's face should have been a warning. Boz had grabbed him by the collarbone and threatened to cut his throat. "You little son of a bitch," Boz snarled, "I'll kill you right here and no one'll ever find your bones." Then he'd hauled out a bottle of the brandy that he'd stuffed in his coat pocket and taken a heavy draught. That had seemed to stabilize him.

They stumbled on. Kibosh's route markers—the chalk marks at junctions with other tunnels, the arrows scratched in posts—were all but invisible to Boz. Kibosh pointed them out to him, but it was clear that Boz, on his own, would miss most of them. Kibosh began to think that it might be possible, at some point, to run ahead, to hide, and lose this insane oaf inside the mountain. But at one point, when he had begun to edge farther and farther ahead, a bullet spattered past him, on the rocky edge of the drift. He looked back, hearing the heavy, shocking boom, to see Boz brandishing the automatic pistol, eyes blazing in the glare of the flashlight.

"For God's sake, don't do that!" Kibosh exclaimed. And almost immediately, there was a blinding cascade of sand and grit, dislodged by the shock of the weapon firing.

Boz shouted, "Then don't get so far ahead! I swear, the next one is in your back!"

Boz began to lose track of time. He declared a rest. They had entered a largish chamber. Men had hollowed out this cavern, clawing at rocks to release ore from which gold could be sifted. Their flashlights played on the walls and ceiling.

"This is hell," Boz declared. "We're going down, ain't we? We're going down all the time, to the center of the earth."

"Some of the time," Kibosh said. "But what difference does it make? There's as much above us as there is ahead. I think."

"You think? Why, you lousy old bastard, don't you know? Are you lost? You're lost, ain't you?"

He looked around, close to panic. He wanted to go back. But when he paced back to the entrance to the chamber, he saw another drift, not far to one side. He paused. Could that be the way they had entered the chamber? He wheeled around and came back to where Kibosh was sipping at a jar of water.

"Are we lost?" Boz demanded, his eyes wild.

"No, we ain't lost," Kibosh said, as calmly as he could muster. He felt superior now. "But I'm the only one knows the way on." He let that sink in. A few things had become clear to him as they had slogged through these dusty, infernal passages. Once they got out, Boz would have no further use for him. If he could contrive to get them lost—a little lost—the man might collapse before he did. The passage of time seemed greater to Boz than to

Kibosh. It was a phenomenon even of outdoor trails, when you were stuck behind someone who knew where the end of the trail was, how much farther it was to camp, to the water—that could drive a man bats. It was infinitely more the case when one was stumbling inside the guts of a mountain.

At this point, Kibosh reckoned, they were more than half-way. Boz had no notion of what remained. They had not descended nearly enough, to a grade more in keeping with the exit at the river. But he knew Boz would be spooked by this. Kibosh figured he could take the wrong way on one of the cross tunnels and still find his way out. But maybe not. After all, he'd only been clear through once, and back. And at what point might Boz simply panic and kill him?

"I gotta warn ye," Kibosh said, "a man alone in here could wander for the rest of his short life."

Boz backhanded him across the mouth. Kibosh tumbled away and struck his head against a rock. "You filthy little prick," Boz rasped, leaping on him. "Don't even think about it. I won't shoot you. I'll beat you death with my bare hands! I'll strangle you and gouge your fuckin' eyes out with my thumbs! Now get your ass up and get us out of here!"

Kibosh was dazed. He got to his feet and hoisted his pack. He didn't say a word, but trudged on. One thing he didn't want, he realized, was to spend his last hours inside this hole with this wretched maniac. It was too sordid a way to die.

As he'd expected, Boz was terrified by the descents. "We're going into the pit of hell," Boz said. "If I ever get out of here, I'll never so much as drive into a tunnel I can see the end of."

It was noticeably warmer. Boz said they were nearing hell. Kibosh thought he'd made a joke and almost laughed, but realized that the man had that nightmare lodged in his head. It was an actual fear. At one of their rests, he said, "Ye musta had a religious upbringin'."

Boz nodded. "Them damn Baptists in Georgia harped on it all the time. Same in Texas. Hell! That's all they talked about. Lake of fire." He shuddered. "I seen the pictures in the churches, in Serbia. Awful. One thing about them Muslims, though, none a that shit in a mosque. But we dynamited those fuckers, anyway. We made hell for 'em." He laughed, grimly.

Onward they went. At one point, Kibosh thought he was lost. Then he realized that they'd taken the wrong passage. He could no longer see any of his marks. A tunnel, back a ways, had been blocked. He said they had to go back to it. This scared Boz. He had lost all track of time. But he doggedly backtracked with Kibosh, and when they came to the blocked passage, he dug in with his hands to help clear away the debris. It wasn't as bad as it had appeared. Kibosh had feared that the route was blocked by a massive collapse, but it was only a minor fall of rock and sand.

They were now, he realized when they got through, no more than a hundred yards from the exit. Just thinking of it scared him. They could have wandered forever—well, not forever, obviously—within a stone's throw from freedom.

Kibosh decided to halt. The air was fresher, but he didn't think that Boz, sweating and drunk, dazed by exertion and fear, was aware of it. Kibosh couldn't go on, not knowing what would happen once they saw the exit. He knew that it was still night. As they sat, drinking water and brandy, he said, "Boz, I got to know. What's gonna happen?"

"What do you mean?" Boz said. "At the End?"

"Yeah, at the end," Kibosh said.

Boz leaned his head back against the wall. Little grains of sand sifted down, sticking to his sweaty skin, but he didn't care anymore. He closed his eyes and after a moment, he said, "At the End, the Devil comes."

"Ah," Kibosh said, understanding now. "And who's he? I mean, what's he like?"

"He's a beast . . . he's awful," Boz said, his eyes still closed, letting his mind wander. "He's wet, hairy . . . big red eyes, like coals burning, teeth like daggers. He's huge and powerful, with long claws. He chooses the ones he knows. He takes them away."

"But what does he do with them?" Kibosh asked. He was momentarily distracted by this vision.

"He devours them, but they ain't eaten. No, he tears them into little pieces, but they ain't torn up. His hands are like ice, but they burn. It's awful, like you're chewed up, ripped apart, but you're still there."

Hands? Kibosh thought. "Is he a man? Does he have feet?" he asked.

"No, he ain't a man, but he's like a man. He's like . . . like a wolverine, or a badger. Ferocious."

"A badger?" Kibosh wondered if this was a joke. He wouldn't have thought Boz was capable of joking at this point.

"Like a monster badger-bear. Only he don't go on all fours, he don't have a hide, but his skin is like hairy leather. He walks sort of in a crouch. And his feet, they're like a turtle's," Boz said. "Or maybe a huge lizard. Claws. He's got a huge prick, giant hairy balls. He smells like shit, like he was dead."

Kibosh felt a hysterical mirth rising in him. This was too crazy, a Sunday school fantasy. Well, not any Sunday school he could remember. But a joke. From the tone of despair in Boz's voice, though, he could tell that on some level he believed this.

Kibosh coughed and cleared his throat. It was time to get serious. "Actually, I was meanin', what happens when we come to the exit."

"The exit?" Boz said, uncomprehending. And then he must

have caught something in Kibosh's tone. "You mean we're there?" The relief was plain on Boz's dirty face, in the dim light of the flash. "How far is it?"

"'Tain't far, but we got a couple a jinks," Kibosh said. "What are ye gonna do?"

"Do? Why, damn it, man, I'm gonna run! I'm gonna run across the field under that sky and I don't believe I'll stop running."

"I mean . . . what about me?" Kibosh said. "I want ye to know . . . it's like I never seen ye. As far as I'm concerned, ye can go anywhere ye want and nobody'll ever hear a bad word about ye from ol' Kibosh."

To his surprise, Boz smiled and reached out and hugged him. "Don't you worry, old man. You got me through. That's all I care about. I'd never harm you. Shit, man, we just slogged through the outskirts of hell together! We're buds." He was genuinely grateful. He opened his last bottle of County Fair. He took a deep swig, coughed, and handed it to Kibosh. "Don't you fret," he said, "I'd never put the kibosh on *you*." He laughed.

Kibosh drank and handed the bottle back. "Well, it has been a little bit a hell, ha'n't it?" He grinned uncertainly at the young man. "The outskirts, ye said. I like that. The suburbs, ye might say."

Boz drank again and screwed the lid back on tight and put the bottle in his pocket. He got to his feet with new vigor. "The city limits, maybe . . . and back, buddy. And I couldn't've done it without you. Now come on, let's get the fuck out of here."

Ostropaki

He was running up the hill through the forest, the branches slashing at his face and his breath coming in flashes of cold steam burning his chest and his throat, and below him the pursuers were shouting to one another, their voices high and excited, as they heard his gasping and his clumsy breaking of fallen limbs and crashing through the underbrush. And all the while a mechanical heart was buzzing in his breast pocket, calling to him. No time for that. He couldn't stop. If he was caught he'd be killed, murdered. Forced to kneel with his hands bound behind his back and wait, cringing, for the blow.

Then he awoke. Like that, it was over. Edna was prodding him. She said, "The phone! The phone!"

"I'm awake," he said, as calmly as if she hadn't been nearly punching him in the shoulder. He reached out and picked up the phone. "Tucker," he said.

"Vern? This is Max. I know it's late, but I thought you'd want to know right away. I think we've found Ostropaki."

"Alive? You're kidding. Where?"

"Would you believe Brooklyn?"

Tucker felt a coldness he hadn't experienced in some time, not since Vietnam. "When you say 'we,'" he said, "exactly who do you mean?"

"Me and Aaron."

"Does Aaron know you're calling me?"

"He thinks I'm calling Barnes, the night controller. Which," Max said, "I'll be calling next."

Tucker's brain processed all the permutations of this information very quickly. If Ostropaki was in Brooklyn and had not contacted him, or the DEA . . . and Max Kravfurt was calling Tucker first, before he contacted his controller . . . then Max had been following some sort of lead and at the end of it was Ostropaki, whom Max hadn't expected to see but whom he knew that Tucker would be interested in.

"Was this a tip?" Tucker asked. Max said it had been. "Let me guess," Tucker said. "Anonymous? A phone call? To you, specifically, or just the department?"

"Me," Max said. "I'll make it quick, then I got to go. Caller asked for me, said a man would make a delivery at a parking lot. One individual would get in the car. The driver would cruise while the individual checked out the goods. They would be in cell-phone contact with another vehicle. Caller didn't know where that car would be. If the goods were okay and if the party on the other end said the money was okay, the driver would stop at some pre-arranged point and the individual would hop out with the goods and get in another car, which would be going the other way. We barely had time to make the scene, but we spotted the car, followed, and the first stop he made was to pay a toll at the Triborough Bridge."

"The guy with the goods got away," the colonel said. "But you tailed the deliveryman? Have you arrested him, then?"

"For what?" Max said. "Giving a guy a ride?"

"So, you don't have the goods and you don't have the money, either. How do you know it's—"

"Ostropaki? I saw him, once, remember?"

"And where is he now?"

Max gave the address in Brooklyn.

"What will your report say?" the colonel asked.

"Blown lead," Max said. "It looks suspicious, but that's all. We did the best we could. We didn't know in time to set up anything. I'll be asking Barnes if I should question him, pick him up, whatever. My guess is that Barnes will tip off the NYPD, they'll watch him, pick him up sometime soon on some unrelated charge, and we'll be notified and have a chance to talk to him. I imagine that, at that point, you'll be notified."

"I imagine I will," Tucker said. "Well, thanks, Max. I appreciate the heads-up on this. It's good not to have it sprung on one."

"Just keep me in mind, Vern, if it works out for you."

"I will Max. You'd better call Barnes now."

When he set the phone down, Tucker lay back in the bed. Edna drew close, and he put his arm around her but continued to stare into the darkness of the bedroom. She didn't say anything. It was her way. He was grateful. He was also tired. It was nearly four A.M. Out in Montana—he subtracted two hours—it was almost two.

"Get some sleep," he said to Edna. He lay there until she fell asleep, then rose and went to the shower. Afterward, he left a note for Edna, explaining that he was going in to the office. He didn't mention Ostropaki, only that he'd call later, that lunch might not be possible.

It was raining pretty steadily. Once in the car, he tried to call Jammie. The service said, after several rings, "The party you are trying to reach is either out of range or otherwise unavailable. Please try your call later." As he was entering his office, however, the phone was ringing. It was Jammie.

"I was going to leave a message," Jammie said. "What are you doing there at this hour?"

The colonel explained about Ostropaki.

"I thought he was dead," she said.

"Apparently not. What do you know about him?" the colonel asked.

"He was a contract agent, wasn't he?" Jammie said. "Or was he—"

"More?" the colonel broke in. "In a way. But this is not a good time to discuss it. What are you calling about? It's pretty late there."

"How about Max?" she asked.

"You know Max? He's just fishing for a job. He hates working with Barnes and those guys. Are you in your car? What's going on?"

"We may have found Bazok," Jammie said. She explained that she was on her way to meet Joe Service, up some back road. The cell phones had some kind of interference. She had stopped to use a pay phone at the village en route. "He thinks he may have your man cornered."

"Badger in the holt," Tucker said. "This could be dangerous. Be careful. But what about Franko? Any word on him?"

"For all I know, Bazok may have found Franko," Jammie said.

"Where did he go to ground?"

"The situation's not clear to me yet," she said. "Somewhere out in the boonies. Communication isn't good. That's why I'm on the road." She didn't mention the mine.

"Quite a morning," the colonel said. "Raining here."

"Dry and clear here," Jammie said.

"You know . . . I've got a lot on my plate," the colonel said. "I think I'll leave this to you and Joe. I take it no local yokels are involved?"

"Really?" Jammie was surprised. "No, the locals don't know anything about it, as far as we know."

"That's good," the colonel said. "Let's leave it to Joe. How are you two getting along? You three."

"Joe was a little jumpy at first, but we're cool. Helen is leery of me, but she's okay."

"Leery? Ah, girl stuff? Well, she'll get over that. Now, you can offer your assistance with the badger, make suggestions, but let the decisions be Joe's. Let me know as soon as it's resolved. I'll probably be at the office, at least for a while yet, but call my cell number."

"As you say," Jammie said. "Are you expecting to see Ostropaki?"

"At some point, I imagine," the colonel said. "But probably not immediately, maybe not even today. It depends on how things turn out. Why?"

"I was wondering if you shouldn't come out here," Jammie said. "It may not be easy to get the badger out of his fort without involving the locals. You could be a big help with that. Bazok may know about Ostropaki."

"I would think so," the colonel said. "But it can't be helped. Let Joe run this, but if the badger looks like he's getting away . . . don't let him."

That was pretty clear. "Should I pass this on to Joe?" she said. "What about Franko?"

"Franko is Joe's job. He's got my instructions. Bazok . . . that's a matter for our disposition—yours, as it happens. So, no, I don't think it's necessary to confide in Joe about Bazok. Joe has badgerlike qualities himself. They're famous diggers, you know."

Jammie almost laughed. "Badgers?" she offered in a comic accent. "We don't need no stinkin' badgers."

Tucker was silent for a moment, but the best he could offer in response was, "Oh, dear." Then, "All right, call me as soon as you can. I may need some help on this other business."

"That might be a good idea," Jammie said. "Maybe you should hold off on meeting with Ostropaki until we're through here."

"Well, we'll have to see what develops," the colonel said.

Jammie saw Joe on the road, well down the hill from the Seven Dials. He hopped into her car and told her to take it slow, with her parking lights only. "This road's a little hairy for no lights," she said.

"You can do it," Joe said. He seemed in high spirits. "Did Paulie get the message? I couldn't be sure how much got through. Damn these mountains and phones."

"He said he thought you had Boz cornered, in this mine," Jammie said. "Isn't that right?"

"We haven't seen him," Joe said, "but Frank's truck was parked up there. Luckily, Frank had a key, so I coasted it down to this turn-out here—logging trucks use it. Just pull in. We can hike up."

The big Dodge Ram was parked next to the Durango. Before they started up the hill, Joe selected some armament. He took the H&K and offered Jammie an AK-47. "Have you ever used one of these?" he asked. She said she had.

As they made their way up the hill he explained the situation. He assumed that Boz had taken refuge with the old recluse Kibosh. The fact that the light had been on, then turned off suggested that Kibosh was aware that he was harboring somebody dangerous, but that Kibosh was still able to act with some freedom. They hadn't noticed any activity since they'd arrived. Frank was still on watch. He was armed with one of Joe's shotguns. Joe had decided that it would be the most effective weapon for Frank, who wasn't a hunter, no kind of shooter at all.

"I don't suppose you have some stun grenades or tear gas on you?" Joe asked her.

Jammie laughed. "Is that your plan?"

"It'd sure be handy," Joe said. "Any other suggestions?"

"Let's get a look at the situation first," Jammie said.

Frank was relieved to see them. He was standing well back from the entrance to the mine, among some ponderosas. "No movement," he told them.

Jammie sized up the situation. It seemed clear. The obvious solution was to wait for Bazok or Kibosh to come out as they normally would, in the morning. If one or the other showed in some reasonable time, they could easily position themselves on either side of the door, with another shooter in good cover back a ways to one side. With any luck, regardless of who came out, they'd be able to take that man. If it was Bazok, that would be all that was required. If Kibosh, it would remain to flush Bazok out, and there would be no reason for restraint. Kibosh, of course, would be able to inform them how well, if at all, Bazok was armed. Frank volunteered that Kibosh, at least, had a .30-06 deer rifle that fired a single shot at a time.

But, alas, the element of the tunnel system made it a different game. Frank explained to Jammie that Kibosh knew a route through the mountain with an exit at the river, not far from Frank's place. Paulie, at the other end with Helen, knew the exit that Kibosh had used before. The question was, Where was Bazok most likely to be right now? Sleeping unawares here, or on his way to the other side?

"I think we have to assume the tunnel is in play," Joe said. "Maybe Kibosh hasn't told him about the route, and even if he has, it probably wouldn't be Boz's preferred approach to Frank's place. But if he knows we're out here, that'll be his escape hatch."

Jammie saw the point. They could wait here for hours, in the belief that Boz was unaware of their presence. Or they could force the issue, drive him toward the other exit.

"I hate to give up the easy option, by letting him know that we're here," Joe said, "but we could sit here until ten o'clock, maybe later, waiting for him to wake up and come out. Without easy communication with Paulie and Helen, someone has to go back, and pretty quick, to man the other end."

Jammie agreed. The people on the other end would have to wait, too. The communication problem was critical. Also, where should they put their main guns?

What was needed was a SWAT team. "I think it's time to call the colonel," she said. Then she waited patiently while Joe argued her out of that.

"Okay," he said, "that's settled. Now, two reasonable assumptions: they don't know we're out here yet, and Kibosh is still alive. Boz will need Kibosh's help to get through. Let's say he is able to get that help, willingly or coerced. How long will it take them, Frank? The minimum?"

Frank said that the best he could recall, Kibosh had told him that he could get through in a couple of hours. Frank was skeptical of that figure—that had been a few years back. There was no telling what the tunnels were like now. Two hours would be the absolute minimum. More like three or four.

"Could they possibly make it in an hour?" Joe asked. "Just in theory?"

"No way," Frank said. "If it were a straight path, it would take an hour to walk it."

But he was not happy about Joe's idea of starting the hare. He feared that Kibosh was in too great a danger that way. He was for waiting, on the chance that Kibosh would come out, probably quite early. "He's an early riser," Frank said. "For all we know, he and Boz are getting along fine in there. Probably snoring away. Kibosh is a friendly old cuss. He'd take in a wounded bear, I'm afraid."

"That's about what he's done," Joe said. "Face it, Frank: your friend is in mortal danger just sitting next to this maniac. You saw how he was at the house. The longer we wait here, the greater the danger becomes."

Frank wasn't sure. Waiting seemed such an ideal solution. "Let's wait till dawn, anyway," he said.

"It's not going to happen," Joe said firmly. "In about five minutes I'm going in. If Boz is in there we'll have an exchange of fire. If all Boz has is the rifle, Kibosh's main danger will be from us. I hope Kibosh isn't hurt. The chances are . . . fair. The chance of us nabbing Boz by waiting is only slightly better. If we don't get Boz—or, God forbid, Kibosh—then Boz will have a hostage and I don't like your friend's chances at all."

Frank gave in.

"Here's how we do it," Joe said, glad the arguing was past. He was ready for action. He outlined his plan to them both. When it was clear and they accepted it, he told Jammie, "You stand on the near side of the entry, Frank on the far side. I'll bring up the truck. You'll be ready to fire at Boz, as soon as you're sure of your target, Jammie.

"Frank, just fire in the air, make some noise. If they're not in there and we can be fairly sure that they've made an attempt to get through, at least one of us will have to stay here to make sure they don't double back. I guess that'll have to be you, Jammie. Frank can stay, if you like, and I'll have maybe a half hour to get to the other side."

Jammie shrugged. "Let's see what happens first; then we can figure out the rest. Somebody could get hurt."

Joe accepted that. He saw them stationed, then ran back down the hill. He set the H&K submachine gun on the seat of the Dodge Ram and stuffed extra clips into his pockets, Boz's Glock into his belt. Then he revved it up. "Here we go," he said to himself, and started his run. He raced the big truck up the road, the lights on, and at the little clearing before the entrance to the mine, he swerved and floored the accelerator. The big truck plunged into the frame structure of the entry with a splintering smash. Just before impact, he had a glimpse of Jammie jumping out of the way.

The impact was greater than he had imagined. Having slipped the shoulder harness of the seat belt off so he could duck down to avoid any gunfire, he was thrown violently against the steering wheel. He could hear the shotgun blasting. Great! And there was, as yet, no fire from the AK-47. Momentarily dazed, he found the H&K and crawled out of the wreckage, incongruously thinking that the colonel was going to have to pay Frank for damage to his truck.

The dust was totally obscuring. He decided that the best thing was to crawl under the truck, with its high clearance. Jammie was calling, "Kibosh! Get down! Get down!" The shotgun was still blasting, then stopped. Joe crept forward. Through the wreckage of the room he could see no sign of any movement. One headlight was still on, but the truck's engine had died.

He crawled on. Within a few seconds he was certain of what he had expected: the living space was empty. The entry into the drift was open. They had gone. But how recently?

"Okay!" he called out. "They're running!"

Jammie appeared. She saw the situation. "They may not have gone far," she said.

"You want to wait here?" Joe said. "Or pursue them? We'd be in trouble in a hundred feet if Boz is waiting for us."

Jammie insisted on venturing at least a little ways into the tunnel. Unfortunately, they had only the single headlight of the wrecked truck for illumination.

"I've got a light in my car," Jammie said.

"Well, get it," Joe said. "Time's wasting. I'll stay here with Frank."

She was back in ten minutes with the car. The light she brought was sufficient for them to venture into the tunnel far enough to convince them that Boz and Kibosh had bolted for the other exit. The tracks of the two men were easy enough to follow. Jammie was all for pursuing them.

"No," Joe said. "For all we know, they've got an hour's head start. That's too much. I think you or I could hold this end, in case they double back. The place to wait is at the mouth, here. With any luck, we can maintain some kind of communication. But I'm for getting to the other end."

Jammie conceded the point. She would stay.

Joe and Frank raced down the hill. While Joe drove recklessly down the mountain, Frank tried to call Paulie. He was unable to get through until they reached the freeway. "Keep a good watch," Frank told him, explaining what had occurred. "We'll be there as quickly as we can."

In fact, it took them more than a half hour. Joe drove straight across the meadow, bouncing over rocks and hoping he wasn't going to rip out the transmission. At last, however, he had to cut the lights, and he stopped. They piled out of the Durango and raced over the ridge and down to the river.

The river was freezing, much swifter and deeper than Joe had thought. It seemed only a foot or two deep, but once they were in the water it proved to have much deeper holes and was flowing quite fast. At one point, he lost his footing and was swept downstream, barely keeping the H&K aloft. But he regained his feet and saw that Frank was already on the bank.

"It looked like such a placid stream," Joe said, shivering when he caught up to Frank.

"There's places to wade, if you know the stream," Frank said. He was wet only to his knees.

It was still very dark, but dawn was beginning to show in the east. Paulie appeared. "The entrance Kibosh used is up there," he said, pointing at the cliff.

The entrance was little more than a dark spot, apparently seventy-five or eighty feet above the gravelly talus that sloped up from the river's edge, here, to the base of the cliff.

"As soon as the sun gets up," Paulie said, "in about twenty minutes, the rays will strike the ridge up there and then the edge of the sunlight will quickly begin to drop down, lighting up that whole cliff face. It's quite a sight, just a blaze of red and gold."

Morning mist was rising off the river. It was cold.

Helen was waiting in the sparse shelter of some low brush, about fifty feet downstream. She had the other Glock and Paulie had the little .410 shotgun. Joe wished he had thought to bring another gun; the guns were back in the Durango, across the river. He sent Frank back to get the other AK-47 and the Stoner rifle. "Be sure you get plenty of ammo," he told him.

Boz had never been so glad to see anything like that pale patch of sky at the mouth of the tunnel.

"By God, Kibe, we found it!" he exclaimed. He ran to the opening and suddenly caught himself. "Jesus Christ!" There was a huge drop to the river. Another step and he'd have fallen to his death.

"Now what?" he said as Kibe came up beside him.

"Aw, don't worry," Kibe assured him, "there's a path. Jist gotta take it easy." He paused and looked out. He was dead tired, to say nothing of still being dazed from when Boz had knocked him against the rock back there. He felt a little shaky. "I believe I'll set a spell," he said, "till I get my bearin's."

"Might be better to wait till it gets a little more light," Boz agreed. He looked dubiously at the narrow path. From up here he could make out the top of Frank's house, beyond the ridge. Daybreak was a broad swatch of deep purple and red, staining the sky beyond the black silhouette of the mountains to the east, and growing redder by the minute—you could almost believe it was a massive conflagration over there, a forest fire. The sky above was lighter, especially toward the east, but many stars were still visible. Everything nearer at hand was in deep shadow. The path, what Boz could see of it, was at least a couple of feet wide, quite manageable. But like Kibosh, he was leery of trying an immediate descent. He didn't feel all that stable himself.

He sat down by the opening and felt around for his remaining bottle of whiskey. He comforted himself with a long draught. He looked over at Kibosh, who was drinking from a jar of water. Now was as good a time as any, Boz thought, to get rid of this encumbrance. He unconsciously felt his pocket, where the Star automatic nestled. But then it occurred to him that he still had to get to the house. Kibosh might come in handy as a hostage.

"Kibe," he said, warmly, "you're a good man. You got us through. I thought I'd die in there. But we still got a ways to go."

"Sun'll be up soon," Kibosh said. He'd noticed Boz's gesture toward his pocket. He reckoned that his night of terror was not over yet. He wondered if he'd have a chance to push this bastard off the side. He would do it cheerfully. He was worried now, about his friends. Would they remember this exit? He hoped so. But what if they hadn't come to Seven Dials last night, after all? There was a good chance that he and Boz had undertaken this trip through the mountain in the dead of night just from being spooked by a bear, or a curious nocturnal badger that had come snooping around the Seven Dials, drawn by the smell of the sausages in the smoker. It could have been nothing more than a curious skunk! Maybe no one had been outside the door of the Seven Dials at all. Maybe Frankie and Paulie were still sleeping over there, at the house.

The sun was rising quickly but hadn't crested the mountains. Kibosh knew it would soon illuminate this cliff face, a grand sight if you were out there on the meadow. The morning fly hatch would be coming off along the river, which he could now see was blanketed with mist, below them. The trout would be rising. It would be a great thing to be down there with a fly rod, he imagined. Probably, at this time of year, some kind of *Trico* hatch, followed by some *Baetis*, maybe some caddis. He could weep.

"It's getting pretty light pretty fast," Boz said. "Time to go." He hefted the deer rifle and gestured for Kibosh to lead.

So there goes that chance, Kibosh thought. He picked up the backpack.

"Leave it," Boz said. "We don't need it no more. We'll have to move fast, once we get down from here."

They stepped out into the still dim daylight. Above them, the sun was catching the top of the cliff. They began to move cautiously down the path.

Below them, Joe saw the two men leave the hole in the wall and set out on the path. At last! Until this second he had feared the worst. It occurred to him suddenly that he could have been wildly, completely wrong, that Boz might not have been in the Seven Dials at all. The only evidence was the presence of Frank's truck, but Boz could have abandoned it for any number of reasons. He could have allies, supporters he had contacted, who had come and picked him up. He shook his head, marveling at his failure to take that into account. But here they were, moving along the cliff wall like silhouette ducks in a shooting gallery.

He hoisted the H&K. From this steep angle he could see only the head and shoulders of Kibosh and more of the upper body of Boz. The angle was miserable. It was too far for the H&K.

Paulie had explained that the trail came down to their right, then switched back and headed toward them. From their position among the jumbled rocks they had very good cover. The trouble was, as the two men approached, Kibosh would be in the line of fire for much of the time. The best thing would be to wait until the hikers reached a point about fifty feet from the very base, the talus. At that point, they would be no more than a hundred feet away. There was a path that led down to the river that angled farther to their left. Helen was down there, well hidden in the brush. If the two men got that far, they would pass within touching distance of her.

Joe looked at Frank, crouching nearby in the rocks. He was clutching the Stoner rifle gingerly, the tension evident in his face. "You okay?" Joe asked.

Frank looked up and nodded at him. "Ready as I'll ever be," he said. "Do we just wait for them?" It seemed too easy.

"He's got the rifle," Joe said. "If I can get to that rock there"—he pointed to a large rock at a point where the men on the path would pass, about three feet above—"I'll be below him. I'll shout for him to drop the gun. If he doesn't drop it, I can take his legs out."

"You'd be in my line of fire," Frank said. "I'm not much of a shot and I don't know this gun . . ."

"You'll be all right," Joe said. "Just remember what I showed you. When he gets to the farthest point of the descent, before the trail switches back, I'll make a dash. If he sees me, Kibosh will be in our line. But maybe I can creep a little closer now. It's worth the risk."

To Paulie, crouched a little farther down the trail, Joe called softly, "Hold your fire. That shotgun will be as dangerous to Kibosh as to Boz. It could be useful later, though."

Joe looked at the field of broken rocks between him and the covering boulder. It was in deep shadow. He crept out and began to make his way, in a crouch, across the space. Above him, now farther away than initially, he could see the two men carefully picking their way down the ramplike path toward the switchback. He scuttled forward, missed his step, and banged his knee painfully on a sharp rock. It was painful, but he didn't cry out. Worse, however, the H&K had also banged against a rock. He saw Boz turn sharply, and Joe lowered his face to the rocks, afraid that the paleness of it would be visible. He waited.

Boz heard a metallic noise. "What was that?" he said to Kibosh, stopping and crouching.

Kibosh turned. "What was what? I didn't hear nothin'."

"You didn't hear that clank?"

Kibosh shook his head. "Rock," he said confidently. "The sun warms the rocks and they expand. They'll be more falling." He pointed upward. The sun was rapidly creeping down the cliff. As if in demonstration, a fist-sized rock came tumbling down, twenty feet away, struck a projection of the cliff, and spun out into space. "Little by little," he said, "this mountain is falling down."

But he had heard the clank, all right. His heart bounded within him. Boz seemed convinced, however. He leaned back against the cliff and drank from his bottle.

"Almost dry," he said. "Hope they didn't drink all my vodka back at the house." He bared his teeth in his dirty, bristly face. It was a smile. He drank the last of the whiskey and then hurled the bottle out in a great arc. It smashed on the rocks below. He laughed. "No one there." Suddenly a thought struck him. "You had another bottle in that pack, didn't you? Damn! Go back and get it."

"You want me to go back?" Kibosh asked.

Boz reconsidered. The narrow path had been quite scary when they were farther up. Now that they were only twenty feet or so from the ground below, as rocky and jagged as it looked, he felt much more secure. Even if he fell here, the worst that was likely to happen was a broken leg, not death. The thought of climbing all the way back up there, in his spacey condition, was not appealing. He figured he could cover Kibosh with the rifle, in case he tried to escape . . . but what if he ducked back into the mountain? There was no way he was going to go back in there after him.

"To hell with it," he said. "I'll get more at the house. Come on, let's go."

The bottle had crashed not far from Joe. It had startled him, then he'd realized what it was—just Boz heaving an empty bottle. He lay there, his face still down. Finally, he dared to peek upward. The men were moving. But they had made the turn and were coming his way. He was lying in the open, no real cover, just small rocks not much bigger than a bushel basket nearby. And the sun was racing down the face of the cliff. If it reached him he would be too obvious to be missed, unless the men had already passed. He lay still and begged Kibosh mentally to hasten, get past him.

A gentle breeze, stirred by the warming air above, began to shift the still dense mist off the river and toward the cliff. The cold fog rolled over Joe.

Oh, yes, he breathed. Now he could hear the men's shoes scraping on the path. He glanced at the H&K. It was set on automatic fire. The clip would empty in a second. Did he dare to set it on the three-shot cycle? Would it make a noise? He decided against it.

The steps came closer. Somehow Joe kept his face down. The mist helped. They were abreast of him. Moved another step beyond. He scrambled to his feet.

"Drop it!" Joe yelled.

Boz spun, lost his footing for a second, and reeled back against the cliff, sitting down roughly. He hoisted the rifle to his shoulder, pointing in Joe's direction—the scope was a nuisance at this range. Kibosh stooped, found a rock, and hurled it at Boz. It struck him on the shoulder as he fired, the shot going wild. Boz swore, racked the bolt back and forward to bring another cartridge into the chamber. Kibosh began to run down the ramp, toward Paulie's position. Boz looked first in the direction of Joe's voice, but all he saw was mist. He turned toward the running Kibosh and lifted the rifle.

Frank fired, a full clip of .223-caliber bullets. The rifle made a continuous string of flat punching noises. The bullets spanged off the rocks above and to the left of Boz.

When Boz slipped, Joe had found that his target was obscured by the rocks in front of him. He scrambled up, slipping and scraping his ankle and lurching against another sharp rock, desperately seeking an angle of fire.

Boz turned and raced back up the path, in a crouch. Joe twisted, off balance, and pulled the trigger on the H&K, spewing an entire thirty-shot clip into the cliff face in three seconds. In his haste, he'd forgotten the autofire.

He scrambled after Boz, ejecting the clip and finding another, stumbling, half-falling. He had to stop to jam the clip home. And now he discovered a further difficulty: how to get up onto the ramp? Above him, he could see that Boz had made the turn and was chugging rather more slowly up toward the cave entrance. He could even hear the man's gasping breath.

Joe clambered onto a boulder, then hopped to another. The H&K was an annoyance, but he wasn't about to abandon it. Behind him he could hear Frank, who had finally remembered Joe's instruction of how to put another clip into the Stoner rifle, and also to switch to semiautomatic fire: he was firing slowly spaced shots—light, cracking shots, the bullets ringing off the rocks. His angle of fire would not provide much of a target, Joe knew. Then he heard a loud crack from above as Boz fired back, followed by the racking of the bolt.

Joe hauled himself onto the path, on his belly, swinging his leg up, confident that Boz couldn't have a fair shot at him. He got to his feet and raced up the path.

He made the turn and started up the longer run of the ramp. Far ahead, he could see Boz laboring, crouching with one hand against the cliff face, the rifle in the other. Joe stopped and yanked out the retractable skeletal buttstock and took aim, taking care this time to move the fire selector to single fire. He fired four evenly spaced shots, to no visible effect. Then Boz disappeared.

Joe raced on, his breath tearing in his throat. When he reached the top he stopped short of the mouth of the opening. Oh, for a grenade, he thought. Boz was in an unassailable position. Joe had no idea how the tunnel lay, but he supposed that it ran straight back for at least a short distance. Boz could take his stand there, and if he could work the bolt fast enough, he'd be able to shoot three, four, maybe five attackers, who would have to enter more or less one at a time.

"Boz!" he called. "It's no use. You might as well save us all some trouble. You can't come out and you'll never make it back. We've got the other end blocked."

There was no answer. Joe hadn't expected one. He listened. All he could hear was the breeze and an occasional stone rattling down the cliff from above. He leaned against the cliff to recover his breath and to rest his aching legs. He looked off at the view, the sun over the mountains to the east turning the trees to green from black, a raven soaring, the silvery thread of the river in the distance.

If I had a cowboy hat, he thought, I'd hang it on the barrel and extend it out to invite a shot. But he had no hat. He wiped his brow and waited for Frank, trudging up the path, followed by Helen. There was no need for them to hurry, they knew.

When Frank arrived he rested his back against the cliff and breathed for a minute, then straightened and said, "Sorry, Joe. I'm not such a good shot."

Joe smiled wryly. "Ah, you know how it is . . . you take it out of a case, throw it in the back of the car, take it out . . . the sights get totally out of whack. Anyway, it's a hell of a shot to hit a running target at that range. You did fine." Joe knew that Frank was never going to actually fire at Boz, but any kind of fire was helpful.

He looked down at the H&K, moved the lever to the three-shot position. "I think he's gone in deep," he said. "Probably thinks he can walk all the way back. But we have to find out. I'm going to jump across to that opposite wall, low, firing bursts. When I go, you just stick the barrel in the entry and let a whole clip rip. Okay?"

Frank looked at him, his face streaked with sweat and dust, his glasses smeared. "Give me another minute," he said. He breathed deeply, checking the clip. He took it out, decided to replace it with a full one, then delved in his pockets for cartridges to reload the partially depleted one. He stuffed that one in his shirt pocket. "Okay," he said.

Joe nodded and dove for the opposite side of the opening, firing as he went, then flattening himself as best he could against the wall while Frank stuck the Stoner around the corner and emptied a full clip into the drift.

No response. Joe got to his feet and moved into the drift. He could see now that the drift angled upward. Their shots would have struck the floor perhaps twenty feet within. Frank entered beside him, inserting a fresh clip and racking the slide back and forward.

"Got our hands full now," he said.

Helen arrived and peeped in. "Now do we call the colonel?" she said.

"No," Joe said. "It would take a company of troops to get him out. The colonel won't send them. But"—he smiled wearily at both of them—"at least we're out here, and Bazok isn't. We know where he has to come out. Don't we?"

"Kibosh knows," Helen said. "He's down there, being comforted by Paulie."

"You want to stay here?" Joe said to Helen. "I'll go down and talk to him."

"Take your time," Helen said, "but someone better bring me some water, pretty soon, and maybe some coffee. A doughnut would be nice, although the thought of it gags me at the moment."

Kibosh had recovered when Joe found him with Paulie. Joe explained the situation to them. They listened to Kibosh's account of the nightmarish trek.

"I don't b'lieve he'll git very far," Kibosh said. "He was awful scared in there, panicky. An' he didn' seem to have any notion of the signs I made. Been drinkin' awful heavy, too, since we got up yesterday mornin'. Lord, I didn' know if I'd see this mornin'. I'm grateful to ye."

In response to Joe's careful questioning, Kibosh opined that Boz might get no farther than a few hundred feet into the interlocked drifts and shafts of the mines. "He's got a horror of it," he said. "It's a real hell to him. But the man's got guts, ye gotta give him that. The thing of it is, he could stumble on one a them other passages and find his way out, on this side. I don't know how many exits there could be. Probably not more'n a half dozen that a man could get through. I never explored the whole thing, not on this side. But I reckon he won't find none a them. I reckon he'll give out, afore too long. Did he snatch up that pack of mine?"

Joe said he hadn't seen the pack. "What was in it?"

"About three a them packs of Twinkies," Kibosh said, "a jug a water, a fif' a whiskey—he'll be glad a that—some rope. Lessee, what else?" He thought. "Oh, a can a sardines. A little jar a them pickles, whatcha call 'em, gherkins. Some matches, my good pipe, and some terbaccy. That's about it."

"Pickles?" Joe said.

"I jist grabbed 'em off the shelf," Kibosh said. "An' the flashlights, a course. Two of 'em."

Joe asked which was the most likely alternate exit. Kibosh pointed downstream. There was a very old mine down that way that he had actually taken the time to investigate. He was pretty sure it closed off before it reached a drift that would communicate with the one Boz was in. But it was possible that if it wasn't much of cave-in, a person could get through. If he was desperate enough.

"He's desperate enough," Joe said. "Come on, we'll take a look."

Kibosh sighed. "I'm dead beat," he said. "I could use some grub. An' we'd need some flashlights."

Joe nodded. "You're right," he said. "We better regroup. Boz is in there, though, and aching to get out, I'm sure. I think you're right—he won't try to make it out the other side. Paulie, can you take Kibosh back to the house and get what we need? Helen and Frank and I will stay here, keep watch. Oh, and try to get through to Jammie, explain what happened. I think she can come on over. I'm with Kibosh . . . Boz won't try to backtrack."

Parannoniac Arrest

Colonel Tucker was in his office for hours before he received a call from the deputy director of operations. In that time he did little more than sit and think, doodling with a pencil on a pad while he tried to sort out the meaning of Ostropaki's reappearance, and the possible problems that lay ahead.

The obvious inference was that Ostropaki had lied, that the whole operation had been a setup, including "Franko." Ostropaki must have been working with the drug dealers—if not from the start, then at least for some time. They had colluded to set up this "interdiction" operation in order to mask their real trade routes. It was a shell game. And when the war began to get too close, they shut it down, by "eliminating" first Ostropaki, then "Franko." The colonel wondered if there had ever been a real "Franko," or if that was just fiction, too. If so, little wonder that the redoubtable Joe Service had been unable to find this mysterious nonperson.

He got on the computer and logged in to see some files on the operation. He jotted down a column of figures representing drugs seized, along with money, in the various intercepts of this operation. The whole thing had run for more than two years. Counting seizures in ports, on the sea, in Italy, and so on, he came up with a quick rough figure of more than two thousand kilos of heroin and opium, plus upwards of a million dollars in actual cash of various denominations. More than a dozen drug runners had been arrested and prosecuted; others were killed in fleeing, or in violent confrontations. Vehicles were impounded, including boats. All of this with no loss of life to any agents of the DEA, except the "adjunct agents," Ostropaki and "Franko."

There was no denying it: the "Pannonian Putsch," as some DEA wag had dubbed it, invoking the ancient Roman term for those hinterlands of the empire, had been a resounding success. In fact, some had taken to calling it the "Parannoniac Arrest," playing on the constant atmosphere of distrust and betrayal that had seemed so typical of Balkan dealings.

He wrote PANNONIA in large block letters on his pad, then began to analyze the figures again. Quite a few of those seizures were not verified, merely estimated. This was particularly true of the seizures at sea, where items were frequently cast overboard during chases by coast patrols and/or international police agencies. And there was frequently no real verification that all of the materials seized were analyzed before destruction or being turned over to local authorities—conceivably a large percentage could have been other substances, only resembling a bag of heroin, say.

Quite a few of the people arrested were highly expendable types, either untrustworthy or incompetent, and no loss to the smugglers. There were, in fact, no major figures in the trade arrested and prosecuted. Indeed, the major losses to the campaign were Ostropaki and "Franko." Even the million-plus dollars dwindled to what might be considered a normal loss in this trade, the cost of doing business.

When looked at with that kind of harshly critical eye, the Pannonian Putsch began to look like a farcical Keystone Kops raid. But the colonel was unconvinced. Any operation could be made to seem a failure. You went up on Route Pack Six, destroyed a SAM site, bombed the railroad, the steel mill, and had a possible MiG kill and the analysts told you the next day it was a wash, hadn't slowed the Cong at all. Still, they'd known you were there, and you were coming again today, and tonight. Maybe it was a similar run, here. It all depended on Ostropaki.

He noted, incidentally, that one of the more active DEA agents in these interceptions was J. Sanders. She had really gotten her feet wet in this operation, he recalled. It was how she had first come to his attention as a potential recruit to the Lucani.

The phone rang shortly after nine. It was the deputy director's office, asking for Tucker's presence. He said he'd be right in. Before he made his way to the DDO's office, he tore off the sheet of paper he'd been doodling on, to stick it into the shredder. He saw that he had unconsciously overwritten PANNONIA to make PARANNONIAC, and then made bold the letters that spelled PANIC. For some reason, this lightened his spirits.

"Vern, do you remember a fellow named Theo Ostropaki?" the DDO asked when he entered. The DDO was a stocky man who often wore what struck Tucker as a civilian version of marine dress khakis, smartly tailored tan or at least light brown gabardine suits, to go with his ex-marine brush haircut. He was generally genial, though not particularly so this morning.

"Of course you do," the DDO answered his own question. "Man, that was a sweet operation! We put a real dent in the flow of that pipeline. Well, can you believe it, he's surfaced! In Brooklyn!"

The colonel managed to look surprised. He listened to the whole account, a hastily paraphrased version of Kravfurt's report. "What does this suggest to you?" the DDO asked with the shrewd look of a used-car salesman.

"It sounds like the reports of his death were exaggerated," Tucker said.

"Heh, heh," the DDO said, with no joy. "I believe I've heard that one. But beyond that?"

"Our assumptions of Ostropaki's role may have to be reevaluated," Tucker said.

"*Your* assumptions," the DDO amended. "But, what the hell, you had to draw reasonable conclusions from inadequate intelligence—your own intelligence, I might add." He was being generous, not actually kicking butt.

Tucker listened closely, trying to read any nuances here. He reminded himself of the panic inherent in paranoiac. The DDO, he realized, was more concerned to establish firmly who was responsible for this debacle than to seriously examine the merits of the operation. Tucker could not detect any suspicion in the DDO's remarks that he thought his actions had been other than inept.

"Sir," Tucker said, eschewing any familiarity by not using his superior's first name, although they were on good terms, "I take full responsibility. I've got to admit, it looks like we—I—accepted too readily Ostropaki's evasions and explanations. But if you'll allow me a word of caution here . . . sometimes in the morning mist the ducks look a lot like the decoys."

The DDO liked that metaphor. He narrowed his eyes with a little half smile, perhaps recalling some morning in the blind. He opened a desk drawer and took out a large black cigar. "Care for one?" he said. "They're not Havanas, but good chewers, Honduran. No?" He put the cigar in his mouth and began to chew, gently. "Okay, Vern, I take your point. Why don't you get up there to Brooklyn and see which of these ducks can fly? It looks a little murky right now, but no need to panic. Hell, we may end up giving this guy a medal. But if it plays out like it sounds, it's your mess. I'm going to let you clean it up."

There was a slight emphasis on those closing words. Tucker relaxed. The DDO would be happy if all this could be explained in some defensible way. And if not, even a familiar plot line might suffice: it wasn't as if the community was unfamiliar with the sad story of a contract agent who had played a double game. Happened all the time. The manly thing to do was own up to a mistake and then sweep it under the carpet.

The DDO even rehearsed the well-known scenario: Ostropaki had allowed them to snatch a few shipments, diversions, so that the real shipments got through. The "real dent in the flow" was instantly reduced to a paltry leak. The best deal might be to find out if Ostropaki could be turned again, give them a real handle on the main villains. That would get Ostropaki out of the country, away from congressional oversight committees and possible publicity of their failure.

"The NYPD's task force is going to pick him up the minute he shows his face," the DDO said. "They're happy to cooperate. It was our coup that identified him. They'll want some quid pro quo, of course. I'm counting on you to handle this with discretion, give them something, but don't let them see that our faces are red. Don't be arrogant, Vern. We can't just hustle this guy off to some safe house. It's got to be done in plain sight, with them looking on. Think you can handle that?"

That was a nasty swipe. As much as to say, You blew it, you bungler. Now make us look good.

"I'll get on it right away, sir."

In fact, the shuttle got him from National to La Guardia a little after eleven o'clock. Ten minutes later, Max Kravfurt was driving him to a rendezvous with a Detective Porter, in Brooklyn.

"How are you getting along with Barnes, Max?" the colonel asked, as they drove.

He listened with interest to Kravfurt's cautiously worded complaints about bureaucratic pusillanimity. Tucker wanted to hear genuine gripes, not sour grapes. He had sounded Kravfurt out in the past on this and found him a potential candidate for the Lucani. Now was a good time to audition Kravfurt's song, to hear if he at least got all the notes right.

"You don't have to sugarcoat it, Max," he said. "We're in this together. You should have seen me kissing the cardinal's ring about an hour ago. What a desk jockey!"

Kravfurt was eager to yodel. He immediately launched into an aria about an operation he'd been on a few months earlier.

"Are we talking about that Congressman Heller sting?" the colonel asked at one point, interrupting the diatribe. "I didn't know you were involved in that. Who else was on the case?"

"It was a cousin of mine who tipped me," Kravfurt assured him. "We grew up in the same neighborhood as Heller. Mike knew him better than I did. He called me, said Heller was living pretty rich, new cars, a house in Florida, shtupping some kid half his age, a dancer at Tori's. Twenty-year marriage crashing. Worse, he's hanging out with some old neighborhood mopes. Well, you know a congressman: he's got backers, they throw him stock tips, pad his campaign fund—he's bound to be doing all right. But it was more than that. These are mob guys, dealers, he's hanging with. They're cutting him into the distribution end, and Heller's into the coke himself. He was making an ass of himself.

"I developed the whole case, me and Aaron. Then what happens? When I set up the buy, Heller sends some hood Aaron remembered from that LaGuardia case, doesn't show himself. We brought in that babe that worked on the Franko stuff overseas, Jamala Sanders—you remember her?"

"Sanders? Sure. Why her?" the colonel said.

"She can look black," Kravfurt said. "Plays it real good. And she hasn't been seen around here. Anyway, she's the buyer. When Heller doesn't show, she pitches a monumental bitch, takes a hike.

Smart gal. So we go through the whole thing again. Aaron tells Heller that she got spooked, something about the contact. She thought he was a rat, maybe working off a rap for the feds. Heller says that's bullshit. Anyway, to make a long story short, he finally agrees to meet her himself. We had a man with a long lens, got photos, tapes, the coke, marked money he deposits in his own bank account, the whole schmear."

"So what happened? How did Heller walk?"

"Politics," Kravfurt said, a clear, pure note of disgust. "Somebody owed somebody. All I know is Barnes calls me and Aaron in, says the evidence was tainted. We're transferred to another case. Lucky we weren't sent to another division, even fired. We'd messed the whole thing up. Heller quits Congress, pleads bad health. That was the deal they worked with him, obviously. He's down in Florida, now, free as a bird."

This was the sort of thing that the colonel wanted. He could check it out with Jammie. The sooner the better. But first, Ostropaki.

Detective Porter and his assistant, Detective Cook, met them in a coffee shop on Flatbush Avenue. Some NYPD undercover cops were watching the house. It was an apartment building, actually, an older place just a few blocks away. A number of Muslims lived in the building, Albanians. Ostropaki could be staying with any of them. They couldn't be sure which apartment. The plan was to wait for him to come out. As soon as he tried to drive anywhere he could be pulled over for some real or imagined violation. Then Porter and Cook would be called in. Ostropaki would be taken to the precinct. Tucker could talk to him there. If necessary, some coke could be "found" in the Ostropaki car.

"That won't be necessary," the colonel said. "We've got legitimate reasons to ask him questions about operations outside the country. But if you want to . . ."

Porter and Cook could wait on that, they said. They'd like to see what came out. "Hell, with any luck," Cook chimed in, "the guy will be making another delivery."

They all went for a drive-by, to look at the house. It was an ordinary brick building, three stories, no elevator. Four apartments on each floor, but from what the undercover guys had seen, it looked like a couple of hundred people lived there, Porter told them. Well, maybe not that many, but many more than one would expect. Could be a violation of housing ordinances—a dozen apartments converted into two dozen, or more. Almost bound to be. Foreign types coming and going more or less constantly. Nobody seemed to work. Women in shawls, men in funny hats.

The four men returned to the diner to wait, chatting, talking shop. Tucker was anxious to get away, not only from the detectives but from Max. He wanted to call Jammie, find out what was going down in Montana. He had a feeling that Joe would be able to wrap that up. Maybe the thing to do was simply go back to the Manhattan office with Kravfurt, since Ostropaki didn't show any sign of moving. He and Max could always be called when the pickup occurred. The only thing was, he wanted to be on the spot, in case Ostropaki began to talk. Tucker wanted him to talk, but not too freely. He wanted to get Jammie back, now. Let Joe do his thing.

About one, the watchers called in. An unexpected type had shown up at the apartment house, in a cab. A burly man in a black suit, carrying a briefcase. He'd gone into the house.

"A delivery!" Cook declared. "Mr. Big! Let's go in."

"Mr. Big?" Porter laughed. "We don't have a make on him. We don't know which apartment he went into. Maybe he has nothing to do with our delivery boy. We'd never get a warrant on that."

"A burly guy, in his sixties?" Cook said. "We give him an ID! Sounds like Boomie Karns," he said.

They amused themselves trying to attach a name and face to this "burly" visitor. About forty minutes passed, and Tucker began to think that he could reasonably plead a lunch date. He had a feeling that if Ostropaki had been up all night, he might not be going out, if at all, before late afternoon. By now, he thought, Jammie and Joe had probably taken care of Bazok. He was anxious to know.

Then the word came: Ostropaki was on the move. The detectives took their car, Tucker rode with Kravfurt. The cops had allowed Ostropaki to get well away from the house but stopped him before he got on the freeway. The cops had pulled him over on a side street.

"Thanks, guys," Porter told the uniforms as he approached Ostropaki's car. "We'll take him. Get this car towed. We'll want a thorough search of it."

The colonel and Kravfurt watched from their car. "That's him, all right," Tucker said. They followed the detectives to the precinct. The detectives had Ostropaki in an interrogation room when the colonel and Kravfurt entered.

"Colonel!" Ostropaki said. He looked relieved. He smiled and stood up to hold out his hand. But the colonel ignored it, giving him a cold look. Ostropaki, chastened, sat down again.

The colonel took a chair across the table from Ostropaki. A tape recorder sat on the table, but not turned on. The colonel knew that they were being recorded, however. This was a delicate moment.

Tucker gestured at the tape machine and asked Porter, "How does this work?" Porter showed him. Tucker turned on the machine and gave the date, the time, the place, then identified himself and those present. Ostropaki watched quietly.

"The subject is known to me as Theodore Ostropaki," the colonel said. "Is that your correct name? Please speak up. Give us your nationality and date of entry to the United States, how you arrived . . ."

Ostropaki was very cooperative. He had entered two days earlier, was visiting friends and professional contacts. He gave the address of the apartment and the names of the friends. They were Albanian immigrants. He worked for an international refugee organization and was here to provide information about missing relatives, that sort of thing. It all sounded quite legitimate and reasonable. The colonel had his passport. It had been issued by the Albanian government, where he now resided. The date on it was a week old.

The colonel asked him about that. Ostropaki explained that he had been a refugee himself. He'd been caught in the outbreak of hostilities in Kosovo and had fled with people who protected him, to Albania. There, for many reasons, he began to involve himself in the refugee problem. Ultimately, he went to work for the agency that had helped him. He hadn't needed a passport before this, his first trip out of the country.

"What did you do in Kosovo?" the colonel asked.

"I was sales representative for a large firm in Athens," Ostropaki said. "Building supplies. I traveled all over . . . Bosnia, Herzegovina, Serbia. I have very good languages, you see. I speak Serbo-Croatian, Bulgarian, Romanian . . ." He went on, describing this good, well-paying job. He seemed calm, as if he knew that all this was a mere formality and soon he would be allowed to return to his friends.

"Where were you going just now?" the colonel asked.

"Breakfast," Ostropaki said. "I was up late last night and slept in."

"What were you doing last night?" the colonel asked.

"I had to meet a man whose family is still in Serbia," Ostropaki said. "He works what he calls a graveyard shift? In Serbia he was surgeon, here he is emergency-room technician at a hospital in

Manhattan—I think he operates the machines that say if one is still alive, something like that. I delivered to him some letters from his family. He has an uncle in Albania, at one of the camps, waiting to return to Serbia." He gave the man's name and where he worked.

The colonel looked up at Porter, who nodded to Cook, who left the room, obviously to check on this alleged hospital technician. This was not going as they'd expected. Every one of the officers in the room had the dull feeling that the man just described would turn out to be a solid witness for Ostropaki. The colonel, however, felt his spirits lift.

"I was hoping to see you, while I am here, just a few days," Ostropaki said to the colonel. "You were so"—he hesitated, then found the right word—"amiable, when we met in—"

Before he could say "Athens," the colonel reached over and punched the stop button on the recorder. He got up and went outside. Porter and Kravfurt followed.

"Well, that's a loser," Tucker said in the hall, with a rueful look on his face. "We interviewed him in Athens a couple of years back, thinking he might be a useful correspondent, since he traveled to Serbia quite a bit. Then we lost track of him. Nothing came of it."

"That was your interest?" Porter said.

"It looked different," the colonel said. "There was always the possibility that he might have contacts with the Zivkovic group, in Serbia. But now, it sounds to me like someone set him up. What do you think?"

"Why would someone set him up?" Kravfurt said.

"Who knows? Maybe to discredit him with this refugee organization," the colonel said. "It could have been some internal dispute. These people are notoriously divided among themselves. One faction opposes another, and they're all engaged in the same cause! Or it could have been some Serb group that found out about

Ostropaki's mission, got some inside information on this meeting with the doctor, or whatever he is."

Porter seemed to buy it, especially when Cook returned with the news that Ostropaki's contact was an emergency-room technician at the hospital. Porter was disgusted. He had wasted his day, and his men. "What do you want to do with him?" he asked the colonel.

"I'd like to talk to him some more, see what he knows. He might have some useful information about other people we're interested in, people who also disappeared during the NATO bombing. But I think it would have to be in a more congenial setting. If by chance he comes out with something of interest, I'll let you know, of course. In the meantime, perhaps you could run a record check on this ex-surgeon fellow who works at the hospital. Doctors have been known to have drug associations. If that proves questionable, we know where Ostropaki is."

Porter muttered something derisive and said, "Yeah, take him away. I'll get a release for his car. Don't forget to call. You owe us one."

The colonel ushered Ostropaki out of the precinct station. It had helped that Ostropaki's rental car had been clean. To Kravfurt, he said, "Theo can take me back to the airport. I'd like to chat with him about his experiences."

Kravfurt said, "Fine. Don't forget me, Colonel. This looked like a good thing."

The colonel assured him that he appreciated being called and said Max could expect to hear from him before long. As soon as Kravfurt had gone and they were driving away, the colonel said to Ostropaki, "Was that you who called?"

"It was a friend of mine. I told him to ask for Kravfurt, because he was with you in Athens, that time."

"So, Theo," the colonel said, as they drove toward La Guardia, "how did you manage not to get killed? I thought the Zivkovic people were on to you."

"Oh, they were. The minute I returned to Belgrade, I was arrested. Vjelko was behind it. He was tight with the regime. They were all in the drug trade. They kept me in a rather nasty jail, questioned me about Franko. But I had nothing to tell them."

The colonel could tell from his reticence that it had been a painful and humiliating experience, not to say potentially fatal. It was clear that Ostropaki was not eager to talk about it, but it was necessary. The colonel pressed him. The story was a depressingly familiar one of beatings, threats, torture, and terror. Of particular interest was the degree of cooperation between an outright gangster like Zivkovic and the highest reaches of the regime, including the police.

"Finally, they put me in a camp," Ostropaki said. "I thought they would kill me there. They killed so many. Sometimes, one of Vjelko's men would come to question me again. One of them, a very bad man named Bazok, was especially crude. He asked me about Franko—did I know him? I didn't know who he was talking about, I said.

"I think because I was a foreigner it saved me. At last, one of my old construction customers in Belgrade, a friend of mine, heard I was there and began to ask questions. He was important to the government. They drove me into Kosovo in the middle of the night, pushed me out of the car, and told me to start walking. I thought they would shoot me, but they didn't. I was telling the truth about the refugees, you know."

"It sounded authentic, anyway," the colonel said. They found a spot in the US Airways parking lot at La Guardia and walked to the terminal. "Why did you go to such lengths to contact me?"

"Colonel, I am worried about you. I was coming to the United States, anyway, and I thought it would be a good opportunity to meet with you."

"You're worried about me? Why didn't you just call me?"

"I didn't think it would be wise. I'll explain. You remember that we talked once about the difficulties you had with getting your country to carry through on their drug policies? Yes? I thought you were trying to recruit me."

"Well, as to that . . . ," the colonel said, hesitating. "But I did recruit you, on the Franko operation."

"Yes, but you insisted we keep the Franko connection to ourselves," Ostropaki said. "I don't accuse you! You were right to do so, as events proved. The effect was the same. It was better that I not know too much. Do you think we could stop for some coffee? Or are you in a hurry?"

"I have all the time you need," the colonel said. They bought coffee at a food stand.

"Last week an American woman came to see me, in Tirana," Ostropaki said. "I had seen her before. She was with some US AID officials then. This time she came alone. She asked me questions about my involvement with the DEA. I didn't know what to say. She showed me a picture of you. I admitted that I had met you, in Athens. I told her that you had asked me some general questions about Serbia, where I had been, what I had seen."

This was the genuine Balkan reserve, the colonel thought. Perhaps it was too much to call it paranoia. "Why didn't you tell her about working for us?"

"She didn't offer anything," Ostropaki said simply. "She didn't even say she was with the DEA. She never mentioned any specific operations—not a word about Franko, at first. Just asked if I had supplied information or had otherwise assisted the DEA in Serbia. So how could I think that she knew anything, or that I should share what I knew? Besides, she seemed interested in something else. She showed me a photograph of Franko, taken in Kosovo, it appeared. Did I know this man? I told her I didn't know him. She asked me if I had ever heard of an American agent named Franko Bradovic. From a village named Tsamet, in the mountains. I told her I had driven through Tsamet, once, but I didn't know this man. Finally, she asked me if I'd ever heard anything about an inner group, within the DEA. Whether you had mentioned such a group."

"What kind of group?" the colonel asked. "Some ultrasecret agency? A special task force, perhaps?"

"Perhaps," Ostropaki said. He pushed his coffee away with distaste. "That was the sort of thing I asked her. But she said, no, it was not an official group. It was independent agents who had, perhaps, agreed to assist each other in extralegal activities. She didn't elaborate."

"Aha!" the colonel said. "Corrupt agents, working with the smugglers, eh?"

"That's what I assumed," Ostropaki said. He looked quite neutral, but a little self-conscious.

"Well, there are such agents, as we all know," the colonel said. "It's a major problem in drug enforcement. More so than in any other aspect of criminal law—not just undercover agents, but administrators, even prosecutors and judges. It's the money that's involved . . . so much money. But you're well aware of this; we've discussed it."

"But to have these suspicions raised in the same breath as your name!" Ostropaki said. "It's outrageous. After all we did, with Franko. Oh, Colonel, that was a beautiful thing. Poor Franko. I felt so bad."

"Ah, I wanted to ask you about Franko," the colonel said. "What did you hear about him?"

"Don't you know?" Ostropaki was saddened to have to tell him that he had heard, from one of his torturers, the monster Bazok, that they had captured Franko. "They lie, of course," he said, "pretending to know more than they do. But it seems they knew some things about Franko that I didn't. He was captured with some KLA terrorists, they said. He had resisted their persuasion for a long time, but eventually he told them everything. That's how they discovered my perfidy.

"I insisted that I didn't know the man, but this Bazok, he said he knew all about our collaboration. Well, that's how they talk, of course. But I understood, from what Bazok said, that Franko didn't get out. This Bazok, even after what I had seen and been through, he made my hair stand on end, describing some of the things that Franko had endured. Still, you know . . . why did they continue to be so interested?"

"I see what you mean," the colonel said. "If they had gotten so much information . . . but I dare say, the rationale given was that they must verify one prisoner's confessions with another's."

"Precisely. But I must ask you, Colonel . . . please forgive me . . . but is there anything to this woman's suspicions? I'm sorry— I'm a man of the world, you understand, a skeptic but not a cynic." He looked the colonel directly in the eyes.

"None whatsoever," the colonel said simply. "Quite the reverse."

"I didn't believe it for a second," Ostropaki said. "But I felt that I must hear it from you. Franko affected me very much, you see. He was a good man, a decent man. That is why I contacted you about him. I felt that he was exactly the sort of man you were thinking about, when we spoke in Athens. An idealist. But in this world, in war, especially in the Balkans, an idealist is just . . . what is the idiom, 'a fish in a barrel'?"

"That's . . . that's close enough," the colonel said. "Tell me, what else did this woman have to say about Franko?"

"Nothing. She had the snapshot, but that was all."

"So you didn't get the impression that she actually knew anything about him, beyond a name?" the colonel said.

Ostropaki shrugged. "It didn't seem so."

"And what was her name?" the colonel asked.

"Sanders. A tall, slim young woman, with frizzy reddish hair. She seemed quite capable. Very efficient, cold. You see why I was worried. I thought I must tell you as soon as I had the opportunity, but privately. So, as there was a task to be done here, I took the chance of being arrested."

"It was a smart thing to do, but risky." The colonel glanced at his watch. It was after four. His flight would not leave before seven. In Montana, it would be two in the afternoon.

"This Ms. Sanders," the colonel said, "she has worked for the DEA, in the past. But I believe she transferred to another agency. What agency did she say she worked for?"

Ostropaki looked thoughtful. "She never really said," he replied. "She showed me some identification, with a picture, and I think—foolishly it now seems—that I took it to be . . . well, I'm not sure what I thought. Some U.S. agency. You have so many, with different initials. I'm sorry."

"This was last week," the colonel said. "Did she seem to know that you were coming to the States?"

"No. But it was not a secret," Ostropaki said.

"How long will you remain in the U.S.?" the colonel asked.

"Until the end of the week," Ostropaki said. "I have to see about some refugees, provide the documentation they need to stay in this country. Here, let me give you my telephone number."

They exchanged numbers, and the colonel promised to call him before he left and, if possible, to return to New York to see him. He was very grateful to Ostropaki, he told him, and delighted that he had survived. They had feared that he was dead. It was possible that they could work together sometime in the future. But for now—the colonel glanced at his watch—he had to run to catch the shuttle.

He did not catch the shuttle. Anyway, it wouldn't leave for a couple of hours. But he had to get free of Ostropaki. Instead he went to the operations office, identified himself, and was allowed to use a private telephone. He tried Jammie's cell-phone number. There was no response—"The party you are trying to reach is either out of range or otherwise unavailable," said the voice. He really wanted to contact Joe Service, but, of course, Joe had not provided him with any contact number.

He called the DDO's office and, luckily, caught him before he left for the day. "You were right, sir," he reported. "We may have to give Ostropaki a medal." He went on to explain what had happened, but he left out any mention of Ostropaki's need to contact him, attributing the false betrayal to a rival, as he had with the NYPD. Nor did he mention Jammie Sanders.

"I just wanted to let you know right away, sir," Tucker said. "I'll have a full report for you, but I've been talking to one of my people, and it looks like I might not get back to Washington this evening."

The DDO said that was fine, the report could wait. He was obviously pleased.

Next the colonel called Agnes and asked her to run down, if she could, a phone number for Frank Oberavich. While that was in progress, he called Dinah Schwind, in Seattle.

"When you suggested Jamala Sanders for the Butte job," the colonel asked her, "was that your suggestion, or hers?"

"I didn't suggest her," Schwind protested. "*You* suggested her. Oh, you mean when I told her about the situation? Mmmm, let me think. I guess . . . well, you could say that she volunteered. Why? What's happened? Is Joe—"

The colonel cut her off. "Did she ever approach you about the L— about the group? Not by name, necessarily, but about groups like that?"

Dinah had to think. "I'm not sure," she said. "It was a topic of conversation between us, from . . . oh, way back. You know, when agents are grumbling about the bureaucracy, the politics. . . . But if the question is did she ever inquire about my knowledge of the existence of any such group? No, I don't recall her doing that. When I broached the idea, though, she jumped right on it. I told you that."

Tucker quickly briefed Schwind on his meeting and conversation with Ostropaki. "Which raises the question," he said, "what does she want with Joe?"

"Joe?" Dinah said. "Don't you mean Franko?"

"Well, maybe it's two questions," the colonel said. "I was looking at the files on that operation this morning, and I don't recollect any indication that she knew about Ostropaki. She could have. But she worked only on the receiving end of his intelligence."

He felt insecure about this telephone conversation, so he didn't say what he was thinking: his impression was that Jammie hadn't heard about Franko before she was recruited for this present mission. But Kravfurt seemed to know about Franko, and Sanders had worked with Kravfurt. . . . Only, what would she have heard beyond the name? Franko was ostensibly a straightforward, unnamed DEA asset, controlled by Ostropaki. It was impossible to know what the extent of scuttlebutt might be among agents.

More to the point: if Sanders was investigating the Lucani, what would be the value to her of Franko?

Dinah was thinking along the same lines. She had reported her conversation with Jammie to the colonel, with some omissions, to spare his feelings. Joe would interest Jammie, she thought now, as a potential weak link in the Lucani organization. Then another thought intruded: what if Jammie's interest was, in fact, Bazok?

Apparently, the colonel had reached that same point in his thinking. "Bazok?" he suggested, almost idly.

The answer to that hardly needed to be spoken: Bazok would interest Jammie only if she was working for some other group, or agency—say, the international tribunal. Or . . . Zivkovic. Such a possibility was breathtaking for Schwind.

The colonel seemed to read her mind, three thousand miles away. "It's not unheard of," he said. "Theo and I were discussing something along those lines, in a slightly different context." He paused for a moment, then said, "Presumably she would be known to Bazok."

The line was silent while they both pursued that thought.

"Here's a notion," Tucker said, finally: "Say Bazok was . . . what's the term? . . . a badger bait? Badger hound? You know, the expendable dog one thrusts down the hole—"

Quietus

"**T**he responsibilities of command" was a phrase that Joe Service could not recall ever having employed, and yet it seemed unavoidable. Perhaps he'd heard it from Colonel Tucker, but he couldn't recall the context. It sounded like something that Tucker might say. But at the moment it was an issue for Joe. He had a drunken, armed mass murderer wandering around inside a mountain, presumably lost and in a state of desperate panic.

To apprehend this maniac, he had a crew of three men and two women. Two of the men were willing but less than competent for the task; one was willing and competent, definitely useful, but aged and exhausted. The women were competent, but at least one of them was overmatched physically, while the other had ambiguous motives.

He had a communication problem between the elements of his crew. There were also ominous, omnipresent dangers of public exposure, complications of law, and . . . what else? Oh yeah, they were all dangerously tired, from both their morning's exertion and their lack of sleep. Joe was no exception. Maybe that was why he had shunted aside the problem of multiple exits.

To be sure, Joe was aware of the exit problem, but he had largely discounted the possibility that Bazok might backtrack to the Seven Dials entrance. Kibosh had convinced him that Bazok was so confused, so demoralized that he would never attempt to go all the way back, and even if he did, he'd never find his way. Joe wasn't so sure, on reconsideration. The man was desperate, and desperate men do things you can't predict.

The communication problem was keyed to the exit problem. There was no response on the cell phone from Jammie. Joe felt that he'd made a mistake in leaving her on the other side. He could use her more effectively here. But then if she were here, one of the incompetent men would have to take her place over there. Damn the pressures of command. Joe longed for the days when it was just him against a quarry, or at most him and Helen.

There was nothing for it: he'd have to send Paulie or Frank to find out what was amiss with Jammie. One of them, or even both, could take Jammie's place and send her back to this side, where the action was most likely to be played out.

Frank had a suggestion: why not use the dogs at the Seven Dials entry?

"You mean, to track Bazok?" Joe asked. "Would they go in?"

Frank said they would. They weren't trained tracker dogs, but they would go after Bazok. "They've got a taste for his blood," he said. "He killed their brothers. Dogs don't forget that."

Joe didn't quite believe this. He thought it was attributing human feelings to dogs. However, he didn't know anything about dogs. Maybe it was so. "But," he said, "what if they get lost? Then what? What if you get lost, assuming you'd be with them? Then we'd have to look for both you and them. I don't know . . ."

Still, there were attractive advantages to the scheme. It would expand Joe's available manpower. The dogs might drive Bazok out, or at least keep him from backtracking. "How about this?" he suggested. "You take the dogs into the tunnel, on a leash, but no farther than the first side tunnel. That ought to prevent Bazok from using that exit, and there would be no risk of anyone getting lost."

Frank was convinced that the dogs would follow Bazok's scent. They wouldn't get lost. But he had no appetite for accompanying them deep into the mountain, so he agreed to Joe's suggestion. Only now Paulie volunteered for the job. He claimed to have better command of the dogs—Frank conceded that—and anyway, it might be better if Frank manned the house, to answer phones, either from the searchers or from outside.

Joe sighed and agreed to that. Once Jammie returned, she and Helen could cover the exit from which Kibosh and Bazok had emerged, now more than an hour ago. Joe and Kibosh could explore some of the other possible exits on this side. In the meantime, they could all get a little rest, keeping a watch on the exit, until Jammie returned.

Frank and Paulie went off to get the dogs and rustle up some food and drinks for the searchers. Kibosh slept, curled up in the shade of some pines along the river. Helen crouched just inside the mine exit, waiting and watching. Joe lay down for a while near Kibosh, but he only dozed. They were within visual range of the other possible exits—Joe kept an eye on them.

Soon enough, Frank returned with sandwiches, coffee, beer, and some cookies he'd found in the pantry. "They're only store-bought," he apologized, meaning the cookies. Joe ate his share anyway, without complaint. He glanced at his watch. Paulie had been gone for forty minutes. It was a little early to expect Jammie, but Joe asked if she had called in. Frank said she hadn't. He hiked off to take lunch up to Helen.

On his way back down, Joe told him to let him know as soon as he heard from Jammie. He was getting restless, now, eager to wake up Kibosh, snoring in the shade, and get started on their part of the search.

It was a beautiful early-fall day in Montana, just a few fluffy clouds drifting over the mountains, an idle breeze stirring the brittle leaves of the alders. Joe lay back and watched a large hawk, or possibly it was an eagle, drifting lazily a couple of thousand feet above the river.

Man, oh man, he thought, I love this country.

Boz had found a hole. He had begun to fear that his light was dying. He was sure that it was much dimmer. Fortunately, there were some extra batteries in the pack that he'd made Kibosh leave behind. And, of course, he had Kibosh's flashlight. That comforted him. He was lost, however. He hadn't seen anything that looked like a chalk mark on a stone facing, or any of the scratches or other signs that Kibosh had pointed out, in quite a while. He had no idea when he'd quit noticing them. He still felt that all he had to do was backtrack a little ways and he'd come across a mark. But first he had to rest.

He sat down with his back resting against a wall. He drank some whiskey, then some water. He was amazed to find the gherkins that Kibosh had packed. They were delicious. He ate several. Then he rolled on his side, curled up, and fell asleep. He slept for only a few minutes, although it seemed longer. He awoke because he remembered he'd left his light on. That was foolish. The sleep was a good idea, he realized, but it wouldn't do to simply crash right here in the middle of the passage, in case pursuers came along, as he was certain they would.

A canny idea popped into his head: he could find a niche, or a little gallery, and take a nap. He needed the rest, and with his light off he wouldn't be seen. Joe Asshole and his pals would come along and he was bound to wake up in time to ambush them, and then they'd guide him out! It was perfect. He got to his feet and began to look for the ideal spot. Within ten minutes he found it, a little chamber not much bigger than old Kibosh's crib, just off the passage.

He crawled in there and made himself comfortable, turned off his light, and fell deeply asleep. His last conscious thought was that this was bliss, real peace. After a short time, he began to snore loudly. This was not something he had considered, but of course, he wasn't aware of it. At first he slept as profoundly as he had ever slept in his life, but soon he began to dream.

His first dream was very good, an erotic dream. It involved the Muslim girl. She was being very accommodating, eager, and as aroused as he was, which was totally. But when he was close to ejaculation, the dream inexplicably but relentlessly turned ugly— he was slipping in a morass of slimy bodies, corpses and snakes and worms. He almost awoke but instead managed to segue to another dream, concerning railcars and then a campfire under a bridge, with other hoboes about. Very chummy and cheerful, at first. But one of them was bothering him, an old man making lewd suggestions, then groping him, and he was rolling closer to the fire. He escaped that development by running the dream back, but inevitably it deteriorated: the fires getting closer, threatening dark figures, the gropers and callers, some of them dead people with ugly, slashed throats and tongues coming out of their wounds. . . . There were animals here, too, snakes and rats, spiders, and a clawing, snarling beast with shaggy hair and ferocious teeth, tunneling after him. He couldn't escape this implacable, persistent creature. He woke up in a sweat.

It was utterly dark. He panicked, but gradually he got a grip on himself and found his flashlight. He was in the mountain. He was drenched with despair. He opened the pack and drank some whiskey, then water. He was extremely thirsty, but he knew better than to drink all of the remaining quart of precious liquid. The whiskey calmed him.

When he could think, he realized that he had to go back to the exit. It no longer mattered what awaited him outside. He couldn't stay in here any longer. This decision steadied him further. He would go on out and, if it worked out that way, he would surrender. At least he would be safe. But there was always the chance, he thought, that he could still win. He'd make it out and his pursuers would have gone, or he could elude them. Regardless, he was coming out.

He set off back the way he had come. Focusing now, he could see signs of his passage, footprints, an overturned rock. He thought he recognized the route. He felt more confident. It occurred to him that he might have slept for twelve hours, perhaps longer. By now it would be dark again. Joe Asshole could well have given up. Why wouldn't he?

When he thought about it, he had no idea why Joe Service was pursuing him. Just because of that stupid business in the house? He wished that he had killed them all. He should never have screwed around, distracted by that stupid girl. It was her fault, the prick teaser! Still, it would have been great: bend the bitch over a chair and fuck her brains out, the bound men looking on, tongues hanging out in lust and envy. Then, just as he came, he'd cut her damn throat and, after, all the others. Goddamn, what a scene that would have been!

Franko, he could understand. Franko was just protecting his goods; but what was in this for Joe Asshole and that girl? It didn't make any sense. By now, he thought, they would have given up and gone away. Franko would still be hanging around. Where was he going to go? They could make some sort of deal. If not, he'd just top Franko and his fruity little hippie pal, and then he'd find the goods and could go back to Zivko and tell them it was all done, and they'd get on with having a good time.

He entertained himself with these thoughts as he stumbled along, imagining raping the woman in various ways, shooting or stabbing the men . . . and then he realized he had left the rifle behind, in the niche where he'd fallen asleep. To hell with it, he thought. He still had the Star. He wasn't going back for that damn rifle, it was too clumsy anyway, and besides, he wasn't confident that he could find that niche. And with that, he realized that he was still lost.

He shuddered with dismay. It was night outside by now, he thought, and even darker in here. He was as close to hell as a living man could get, he figured. He could pass within ten feet of an exit and never see a patch of natural light, because it would be dark outside. What an awful, awful thought! He wanted to roar, to scream, but he knew it would never be heard. Perhaps he had screamed. He wasn't sure.

"Help!" he shouted, a little tentatively, then louder and longer. There wasn't even an echo, just a dull sound muffled up by the mountain. It was swallowing him alive.

For some reason, it seemed to him that it would be better to crawl, that he'd naturally find his way out that way. But when he got on his hands and knees the occasional stone hurt him, and he only did it for a short distance before he came to his senses and realized it was pointless. He stood up and remained in one position for a period of time, his mind numb. He moved on in a hopeless trudge. If he just kept walking, he told himself, eventually he had to walk to an opening. It stood to reason. Just keep walking. He fished out the whiskey bottle and took a sip, not wanting to finish it, not wanting to be caught, finally, without even a drink. He shuffled on.

Paulie shook his head at the sight of Frank's truck, protruding from the ruined entrance to the Seven Dials. There was no sign of Jammie. He left the dogs in the cab of his own pickup while he organized his gear, a backpack with necessary supplies, including a flashlight, plus one of Joe's pump shotguns. It would be a hassle handling this gear and the leashes, but he felt he could manage. The dogs were certainly eager. As soon as he opened the door, they leaped out and ran immediately into the entrance. To his dismay, they did not stop when he called. He ran after them, but he was brought up short at the entrance. He stared into the ruined interior, reluctant to enter the tunnel. He hadn't visualized this. Going into a tunnel . . . it was exactly like entering a cave. He couldn't move.

He called to the dogs: "Bruno! Sylvie!" There was no answer, no sound at all. They had run into the dark tunnel.

"Jammie!" he cried. Once again, the cave swallowed the sound. He stepped back out, into the sun. "Jammie?" There was no echo among the tall, aromatic pines, in the warm sun. And no answer. He thought he heard something, but it was only a jay, up the slope. He called again, louder. No answer. A squirrel chattered. The wind soughed in the tops of the pines.

What to do? He thought of sounding a car horn, but he wasn't sure that was a good idea; it might alert Bazok. Then he realized that was a stupid notion. He took a breath and bravely stepped inside.

Poor Kibosh, his place is a mess, he thought. But then . . . it was always a mess. We'll fix it up for him when this is over, he thought. He switched on his flashlight at the gaping opening into the tunnel at the back of the room. He called the dogs again, then, "Jammie!" The sound was absorbed in the mountain.

There was nothing for it; he had to go in. When he reached the first side tunnel, he stopped. This was as far as he would go. Joe had said as much. The dogs were loose, inside, but it would be foolish to go after them.

Where was Jammie? He cast the beam down the side tunnel; he could see about fifty feet before the tunnel angled away—just an empty, abandoned tunnel. He turned the beam to the main drift. Again, he could see some fifty feet before the tunnel floor dropped lower. He should go back, he thought. Look around outside for Jammie. Maybe she had climbed up on the ridge, trying to find high ground to make phone contact.

He never heard the shot. But he knew it was a bullet. It knocked him backward. Paulie felt a great weight in his chest, an enormous lump that he couldn't swallow . . . then everything got truly black.

Relations

Joe was surprised to see that Jammie looked fairly fresh. She had even changed clothes, he noticed as she waded across the stream, a Cordura sports bag in one hand, the AK-47 in the other.

"Ah, the SWAT team's here," Joe remarked, giving her a hand up the bank.

Jammie sat down on a rock to pull on her boots, which she'd slung around her neck. She laughed. "Sure you don't mean TWAT team? Oops, bad joke—that's what the D.I.s yelled at us in school."

Joe seemed disconcerted. "What school is that?"

"You don't want to know," she said, standing up. "Ready for action, Cap'n." She saluted like a music-hall sailor.

She looked ready for action, Joe thought. The jumpsuit might ostensibly be military in intent, but the tailoring bespoke a different objective. The effect was unsettling. Joe couldn't help but notice that the zipper of the jumpsuit had a large ring dangling from the clasp. It had been pulled down far enough to reveal the cleavage of her breasts.

Jammie caught his eye on it and said, in a low voice, "One yank and it's off."

Joe's mouth twitched. It was as much smile as he could muster right now. But unthinkingly, he glanced up at the opening to the tunnel.

"She's at least a hundred feet up there," Jammie teased. She set her hands on her hips and arched her back, as if stretching. Her breasts pressed against the nylon, flattening only slightly and revealing the outline of the nipples. "You only go around once, Joe . . . grab the ring."

Joe chose to take it as a joke, ignoring the undertone of a genuine invitation. "Helen's too speedy," he said. "We'd never have a chance. 'Preciate the offer, though."

"Never turn down a willing woman," she said. "Or so my daddy used to say."

"Daddy probably knows best," Joe said, "but we don't have time to play right now."

Jammie looked momentarily chagrined, but she smiled. "Lighten up, Joe. You work too hard. Why? What's in this for you? You're not one of the Lucani."

"No?" Joe said. "I thought I was. That's what they keep telling me."

"You'll never be one of them," Jammie said. "You're an outlaw. They just want to play at outlaws. They're a bunch of scouts. I think you turn them on—you turn me on—but they'll never let you in. Not really."

"They?" Joe said. "How about you?"

"Hey, I'll let you in," she said with smirk. "I'm an outlaw myself. Outlaw Love—sounds like fun."

"Not a Lucani?" Joe said.

"They're more fun than the stuffed shirts," Jammie said. "But I'll never be a Lucani, any more than you." She had hooked a finger into the big ring and was gently tugging the zipper, first a little lower, then back up. She reached out and took his hand and brought it to her left breast, then suddenly zipped the garment open enough so that it was exposed. It was very full and the areola was large and dark, the nipple standing out. Joe's hand involuntarily closed on her breast. It seemed to pulse with heat.

Joe snatched his hand away. "I don't have time for this," he said.

Jammie zipped up. "No? Well, let's see . . . that leaves riches."

"What are you playing at?" Joe said.

"You're not concerned what the Lucani think," Jammie said. "You're not tempted by a lady's tender offer. What does interest you? You see, Joe"—she stepped closer, her voice no longer playful—"there's a lot going on here that you know nothing about. Money, politics, careers, lives even . . . and you're the one who seems to be just playing at it. You and Helen. These others"—she tossed her head in the direction of Frank's house—"they're just bystanders—innocent or otherwise. So what's your game?"

"It doesn't even remotely concern you," Joe said. "But let's get back to the present. What's your thinking? What do you think we should do?"

"I think we should button it up. Time to boogie."

Joe was surprised. "Just bail? What about . . . ?" He gestured toward the mountain, his hand sweeping back toward the house.

"What's the old playground chant?" Jammie said. "Find 'em, feel 'em, fuck 'em, and forget 'em. Eh? You and me and, if you insist, Helen . . . we just pack up and blow. Bazok . . . he'll never get out of there. He's as good as dead already. Frank and Paulie, they'll never say shit. Frank's worried about his dope farm . . . Paulie vell, ve haf vays to make him *not* talk."

"No," Joe said, "too many loose ends. Besides, I've got an interest—which, as I said, is none of your business. I'm not going to leave until I'm sure that Bazok is taken care of. Anyway, you left out Kibosh."

"Kibosh?" she said, her forehead wrinkling. "The old man? Collateral damage, I'm afraid . . . Bazok will take care of him, as soon as he's sure he doesn't need him. But he was a hermit, wasn't he? Folks will just assume he got lost in his abandoned mines. I doubt there'll even be a search."

It was Joe's turn to look puzzled. "Didn't Paulie fill you in?"

"Paulie? What about Paulie?"

"Didn't you see Paulie?" Joe said. "At the Seven Dials? I sent him over there to relieve you, with the dogs. I thought that was why you came back."

"I must have passed him on the way back," Jammie said. "I got bored. The cell phone didn't work. I think the batteries are dead. Anyway, it looked like it was time to wrap. So . . . Kibosh escaped?"

Joe explained what had happened.

Jammie nodded. "Well, even better. Bazok is definitely compost now. Kibosh . . . he won't be calling CNN, and nobody'd believe him anyway. Party's over. Let's sweep the dirt under the carpet and leave the dishes in the sink."

"What dirt is that?" Joe said.

"Well, for instance, I take it Paulie's got a camp up the creek a ways," Jammie said. "That'll be where he stashed the shit." She caught Joe's puzzled look. "You don't get it, do you? The guy walked out of Kosovo with half a mil in heroin, lists of names, maybe useful evidence. I'll go check it out, make a clean sweep, and we can catch the stage to Yuma."

Joe took a deep breath, then puffed it out. "I see. And what do we do about Paulie? The colonel sent me here to get Paulie. He wanted to talk to him. That's my contract."

"I talked to the colonel, on my way back," Jammie said. "Sorry. It seemed wise. Forget Paulie. The colonel's not interested in Paulie now. Anyway, it looked like you had Bazok cornered. No more Bazok, the job's done. Zip, zip." She ran the zipper down, then up.

"The colonel's not interested in Paulie?" Joe said.

"Franko," Jammie said. "He doesn't even know who Paulie is. He's not interested in Franko anymore. No need for him to know. That's what you want, isn't it? Keep Paulie out of it? You can explain it to the colonel, if you like. I don't know what your deal with Paulie is, but it's your business, as long as it doesn't involve the heroin. Me, I'll go check out Paulie's camp."

Joe had listened to her, but now he shook his head. "You do what you like," he said. "You and the colonel want to forget about Paulie, that's fine with me. But Bazok . . . I'm not leaving here until I know he's—"

"Dead?" Jammie said.

Joe didn't answer. He started off toward the pines where Kibosh was still snoozing. Jammie stared after him. Then she followed.

"Okay," she called after him. "I'll help you take Bazok. Then I'm F.O.B."

Joe stopped in the shade of a copse of aspens. "Deal," he said. "Kibosh knows a passage that he thinks communicates with the main drift. I figured he and I would go in, try to get a jump on Bazok."

"It's a plan," Jammie said. "Where do I bat in this lineup?"

"It depends on how it plays out," Joe said. "Kibosh thinks, and I agree, that it's a good chance that Bazok will be so demoralized that we'll be able to simply grab him and lead him out. He may not resist. Even if he does, I should be able to keep him pinned down while Kibosh comes out and gets you. The two of us should be able to handle him. The idea is to take him alive, right? The colonel will want to talk to *him*, at least."

"You don't want to be worrying about what the colonel wants," Jammie said. "In there? It's like being tied up in a gunny sack with a badger and tossed down a well."

"If it gets too rough, I'll have to take him down," Joe said simply. "What I'm more worried about, though, is if he gets between us and this exit . . . you and Helen."

"We're just girls," Jammie said sarcastically. "But if you think we can handle him. . . . Seriously? How about, Helen hangs at the entry with one of your alley sweepers while I go inside, maybe fifty feet or so, and find myself a good position. If I see him approaching, I'll backtrack, and we'll have time to get down the trail. It shouldn't be a problem. If he's in his berserk mode, we'll just stay out of his way. He can't get far, out here." She indicated the river, the broad meadow beyond.

Under the circumstances, they really couldn't make much more of a plan than that, Joe thought. He had a vision of Bazok, pinned on the cliff trail, with Jammie and Helen covering him below and Joe above and behind him. He'd have to throw it in. It would be a neat conclusion, only Joe had no illusions: it was bound to go differently. But at least they had a notion of how to proceed.

"Okay," he said, "I'll get Kibosh. You can brief Helen."

"No good-bye kiss, Joe?" She tugged at the zipper again. "Last chance."

Joe shook his head at her levity and disappeared through the trees.

"**H**ey, girl," Jammie called as she arrived at the mouth of the mine, her breasts heaving slightly from the climb. They were all but entirely exposed, the zipper drawn down almost to her belt.

Helen stepped out to greet her, blinking against the bright sun.

"Dispatches from Napoleon," Jammie said.

"Napoleon?"

"The Little Corporal," Jammie explained, gesturing over her shoulder.

"You mean Joe?" Helen said.

"The very same. We have a plan of battle. He goes in down there." She pointed—they could see Joe and Kibosh making their way up the talus slope toward some caves. "And I go in up here. Classical pincer movement, right out of Clausewitz. Bazok is all but maggot-munchy."

"What about me?" Helen said.

"You stand guard," Jammie said. "Just in case Bazok gets by me."

"That doesn't sound like much of a role," Helen said.

"I'll trade ya." Jammie extended the AK-47 she carried.

Helen ignored the gesture.

Jammie nodded and said, "I don't blame you. Why risk your ass for these pricks? There's nothing in it for you, is there?"

Not as much as I'd like, Helen thought to herself, but she wasn't about to admit it to Jammie. "Joe is in it," she said.

Jammie nodded. "Yeah, he is. The question is, Why. What's in it for him?"

Helen was not about to go into the details of Joe's rebuilding schemes. It didn't concern anyone but them, and it seemed unlikely that Jammie would understand. "Joe has a contract," she said. "He likes to carry out the contract. It's a point of honor."

"Oh, how I love honor," Jammie said with a little laugh. "It's the old fallback position when an operation has lost its focus. You guys should have bailed on this one days ago. Well, you anyway. Joe has his own reasons, I'm sure."

"What?" Helen said.

"Gee, you haven't given it much thought, have you?" She regarded Helen thoughtfully. "Maybe Joe and the colonel left a few things out. There's a lot of money involved. Didn't they fill you in?"

Helen looked dumb.

Jammie shook her head. "Your newfound friend Paulie walked with a lot of goods, money too. Joe didn't say anything about that?

I wonder why? Maybe it's just between him and the colonel . . . and Dinah Schwind, of course."

"Schwind!" Helen said.

"Oops . . . gotta learn to keep my mouth shut," Jammie said, then sighed. "What the hell, why should I cover for them? You and me are bath buddies, aren't we? Naiads of the natatorium? You're out here riding shotgun, you deserve to know. Joe and Dinah . . . how should I put it? They're a little tighter than agent and control. Didn't you dig that?"

"I could see she was interested in Joe . . ."

"But not the other way 'round?" Jammie shook her head with a slight smile. "Well, I'm sure he's not really, really into her . . . except about six inches, anyway. But that's how men are—as long as they can wet the wick, the banns can wait."

"What do you know about it?" Helen said. She kept her voice even.

"Just what I heard from Dinah, before I got roped in on this goofy badger game. I know her from old school days. That's where we first met the colonel. Dinah was very good on the oral exams— that's how she got into the Lucani."

"How did you get in?" Helen said.

"Not that way," Jammie said. "Dinah's special at that. I think she's one of those gals who find the missionary position oppressive. Although, I dare say she can tolerate a little man-on-top, now and then—and your Joey's not so heavy, is he? But it's a little late for gossip. Time to soldier." She stooped to pick up her gear bag.

"What's in there?" Helen said. She was trying to distract herself from these malicious jibes.

"Just some toys, in case I get bored," Jammie said. "Wish me luck." She slung the AK-47 over her shoulder.

"I don't believe that stuff about Joe and Schwind," Helen said.

Jammie gave her a glance of pity. "You know what they say—'Someone's in the kitchen with Dinah.' Stand by your man, honey. But don't forget—he's just a man." She started into the cave, then stopped, turning to look back. "I'll tell you what . . . and this is my honest, sincere opinion . . . if I were you, I'd skedaddle before we come out of here—whoever comes out of here. Just a bit of wisdom from your worldly fellow nymph."

Helen stared at the woman. Turned sideways, Jammie's posture accentuated the exposure of her breasts. She didn't trust Jammie. There was something wrong. But she knew that there was something between Joe and Schwind. She'd sensed it before. Was there something, as well, between Joe and Jammie? She'd seen them standing in the trees, down by the stream, standing very close. But she'd been unable to see much.

"What were you and Joe talking about, down there?" Helen asked.

"Oh, just Clausewitz," Jammie said. Then she glanced down at her breasts, aware of Helen's stare. "Oops. Nothing serious, my dear, honest. Joe's not really a tit man anyway, is he?" Then she vanished into the interior.

Helen stood on the path, fuming. The bitch! she thought. She looked around. The sky was clear except for a handful of puffy clouds. Nothing stirred in the grand panorama except a few birds, magpies she thought, flapping and calling around the trees along the glittering stream below.

What was she doing here? Backing up Joe. Maybe Jammie was right: she ought to scram. But after a few frustrated minutes, running Jammie's remarks back and forth through her mind, she knelt to rummage in the backpack for a roll of duct tape: Joe had suggested mounting the flashlight on the barrel of the shotgun, just in case. Now she took his advice. Then she went into the tunnel.

She had hardly gone fifty feet, just beyond the point where there was no longer any illumination from the entrance, when she came upon Jammie's gear bag. It sat, not nearly so full as it had seemed, next to the AK-47, leaning against the wall.

Kibosh was willing but skeptical. "He'll die in here," Kibosh said as they made their way into the mountain, "and I might find his bones in a year or two of lookin', though to tell ye the truth, I don't reckon I'd spend my Sundays doin' it. But by golly, I wouldn't want to be in his shoes neither. It'd be a hell of a miserable way to go."

"Not as miserable as the one he gave to a lot of others," Joe said.

It did not take long for them to reach their first serious obstacle. The floor of the tunnel they were in had been gradually sloping upward more quickly than the ceiling. Finally, there was little more than a crawl space, scarcely large enough to admit a man of Joe's size. Kibosh was skinnier. He crawled forward with the light while Joe waited. Soon he crawled backward out of the hole. He seemed puzzled.

"I coulda swore this was a walk-in drift," he said. "But it just plumb peters out."

They were sitting on the floor, and Kibosh picked up a handful of sand and let it run through his fingers. "This ain't no recent cave-in," he said. He looked around and picked up a sliver of what looked like wood, sniffed it, then tasted it. "That there's a bone," he said. "This has been used by a lion. There's quite a few of 'em about, more than there used to was."

"I never thought of these mountains as being like this," Joe said. "They look so solid, and yet they're just honey-combed with these passages and tunnels."

"A mountain's a livin' thing," Kibosh said. "Quite a lot goin' on in 'em. Lions, bears use 'em, even badgers—though they like to dig their own, mostly. They're diggin' machines. Well, we'd best backtrack."

Soon they found where they had gone astray. A fall had masked off another tunnel. They picked at it for twenty minutes or more, dragging larger rocks away. It was loose at first, then more tightly packed, but finally loose again, and they were able to push through into a man-sized passage.

"Hard work," Joe said. They paused to drink water. "You seem to have an idea where you are," he said to Kibosh. "How?"

"Why, I don't know," Kibosh said. "I just al's seemed to have that sense. Ye get turned around, sometimes. But I al's had that sense of it. Kind of a feel. Where we are now, we been steady goin' up, an' a little to the right, all the time. I reckon the main route, if ye want t'call it that, is on a bit more to the right and higher yet. That'd be where Boz orta be, if he ha'n't strayed off into another whole system."

They went on. Joe had lost track of time, or would have, but now he was surprised to see by his watch that they had been in the mountain for only a little more than an hour. They investigated several galleries, as Kibosh termed them, to no avail. One passage came to a full stop with a cave-in, quite old according to Kibosh. Another angled back toward yet another exit.

"Do ye want to take a break?" Kibosh asked. "Ye could foller this tunnel here and it'd get ye to a point downstream of where we started, by about a quarter mile or more."

"How long would that take?"

"Fifteen minutes."

Joe thought about it, then decided to push on. It was well that they did, for in another twenty minutes they came to a cross drift that Kibosh said was almost certainly bound to intersect with the main passage. But he wasn't confident how far it was.

"How can you tell?" Joe asked.

Kibosh said he could tell from the size and condition of the drift. It had been worked pretty thoroughly. "Musta found some gold in here," he said. "I'll have to 'member this. See, they worked these galleries here and there, laid these old boards . . . kinda rotted now. See?"

"Why did they stop?"

Kibosh looked at the dirt, inspected some flecks of minerals he pointed out to Joe. "It's a sign, but not real promising. They had to've assayed, an' prob'ly didn't find it rich enough. Maybe they jist got tired. Found somethin' better over yonder. Maybe they got sick. Who knows?"

Joe was weary of being in this hole, but he didn't say anything. It wouldn't do to quit now. They pressed on. Within fifteen minutes they were into the cross drift that they'd come upon earlier. But after they had traveled along it for a while, Kibosh remarked that it seemed to be quite a bit farther to the main passage than he'd reckoned.

"Seems like it keeps bending back," he said. They stopped and reconnoitered a bit, exploring some of the galleries they had passed. At one point, Kibosh paused and sniffed. He said he felt a draft—did Joe feel it? Joe wasn't sure. They hoisted their gear and went on. Within a short time Joe and Kibosh found themselves in an easy passage, and not long after, they came to a recently collapsed cross tunnel.

"This could be it," Kibosh said. "It heads the right way." Together, they managed to clear away enough debris to squeeze through, and from there it was a short walk until they entered a large chamber.

"By damn," Kibosh said, "this here's the chamber where I stopped with Boz. An'"—he broke off to cast his light about—"he ain't been back here. I bet he's still betwixt us and the main exit."

All right, Joe thought as they set off. They moved at a good pace, Kibosh as confident of his whereabouts as if he'd been on the corner of Park and Montana, in Butte. They had not gone far when he suddenly snapped off his light and turned to stop Joe. "Up ahead," he whispered.

There was a faint glow ahead. The two men moved forward softly. Joe took the lead, with the H&K at the ready. They came to a bend and then around it and there, some fifty feet beyond, was Bozi Bazok. He stood hunched, a light in one hand and a pistol in the other, his back humped with the old canvas pack. He wasn't walking, just standing and talking.

"You little whore," he muttered, "who the hell do you think you are? Keep walking. Come on." He trudged forward, still talking. The two men followed, keeping their distance.

"There's bandits up in these mountains," Boz said. "Taliban! Ha, ha! I'd like to see them. I'd blow their fucking brains out. I'll blow yours out too. Come here," he said, stopping. "That's it. Get down on your knees. I'm gonna do it right now! Oh, quit whining. Come on." And he shuffled on.

Kibosh plucked at Joe's sleeve. They stopped and let the man stumble on, still jabbering—"*Balijas!* Bozi Bazooks! You don't stand a chance! Haw!"

"Sumbitch is plum loco," Kibosh whispered. "But I'm damned if he ain't found his way. If he just keeps walkin' he'll walk right out. The wimmen'll be up ahead. Hadn't we orta do somethin' fore he gits there?"

Joe knew he was right. "Let's take him. You lay back. He's in terrible shape, but if he starts popping that pistol it could get dangerous. Stay against the wall, or lie on the ground."

"I got a better idea," Kibosh said. "How 'bout I call to him, flash my light? He'll come. Ye stay back, in the dark, and we might lure him back to the chamber, where they's a little more room. Ye could take him there."

This seemed a better idea, Joe thought, but it might be dangerous for Kibosh. The old man was willing, though. He felt that the larger chamber would be less dangerous if bullets started flying. Joe consented and began to backtrack, while Kibosh went forward.

"Boz!" the old man shouted. "Hey, Boz!" He flashed his light down the passage. "This way!"

Boz whirled around. "Wha'? Kibe? That you, Kibe? You come back for me!"

"This way, boy!" Kibosh yelled. He waved his light but, mindful of Joe's warning, retreated around the bend. He kept calling, always staying out of view as they fell back, careful to keep a bend between them and Bazok, his light flashing on the walls to show the route.

Boz stumbled back toward them, overjoyed. "You came back! You're a hell of a man, Kibe! Wait up!"

When Joe and Kibosh entered the chamber they doused their lights, waiting on either side of the entry. A moment later, Bazok burst into the room.

"Where are you, Kibe?" he yelled. He stood in the middle of the chamber, the Star automatic in hand, looking around wildly.

Joe was in the act of flicking on his light when the dogs burst into the chamber, howling. Bazok whirled. "Get away! Get away!" he screamed as the dogs attacked. He fired the Star wildly.

"Get down!" Joe yelled to Kibosh, as bullets ricocheted about the chamber.

The dogs snarled, tearing at their quarry. Bazok's light flew against a wall and went out. In the darkness, Joe and Kibosh could hear the dog's teeth snapping, the rending of clothing, the screams of the victim. Then it was almost silent, with only the panting of the dogs.

Joe flipped his light on. The dogs stood back from the mangled corpse of the killer, a wretched, torn bundle in the middle of the room. Their eyes glowed in the light, but they didn't move. Then they padded forward and nuzzled Joe.

Joe shone his light on Kibosh, who was crouched against a wall. His eyes were wide, but now he stood up, cautiously. "Good dogs, good dogs," Kibosh said. The dogs came to him, their tongues lolling out. They knew him. Kibosh petted them and took hold of their collars.

Joe went over to Bazok. He was dead, his throat and face torn viciously, the blood still spreading around him. Joe had turned to say something to Kibosh when another voice broke in.

"Hold them, hold them," Jammie said. She stood at the entry, her gun in both hands. She had pushed her night-vision headgear back off her forehead. The dogs were straining in Kibosh's hands. "If you let them go," Jammie warned, "I'll shoot you first."

Kibosh hushed the dogs. He looked from Joe to her and back.

"Keep them calm," Joe said. To Jammie, he said, "Well?"

She stepped forward, motioning Joe toward Kibosh and the dogs. "Help him hold them," she said. When Joe moved over to take one of the dogs, she sidestepped toward Bazok. She glanced down briefly and kicked him. The limp reaction told her what she needed to know. She turned her attention back to the two men and the dogs.

"Kind of a standoff, hey?" She laughed lightly. "If I shoot you, the dogs get loose, which could be a hassle. That stupid Paulie . . . I could kill him." She uttered a bark of laughter. "Well, you can't kill a man twice, can you? Which leaves you guys."

"So, you're the cleanup hitter," Joe said. "Is that it?"

"Very good, Joe. I like that." She seemed calm, assessing the situation.

"And who's the coach?" Joe asked. "Tucker?"

Jammie shook her head, impatiently. "Don't be silly," she said. "You're smarter than that . . . or maybe I overestimated you. It's all about money, Joe. Nothing complicated. I offered you a chance . . . but you didn't bite. I guess"—she lowered her aim—"it'll have to be the dogs first."

Helen's light flashed in Jammie's eyes. Jammie swiveled, but it was too late. The shotgun roared. Jammie was thrown back like a rag doll, flopping on top of Bazok, arms flung wide.

Joe approached Helen and tried to embrace her, but she held him off with an elbow. She pointed the barrel of the gun so that the light played on the bodies, their blood mingling on the dirty floor.

"Make sure they're dead," Helen said.

Joe knelt to inspect the bodies. He stood up. "Can't get any deader," he said.

Helen let out her breath and lowered the gun. Joe put his arm around her. She stared down at the crumpled wreckage of Jammie. "My God," she said. "Why?"

Joe picked up Jammie's laser-aimed Llama and the NiteOwl headset that had been thrown from her head. He held them up to show Helen.

"She would have killed you," he said. "She killed Paulie."

"Why?"

"What does it matter?" he said.

"It matters to me," Helen said. "She didn't know us. She didn't know anything about us."

"We were just in the way," Joe said. "She was a determined woman. Dedicated, you could say."

Romance

In the living room of the third-floor back of an apartment building a few blocks off Flatbush Avenue, Roman met an Albanian Muslim man to whom he gave one thousand dollars. A young woman was then brought into the room and introduced to Roman as Fedima. She was dressed like an American girl, in Levi's and an oversized jersey that bore the logo of the Mets. She wore Adidases. Her hair was black and tied in a ponytail. She was very pretty, a little thin, Roman thought, but with large, luminous brown eyes. She was wary. But for her diffidence, she reminded him of Helen, in fact.

The Albanian had explained the situation before the girl was produced. She had been through hell, he told Roman. Her abductor, a Serbian irregular with the *nom de guerre* of Bozi Bazok, had raped her, of course, many times. She was lucky he had not murdered her, as he had murdered all of her family, before her very eyes. He had cut their throats, mostly, but some he had simply shot. Fortunately for Fedima, the *bashi-bazouk* had needed someone to help him escape from Kosovo—he feared that he had been cut off from his outfit by the Kosovo Liberation Army.

This young woman was a very great heroine, the man told Roman. They would write songs about her. Despite her terror, her grief, and, it must be admitted, her ignorance of how to reach Al-

bania, she had managed to convince the *bashi-bazouk* that without her he would perish. In fact, they stumbled into Montenegro,
after enduring horrendous nights of snow and very little food or
drink—and for her, repeated abuse by the *bashi-bazouk*. Whereupon
she had escaped and fled to Albania, perhaps through the inten-
tional negligence of this Bazok, who had tired of her and no longer
needed her assistance.

By then there was no sense in returning to Kosovo—no possibility, in fact. Refugees were streaming out of that land. Ultimately,
Fedima found safety in a camp run by an international agency, and
from there she was sent first to Sweden, then to America.

Alas, she was a ruined woman. Luckily, she had not gotten
pregnant. But she would never find a Muslim husband. She was
learning English, taking courses at the high school. She hoped to
go to junior college. She would become a secretary, perhaps. She
might even find an American man who would marry her. In some
ways, the man said, she was lucky. She was alive, at least.

If Mr. Yakovich could help her, that would be wonderful.
They—the family with which she was placed—got very little assistance from the international agency for taking her in.

"What happened to Bazok?" Roman inquired.

Apparently, he had gone back into Serbia. Who knows where
he was now? Such a man will find justice, eventually. Allah does not
forget. Very likely Serbia was now no longer a safe place for him.

"You understand," the man said, evidently mindful of Roman's
Serbian name, "that we do not blame the Serbian people, as such,
for this tragedy. There were very bad people among them, but the
Serbs have come to their senses and have rejected these gangsters.
Now something must be done for the victims of their cruelty. Repa-
rations must be made."

"Yes, yes," Roman said, absently, wondering how much this
would ultimately cost the Liddle Angel.

That was when Fedima was brought in. An old grandmotherly type was also present. "I bring you greetings," Roman said in Serbo-Croatian, "from Franko." He had been instructed by Helen to tell her this.

The reaction was amazing. This downcast little woman flew to him, her eyes ablaze. "You have seen him? He is well?" she cried. "Where is he?"

"I have not seen him," Roman said, "but I am told that he is well. He is in Montana. He wishes to see you."

"Montana," she breathed. "He wishes to see me?" She clasped her hands in rapture. Then suddenly she was downcast again. "No. It is impossible. He will not want to see me now."

No, Roman, assured her. He had been told. It was certain. Franko wished to see her. If she was willing, Roman could take her to him.

Apparently, she was not willing. She was too mortified, too ashamed. But the old woman remonstrated with her. If a man such as Franko, of whom she had heard so many great things from Fedima, still desired her, it was impudence to refuse him. They argued about this while Roman waited patiently. Ultimately, the desires of the girl and the old woman merged. Now the only point was how it could be effected.

This was not so easily determined. A long discussion began, with the man, the grandmother, others who came in. The girl sat quietly in a corner while they talked. The family could in no way allow the girl to go with Roman, a stranger and a Serb at that. After all she had been through! No, it was impossible. There were also complications of her legal presence, her status as an immigrant. Roman and the man withdrew to another room, to drink a glass or two of slivovitz. Funds were mentioned. Roman mentioned a figure. A ridiculous counterfigure was suggested.

By now it was getting on toward dinnertime. An impasse had been reached. Roman was thinking he would go to dinner, call Helen, and find out how much she was willing to pay.

At this point, Theo Ostropaki appeared. He was just a visitor, it seemed, but he was a representative of the agency that had sent Fedima to Brooklyn. Fortunately, he happened to be in the country on business. As a person interested in Fedima's welfare, a man of authority, and a neutral—that is, neither a Serb nor an Albanian—he was a perfect intermediary. The others withdrew. Roman and Ostropaki conversed in English.

"This young woman has endured so much," Ostropaki said. "I have a passing knowledge of her circumstances. She has lost her entire family. These people are only distant relatives; they have taken her in out of a sense of Muslim charity, a very great principle in their culture, you know. You can understand their reluctance to entrust her future to a . . . well, to you."

Roman was impassive. He listened, then he said, "I am a Serb because my mother said I was. Otherwise, I am also a Jew for the same reason. It has no bearing, what I am. I am not buying this girl."

"Oh, no, you misunderstand me," Ostropaki assured him.

Roman ignored his comment. "I am here because another young woman, a rich American woman from Detroit, asked me to find Fedima Daliljaj, if she was alive. Of one thing I am sure: if Helen Sedlacek is interested in the girl, she will be safe. If these good people need to be paid for taking care of the girl, Helen Sedlacek will pay a fair sum."

"Who is this Mrs. Sedlacek?" Ostropaki asked. "How did she hear of Fedima?"

"Miss Sedlacek," Roman corrected. "She is the surviving child of a Detroit businessman. I don't know how she learned of Fedima Daliljaj. I am only telling you that she has heard of her. She wants to help her." Then he remembered something else. "She wants to help her rejoin her betrothed." This was only an assumption on Roman's part, but it was based on an impression he had gained from Helen's request.

"Who is this betrothed?" Ostropaki said, surprised. "I have not heard of Fedima being betrothed."

"I think it must be a man named Franko, who lives in Montana."

"Franko!" Ostropaki was astounded. "Franko Bradovic? He is alive? Are you sure?"

Roman was not sure. He had no idea who Franko was. Helen had not informed him. But if Mr. Ostropaki wished, they could call her, at a number Helen had provided: Frank's number.

Mr. Ostropaki wished. Within minutes they had reached Helen by telephone. Ostropaki talked to Helen for a long time. To Roman, they seemed to be haggling endlessly, but Roman paid little attention—his stomach grumbled.

As if in response—perhaps the old woman had heard the borborygmus from the next room—soup with filled dumplings was brought in, along with sweet-and-sour cabbage and some rolls that Roman recognized as *klovac,* but which they called by some other name. He sat to eat and shortly was joined by Ostropaki.

"Do you know," Ostropaki said, when the meal was finished, "I am sure that this can be worked out, but I am rather surprised at Franko—or Paul, to give his real name. I knew him well in Kosovo, but he never mentioned Fedima to me. That is, I knew he was staying with the Daliljajs, but there was no mention of the girl."

Roman had nothing to say to that, having no knowledge of the situation whatever, but he remarked, "Perhaps he did not feel it was proper."

"You mean, not germane to our business?" Ostropaki said. "Well, it wasn't, to be sure. But when a man is in love, and he is concerned about the safety of the people he is with, as he was—he mentioned it more than once to me—I would think he would mention the woman to whom he is betrothed. I had always the impression that he was not a romantic type of man, if you follow me."

Roman did not. "She is very pretty," he said. Now that his belly was full, he was content to discuss anything at length.

"She is also very young," Ostropaki said. "Much younger than Fr— Paul. But more important, he is what I call a 'rover'—a wanderer. Such men do not marry. They may have idle romances, but soon they are off to a new place, new romances."

"Montana is not his home then?" Roman said.

"It is, and perhaps he has decided to settle down. I wish I could have spoken to him, but evidently he was not immediately available. Later, we can talk, I hope. Please tell him, when you see him. But now, let us see what arrangements we can make."

Negotiations began in earnest. Helen had agreed to a fee that Roman felt was excessive, but it was within his means to pay. The question arose: what about chaperones? Roman didn't see why Fedima would need a chaperone; he would accompany her to Butte. That was rejected; she must be accompanied by members of her people. Roman balked: he could see the entire family emigrating to Montana, at Helen's expense. But at a certain point, the question was aired: what if the girl, once she had been reunited with her . . . suitor . . . preferred to return?

This was a breakthrough. From that point on, Roman knew that it was a matter of deciding who would be the person who would go and determine that the girl wished to stay and, if she didn't, would be available to escort her back to Brooklyn. Questions of whether there were mosques in Butte, other Muslims, what sort of food was available, where she would sleep, and so on, could be resolved.

Just when Roman was beginning to think of eating again, an agreement was reached. The old woman would accompany Roman and Fedima on the airplane. Round-trip tickets for both must be provided—beyond the other agreed-upon funds.

It is not the easiest flight from La Guardia to Butte. There are other routes, but the one agreed upon was via Cincinnati, Minneapolis, and Great Falls. It took all of the following day before the plane dropped down over the Continental Divide and ground to a shuddering halt on the runway, at what seemed to be the end of earth.

The old lady, who had spoken only a few words to Roman the entire long day, looked on as the party of Helen, Joe, and Frank approached. Helen embraced Fedima, then, in her best Belgrade Serbian, welcomed her to Montana and introduced "Franko."

The girl stared at Frank. He had shaved and was wearing a suit and a tie. This was a critical moment. Everyone except Roman, who was tired and bored, looked at the two young people expectantly.

Frank shook Fedima's hand.

The girl looked around the small airport, momentarily alive with families and friends greeting the disembarking passengers. She could see no sign of her Franko. She looked at Roman, but he was no help. Then she looked at the very pretty woman who was no more than her own size, accompanied by a handsome man who could have been her brother. The woman, Helen, nodded her head so slightly that it almost could not be noticed, and there was a serious look in her eye.

Fedima understood. If asked, she could not have said what, exactly, she understood. But it was something important. She turned to Roman and said, "It is well."

Helen took the ladies to the Finlen Hotel, where she had retained two suites, one for her and Fedima, the other for the duenna. The men returned to Frank's place. Helen took the women shopping, then to dinner. Then she and Fedima settled in for a long talk.

Joe took Roman for a walk while Frank cleaned out a room for Fedima, in case she decided to stay.

Roman labored up the grassy slope to the ridge, slipping in his smooth-soled street shoes. He stood to catch his breath, his hands clasped behind the black suit, looking down on the river where it ran along the cliff. "Very peaceful," he said, but he didn't sound impressed.

"Yes, it's beautiful," Joe said. "Perfect. Come on, I'll show you where Helen and I want to build."

"You staying?" Roman said, surprised. "Helen, too? Way out here?"

"Of course." Joe walked him up on the ridge and away from the stream to a broad meadow backing against a large rock outcropping about the size of a church. This was a site, Joe said, that would be ideal. He pointed out where a road could be routed, where a well could be dug, and so on. The site had a good southern exposure, and from there Frank's house was not visible, although one could see the windmills spinning. Perfect privacy.

Roman grunted—whether appreciatively or not, Joe couldn't tell. "Well, we've got work to do," Joe said. They trekked down to the site of Paulie's camp. Joe explained what they were looking for. Roman would look about outside for possible hiding places while Joe checked out the tent.

As soon as Roman was engaged, Joe set to work. There were an awful lot of books for a camp, three wooden crates of them. And a laptop computer. Joe didn't bother with that—Helen had the computer expertise. What Joe sought was a handy journal, or a notebook. But in the course of looking for one, he could check for other goods. There was nothing of that sort, he soon realized. He hadn't expected to find any. Jammie had been either lying or simply wrong. But he did find the notebooks.

They were resting in plain sight, on the footlocker by Paulie's camp bed. There were four journals, beautifully bound in hardboard covers that were printed with Egyptian emblems. The journals were labeled: *India, Kashmir, Balkans, Montana*. They were fishing journals. Inside were many sketches of fish, evidently drawn by Paulie, using colored inks. And the notations below the pictures, or alongside them, indicated the date, place, time, weather conditions, water conditions, numbers of fish of various types caught, along with occasional remarks about the day—"high, thin o'cast, fine for b-w-o, later good breeze sw—hoppers and mayflies . . ."

There were also ink sketches of plants, flowers, certain views of hills or a creek, occasionally a bird, or persons—a talented artist's snapshots, things he'd seen on his way to and from the fishing.

Joe leafed through the Balkan book, admiring pictures of a man with a big mustache, wearing a turban and smoking a long pipe; two girls in Balkan peasant dress (Joe presumed), carrying bundles of sticks, laughing, pretty; one very attractive sketch of a farm girl, washing her naked upper torso, who much resembled Fedima. A horse wearing a hat, a dog sleeping, a minaret poking up through the trees. Some of these had been colored with water paints later, it seemed.

Paulie was a skilled artist, but it was clear that his aim was not art but accuracy. There was, for instance, a whole page of sketches of the innards of what Joe presumed was a fish: intestines, gills, organs—an eye, a tongue, something that might be a kidney. There were many very striking colored-ink representations of fishing flies, and drawings of how the flies were arranged on the fly line itself when more than one fly was used.

Joe looked for any notation that might suggest some activity other than fishing, but there were none that he could see. It was a brilliant piece of work, beautiful even, probably the sort of thing that anglers would treasure.

He idly flipped a page and there was Jamala Sanders. She was standing in a village street, hands on hips, wearing a khaki outfit, her hair pulled back in a puffy ponytail. She looked very handsome but intent on something up the street. She was shod in a stylish version of cowboy boots, not quite the real thing. A little notation said, "Am. woman, Tsamet."

Joe hurriedly paged through the book and found three more small sketches of Jammie: one just a tiny head, full face; the others larger, barely sketched cartoons of her striding by a building and by a tree. And near the back was a full-page, ink and water color-enhanced drawing of Jammie nude. It was a great picture, Joe thought. She was lounging by the side of a stream, among the grass, tiny blue forget-me-nots at the stream edge, her arms back to support her on her elbows, with her full breasts exposed, her legs apart to clearly display profuse pubic hair that did not succeed in obscuring the artist's characteristically meticulous delineation of her vulva. There was a remarkable grace to the disposition of those thighs. And the look on her face . . . a knowing smile. It was Jammie, to the bones. The notation read: "Emerging nymph."

Joe examined the rest of the book carefully but could make no sense of the notations beyond their ostensible reports on fishing. Possibly these notations contained some evidence, but it wasn't available to Joe. The other books were the same: fish, birds, bugs, girls, views.

Roman returned, having found nothing. Joe sighed. "I'll have to pack all this up later," he said.

"You need help?" Roman asked.

"You mean, you'd stay?" Joe said.

Roman shrugged. He had nothing else to do.

They hiked back to the house. Joe carried the books, stashing them in a safe place. The colonel had called. He was in Butte, with Schwind. Joe called his motel, to give him instructions on how to find Frank's place.

There was still plenty of light when Tucker and Schwind arrived. They were tired from traveling, but they were eager to inspect the scene. Joe provided wading boots for the stream, and now that he knew the crossings better, he guided them across. As they hiked, he gave them a graphic description of the events.

The bodies were undisturbed, lying exactly as they'd fallen. He watched while Dinah Schwind calmly went about inspecting the wounds, trying not to move the bodies more than was necessary. She seemed unperturbed by the situation. Schwind was methodical, but it was not, after all, a clinical examination. She was soon done, and they walked back to the mouth of the tunnel.

The colonel gazed out on the broad scene before them. "Who owns all this?" he asked.

"Frank owns up to the center of the stream—I guess that's the usual way, out here. Some of the rest is Bureau of Land Management, some is old mining claims, some is state forest. Frank says an old lady in Great Falls owns a huge chunk. I'll take you over to the Seven Dials, where Paulie is," he said. "That's owned by Kibosh—Lester Collins. He filed a mining claim, several years back. . . . I'm not sure of the legal status."

"I'll find out," the colonel said. He nodded at Schwind, who made a note. "Where's Collins now?"

"He's there, fixing it up," Joe said. "Couldn't talk him out of it. I offered to put him up in town, but no. He's agreed to leave the murder scene alone."

"We'll have to remove Martinelli's body," the colonel said, as if thinking aloud, "but maybe we can leave these two. I'll have to see if we can't get the ownership rights to the site." He peered back into the tunnel. "A little well-placed explosive could seal it off. Appropriate tomb for those two, you might say."

Joe expressed no surprise, no objections.

"What's your take on Collins?" the colonel asked. "Is he going to tell stories?"

"No," Joe said. The colonel asked for no further explanation. "And neither will Frank."

"Yes, Frank Oberavich," the colonel said. "You left him out of your report, Joe. But," he hastened on, "no harm done, I guess. Well, my dear"—he turned to Schwind—"we've got our work cut out. Better get moving."

"Don't you want to go over to the Seven Dials?" Joe asked.

"Tomorrow," the colonel said, "unless you think Mr. Collins is nervous about the body. Schwind can get it removed. We have some people due in . . ." He looked at his watch. "Probably waiting for us, in Butte."

"Aren't you forgetting something?" Joe said.

"Ah. Of course." The colonel took an envelope out of his coat pocket and handed it to Joe. "Your fee. We didn't discuss it, but I think you'll find that adequate."

For once, Joe was surprised. He took the envelope and stuffed it in his pocket without looking at it. "I wasn't thinking of that," he said. "There's a lot of details . . ."

"All in good time, Joe," the colonel said. He began to ease gingerly down the path, but within a few steps he felt more at ease and walked casually. He was from this country, after all.

When they had waded the river and were walking back to the house, Schwind jogged ahead, already tapping at her cell phone, shaking it, looking at the sky wonderingly. She was on the job.

The colonel lagged behind with Joe. "You want to know about Sanders," he said. "We don't know the whole story yet, but it's unfolding. We've found Ostropaki. I guess you didn't hear about that? No, Sanders wouldn't have had any reason to inform you. Anyway, he's helping us put together the pieces."

"Paulie had met her in Kosovo," Joe volunteered.

"Martinelli? Did he? Well, that's interesting. What else did you find out? How did he get involved?"

"He was just fishing," Joe said. He talked about the notebooks.

"I'd love to see them sometime," Tucker said. "Fly-fishing, eh? You know . . ." He stopped and looked back at the river. "It's a religion out here."

As they approached the house, the colonel nodded toward the barking dogs. "What will happen to them?" he asked.

Joe said that Frank had not decided, but he was concerned.

"Dogs that have killed . . . ," the colonel said. "It might be a problem. They're no trouble to you, or others? I'd hate to see them destroyed. I'll have a word with Oberavich. They might profit from a training session."

A few days later, having exhausted themselves cleaning up Paulie's camp, Joe and Helen strolled up to their building site, just to take in the view. After they had admired the scenery, Helen said, "We should move quickly on this."

"What do you mean?" Joe said.

"Get the papers signed."

"That's no problem," Joe said. "Frank is cool."

"He's cool," Helen agreed. "It's Fedima. She's a farmer, you know. She has plans."

Joe was taken aback. "Already!"

"Oh, yes. She's looking out for her family, you know."

"Her family! She doesn't have a— You mean Frank?"

"And the kids. There'll be kids, starting in about nine months, I'd guess."

Joe looked around in dismay. "Kids."

"Don't worry, Joe, we'll have plenty of room. You should take up fly-fishing, you know."

"I'd rather wrestle," he said.